Jessica Blair grew up in Middlesbrough, trained as a teacher and now lives in Ampleforth. She because a full-time writer in 1977 and has written more than 50 books under various pseudonyms including *A Distant Harbour, Storm Bay, The Other Side of the River, The Restless Spirit, The Seaweed Gatherers, Portrait of Charlotte, The Locket, The Long Way Home, The Restless Heart, Time & Tide, Echoes of the Past, Secrets of the Sea, Yesterday's Dreams, Reach for Tomorrow, Dangerous Shores, Wings of Sorrow, Stay With Me* and *Sealed Secrets* all published by Piatkus.

For more information about the author visit: www.jessicablair.co.uk

D1386664

The Red Shawl

Jessica Blair

piatkus

PIATKUS

First Published in Great Britain in 1992 by Judy Piatkus (Publishers) Ltd
This paperback edition published in 2010 by Piatkus

A CIP catalogue record for this book is available from the British Library.

ISBN 978-0-7515-4503-6

Typeset in Sabon by Hewer Text UK Ltd, Edinburgh
Printed and bound in Great Britain by Clays Ltd, St Ives plc

Papers used by Piatkus are natural, renewable and recyclable products
sourced from well-managed forests and certified in accordance with
the rules of the Forest Stewardship Council.

Mixed Sources
Product group from well-managed
forests and other controlled sources
www.fsc.org Cert no. SGS-COC-004081
© 1996 Forest Stewardship Council

FSC

Piatkus
An imprint of
Little, Brown Book Group
100 Victoria Embankment
London EC4Y 0DY

An Hachette UK Company
www.hachette.co.uk

www.piatkus.co.uk

JOAN

in memory of the night we sailed
out of Harstad
and felt
the call of the North

Chapter One

The icy wind, born in the frozen wastes of the Arctic, had blown thousands of lonely miles across the cold, grey sea. It swirled over the bleak North Yorkshire moors, beating at the stunted heather, rippling the pools of melted snow and chilling the drifts which remained on the north-facing slopes of the gullies and valleys. The snows of January 1780 had felt an unusual touch of warmth so early in the year but now the wind reminded them that, on these desolate heights, February could bring the worst of the winter.

It howled with extra vigour as it swept over the edge of the moors and lashed at Pickering, overlooking the fertile vale on which the market town based its workaday prosperity. It sent merchants, their trading done, hurrying to the comfort of their fireside in their solidly built mansions; it drove housewives to hasten their last purchases in the market so that they could sooner seek the shelter of their cottages and warmth in the cup from the kettle on the reckon; while poorer folk were sent scurrying to their hovels hoping that the rotting thatch would hold against the buffeting.

Its chill bit deep into Ruth Harwood's bones as she stumbled along the soggy path between Pickering and the tiny hamlet of Cropton, crouched on a spur of a hill five miles to the east of the market town. Her slim, abused body sought warmth in the tension which gripped her shoulders, hunched against the frenzied wind.

She drew her torn shawl tighter around her worn, fustian dress, holding it at her throat with her right hand while her left gripped the piece of ham hidden beneath its folds as if her very life depended on it. If she returned home without it, or was late, she would feel the savage slash of her step-father's belt, and in his most sadistic moods he used the buckle end on her. She shuddered, recollecting the ugly weals and blue-black bruises which marked her.

Ruth quickened her slithering steps. She must snatch a few precious, prearranged minutes with David Fernley. They were the only comfort in a harsh and drab life. He was the only person who gave her hope. She needed to know he was nearby, that he would always be there, otherwise her whole world would collapse and she would not be able to face the emptiness.

She turned towards a byre standing in the corner of a field a quarter of a mile from the cottage in which David lived with his mother and father, his brother and two sisters.

How Ruth envied them their closeknit family life, happy in spite of the harsh existence. But at least Kit Fernley had a steady job as a confined labourer to the squire.

He worked hard, tilled his own little plot around the cottage for potatoes and vegetables and was allowed to keep and graze a cow. Hopefully, one day, she would be taken into that family group when she married David. It was that thought, held in her own secret mind, which made life bearable.

The day darkened. Ruth, her eyes troubled with anxiety, glanced upwards. The strengthening wind drove the first clouds from the north scudding across the sky. Spots of rain stung her pale face. She broke into a half run and stumbled through the sacking hanging over the byre door just as the first swish of heavy rain soaked the old, stone building.

She stood, her chest heaving, her slender body relieved to be free of the buffeting, her eyes piercing the gloom, looking for David. The light which filtered through holes in the roof, and through the tears in the skin across the windows, revealed only the cow, which lay contentedly chewing its cud among some old straw at one end of the byre.

Panic seized Ruth's heart. David was not here! Why? Where was he? She had felt sure he would be waiting. Oh, he must come. She must see him, if only for a few moments, just sufficient to draw strength to endure her mother's spiteful tongue and step-father's fists. How long could she wait? She frowned and turned in anxious agitation to the doorway.

Dropping the ham on the floor, she drew the sacking back and peered through the veil of lashing rain, but there was no one. The wind howled, its shrieks filled with mockery.

3

With a sigh she let the sacking fall into place. David had said he would be here. She had never known him break a promise. She could wait a few minutes. Ruth slid the shawl from her head and let it drape round her shoulders. She ran her hands through her lank hair, remembering the time thirteen years ago when, as a child of five, she sat on her mother's knee while her mother ran a brush gently through it, making the copper-tinted tresses shimmer in the autumn sunshine. Those had been happy days, poor though they were. But suddenly they were shattered when, that Christmas, her mother had married Nathan Cornforth, the brutal man who was not Ruth's father.

He had resented her as an intruder and, in spite of her mother's pleading, had refused to let his step-daughter take his name. So Ruth had grown up with her mother's maiden name, evidence that she was a bastard, a stigma which marked her life and made her the butt of other children's cruel teasing. Only David stood up for her and protected her from the barbs.

Her step-father, a day labourer who, with his drunken ways, inspired no confidence, survived on the good nature of the squire who had compassion on an ever increasing family. Some said it was because of Ruth but her step-father afforded her no credit for that and never let her forget that she was not his true daughter.

At first, the mother had comforted the child whenever her husband was absent for she dare not show one morsel of affection for her in his presence. But, as Ruth moved into teenage years, her mother's solace waned and vanished in a sea of jealousy. Rebecca Cornforth saw her daughter developing into an attractive young woman. She envied Ruth her youth and beauty and the lithe, firm body which any man would be glad to take. Ruth's proud, high cheekboned features, her air and carriage reminded Rebecca of her father, so different from the man she married.

In envy, Rebecca sided more and more with her husband against her daughter. She gave her the poorest of rags when she had finished with them and Ruth could not remember the last time she had had something unworn. She came to expect her only food to be scraps thrown from the table, not knowing that, secretly, her mother was delighted to see her daughter lose weight and with it the attraction she had noticed reflected in her husband's lascivious eye.

Ruth glanced at the doorway. If she did not go soon, she would be late with her step-father's meal and that raised the spectre-like image of him, fist raised, his face taut in sadistic pleasure as he relished the pain he would inflict on her. She should go but she wanted to stay. She fiddled nervously with the ends of her shawl as she paced up and down.

Suddenly she stopped, her mind frozen by the half-heard sound. She inclined her head, listening intently. Had she been mistaken? She strained to hear above the lashing rain. No! There it was again. It grew louder. Someone was running. David! It must be. The thought sent joy coursing through her.

Three quick steps took Ruth to the doorway. She jerked the sacking aside and saw a figure, dark against the rain, bent to the buffeting wind, shoulder half-turned as if forcing a way through it, running towards the byre. Nearer and nearer. David! A smile broke across her face.

She ran her free hand through her hair, conscious of a desire to look her best.

She stepped to one side as David burst through the doorway out of the rain. She let the covering drop back into place and swung round to face him. He was throwing off the piece of sacking which had kept the shoulders of his sleeved waistcoat dry as he ran from home. His buckled shoes and hand-knitted stockings below knee-breeches were spattered with mud. There was laughter in his eyes as he held out his arms to her.

She flung herself to him and buried her head against his chest. She drew comfort and confidence from the feel of his tall, straight body, broad for its eighteen years, toughened by an unyielding life on the land, which brought little reward. His face beaten by the sun and wind, swept by the rain, already bore marks of that life but there was still the thrust of youth about his dark, deep-set eyes and a determination about his firm lips which strengthened the feeling of protection she drew from him.

'Thee's trembling, luv.' David eased her gently away from him so he could look into her eyes.

She met his searching gaze. 'I thought you might not come when it was silin' down.'

'Rain wouldn't stop me. Sorry I'm late but I had to talk to Pa and Ma.' David paused. Concern clouded his eyes. He raised a hand and gently fingered the bruise on her left cheek. 'Ruth . . . ?'

'That's nowt,' she hastened to reassure him as she took his hand in hers and started towards the corner of the byre. 'That was last night.'

David frowned. 'Why?'

She shrugged her shoulders. 'Why?' She gave a half laugh as she flopped into the hay. 'He don't need a reason when he's drunk.'

David stood staring down at her, fury and anger threatening to burst free. His knuckles gleamed white through his clenched fists. How could anybody lay a hand on Ruth? How could anybody get pleasure from inflicting pain on her? His lips tightened.

'Is thee telling me everything? That drunken sod didn't . . . ?' The words demanded the truth, and then came sharp with resolution: 'If he did, I'll knock t' living daylights out of him?'

Ruth's attention was riveted on David standing over her. He looked so tall, so powerful, those clenched hands ready to avenge her. She saw his muscles ripple beneath his coarse shirt. His jaw was tight and his eyes half closed as if visualising a confrontation with her step-father. Ruth had never seen him like this before. He had never threatened what he would do. He had expressed his horror at the beatings but had never mentioned retaliation. She felt herself gripped by a strange elation, a feverish belief that the end of her troubles was in sight.

'No, there was nowt else, and I've had worse thrashings,' she started. Uttering that word had reminded her that she must not be late home. 'Davey, I can't stay long, or I really will catch it in t' neck. It's market day, remember?'

David knew only too well what that meant. He dropped into the hay beside her and took her hands in his. 'Been thieving again?' he asked, knowing his frown of disapproval meant little against Ruth's step-father's threats.

'What else can I do?' Her eyes questioned him. 'If I don't get his meat he'll beat me.'

'Aye, but if thee gets caught – it's deportation!' His voice was cramped with horror. He dreaded the worst, the loss of Ruth for ever.

'David,' she said gently, 'I won't get caught. Better to risk that than a belting. He allus comes home drunk on market day, and if I cross him I pays.' Her brow furrowed. 'I must be off.'

'Not yet!' David tightened his grip on Ruth's hands, preventing her from rising. 'I've summat to tell thee.'

Her eyes fixed on David, puzzled at the gravity on his face as he stared at their linked hands.

'Well?' she prompted.

David looked up. 'I'm leaving – gannin' t' Whitby!' The words came sharply, beating at Ruth like the rain lashing the byre.

Her eyes widened in disbelief. She gaped at him. Incredulity turned to horror as the nightmare bit into her numbed mind.

'What! You can't! Why? WHY?' Her voice rose like the cry of a stricken bird doomed to die on the moorland wastes.

Ruth's distress tore at David's heart and he wished he could spare her the pain. He ran his broad, rough fingers down her smooth cheek with the same caressing touch which had so often given comfort to the girl he loved. Then, she had responded with warm, reciprocal feeling. But now there was no reaction. It hurt him to see her grey eyes filling with tears.

'I'm gannin' for us, lass,' he explained, his voice gentle.

'It's the only chance we'll have. There's nowt here for us. I can get work only now and again. What sort of life's that?'

'We'll manage. I don't want you to gan.' The sadness in Ruth's eyes was touched with pleading. 'You're the only joy I have.' Her words choked on a sob. Nausea gripped her. She saw compassion and sorrow in David's eyes, but there was also a grim determination which she had never seen before. It drove her into a deep well of despair and her very being seemed to crumble as if her lifeblood was draining away. She could no longer hold back the tears and as they flowed, like a moorland stream in spate, she slumped against him, her head buried hard against her chest. Sobs racked her body. Life would be hell without David near. She wished she could curl up in a corner and never wake up to the loneliness which awaited her.

He let her cry, holding her close, stroking her hair with the lightest of touches and rocking gently as a mother would comfort a young child.

When he felt the sobs subside, David spoke with a voice which caressed. 'I'm gannin' because I love thee. We'll be together soon, lass, I promise.' He eased her from him and gently raised her head with a finger under her chin. He looked deep into her eyes, then, leaning forward slowly, kissed each of them in tender compassion to drive away the last of the tears.

'But why gan, Davey?' Ruth asked, still bewildered by his announcement.

'There's nay future here,' he replied.

'But your pa's all right . . .' started Ruth.

'Oh, aye,' cut in David, 'Pa's content as a confined

labourer – he's certain of work and regular money. And with Ma skivvyin' three days a week at the hall, they manage. But there's only occasional work for me and John. He's prepared to bide his time until he's a confined labourer. I'm not.' His voice hardened with determination. I want something better than a life of poverty in Cropton. I want a decent home, and fine clothes for thee. I'll have a better chance to get them in Whitby. I know I can do it. I WILL do it! One day thee'll be proud of me.'

Ruth listened in amazement as the words poured out unabated, like a moorland fire once it has a hold on the tinder-like heather. The tenacity and eagerness in his voice transmitted their passion. She could feel his excitement as he looked into the future.

'Then tak' me with you,' she begged.

The brightness in David's eyes clouded over. 'I can't. Thee'll be all alone in Whitby after I sail with the whaleships.'

Ruth's breath caught in her throat. 'Whaleships! Not the whaleships!' Her eyes widened with horror and wild despair. 'I'll niver see you again! You'll die in the Arctic!'

David gave a half smile as he placed his hands firmly on her shoulders. 'Course I won't. I'll be back in five or six months.'

'Months!' she groaned, rolling her eyes in distress. 'What on earth gave you such a fool notion?'

David pulled her gently to him and cradled her against his chest. 'I was nine . . .' he started.

'Nine?' Ruth jerked her head up in surprise.

'Aye. Pa took me to Whitby when he went to see about selling hides and sheepskins for the squire.' David's mind

10

spanned the years, recalling the busy, bustling Yorkshire port which sent its ships to all corners of the known world; the ships with their tall masts soaring high above the quays, their rigging trellising the sky; the pungent smells of fish and rope; the incessant screeching of the gulls as they wheeled in graceful flight, or flapped frenziedly in fight for some tempting tit-bit; and, not least of all, the river and sea swirling into unity between the protection of the two stone piers.

'Pa showed me the whalers,' he went on, 'and told me they sail far to the north, to hunt big whales from tiny boats so that we can have oil for our lamps. I've wanted to sail with them ever since.'

'You niver told me,' she pouted.

'Told no one until today. Told Ma and Pa this afternoon, that's why I was late,' he explained.

'What did they say? Didn't they try to stop you ganning?' Ruth would have been surprised if David had secured their blessing readily.

'Course they did,' he said, 'but I finally persuaded 'em. So now I can gan and earn good money on a whaleship. After the first voyage, I'll come for thee.'

'But you don't know if they'll tak' you on for this season.'

'If not, I'll find some other work and gan to the whaleships next year.'

'Then you'll be gone longer,' she cried. The prospect of even longer without him made her voice sharp with despair. 'What will I do? Please don't gan!'

'I must, luv.' David frowned. He knew the pain he was causing, but he also knew that the only way for a better

11

life was to go now. Ruth would come to realise it and would thank him one day.

She twisted round, pushing herself from his arms, and facing him with fury in her eyes. She sniffed back her tears and brushed her hair away from her cheeks. 'You're only thinking of thissen. What about me? You're leaving me to a livin' hell with no one to turn to.' Her words blazed at David as she tried to shame him into staying. She sprang to her feet and her face flamed angrily down at him. 'You don't care about me. If you did you'd stay, or else tak' me with you.' Her lips curled in contempt. 'You're just abandoning me. You won't . . .'

David had scrambled quickly to his feet. He grabbed Ruth and jerked her to him. His eyes met hers, unflinching. 'I'm not abandoning thee! It's to help thee escape, to get a better life for us, to be rid of poverty.'

'If you loved me . . .' Her cry was cut off.

'Course I love thee. That's why I'm gannin'.'

'It's not.'

David crushed her to him and his lips came down fiercely on hers, stifling the hurtful words which threatened to engulf them both. Ruth gasped at his unbridled passion. He had never kissed her like this before. She resisted for a brief moment. Then she was swept along on a tide of sheer joy, her anger forgotten.

Her arms came up around his neck and she clung close to him as she returned his kiss. Her mind, cleared of its boiling fury, began to see a way in which she might still persuade David to stay. Show him what he would be missing if he went, show him how she could please him even more. So far their loving had gone no further than cuddling and kissing. There had been times when the temptation to give way to their desires was great but Ruth had always held back, remembering what had happened to other village girls who had gone too far. But now, she was prepared to go to the limit if it would hold David to her.

Her lips trembled and sent a renewed hunger coursing through David's veins. She felt his passion intensify and in the sensation her legs weakened. Her knees gave way and she sank into the hay, taking David with her, their lips still pressed together.

'Ruth, Ruth, I do love thee, I do. Niver forget it,' he gasped when their lips parted.

'And I love you,' she whispered. She caressed his face with her hand. It strayed across his chin and down to the buttons on his shirt. She unfastened two of them and slid her fingers teasingly across his chest.

David pulled her closer and there was desire in his kiss and eagerness as his hand smoothed her breast.

Her fingers moved across his belly to the top of his breeches. Soon she would have David in her power, able to bend him to her will, able to make him stay and forget Whitby and the whaleships. She pressed her warm, soft body closer to him, whispering into his ear, 'I love you, David.'

He moaned under her gentle caressing hands and she sighed as his finger marked the furrow between her breasts. 'I'm yours, David, take me!'

Suddenly he broke the kiss and rolled away from her. He lay spreadeagled in the hay, his eyes fixed on the roof, his body heaving with deep breaths as he fought to bring his craving under control.

Ruth, her mind pounding as it was torn between her own desire and the thwarting of her plans, sat up and stared wildly at him. 'What's the matter?' she snapped. 'I thought you said you loved me.'

'I do, Ruth, I do.' David turned his head and saw annoyance in her eyes. 'But this is not the way; this is not the time. When I come back from the whaleships, when I can tak' thee to Whitby, when I know our future's safe, then I'll love thee as you want me now.' He sat up and came closer to her. He pressed her pouting lips with his fingers but she took no notice and kept her eyes downcast. 'Please, try to understand,' he went on. 'What I'm doing will be best. It'll mean a new life, we'll be better off and you'll be able to forget all the brutality you've suffered.'

The word startled Ruth. She glanced up at him and he was disturbed by the frightened look which flashed into her eyes like some cornered animal. 'Oh, God, I'll be late. He'll be waitin' for me.' She scrambled to her feet, straightened her clothes, and grabbed her shawl from the hay. Panic gripped her as the vision of her step-father, belt in hand, drove all other thoughts from her mind. Maybe, just maybe, he had lingered at the inn longer than usual, maybe the rain had deterred him from leaving Pickering. Maybe she would still be home before him.

David was on his feet beside her. 'Calm down, Ruth, calm down,' he urged.

'Could you if you knew you was going to get a belting? I must be off.'

As she turned, David grabbed her by the arm. 'I'll come with thee an' see he don't touch thee.'

'An' what happens after you've gone? I get it worse.'

14

Ruth was wild-eyed. Desperately she shook herself free from David's hold. She ran across the byre and bent for the ham.

'Ruth, I'll see thee afore I go tomorrow,' he called.

She froze. She straightened slowly and looked round at him. 'Tomorrow!' she gasped.

David nodded. 'I must beat the snow that's coming. Thee knows how it can be on the moors between here an' Whitby.'

'So we won't be coming to our byre any more.' Ruth's voice trailed away in dejection. She stared at him for what seemed an eternity. Disappointment, hurt, betrayal and accusation all crossed her face and raised an agonising torment in David's very soul. Broken-hearted, tears streaming down her face, she turned, pulled the sacking aside and ran out into the pouring rain.

David gazed at the sacking swaying in the wind. He flung himself forward and tore it down.

'Ruth!' The wind tossed his word away. His eyes narrowed to pierce the gloom of the driving rain. There was no one. Ruth had gone.

Mud squelched through Ruth's toes as she slithered and slipped towards the hovel she called home, though there was no home there as far as she was concerned. All it provided was a dry corner and a roof over her head.

She was not aware of her wet clothes clinging miserably to her body. She was empty of all emotion, numbed by those three words: 'I go tomorrow.'

She gasped for breath, but dared not slacken her pace. Maybe she would be in time. Maybe . . .

A figure appeared in the doorway of the cottage.

Fear struck.

Ruth's step faltered. She saw her step-father, big, powerful, his shoulders hunched like some demon about to strike. He reached to his waist. A moment later he held his belt between his hands and then let one end drop beside him. The buckle dangled near the ground! She stopped, frozen by the thought of the hard metal biting into her flesh.

'C'm on, y' bastard!' the voice boomed at her. 'C'm 'ere!' Ruth could not move. 'C'm on! Where y' been? Whorin' again? Where's my meat? Hell, if you've lost it . . .' His voice trailed off in a snarl. 'Fetch it!' The words came with such viciousness that they startled Ruth. They jerked her back to reality. There was no escaping. Slowly she moved towards the cottage.

Chapter Two

David stepped into the kitchen, into the familiar world of the early Tuesday routine of the Fernley household, a routine which must be followed even if one member was about to break the family unity which, less than twenty-four hours ago, had seemed impregnable.

In the centre of the big kitchen his father sat at the head of a scrubbed, whitewood table. His mother, at the opposite end, was spreading dripping on an oatcake. Betsy and Jessica on one side and John on the other were eating frumenty from wooden bowls. Above the turf fire a kettle hung on a reckon, puffing steam gently from its spout, and beside it fresh oatcakes were cooking on a backstan.

David would always remember this homely scene, as well as that of his parents sitting of an evening in the two wooden chairs beside the fireplace, the long hard day's work over, his father weary but contentedly smoking his pipe, his mother knitting or sewing, to eke out his father's wage.

Kit Fernley, Cropton born and bred, had impressed the squire by his ability and hard-working manner so that he had been offered a secure job on the farm, ensuring some stability and measure of comfort for his family. The hard days in the open had taken their toll and David had seen the lines on the weather-beaten face deepen recently. It hurt him to see the broad, powerful shoulders begin to assume a slight stoop and he knew that the years of scything, of lifing heavy sacks, of handling sheep and cattle, of being soaked by the rain and snow and penetrated by the wind were ageing his father with aches and pains. But Kit never complained and there was always a sparkle in his dark eyes so very much like David's.

'C'm on, lad, what's kept thee?' Kit said, pointing to the empty place at the table. He was sorry to see his son leave but hid his own feelings knowing that he had to be stong for Martha, his wife.

'Been packing, Pa.' David dropped his cloth bag beside the door.

'Got everything?' his mother asked, as he crossed the reed-covered floor.

Their eyes met.

Hers were filled with sadness brought about by the first major upheaval in the family. His pleaded for understanding and her blessing.

Martha was a Pickering lass whom Kit had met one market day when love had blossomed to the exclusion of anything else. When they married, he was made a confined labourer and the squire offered him a rent-free, tied cottage.

It hadn't been easy raising four children on Kit's wage

of a pound a month. The daily labour of household chores seemed never ending but Martha also fitted in three days a week skivvying to earn a few coppers more.

'Yes, Ma, couple o'shirts, my jump-jacket, a jersey and my shoes. I'm wearing my boots, sitha,' replied David, pointing to his feet. He knew his mother would want to know every detail so she could approve.

'Stockings?' she queried.

'Two pair,' said David, as he pulled out his chair and sat down. He looked across at Betsy, who had not even glanced up when he came into the room. She kept her head down close to the bowl as she toyed with her frumenty. David spotted the tears she was trying to keep hidden. 'Hi, Betsy, no crying,' he said and added, 'Thanks,' to Jessica who had brought him a warm oatcake from the hearth.

'I don't want thee to gan,' Betsy muttered. David was her favourite. Maybe it was the bond which sprang naturally between youngest and oldest, or maybe it was because David never tired of doing things for his fourteen-year-old sister, who not only carried her mother's rosy features but also her good-natured temperament. Without doubt, David knew that she was destined for a life in the farming community around Cropton.

'But I've got to,' he replied.

Betsy sniffed and shot an accusing glance at her brother. She felt he was deserting her without any thought as to how she felt.

'Hast tha, lad?' Kit's voice came gruffly, half questioning, half challenging. He had been shocked by David's announcement and a wakeful night spent worrying had not improved his morning temper.

19

David glanced sharply at his father. 'Pa, we went through all this yesterday. Thee knows why. I thought thee'd agreed.'

'Aye, lad, but do thee really know what tha's gannin' to?' Kit urged, looking up from the dripping he was spreading on a freshly cooked oatcake.

'Pa, thee showed me the whaleships. I once met a young chap in Pickering who'd been whaling. He said it's an exciting life.' David's eyes brightened as he recalled the tales he had heard. 'We'll sail to the edge of the ice, and its daylight all the time up there.'

'How can it be?' snuffled Betsy derisively, half to herself.

'It is,' whispered Jessica, leaning towards her sister. 'Shh, don't interrupt.' Jessica wanted David to go on. She sensed the eagerness in his voice. Her eyes, dark like David's, gazed admiringly from an oval face framed by dark hair cascading to her shoulders. She was pleased her parents had agreed. At sixteen, hers was a deep sisterly love, unlike Betsy's adoration. She knew she would feel David's departure but it would be in the more grown-up way of a girl on the verge of womanhood. She dreaded the break in the family, the first loss in her life, but she wouldn't hold David back, for she realised he was going to do something on which he had set his heart and she wanted him to achieve his ambition. She saw in David's departure the possibility of her own escape from farm life which held little attraction for her. It was difficult for a girl to satisfy the restless burning within her, but with David in Whitby the possibility of doing so was greater. She wanted him to succeed not only for his sake but for hers too.

'I'll get paid good brass,' he went on enthusiastically as if there had been no interruption. 'Everyone gets a share of the catch when the ship gets back to Whitby. After six months this lad had come home with twenty pounds.'

'What!' Martha flopped back in her chair and stared disbelievingly at him.

'Rubbish!' sneered Kit. 'He'd no such thing. Get such damn' fool ideas out of your head.'

'It's not rubbish, Pa. He told me . . .' David started to protest.

'You'll believe owt if you believe that,' Kit mocked. 'Besides, lad, remember, if it's right, it's nobbut for six months. What's he do for the rest of the year?' He eyed his son shrewdly, figuring he had made a point.

'It's more than you get,' retorted David. He bit sharply at his oatcake.

'Maybe it is, lad, but you's forgettin' I'm allowed a cow, so I get milk, I can keep a pig and some hens, and I lives rent free on top of twelve pounds a year.' Kit reached for another oatcake.

David swallowed. 'Aye, Pa, but there's a chance for promotion in whaling – there's nowt in farming but hard work every day of the year.'

This talk of big money upset Martha who hoped it wasn't turning John's thoughts the same way. She glanced at her younger son to reassure herself.

Although John was staring goggle-eyed at David, she felt sure he would not follow his brother to Whitby. John was too much of the land. At seventeen there was still a lot of boy in him, though Martha had no doubt that, with

21

David gone, John would approach manhood sooner. He was a fine, strong lad, happy to be helping his pa, even when there was no casual work for which the squire would pay him. His brown eyes always shone, and his square-cut face always glowed with pleasure after a day in the fields or out on the moors. He had an affinity with animals, always looked forward to lambing time and was eager to help when a cow was calving.

No, John would never leave Cropton, nor would Betsy, but Jessica? Martha's motherly intuition told her that Jessica might be another story for she was a lot like David.

Wanting to prevent an argument developing, Martha stood up. 'Finish your oatcake, lad, I'll get some frumenty. What did Ruth say?' Martha went to the hearth and lifted a pan which had been set close to the hot turf. She stirred the contents and spooned some into David's bowl.

'Doesn't want me to gan,' he replied.

Martha nodded but did not press the matter when David offered no more.

The mention of Ruth set David wondering if Ruth was all right. Had she reached home before her step-father? Was he right in leaving her or should he take her to Whitby? But what would she do when he had sailed with the whaleships?

'You finished, Betsy?' Martha broke into his thoughts as she returned the pan to the hearth.

'Yes, Ma,' she replied sulkily.

'Then, sup up your cocoa and get thissen ready for school,' ordered Martha gently. She knew how much her youngest would miss David.

'Don't want t' gan, an' don't want me cocoa!'

'Now, none of that,' Martha scolded. 'You need a warm drink this cold morning.'

'Come here, Betsy,' David intervened to head off trouble. When she glanced sheepishly at him, he winked at her and inclined his head for her to come to him.

She gulped her cocoa, slid off her chair and, with mouth set tight, came round the table.

David fished among the coins in his breeches pocket, coins which he had saved secretly over a long period for the day he would leave for the whaleships.

'Here you are,' he said, putting one arm around his sister and holding up a halfpenny in the other. 'Do as Ma says. No more crying, and treat thissen to some goodies at Mrs Simpson's.'

Betsy's eyes brightened at the sight of the coin and the thought of sweets. 'Oh, Davey, thanks.'

He grinned and gave her a hug as she took the money. Her tears forgotten, and with David's parting assuming some excitement for her, Betsy ran from the kitchen.

Kit drained the last of his tea. 'Well, I must away. Valley Field today.' He pushed himself from his chair and went to the outside door from which he took his cloth coat from a peg. 'Coming, John?' he asked as he shrugged himself into it.

'Aye, Pa,' said John. He stood up and turned to David. 'Sorry thee's leaving, Davey, but best of luck.' He held out his hand and felt it taken in a firm grip.

'Thanks, John,' said David. 'Tak' care of thissen, and Ma and Pa.'

John nodded. There was a lump in his throat. He

slackened his grip, slapped David on the shoulder and went for his coat.

Kit crammed a round, felt hat on his head, and drew himself to his full height for the parting. He eyed David. 'Well, lad, this is it.'

He stood up and came to his father. Their hands met in a grip of deep affection. David saw a dampness in his father's eyes. 'Tak' care, lad. Remember your promise. Back in six months if you don't get work.'

'Right, Pa.' David's voice broke.

Kit knew it was no time to linger. He gave his son a friendly slap on the shoulder and without another word he and John hurried from the cottage.

David turned slowly back to the table to see his mother standing beside his chair, the pan of frumenty in her hands. As usual she was wearing a white apron over her voluminous black dress and a mob cap covering her head. He could never recall seeing her with her hair down.

'Some more, Davey? You need summat warm in thee. I put some raisins in specially.' Martha started spooning into his bowl.

'Thanks, Ma,' he said as he sat down.

'Ma, can I set David?' Jessica glanced at her mother hopefully.

'All right, lass,' said Martha, straightening from placing the pan on the hearth. 'But get bucket on the fire, it's still washday, tha knows.'

Jessica sprang from her chair, delighted at her mother's approval. She grinned at David who returned her smile.

Martha sat down at the table. 'We'll all miss thee, David.' She swallowed hard, holding back the tears.

'And I'll miss you.'

'I'll pack thee some food. Goodness knows when thee'll next get a meal.' Martha went on, needing to be busy.

'Thanks, Ma.'

Betsy, dressed for school, ran into the kitchen. Still clutching her coin, she kissed David. 'Bye, Davey.' She turned, kissed her mother, and hurried to the door.

'Bye, Betsy,' he called. 'Be a good lass.'

Jessica had brought the large bucket to the fire and was filling it with water from the pump in the yard. Soon it would be bubbling and steaming, boiling the clothes. Soap made for the village folk from mutton fat by hall servants under instructions from the squire's lady would be flaked into the water. The smell, wafted on the steam, would soon fill the kitchen.

When Jessica had finished filling the bucket she went outside again to the trough and removed the wooden wash tub, kept immersed so that it did not dry out and crack. She brought it inside to the stone sink under the window and, after bringing some more water from the pump, cleaned the tub ready for the clothes to be pounded with beating sticks.

By the time she had done this, David had finished his breakfast and Martha had packed oatcakes, cheese and her home-made backstan cake into David's shoulder bag.

As he left the table Jessica reached for her brown cloak and woollen shawl from a peg on the door.

'Wrap up well, Jess,' Martha said. The moment she had dreaded all night was near. 'That wind's too lazy to gan round thee. You too, Davey. It'll be a might cold on the tops. And put your pattens on, Jess, to keep your feet dry.'

David shrugged on his coat and pulled a felt hat on to his head. He turned to his mother. 'I'd best be off.'

Martha came to him with outstretched arms. Tears streamed down her face as she enfolded her son and hugged him tightly.

'Tak' care, lad,' she whispered, unable to raise her voice.

'I will, Ma.' He kissed her on the cheek and eased himself from arms unwilling to release him. He picked up his cloth bag and took the shoulder bag with another word of thanks. 'Ready, Jess?'

'Yes,' she replied, pinning the shawl beneath her chin.

David went to the door and stepped outside without another word. If he paused once more he knew he would succumb to the emotion which was tightening his throat.

Martha, her shoulders drooping, leaned against the doorpost and watched her son, with Jessica beside him, stride across the valley towards the slope rising to the moors.

Reaching a small wood close to the foot of the slope, David felt that the break had been made, that now he could pause and look back. The cottage was a mere outline through the gently rising mist. Smoke curled and hung above the roof. A figure still stood in the doorway. David waved. He saw an arm raised in acknowledgement. He turned his back on home.

They started up the long gentle slope leading out of the trees towards the moors. Their feet slipped and slithered on the soft earth. David held out his hand to help his sister.

'I'm pleased you're gannin', Davey,' she said.

David glanced at her with curiosity. 'Glad to be rid of me?' he jested.

'Nay, you know I'm not.' Jessica smiled wryly. 'I'm pleased because it's what you've always wanted to do.'

'I thought no one knew,' said David, surprised at his sister's observation.

'I did because I'm like you. One day I'll leave Cropton, too. One time when you comes home you'll have to tak' me back to Whitby.'

David stopped, stunned by her words. He knew he should tell his sister that girls did not think this way, that she should get such foolish notions out of her head but how could he? Wasn't he doing just what Jessica wanted to do? He couldn't criticise. He turned and looked hard at her. 'Be patient, Jess. Remember, I might not find any work. I might be forced to come home.'

'You'll find a whaleship, I know you will.' Jessica smiled, pleased that David had not disapproved.

'I won't if we don't get on.' He laughed. He turned and started up the hill, taking Jessica with him. 'Tell no one, Jess, not yet.' There was a serious warning in the look he shot her and she knew he did not want their mother and father to suffer more pain.

'I won't,' she promised.

'I told Ruth I'd see her before I left,' said David, changing the grip on his cloth bag.

'Right, I'll leave thee at the top of the hill. I'll get back and help Ma with the washing.'

The roughness of the tufted grass gave way to the confusion of dead brown, bracken. The snows of the late

27

year had held it under pressure through January until the recent unusual thaw. Now the fronds lay sodden and broken as if resigned to a further beating before the freshness of spring brought a new life.

They reached the top of the hill and stopped. The bracken drifted into the short remains of the heather which stretched to the far horizon. With the hillside no longer offering them protection against the wind, they pulled their clothes more tightly to them.

'Looks as though I'll be just in time,' commented David, indicating the heavy clouds to the north. 'Winter's returning. A couple of days and the tracks across the moors will be impossible.'

'No lingering, David, please.' There were tears in Jessica's eyes.

'All right, Jess. Goodbye then.' He looked hard at his sister, then embraced her.

'Goodbye, David, tak' care of thissen.' She stepped back and stood with the wind plucking at her shawl, gazing at him. She wanted to remember him this way. His face filled with brotherly love for her, his eyes bright with determination. David a man, the boy gone forever.

'Davey! Davey! The distant cry, on the wail of the wind, intruded momentarily.

Brother and sister looked at each other. Had they heard a voice or was it imagination?

'Davey! Davey!' the cry came again, battling to pierce the gale.

David and Jessica spun round to see a figure, half running, half stumbling along the edge of the hill.

'Ruth!' David gasped. He dropped his bags on the

28

track and, with Jessica close behind, plunged through the winter-stunted heather.

Ruth stumbled, reaching out as if she would hold on to the two figures before they vanished. She fell and struggled to her feet, only to trip again and lie still, no longer able to summon the strength to struggle on. She began to sob, her face buried in her arms in the cold, wet mud.

David was on his knees beside her. He turned her over and gasped with horror at the sight which met his eyes.

Ruth's right eye was half closed with an ugly blue weal spread around it. A gash on her forehead in which the blood had congealed ran to her eyebrow. Her left cheek was cut and her lips gashed and swollen. Her dress, torn down one side, revealed dark bruises.

'Oh, my God!' Jessica's eyes widened with shock.

Ruth flung her arms round David's neck. 'Davey, tak' me with you. You must! I can't go back!'

'What happened?'

'He was waiting for me when I left you. He was drunk. I got belted for being late. This morning he started on me again.' Ruth shivered. 'He niver let up, reminding me I wasn't his, calling me names. I could tak' it no longer. I told him I'd soon be gannin' to Whitby with you.' She paused and swallowed hard, drawing strength to go on.

'What then?' pressed David.

'That made him worse.' Ruth shuddered at the memory. 'He said I had to stay to work for Ma. When I said I wouldn't, he went wild – hitting me and kicking me, taking no heed of Ma's shouts, shoving her out of the way when she tried to stop him.' The words choked in her throat.

'Damn t' man!' David seethed with anger. 'What sort of animal is he? I'll beat the daylight out of him.'

'No, David, no!' cried Ruth. 'Just tak' me with you.' she pleaded. Then winced and held her side.

'Ruth, you aren't fit to travel to Whitby. You'd not get as far as Saltersgate,' he pointed out.

'David's right, Ruth, you couldn't get there in your condition.' Jessica lent support to her brother.

Ruth looked wide-eyed at each of her friends, her face creased with desperation. 'What am I going to do?' Tears of despair filled her eyes. 'I can't go back.'

David looked at Jessica. 'Tak' her home, Jess. Ma will look after her.'

'But I can't put on her. Besides, that pig'll find me,' wailed Ruth. 'Please stay, David. Please!'

His brow furrowed with worry. He was badly shocked by Ruth's condition, and tussled with the right thing to do. Should he stay, marry Ruth and settle for a life on the land? It would be the simplest way out and would please Ruth and appease all the fears she had of further confrontations with Nathan. But there was doubt in David's mind, for that road would lead to nothing but a life of unrelenting farmwork. His lot would never be better than his pa's – a measure of security, a bare living, but back-breaking, soul-destroying graft, day after day. To derive any satisfaction from that you needed to be born with the smell of the land in your nostrils and the feel of earth in your hands. It was not the same for him as it was for John. That visit to Whitby nine years ago had convinced him. Now a new life was within his grasp; he couldn't give it up. It meant so much to him and Ruth.

He looked hard and pityingly at her. 'I must gan. It's for the best. I'll warn Nathan to leave thee alone,' he reassured her. 'And Pa will see you comes to nay harm. You must gan back with Jessica. There's no other way. Ma will understand.' He helped her gently to her feet.

'It'll be all right,' confirmed Jessica, taking Ruth by the arm. 'You'll be safe with us.'

'David, stay,' she moaned with tears streaming down her face.

A cold bite came into the wind. It whirled and clutched at the three figures on the edge of the moors.

'I can't, luv,' he said. 'Jess, tak' Ruth now.' He kissed her on the cheek. 'Bye, luv, I'll be back to marry thee in the autumn.'

Marry! The word gave Ruth hope. 'Stay and marry me now!' she cried, excitement in her voice.

'I can't, luv. I'd miss the whaleships.' He swung round quickly and strode off in the direction of the Cornforth hovel.

'No, Davey! No!' screamed Ruth as she struggled to be free of Jessica whose grip tightened to detain her.

In spite of Ruth's cries, David kept on walking, letting the wind whisk them away until he could hear them no more.

As he hurried along the rough path, through the stunted heather and dead bracken where the moors dipped to the slope, the picture of Ruth's bruised and battered face haunted him and stoked the fires of his anger.

When an ill-kempt cottage came into view, surrounded by mounds of rubbish overgrown with briars and nettles, he cut down the hillside. A child came out of the open door and, after a few paces, stopped, stared for a moment, then turned and ran inside. A few moments later he saw Ruth's mother appear and lean against the doorpost. One after the other, seven children pushed past her and stood around the doorway staring in his direction.

David was within two hundred yards of the cottage when he saw Rebecca Cornforth lurch and stagger, pushed roughly out of the way by her husband who stumbled out of the cottage and stood swaying, feet astride, in front of his family.

The three youngest children broke away from the group and ran towards David. He did not alter his stride when they reached him and skipped around beside him.

'Our Ruth's gone,' laughed the youngest, looking up at David with a satisfied grin on her grimy face.

'I'm glad,' shouted the girl beside her, and wiped her running nose on her jumper sleeve, shiny with repeated use.

'So, 'm I,' agreed the bare-footed boy in torn trousers and dirty, patched shirt who ran on David's right. 'Pa whipped her good an' hard. Should've seen it.' He chuckled at the recollection. David was shocked by the perverse delight in the boy's tone which was now matched by his sisters' giggles.

'Thumped her reet hard.'

'Should've seen t' blood.'

'Tore her clothes.'

'Y' could see her . . .' grinned the boy lecherously.

David glared at him but did not alter his stride towards the cottage. Nathan Cornforth's hunched shoulders belied his height and hid some of his power in his immense frame. David met the glare which came from dark angry eyes hooded by bushy eyebrows.

For a brief moment he had his doubt! Could he teach this hulk of a man a lesson? He had to! He must! The memory of Ruth fuelled the anger inside him and he did not alter his stride.

'Don't ever touch her again, Cornforth!' hissed David, his eyes narrowing with the warning. He stopped in front of Nathan.

'Like 'ell you'll tell me what to do!' Nathan snarled and spat in contempt. 'Hast she come snivellin' to thee?'

'She's being taken care of. She won't be coming back here. Thee leave her where she is. Touch her again and I'll kill thee.' The words came sharp and incisive and David drew strength from his own boldness.

Nathan's lips tightened. 'You send that hussy back home. She has to help her ma.'

'She ain't coming,' snapped David.

'Ain't she?' Nathan's laugh was harsh and contemptuous. He'd have to show this whippersnapper who was boss. He launched himself at David.

The speed of the movement from such a big man, still the worse for drink, almost caught David unawares. At the last moment he slipped the charge and drove his fist hard into Nathan's face. It jerked him to a sudden stop. David swung round and punched him hard on the side of the head, sending the big man stumbling sideways to pitch

33

to the ground. David moved again swiftly and smashed his fist into Nathan's nose. Blood spurted. He struck again but Nathan ducked under the blow and grasped David's legs. A sharp tug brought him crashing to earth, driving the breath from his body.

With a snarl of triumph, Nathan flung himself forward and smashed his fist into David's cheek. His head reeled. Through half-glazed eyes he saw the powerful body on its knees towering above him. Nathan's fist plunged downwards. David twisted his head and the blow glanced along his temple, causing Nathan to lose his balance. David rolled over, driving his knees into Nathan's side.

He scrambled to his feet but Nathan was just as quick. The two men circled each other, their eyes never wavering, each watching for a sign of attack. Nathan flicked his blood running from his nose. David ignored the trickle from the gash in his cheek.

Nathan sprang, his movement so quick that, although David took a step back, Nathan caught him in a bear hug. David winced under the pressure. Nathan's face was close, an evil grin of triumph from which whisky and beer fumes issued. 'Now y'll pay y' bastard.' He crushed harder. David's mind felt as if it would explode. He must escape or else he was finished. He staggered under Nathan's weight, altered his stance and brought his knee sharply up into the other man's crotch.

Nathan grunted from the pain searing through his body. His face creased in torment. Sensing his grip was about to slacken, David snapped out of the stranglehold. Nathan doubled up, trying to alleviate the agony which coursed through him. David sucked in air, and struck hard at Nathan's face, lancing the flesh above the eyebrow. Nathan swayed. He flung a blow which cut David's forehead but did not stop David's fist swelling his eye and lacerating his cheek. Nathan staggered. David sensed victory. His eyes gleamed in triumph as a measured punch took Nathan on the side of the jaw and sent him crashing to the ground. Breathing heavily, Nathan struggled to get up. His mind urged him to fight but his body was unwilling. He sank back as David towered above him. Once more he tried to push himself up but David shoved him back with his foot.

His chest heaving, his mind oblivious to the yells of the children and the abuse streaming from Ruth's mother, David glared at the man on the ground. 'I've told thee – lay your hands on Ruth again and I'll kill thee!'

He stepped back. Rebecca scuttled to her husband and dropped on her knees beside him. She glared at David, her eyes ablaze with hatred.

'She got what she deserved,' she yelled. 'Stuck-up brat! Just like her father? Damned hussy, too big for her shoes!'

'She's being take care of. Don't try to bring her back,' snapped David. He swung round and hurried away, pausing to douse his blood-stained face in a water trough.

'Don't want 'er back! You can 'ave 'er! Hope the scheming bastard does for thee as y' deserve,' Rebecca screamed after him as she restrained Nathan, who cursed her for not letting him get after David. But she knew that, in his present state, Nathan would only absorb more punishment.

David climbed the hillside, striding out of his system the fury which burned deep. The sharpness in the wind as he topped the rise cleared his mind. The sky had darkened even more ominously. David frowned. He did not like the signs. He needed to be across the moors. He found his bags and lengthened his stride.

Martha straightened from her wash-tub and stood staring unseeingly out of the window. A tear ran down her cheek and plopped into the water in the tub. Her son had gone. Would she ever see him again? Had the struggle all these years been for nought? She sighed, wiped her cheeks and was about to turn her attention back to her washing when she saw two figures appear across the vale. Jessica – and she appeared to be helping someone.

Martha moved quickly to the door and stepped outside. Annoyed that her eyesight was not what it used to be, she narrowed her eyes to try to pierce the distance. The figures came nearer. Who was it? What was wrong? 'Ruth!' Martha gasped and started forward to meet the two girls.

'Oh my God!' Martha was shocked by the sight of Ruth's bruised and battered face on which the blood had congealed. 'What happened?' She thrust the query at both girls as she looked quickly from one to the other.

'Her pa did it,' said Jessica. 'She was on the moor, coming to find David. He asked if you'd look after her, Ma, said not to let her pa tak' her back, and when he comes home from Whitby he'll marry her.'

Martha stared aghast at Jessica. Another lass in the house, maybe against her mother's wishes. Maybe there'd be trouble from Nathan. And marry! David had said he would marry her! This was too much to take in. Martha's mind felt in a whirl but the practical woman exerted herself. First things first. 'C'mon, lass, let's get thee inside and tidied up.'

'Get some water, Jessica,' said Martha when they reached the house.

She went to the kettle which was always hanging on the reckon and poured some water into a bowl. She tested it and cooled it with water from the pump while Martha help Jessica to undress in front of the fire.

Both Martha and Jessica were shocked by the bruised and lacerated body.

Seeing the horror on their faces, Ruth said, 'I'm always like this.' She looked appealingly at Martha, her eyes wide. 'You won't send me back, Mrs Fernley! You won't! Please.' There was fear in the rising tone of her voice.

'Not if we can help it, lass,' said Martha.

She and Jessica busied themselves cleaning and dressing Ruth's battered body as gently as they could. When Martha was satisfied that they had done all they could, she turned to Jessica. 'Tak' Ruth and give her some of your clothes, you're about the same size.'

When the door closed behind the two girls, Martha sank wearily on to a chair. What a day this had been so far! She knew of the friendship between her son and Ruth but she had not expected talk of marriage – not yet. She realised that in the deep recesses of her mind she hoped it would never happen. Something held her back from feeling joy at David's choice. There was something about Ruth which she could not put her finger on, something which made her feel that, although she felt sorry for her, Ruth was not right for David.

* * *

Out on the desolate moors, the wind forced David to hunch his shoulders. He grimaced at his aching body, legacy of Nathan's blows, but did not alter his stride. He had won! There was a new life ahead and he was determined to seize it and give Ruth everything she desired. He strode on towards Saltersgate, the carrier and Whitby.

Chapter Three

David paused at the edge of the hill. To his right the track-way from Pickering plunged over the escarpment and stretched across the dark moors to be lost in the wild horizon. Below him, beside the track, he saw a building, black in the fading light.

David drew a deep breath of satisfaction. Saltersgate Inn! He was ready for a bed. It had been a hard walk, not helped by the pain from his encounter with Nathan. He cut down the slope, sending rivulets of stones rolling before his feet.

He eyed the building apprehensively as he approached it. No light gleamed between the cracks in the wooden shutters. Its silence gave it the air of a dead place, its menace heightened by the wind moaning round the chimney pots and setting the sign creaking eerily on its iron bar fixed high on the wall. He glanced upwards and saw a crudely painted wagon and horses, the wagoner depicted curling a long thronged whip above the horses' heads. Even the sign had an air of menace about it.

David shivered with misgiving and hesitated before thumping on the blackened door. The noise echoed back at him from the depths of the inn and when it died away it left only a ghostly silence. He shuffled uneasily and glanced about him in the gathering gloom, nervous of what the shadows might hide.

Suddenly he jumped, startled by the sharp clatter of bolts being drawn back. The door creaked open slowly, revealing a huge hulk of a man holding a lantern high.

David blinked in the light which sent shadows rippling across the man's face as the wind teased the flame. They made the scarred and rugged features look even more frightening. He saw hostility in the deep-set eyes which glared at him.

'What's tha want?' snarled the innkeeper, his thick lips curling with contempt and suspicion.

'I . . . I've . . . er . . . I've come for the carrier to Whitby,' spluttered David.

'Old Silas ain't 'ere yet.' The reply was curt with irritation. The innkeeper started to close the door.

'Can I wait?' put in David quickly. 'I want a bed for the night.' He eased the bag on his shoulder.

'Not 'ere. No room.' The man spat in the dirt at his feet. 'Tha can wait in t' stable.'

Though David suspected the man was lying, he didn't challenge him. The stable would do.

'Where's that?' he asked.

'In t' yard,' snapped the man with an ill-humoured inclination of his head to David's right.

He glanced round, saw a gateway and nodded. When he looked back, his word of thanks froze on his lips as the door groaned shut. The bolts were rammed home, signalling an end to their brief encounter.

He stared blankly at the door, shrugged his shoulders and turned towards the yard, hoping the carrier would be more friendly.

He found the solid wooden gates, hanging on heavy iron crooks in a six-foot wall. Walking into the yard, he glanced at the back of the inn. In spite of a tiny ray of light showing at one end of a shuttered window and sneaking below a door, it was just as dark and forbidding at the rear.

David shuddered. If the inn was full, why wasn't there more noise and more light? He felt uneasy. He didn't like the eerie atmosphere which hung over the place. It was as if the inn was waiting for some dire happening.

He glanced round. A single-storey building ran from the house on his left. In front of him across the yard was another long low building. To his right was what he judged to be the stable. He hoped the carrier wouldn't be long, he'd like some company. Leaving the stable door open to allow what little light was left in the sky to penetrate the darkness, he picked himself a corner and spread the straw more comfortably. He sat down with his back propped against one of the stalls and fished in his bag, thankful that he still had some of the food which his mother had packed for him.

He ate ravenously and, as he wiped his mouth with the back of his hand, wished he had a drink. Maybe the landlord would sell him some ale, though he didn't relish facing him again. Weariness after his walk, and despondency at the way he had been received by the innkeeper, had fogged his mind. David started. There was nothing to be afraid of. After all, he had faced Nathan Cornforth and won! His exhaustion and depression sloughed away.

He hurried from the stable. Cloud shadows preceded him across the yard, leaving him bathed in the first moon-glow. He headed for the light spilling beneath the back door. There was not a sound apart from the wailing of the wind. David paused at the door. Was anybody there? The landlord must be somewhere in the building. He inclined his head to listen and heard murmurings, growing louder as if someone was coming into the room beyond the door. He raised his fist to knock but before it struck the wood he froze.

'Bloody nuisance, 'im turning up.' The voice, gruff and harsh, was filled with annoyance. 'What y' tell 'im?'

'Sent 'im t' stable, Ben.' David recognised the reso-nance of the inn-keeper's voice.

'Hell! We'll 'ave to get rid of 'im afore the Gentlemen arrive,' snapped Ben.

'Y' mean . . . ?'

'Aye, slit his throat afore Old Silas arrives, then no one will know he was ever 'ere.'

David's heart beat faster. His face drained into white fear. His mind, half-numbed by what he had heard, screamed for him to run but his feet would not obey. He glanced round anxiously. His things were in the stable but to go there would be fatal. Footsteps nearing the door drove him into action. He moved swiftly but quietly and froze in the shadows of the inn and its outbuilding.

The door of the inn opened and a lantern held by the innkeeper cast a wavering pool of light as two men

42

emerged from the building. David pressed himself harder against the wall, cringing back in case the landlord should wave his lantern around and spill light in his direction. But the two men were intent on their task. They crossed the yard towards the stable. Once they disappeared inside, David moved quickly. He stopped near the gateway and crouched in the shadows of the high wall. Why were they prepared to murder him to get him out of the way? Who were the Gentlemen?

He heard a loud curse from the stable. A moment later the men reappeared.

'Where the 'ell's he got to?' snarled the innkeeper, holding the lantern high.

'Snooping. There'll be hell to pay if we don't get rid of him. Let's look ower yonder.'

The men made off towards the buildings at the opposite side of the yard to David. His companion searched quickly while the innkeeper kept watch outside. David dared not move.

'Not here. Let's look around front.'

The wind unveiled the moon which lit the yard with a pale glow. The two men started for the gateway. David stiffened, poised ready to run, when other sounds intruded: the squeak of wheels, the clump of a horse's hoofs, the rattle of a wagon. The carrier! He was safe! The two men stopped.

'Damn it, Silas is 'ere. Now what do we do?' cursed the innkeeper.

'Lad wants carrier so he'll appear when Silas arrives. We'll do away with both of 'em,' hissed his accomplice.

'But Silas'll be missed.'

'Cart found ransacked on t' moor, two bodies – robbers

did it.' He chuckled at the simplicity. 'We get rid of 'em both, and who's to suspect owt?'

David chilled to the bone with horror. Who were these Gentlemen that the innkeeper and his mate were willing to commit a double murder to keep them undetected?

'D' we kill 'em now?' queried Tod.

'Naw. Silas is a wily old bird. Keeps a knife handy, an' he's good with it. Get 'im his beer and let 'em settle down. We've plenty of time afore t' first Gentlemen arrive.'

The rattle of the cart and the carrier's call to his horse drowned out any further exchanges. The carrier turned into the yard and pulled to a halt when he saw the light and the two men.

'Evenin', Landlord Sykes, an' you, Ben Chase,' he greeted them. 'What's brought you out this wild night?'

'Just checking the stable was right for thee, Silas,' replied Sykes.

'Mighty thoughtful,' he returned, puzzled by treatment he had never received before. 'Lost summat, Ben?' he added, noting Chase's restless, darting eyes.

'We'll bring your beer,' Sykes offered quickly to divert Silas's attention. The lad still hadn't appeared and Sykes was puzzled. He would need to check the stable again and the beer gave him the excuse.

'What's gotten into thee?' grunted the carrier. 'Not like thee to play genial host.' In all the ten years he had been spending two nights a week at Saltersgate, he had always collected his own beer and spirits. Never had they been brought to him. Something was not quite right and he was suspicious.

'You isn't allus 'ere to see how I treat my customers,' laughed Sykes. 'C'm on, Ben.' He started for the inn.

'Some cheese and bread wouldn't go wrong,' Silas called after them.

He led his horse forward and halted outside the stable door. David watched every movement carefully and, as soon as the door closed behind Sykes and Chase, slipped from his hiding place and hurried quietly across the yard.

Silas was unfastening the horse from the shafts when David came round the back of the cart.

'Don't unfasten it!' David's whisper had an urgent note in it.

The carrier, startled by the voice, swung round, his hand going to the knife in his belt.

David saw the movement and stopped in his tracks. The moon revealed a small, stocky man, his lined, leathery face alert with suspicion, crouching in an attitude of defence.

David raised his arms sideways so that the carrier could see that he was not armed. 'Sorry, didn't mean t' scare thee.'

At the friendly tone and gesture, Silas straightened. 'Hell, young fellow, didn't hear you coming. Shouldn't startle a body like that. You might get a knife in thee and questions asked afterwards.'

David stepped forward. 'Keep your voice down,' he urged in a whisper. 'Don't want them to hear us.' He inclined his head in the direction of the inn.

Silas frowned. ''Ere, what's going on?' he muttered. This young fellow's attitude only fuelled his suspicion at the strange reception he had received from Sykes and Chase.

Light from the lamp hanging on the side of the cart showed the suspicion on Silas's face, but beneath it David thought he saw friendliness.

'Those two are figuring on murdering us,' he explained.

'What!' Silas gasped. 'Hell, nay, I've been coming here fer ten years . . .'

'My fault,' cut in David. 'Seems I turned up at the wrong time. They want me out of the way. Summat about the Gentlemen, whoever they might be.'

Silas drew a sharp breath. 'Gentlemen? So that's it. But why me? And what do you know of the Gentlemen?'

'Nowt,' replied David. 'You're implicated because of me.' He went on quickly to tell Silas what he had overheard.

'That's a right story, young fellow,' commented Silas, a touch of doubt in his voice as he rubbed his stubbled chin.

'And true,' he urged, eyes darting towards the inn. 'No reason for me to make it up. All I want is a ride to Whitby in the morning. An' I niver heard of these Gentlemen.'

Silas had been studying David. The lad was obviously concerned, and he was right – and there was no reason for him to make up a tale like this. He had a friendly open face and certainly didn't look a fustilugs. Sykes and Chase had been in the yard, so could easily have been looking for the lad, and the reception they had given Silas was definitely out of pattern.

'Right, lad, what's your name?' said Silas.

'David Fernley,' he replied, casting another anxious glance in the direction of the inn.

'Right, David. We act as if nowt has happened. They have two hours afore first o' t' Gentlemen start arriving.'

'How do you know?' asked David, alarmed at Silas's knowledge.

He chuckled. 'Old Silas knows more than they think. Now, c'm on, help me unfasten Sal.' He turned to the leather holding the shafts.

'But we should get away,' protested David.

'Do as I says. Act normal. They'll bring us the beer, and come to kill us when they figure we'll be asleep.'

David went to the other shaft and unfastened the harness.

'Fetch Sal,' said Silas, unhooking the lantern from the cart.

David led the horse from the shafts and as they approached the stable the inn door opened.

'Good,' hissed Silas. 'Pretend to be rubbing her down.' He hung the lantern on a nail driven into the side of one of the stalls.

David positioned himself so that he could see the doorway and took a cloth to the horse's side.

'Thought you were niver coming,' Silas greeted Sykes and Chase when they appeared with a pitcher of beer, half a bottle of whisky, a plate of cheese and a loaf of bread. 'I'm a might thirsty.'

'Ah, you've met the lad,' said Sykes, placing the beer and whisky on top of a corn bin on which a merrells board had been carved.

'Aye, wants to gan with me to Whitby,' said Silas, taking the cheese and bread from Chase. 'We'll get the usual early start in the morning.'

'Then we'll leave thee to bed down,' said Sykes. He glanced across at David. 'Don't let Old Silas get thee to do all his work, lad,' he added with a half-laugh.

'Worth it for a ride tomorrow,' replied David, forcing his voice to be as normal as possible.

When the two men left the stable, David and Silas moved to the doorway. They watched the lantern weave its way across the yard and were relieved when they saw two forms, silhouetted against the light, step inside the inn. The door closed and they heard bolts being shot into place.

'Let's away, lad,' said Silas. 'Get Sal back in the shafts.' He started for the horse.

'We'll muffle her hooves,' David suggested.

'Good idea.'

He hurried to the cart and a few moments later returned with sacking and some twine. They worked quickly and soon had the horse in the shafts.

'Cart'll creak,' Silas warned.

'Can't help it,' said David. 'They won't hear the horse so we'll hope they think we're just moving the cart for convenience.'

'Right. Let's gan,' said Silas.

'I'll get my things,' returned David, and ran into the stable to collect his two bags.

'Aye, and there's no need to leave good food and drink,' added Silas, following David. He removed the bread, cheese, beer and whisky and placed them securely in the cart, while David fastened his two bags to the cart seat.

The cart's creaks and groans sounded like thunder to David and Silas as they led the horse slowly from the yard. David kept an eye on the inn expecting the back door to be flung open at any moment to release Sykes and Chase in murderous intent. But nothing happened and he and Silas breathed more easily when they turned on the track in the direction of Whitby.

'Once Gentlemen hear tell of us from Sykes, there'll be hell to pay. They'll likely come after us,' warned Silas as they climbed on to the seat.

'We'll have to hide, then.'

'Aye. About a mile further on we'll tak' an old track across the moor,' said Silas, flicking the reins to urge Sal on. 'After a quarter of a mile it forks. We tak' the left-hand path to a hollow where we can hide the cart. It's in the middle of some marshy ground. Gentlemen won't expect us to gan that way. Probably don't even know of that track.'

'Who are the Gentlemen?' asked David.

'Smugglers, lad.' Pleased to be imparting secretive knowledge, he leaned towards David. 'They're the men who run the organisation. There are six of them.'

'Smuggling? Here, in the wilds of the moors?' David was puzzled.

'Aye. Goods come by sea, are hidden in various places near the coast and later moved inland to places, such as Saltersgate, by packhorse. There must be a shipment coming tonight. That's why Ben and Tod wanted thee out of the way. Gentlemen want no stranger around when that's happening.'

'Are Sykes an' Chase two of 'em?' asked David, huddling into his coat to keep out the biting wind.

Silas chuckled. 'Not them. These Gentlemen are proper gentlemen, landed folk with money and power. No one knows who they really are – well, only the few who have contact with 'em and they daren't talk. They knows what would happen if they did.' Silas slid his finger across his throat and at the same time drew in his breath sharply. 'They're ruthless, David, kill anyone to keep their secret.'

'Isn't it dangerous for them?'

'Aye, it is, lad. Preventive Men operate on the coast but smugglers are usually too smart for 'em. Most authority turns a blind eye while it drinks smuggled brandy and dresses its ladyfolk in fine silks.'

'Do you know the six?' asked David.

'Nay, lad. And I don't want to.'

'I bet you'd like to really.' David grinned.

'Even if I knew, I wouldn't tell thee. What you don't know won't kill thee.'

'It nearly did tonight!'

Silas laughed from deep in his chest. 'Aye, you're right there, lad, it nearly did.' He eyed David. 'If we get away, keep your trap shut. They won't come looking for us in daylight 'cos we'd recognise 'em. They have their spies and they'll know if we talk about tonight. If we don't, they'll do nothing. Better to let sleeping dogs lie than stir up trouble.'

David nodded.

The last remnants of the clouds, driven by the wind, left the clear moonlight casting a silvery glow across the dark moor.

Silas cajoled Sal on to the old trackway. The cart swayed as it took the slope and David grabbed at the seat to steady himself. Once it was level again, he relaxed his grip.

'Won't the Gentlemen search this track?' he asked.

'Aye, it's possible,' replied Silas. 'But they'll be cautious about crossing the mire even in this light.'

David's eyes darted across the rough terrain, taking in the dips and hollows as likely places to hide should they need to evade the Gentlemen.

Silas guided the horse unerringly and when the track forked he had no hesitation in taking the left-hand trail which narrowed to little more than the width of the cart.

After about another quarter of a mile, the track dipped into a hollow. Silas pulled Sal to a halt, climbed stiffly from his seat and set about securing both horse and cart.

David jumped down. He took a quick all-encompassing glance round the hollow. The moonlight revealed a small amphitheatre on which the heather had not encroached. He figured they were completely hidden from both tracks, but realised that men on horseback could soon surround the hollow and trap them.

He pointed this out to Silas and added, 'Let's leave the cart here and gan back to the main track. There's a good deep ditch near it and we can see what the Gentlemen do from there.'

Silas looked doubtful for a moment but then, seeing David's point, agreed. They slipped out of the hollow and made their way quickly back towards the main way to Whitby.

'Over there.' David nodded, indicating a long deep ditch running parallel to the track. 'If the Gentlemen look like discovering the cart, we'll make off along this ditch. It's cutting back across the moor where I reckon a horse can't follow.'

Silas, narrowing his eyes, looked in the direction indicated by David. 'You're right, lad. You're a sharp 'un, no mistak'.'

They scrambled through the stunted heather, found a suitable place on its west-facing slope, and settled themselves to wait.

David shivered and huddled further into his coat. He was glad of the thick jersey his ma had knitted. Ma! If she could see her son now, crouched on the dank moor like some criminal, his life in jeopardy. And this his first night away from home!

'Here, tak' a swig of this.' Silas drew the whisky bottle from his pocket and grinned at David's surprise.

'Didn't see thee pick that up.'

'Figured we might need warming,' chuckled Silas. He thrust the bottle at David, who hesitated. 'Niver had whisky afore?' David shook his head. 'Then this is a good time to start. It'll warm thee. Just a drop. Don't want thee drunk.'

David took the bottle, put the neck to his mouth and tipped it up. He gulped as the liquid hit his throat causing him to gasp and splutter as he jerked the bottle away from his mouth.

Silas grabbed at the bottle. 'Careful, lad, don't spill it!' As David's grip slackened, Silas juggled it from him and sank back against the side of the ditch with a sigh of relief when he managed to keep the bottle upright.

David swallowed hard and felt a sharp burning sensation all the way to his stomach. He coughed, gasping for breath. Silas laughed and drank deeply from the bottle. He recorked it and stuffed it back in the deep poacher's pocket of his voluminous coat.

David gulped. 'That's like fire,' he gasped.

'Do thee good,' said Silas, settling down as comfortably as he could among the scratchy heather.

'Aye, it has,' muttered David.

A few minutes later Silas grabbed David's arm, jerking him out of the drowsiness which threatened to turn to sleep after his long day and the warming whisky.

'Horses,' Silas whispered. 'Hear 'em?'

David stiffened. Now fully alert, he inclined his head. He heard a faint, distant beat. He nodded. The waiting was over. With all uncertainty drained away, David was gripped by a strange elation, part excitement, part fear – fear of what the outcome could be but excitement at the challenge. He had outfought Nathan Cornforth and outsmarted Sykes. Could he now outwit the Gentlemen if it came to it?

The drumming of the hooves grew louder. It held to a steady rhythm, vibrating with menace. It pounded in David's mind, each beat mocking his ability and undermining his confidence. He had to see what was happening. He started to raise himself on his elbows so that he could peer over the side of the ditch.

'Don't, lad,' Silas hissed close to his ear.

'Must,' rapped David, and continued to push himself upwards.

He peered over the edge of the ditch. The riders were a black mass approaching from the direction of Saltersgate. The sight of them restored David's confidence. Now he was dealing with something he could see, something with which he could cope should the necessity arise. He kept still, eyes fixed on the riders.

Nearer. Nearer.

'Get down, lad!' Silas's note was sharp with the fear of discovery.

David gave a quick shake of his head and, with his eyes still fixed on the riders, ignored the advice.

The thrumming grew louder. Louder.

The moonlight revealed shapes. Six horsemen, three abreast, rode on the main track to Whitby. David's eyes were fixed intently upon them. They rode at a steady canter and from the movement of their heads David knew they were searching.

'David.' The word barely reached him.

Without looking round he signalled Silas to be quiet. He felt a movement beside him and smiled to himself when the carrier raised himself slowly upwards.

'Thought you wouldn't bide,' whispered David.

The only response was a low grunt from Silas whose attention was riveted on the horsemen.

'If they'd kept to this track we'd see them,' called one of the riders. 'They couldn't have got over yon ridge by now.'

'Then they must have turned on to one of the tracks across the moors,' came the reply as the six riders pulled to a halt beside the track.

Though there was the touch of a Yorkshire accent in the voices, the men were well spoken.

'There's too many tracks for us to follow tonight even though there's a good moon.' The first man steadied his champing horse.

'Let's try this one,' a rider suggested.

'No point. If they've used that one they'll run straight into Jethro and his gang with the packhorses, and he'll know what to do.' There was authority in the man's voice.

'So what do we do?' someone asked.

'Back to the inn and get ready for Jethro's arrival. That's the most important thing tonight,' came the reply. 'Sykes should have sent the lad on his way and not offered him the stable. Old Silas won't talk, the lad may know nothing, so we'll leave it. If word leaks out about tonight, we'll find the lad and deal with him then.' The man turned his horse.

For one brief moment his raised head and the moonlight revealed the face beneath the wide-brimmed hat.

David bit back the gasp of surprise which threatened to expose them. He felt his flesh tingle with excitement. It couldn't be true and yet he was certain . . . but he was denied another chance to confirm it for the riders turned their milling horses and sent them into a thunderous gallop towards Saltersgate.

David lay still, watching them grow smaller and smaller and listening to the sound grow fainter and fainter until it faded to silence, leaving him wondering if what he had witnessed had ever happened at all. His mind still cast a doubt but his eyes convinced. He had seen. He had recognised. He knew the leader of the Gentlemen.

Chapter Four

Suddenly David was aware of Silas shaking him by the arm. 'Lad, they've gone! What's gotten in t' thee?'

David started. 'Sorry, Silas,' he apologised. 'What now?' he asked, scrambling to his feet and brushing the dampness off his breeches.

'Ain't any good gannin' on. We'll wait 'til morn. Early start though,' said Silas, stretching his limbs. 'Let's get back to the cart and out of sight afore them packhorses come ower here.'

David fell into step beside Silas and they were soon back in the hollow, but all the time he was haunted by that face. What evil was he up to, what power had he that Sykes and Chase would commit murder for him?

'Here, lad, you'll need these.' Silas dragged a couple of old brown hairy blankets from under the covering on his cart and tossed them to David. 'You tak' the seat,' he said, 'I'll lower the tail-board.'

'Thanks,' David said as he caught the blankets.

He settled on the hard seat and drew his clothes and

the blankets around him to gain the best protection from the cold. He was haunted by the face he had recognised but weariness took over and he was soon asleep.

He was awoken by someone's heavy touch. In the diminishing haze of his dreams, he opened his eyes, expecting to find the Gentlemen with a knife at his throat. Instead he found Silas shaking him.

'Time for up, lad.'

David's mind cleared. He nodded and stretched his limbs, stiff with cold. He gazed upwards. The moon had waned, leaving a pale carpet of stars across the heavens. The wind had stilled and now a silent blanket hung a peaceful canopy over the moors. In those moments of silence when time is held in suspense between dark and light, his mind was touched with doubts. He faced an unknown future. Would it be filled with risks as frightening as those of the past night? What was he doing here, away from the comfort and safety of his home and family? He could easily return and . . . David started and swung quickly off the seat, annoyed with himself for entertaining such doubts. A life with the Whitby whalers offered much – an escape from a life of regular monotonous farming with little reward, a way to taste adventure, a chance for a better life and maybe riches.

'Coming, Silas,' he called.

'Bread and cheese again,' said Silas half-apologetically when David joined him. 'And then a swig of whisky to drive out the night's cold.'

Once they were on the main track, he urged the animal to a sharper pace.

The eastern horizon sharpened against a lightening sky

which sent its glow slowly across the heaven to dim the stars until they faded from sight. The light revealed a wild moor stretching in all directions as far as the eye could see. David was used to the moors above Cropton but these, remoter and far distant from the pleasant farmland between Cropton and Pickering, seemed wilder and filled with a stark desolation which warned the traveller that they would have little mercy on the unwary. They needed treating with respect.

'In all the excitement of last night, I niver got thee asked – why are you ganning to Whitby?' asked Silas, cocking a quizzical eyebrow at David. 'Looking for work?'

'Aye, none at home,' he replied. 'Hoping to join the whaleships.'

Silas pulled a face with a slight inclination of his head. 'Hard life.'

'I'll cope,' returned David quickly, a touch of offence in his voice that Silas should think that he couldn't manage life on a whaleship.

Silas chuckled. 'Don't doubt it,' he said. 'Thee's brawny enough, and sharp witted. Thee'll manage – so long as the press-gang don't get thee first.'

'Press-gang?' David's brow furrowed with a puzzled expression.

Silas leaned forward and dug in his pocket for his clay pipe. 'Here, lad, tak the reins while I light up.' He handed the reins to David, struck a match and lit his pipe. He drew on the stem and, when the tobacco was burning to his satisfaction, leaned against the back of the seat. 'Aye, press-gang forces men into the Navy. Gang'll lay quiet then strike sudden. Navy wants men 'cos of the war.

Things aren't good in the American Colonies. Rebels are getting the upper hand, and, with bloody French and damned Spaniards and Dutch all declaring war on us, it's nay wonder the press-gangs are active. So watch out, lad. Life ain't so pleasant in the Navy fra what I hear.'

'This press-gang just tak's a man like that?' said David with surprise. He flicked the reins but the horse needed little guidance along a track with which it was more familiar than he was.

'Aye, and it's a rough, hard life in the Navy. Few officers care about conditions for the ordinary ratings. Shut their eyes to the bullying and harsh treatment meted out by the mates. Poor food and floggings take their toll. It ain't a life for thee. Better a life on a whaleship, and *that* can be tough and dangerous.' Silas sent a long stream of tobacco juice into the stunted heather.

'Tell me more about the whaleships,' said David, his enquiring mind roused. He saw an opportunity to be forewarned.

'Well, you don't get flogged. Most of the captains are decent. Food's better, at least for a lot of the voyage. But it's a hard life. It's so bloody cold in the Arctic that if you fall in the sea you can freeze to death, just like that.' Silas snapped his fingers. 'And I've heard tell of boats being smashed to pieces by a whale.'

David, wide-eyed, glanced at Silas with suspicion. 'Niver.' He laughed doubtfully.

'It's true, lad.'

David lapsed into a thoughtful silence.

With the sky brightening further every minute, he became even more aware of the bleak moorland. The dead look of winter still oppressed it and snow lingered on the north-facing sides of dips and gullies. Snow at this time of the year needed more to take it away and David felt it was coming in the dark clouds which were intruding on the clear sky to the north.

'Don't look good,' he commented. 'Do thee think thee'll get back to Pickering before there's more snow?'

The carrier screwed up his face as he read the sky. 'Aye, just, I reckon.'

'Thee gans back tomorrow?' asked David, interested to know more about the carrier.

'Aye. I'll be rid of my goods today and have a load ready for an early start tomorrow.'

'What do you carry?' queried David as he handed the reins back to Silas who had spotted a section of the track over which he knew Sal would prefer his hand.

'Veg and fruit fra Pickering when available, but of course there's none of that now, so I've some timber, cloth, butter, eggs . . . anything which'll sell in a sea port.'

'And from Whitby?' prompted David, adjusting his coat to the first touch of the wind.

'Fish, spices, wine, whale oil, whalebone . . .'

'Whalebone?' David's tone showed his surprise.

'Aye. It's not bone really. Hangs in the mouth of the whale instead of teeth. Thin and fibrous. It's used for ladies' stays.'

As they talked, David's enquiring mind took in all the information which the carrier was only too pleased to impart to show off his knowledge.

The wind freshened and both men pulled their coats a little tighter against the chill. David reckoned thick snow would cover the moors before many days were past. Whitby would then be cut off from all communication inland, the sea remaining its only connection with the outside world. But Whitby would not worry. The sea was its livelihood, its passage to the far corners of the known world and to the wealth that brought.

Excitement mounted in David when the town came in sight. A new life beckoned.

Whitby lay along the banks of the River Esk. Houses were crammed into the space between the water and the steep cliffs which rose on either side of the river, but Whitby did not confine itself so rigidly. It spawned its houses boldly up the cliff face on both the east and west sides. The red roofs climbed higgledy-piggledy, seemingly one on top of the other. Terrace grew upon terrace or appeared to be supported by the chimney pots of the row below.

On the east cliff the houses stopped short of the cliff top where the ruined abbey, the ancient parish church with its large graveyard, and the extensive house of the Cholmley family arrested expansion. Along the riverside, upstream of the drawbridge which separated the outer and inner harbours, some fine brick-built houses looked across the water to a few elegant dwellings whose owners lived near their shipbuilding yards, scattered along the west bank beyond Bagdale Beck. The beck, running down from the high ground beyond the town, was a turning point for the west bank part of Whitby which hugged the riverside from the west pier.

Beyond the crowded red roofs, vying for position, the layout of the west town assumed a regular pattern of streets. The houses climbing the cliff face spilled over on to the flat expanse, forming the top of the west cliff. On this side of the river there was room for expansion with every sign that this was happening as the well-to-do moved from the claustrophobic confines of the older parts.

Silas shot a glance at David who had gone quiet when Whitby came in sight. He grinned at the young man sitting open-mouthed and speechless. David did not remember Whitby as such a big place and, although he gaped at what he saw, was drinking in every detail.

As the cart rumbled down the rough slope towards the town, Silas noticed David studying the houses higher up the hillside, partially obscured by a line of trees.

'Posh folk live yonder. New Buildings it's called,' commented the carrier. 'Likes o' ship owners, ship build-ers, merchants. Moved from the old town on far side of the river. More space ower here.'

David admired the imposing frontages of bow-shaped windows and arched doorways. They had a majestic air, an aloofness, as if they were lording it over the rest of the town. The houses spoke of money and elegance, of a finer and richer way of life than he had ever thought about, a life far removed from the one he had known.

There was ease and comfort on that hillside. It might take hard work to get there but at least there was some-thing at the end of it, unlike the prospects back in Cropton. David's eyes narrowed and his mouth firmed into a thin, determined line. 'One day, Ruth, you and I will live there,' he muttered to himself.

Silas gentled Sal over the rough ground, applying the brake when necessary to ease the strain. They moved past the Friends' burial ground and into Bagdale. There were signs that building was taking place to their left where the open ground climbed towards New Buildings. Equally elegant buildings with long front gardens, to keep them aloof from the uneven roadway, could be sited here. On the opposite side there were several houses of various designs and sizes with access by bridges over Bagdale Beck.

David searched his mind and recalled the old buildings and houses packed together, with no room to escape. The yards and garths, narrow and overcrowded, bred a life in marked contrast to the open, elegant proportions of these new developments.

The harbour and ships were obscured from David's view but the red roofs of the old town, flamed by an occasional shaft of sunlight through the gathering clouds, rose towards the parish church and the stark ruins of the ancient abbey on the east cliff. Smoke curled from the numerous chimneys, casting a haze over the whole scene until, above the protection of the cliff, it was whisked away by the wind.

As they rumbled further along Bagdale, David saw the roadway funnel into a street narrowed by the closeness of the buildings on either side.

'That's Baxtergate,' said Silas, pulling the horse to a halt. 'Runs down to the harbour. I'm gannin' up Scate Lane, here.' He stabbed his pipe at the roadway which curved up the hill to his left. 'I'll drop thee, lad. Best o' luck.' He jabbed his pipe back in his mouth and held out his hand.

David bit his lip as he grasped Silas's hand. He felt the parting. Though he'd known Silas for less than twenty-four hours, they'd shared an adventure, each reliant on the other. Now he would be alone in a strange town. 'Thanks for t' ride, Silas. How much do I owe thee?' David started fishing in his pocket.

Silas eyed him and smiled. 'Nay, lad, I wants nowt. You saved my life.'

'But . . .' started David. His eyes locked on Silas with gratitude.

'No buts. Get off with thee.' Silas hastened his words, not wanting to prolong the parting for he had liked this lad. 'If you're looking for lodgings you'd be better on t'other side of the river – and watch out for the press-gang.'

'Thanks,' said David. 'I'll probably see thee again when I'm crossing the moors.' He gave Silas a friendly tap on the arm and jumped down from the cart. He grabbed his bags.

The carrier nodded. 'Good luck.'

'Bye, Silas.'

David watched the cart clatter away. As it turned the curve on the hill, Silas looked back and, with his hand clenched around his pipe, raised it in a friendly gesture of goodbye.

David's lips tightened. He adjusted his woollen cap, eased the bag on his shoulder and set off down Baxtergate. The clamour and bustle intensified the further down he went. Shopkeepers called their wares, carpenters entered the raff-yards of Mr Smales or his rival Mr Barker, to buy timber and deal. David paused at the opening to Bovill's block and mast-making yard where the hammers resounded to the mast-makers' blows. He wandered on, almost overawed by all the activity. People hurried past him, others hastened from America Square and Laskill Square, where families were packed tight in small houses crowded close together. He passed Mr Chapman's sail manufactory, and when he reached the end of the street took his bearing and headed for the bridge which linked the east and west banks.

Bare-legged urchins, yelling and laughing in chase, wove their way through the crowds streaming both ways across the bridge. Sailors called raucously at pretty girls who passed. Faces were averted to hide their blushes as they hurried on with their stern-faced mothers, while others, unescorted and more used to the rough ways of a sailor town, tossed their heads in appreciative disdain or gave as good as they got. Fishermen, housewives, carpenters, shopkeepers, boatmen flowed past David as he stopped beside one end of the bridge and looked up at the wooden arms which extended outwards and held chains by which the bridge could be raised, drawbridge fashion, to allow vessels to reach the wharfs and docks of the inner harbour.

His gaze moved along the river towards the sea. On the west side a quay backed by houses stretched to a long, stone pier. A second pier curved from the east cliff so that, coming close together, the two offered protection from the sea and turned the lowest reaches of the river into the outer harbour.

David jostled his way through the crowds to get to the other side of the bridge so that he could see the inner harbour. Three merchantmen, recuperating after their long voyages, were tied to the wharfs along the east bank. Two whalers, tough, purposeful, revived and ready to search for the whale in the icy seas of the north, were moored in mid-stream.

They were there! Excitement surged through David. The whaleships! The ships he had dreamed about for nine years. He was close to a world he had longed for, a world so different from the one he had left but a world to which he felt he belonged. He must get out to the whaleships and sign on.

Glancing down to his right he noticed an old man, dressed in a thick, knitted jersey, coarse trousers and heavy boots, puffing contentedly at a clay pipe while sitting at the bottom of some wooden steps to which a rowing boat was tied.

David hurried down the steps. 'Tak me t' a whaleship?' he asked.

The weather-beaten face, scored by sea winds, looked up and grey eyes surveyed the young man making the request. They saw a broad-shouldered, well-built youngster, angular-jawed, with skin tanned from an outdoor life. From the bags he carried, it was obvious that he had just arrived in Whitby, possibly from the country. Over the years, the old man had seen scores of youngsters come, believing that their troubles were over once they had reached the prosperous sea-port. The majority had come to escape poverty and squalor but this young fellow did not look like one of them. His clothes were practical, but good and well kept. He certainly hadn't come from the clutches of dire poverty. There was something different about him. Excitement and enthusiasm danced in his eyes. The old man sensed a feeling for ships, rare in most of the young men he had seen come to Whitby eager to go to sea. And few of them wanted to join the whaleships.

The life was tough. It had a reputation for breaking men, and few would flirt with it. But those who did and survived were regarded with a sort of awe as men apart. Maybe this young fellow could become such a man. He had a powerful body, strong from hard work, which was not disguised by his clothes. He looked as if he could take care of himself and the old man sensed a determination which would not be put off easily.

'Which one?' he asked, and drew on his pipe.

'Best!' replied David, glancing enthusiastically in the direction of the whaleships.

'Nay good,' said the old man, shaking his head.

'Why?' demanded David. His eyes filled with disappointment.

'Yon, moored on the east back.' He pointed with the stem of his clay pipe in the direction of the ship. 'She's best. The *Mary Jane*. Seth Thoresby's captain, but there's only a shipkeeper on board. Tak' thee to one of the others?'

David shook his head. 'Only the best for me,' he declared. 'Where's he live?'

The old man chuckled. 'Nay good gannin' there. Disturb Seth at home with that sort of request and you'd be in trouble, then he wouldn't sign thee on. You'll have to wait 'til morn.'

David pursed his lips thoughtfully for a moment then said, 'Right, thanks.' He glanced across the water at the three ships and started slowly up the steps. He was half-way up when a voice halted him.

'Hold on, son.' David glanced back. The old man gave him an encouraging smile. 'You might find Adam Thoresby, Seth's son, in the Black Bull. He'll be able to tell thee if they've a full crew.'

'Thanks.' David brightened. 'Where's the Black Bull?'

'Cross the bridge, turn left and you'll come to the market square. Black Bull's in top corner.' The sailor gave the directions sharp and precise.

'Thanks again.' David hurried up the steps, buoyed by the hope that he might be signed on today. He wove his way through the flow of people crossing the bridge and turned into a narrow street over which the buildings almost touched, as if trying to block out the daylight fighting its way down from above. The street led into a small square. A weathered stone cross stood in the centre, around which farmers' wives and daughters sat with their butter and eggs, crying their wares and hoping to sell them all before it was time to leave for home. If not, they would have to get rid of them at lower prices to the shops in the town or else take them home.

People criss-crossed the square. Mothers, anxious to be home, cajoled their children; sailors, glad to be away from their ships, sought an inn; clerks from the shipping offices hurried about their business; artisans from the shipbuilding yards hastened to their work; four bare-footed, dirty-faced boys, their shirts and trousers torn, played on one corner of the square and were cursed by a drunken sailor for being in his way.

Seeing the half-timbered building with its painted sign of a black bull, David started across the square. He paused a moment to watch the farm girls haggling and bartering to make a sale, before continuing to the corner of the Black Bull where it turned on to Church Street. Houses, inns and shops stretched beyond his sight in both directions. The roadway was rough and, though there had been repeated attempts to level and smooth it, the ravages of weather, horses' hooves and wheels of carts and coaches had rutted it again.

Children ran in chase, scurrying into the narrow yards which climbed the cliff side or inclined to the river. Housewives stood and chatted, others hurried to a shop, old men leaned against doorways, watching the bustle of Whitby pass them by and answered the calls of friends and acquaintances who had no time to stop.

David was about to turn into the Black Bull when a commotion along Church Street drew his attention. People scuttled to the sides of the street, opening a path for a youth who raced through the milling crowd. He ducked and dived, determined not to let anyone or anything stop him.

'Gang! Gang!' he yelled, repeating the cry at frequent intervals as he drew breath.

Alarm spread through the crowds like the incessant turmoil of the sea. Men turned this way and that in panic, trying to find some means of escape and, seeing it, ran as if pursued by devils.

'Gang! Gang!'

Press-gang! David felt a chill remembering the carrier's warning. Bewildered, he looked around him. Where should he go? Run! There was nothing to do but run. Men raced past him, jostling each other to get ahead. The shouts and yells of the pursuers came along the street, growing louder. Then he saw them beating their way through the people who threatened to close in on them in an attempt to help their menfolk escape. The press-gang was nearer, nearer, two of them a short distance ahead of their companions. Someone pushed David and a female voice screamed in his ear, 'Run!' The gang was close.

He started forward, his feet pounding the rough ground. He was aware of someone alongside him. He glanced sideways and saw a burly youth straining to keep ahead of the pursuers. The young man, seeing David hampered by his bags, grabbed one of them and yelled, 'Come on!' As David released his hold on the bag it caught his helper's legs, tripped him and sent him crashing to the ground. With a shout of triumph two men were upon him. David's step faltered.

'Run!' the youth bawled again as he struggled to get to his feet, but David stopped, turned, and in the same movement swung his bag and hit one of the pressmen hard in the face. He reeled backwards, grasping at his head. The young man was scrambling to his feet, the second pressman reaching out for him, but, before the man could get a hold, David shoulder-charged him, sending him crashing into the wall.

'Run!' The bellow from the young man, now on his feet, propelled David forward.

They raced along Church Street between the lines of females, children and old men who screamed encouragement at them and obscenities at the press-gang.

'This way!' shouted David's companion. He broke through the line of people who quickly re-formed to present a barrier once the two young men had passed them.

David followed him across an open square yard with stables on one side and an inn on the other. Raucous shouts came from the street. David glanced over his shoulder and saw that the barrier of people was holding firm against the pressmen. Orders were hurled above the noise of the crowd and David knew that the press-gang had chosen to ignore them and go in pursuit of those who still fled along Church Street.

With their chests heaving from the exertion, the two men sank against the wall of the inn and let the bags slip from their fingers to the ground.

David, thankful for his escape, shuddered at the thought of how close he had been to being taken and forced into an alien life, not knowing when, if ever, he would set foot in England again, even if he survived the bruising work, the bullying and floggings – not forgetting the war.

'Thanks,' gasped the Whitby man. He held out his hand. 'Adam Thoresby.'

Chapter Five

David straightened and gaped increduously at Adam. 'Adam Thoresby?' There was a disbelieving note in his voice.

Adam looked at him with a bewildered curiosity. 'Yes. Why?'

'I was just gannin' to the Black Bull to look for thee. Old man by the bridge said you might be there,' David explained.

'I'd just left. Why?'

'The old sailor said you'd be able to tell me if your father had a full crew,' David interrupted quickly, his face eager, his eyes bright.

'You want to join a whaleship?' Adam raised his eyebrows.

'Yes.'

'Then you'd better come home with me until Whitby quietens down. We'll see what Pa has to say,' said Adam, stooping to pick up one of the bags.

Excitement coursed through David. 'Thanks, I'm beholden to thee.'

'Nay, it's thanks to thee that the press-gang didn't get me,' returned Adam. 'C'm on.'

David picked up his bag and matched Adam's stride as they left the yard.

'What's your name?' asked Adam.

'David Fernley. What happens with the press-gang now?' he queried.

'When they've the men they want, they'll leave,' replied Adam.

'So it's legal?' said David tentatively.

'Oh, aye.' Adam gave a small nod in confirmation. 'Officer in charge of the gang should get a warrant signed by town mayor, but even if it's refused he'll still try to impress men. Greenland men, whalemen to thee, are supposed to be exempt and have a protection note issued to them, but press officer often ignores it, especially with non-specialist Greenland men.'

As Adam led the way through Whitby, David studied him. He wore a short dark-green jacket with a lighter-green muffler knotted at his throat. His fawn trousers came over the top of black bootees and on his head he wore a black beret-shaped cap pulled down at one side. David saw that he was about his own age, broad-shouldered, with an open face, browned by wind and sea spray, and eyes that were dark and full of life.

'Here we are,' said Adam, opening the door of a two-storeyed house in Church Street. The name 'Harpoon House' was carved in a piece of wood over the front door.

As soon as he stepped into the kitchen, David sensed the warm, friendly atmosphere of a close family.

73

When a slightly built woman turned from a shallow stone sink where she was washing some pots, David was immediately attracted by her smile and air of calm serenity. She wore a full dress of grey poplin with the sleeves turned back at the elbows. Around her shoulders was a white lawn fichu and a close-fitting cap of matching material was tied under her chin, framing a pale face.

In a sturdy oak chair to one side of a blazing fire set in a high grate beside an oven with polished, black-leaded surrounds sat a man so much like Adam that David knew this was his father. Adam had not, as yet, grown to the maturity of this man. Although both faces had been weathered, Adam's hadn't the lined depth of years of experience. If David wanted final proof of their relationship, it was in the fire of the dark eyes. They were alert and piercing, but they were the eyes of a man used to gazing at distant horizons. Adam's had the bright, carefree attitude of the young, while his father's reflected the responsibilities which life had bestowed upon him. The older man would miss nothing and would be able to admonish and wither a wayward sailor without a word being spoken, but David also saw the underlying gentleness of a fair, just man. Thoresby wore a waist-length jacket and waistcoat, with a cravat at his throat. His grey-and-black-striped trousers came over the top of black bootees. Dark hair, curling in the nape of his neck, had a natural wave at either side of his head and ran into long sideburns.

'Ma, Pa, this is David Fernley,' cried Adam. 'Just saved me from the press-gang.'

74

'Oh, my goodness!' Emma Thoresby supported herself against the sink as the horror of what might have been flooded over her.

'What happened?' Seth scowled at the thought of losing one of his crew, let alone his son.

'Press-gang suddenly appeared in Church Street. All hell was let loose,' said Adam. 'I fell and would've been taken but for Davey. He turned back. You should have seen him deal with the two pressmen who were on my heels. Laid 'em both low.' Adam's eyes were bright and his voice rose with excitement as he swung his right fist in imitation of a knock-out blow. 'They'll not forget their meeting with David Fernley!' He spun round to David. 'Thanks again, Davey.'

He coloured at Adam's enthusiastic display.

'Thank goodness you were there,' said Emma, as she wiped her hands on her apron. Her voice had a gentle, unhurried lilt to it. It was a voice which warmed and took a person into its comfort. David felt he could listen to Emma Thoresby all day.

'Well done, lad, and thanks,' said Seth, rising from his chair and holding out his hand to David. He stepped forward and felt a hand broad with heavy work, a strong hand with power in the gnarled fingers. 'That damned press officer taks nay notice of the protection for Green-landmen.' Seth Thoresby did not disguise his contempt for the man who would deprive him of sailors. His lips tightened as he reached for a clay pipe and tin of tobacco off the high mantelpiece which crowned the surround of the fireplace. He sat down in his chair and set about charging his pipe.

'Where are you from?' asked Seth.

'Cropton, sir,' answered David briskly, wanting to create an impression on the man he was to ask for a job.

'Ah, country lad,' commented Seth, glancing up from filling his pipe.

'You know it, sir?' David was surprised that a seafaring man should have heard of his tiny village.

'Don't know it, Davey, but I've heard of it. Near Pickering, isn't it?' Seth reached for a spill beside the fire, lit it in the flames and applied it to his tobacco.

'Yes,' replied David.

'What are you doing in Whitby?' he asked between puffs which encouraged his pipe to light.

'Come to join the whalers,' returned David eagerly.

Seth eyed him quizzically. 'Have you, now? Why the whalers? No job back home?' His pipe going to his liking, Seth pinched the glow off the spill and leaned back in his chair contentedly.

'That's part of the reason, sir.'

Seth had seen many young men from the country come for a job. Some came because there was no work for them at home; others to escape the law; others still because their families no longer wanted them. This young man had said money was only part of the reason. Seth was curious.

'And rest of the reason?' he asked, his eyes firmly on David.

'Dreamed about joining the whalers ever since my pa brought me to Whitby when I was nine and I saw the ships.' His voice was filled with passion.

'Can you help him, Seth?' asked Emma. She glanced at David. 'You must be hungry. Like something to eat?'

'Of course he would,' boomed Seth. 'Sit down, lad.' He indicated a chair at the oak table which stood beside one wall.

'You could take him on, Pa,' put in Adam enthusiastically, as he pulled a chair out from under the table for David, before pulling one out for himself.

'Know anything about the life of a whaleman, Davey?' asked Seth, ignoring his son's statement.

David shook his head. 'Only from tales I've heard, and what the carrier told me – and that weren't much. Said you sailed to the Arctic and it's a hard life.' David couldn't hold back his desire to know if Silas had told him the truth. 'Is it true that whales are sixty feet long, weigh sixty tons and can smash a boat to smithereens?' The words poured out as if from some child eager for confirmation of unbelievable facts.

Seth laughed at the disbelief in David's voice. 'Aye, lad, that's all true.' David's eyes widened. 'But it's a good life, if you're cut out for it and are tough enough to tak' it. It's rough, hard work, but it can make a man of you.'

'And you gans to the edge of the pack ice?' pressed David, jerking his chair into a more comfortable position.

'Aye. It gets mightily cold,' warned Seth.

'I'm used to that – winter at home can be cold,' David pointed out.

Seth smiled. 'Aye, it can, but you ain't experienced the Arctic when the weather's vicious.'

'Don't let him put you off,' put in Adam. 'It isn't all like that.'

David smiled and glanced up at Emma when she placed

77

a plate of ham and bread in front of him. 'Thanks, Mrs Thoresby.'

'Enjoy it, lad. You're welcome.' Emma smiled back and gave a David a knife and fork. He sliced a piece of ham, enjoyed the succulent taste and asked Seth, 'What would I have to do if I got taken on?'

'Work damned hard,' boomed Seth. 'Learn the jobs of a sailor, and a whaleman in particular. Handle ropes and sails, clean decks, man an oar in one of the whaleboats, row 'til your back breaks, help with the flensing . . .'

'Cutting up the whale,' Adam explained when he saw David shoot him a puzzled look.

'. . . stow the blubber from the whale, handle the casks and so on,' Seth went on.

David swallowed some bread and asked, 'How long will I be away?'

'That bother you, lad?' Seth asked cautiously, sensing a possible chink in David's enthusiasm.

'No, sir!' David's answer came with an air of conviction which cast aside Seth's doubt.

'We're away 'til August or September, depends how quickly we fill the ship,' he answered David's question.

David nodded and quaffed the tankard of ale which Emma had brought him.

'Well, Pa? Will you tak' him on?' pressed Adam.

Seth hesitated. David looked capable, his actions in saving Adam from the press-gang showed he was quick-thinking and active, his questions revealed a lively curiosity and interest. Seth figured he'd not shirk hard work and would be able to look after himself. He could take to the whaling life.

'You're a well-built, strong-looking lad,' Seth judged. 'I'm taking the *Mary Jane* to the Greenland seas a week today. I'll pay thee fifteen shillings a week, plus a bonus on the catch we mak'.'

'There you are, Davey!' cried Adam. 'You can come with us.' He jumped from his chair, almost knocking it over, and slapped David hard on the shoulder.

But David scarcely heard his words or felt the blow. Fifteen shillings a week! It was a fortune! And there could be more! He could hardly believe his luck. But more important, he'd done it, done what he'd dreamed of for nine years! He was going to sail with the whalers! And fifteen shillings a week for six months. What he could do with that when he returned! His mother and father would . . . 'I'll come!'

Adam let out a whoop.

The firm, decisive note in David's voice pleased Seth. 'Right, lad.'

'And thanks, sir.' He grinned, still spellbound by his good fortune. 'I'm grateful to you.'

Seth eyed him for a moment as he drew at his pipe. 'I'm signing on a sailor. See that you pull your weight and don't let me down. Me and the *Mary Jane* are all that matter to thee from now until you sign off.' Seth wanted no misunderstanding about where David's loyalties must lie.

'Yes, sir.' He nodded his understanding. He turned to Adam and grinned his appreciation of Adam's help.

'Pa generally does a trading voyage to the Baltic for timber when we get back from the Arctic,' Adam explained. 'He'll keep thee on for that. Then it's fend for oursenns until next whaling season.'

'That'll give me time to gan home afore the next whaling voyage,' returned David with a wry smile.

'Oh, hear that, Emma?' Seth grinned. 'Lad thinks he'll want t' come a second time.'

'I'm sure he will,' said Emma, pleased that Seth had taken him on. 'Now, let lad finish his meal.'

As David tucked into the rest of the ham with a relish which gladdened Emma's heart, his eyes wandered round the room. Though it was different, it reminded him of their kitchen at home. Here a kettle, readily available with hot water, hung on a reckon, while across the fire, at just the right convenient height, there was a spit on which the ham he was enjoying must have cooked. He admired the side oven and thought his mother would have liked one. Maybe some day when he had made a lot of money he'd be able to buy her one. The stone-flagged floor was partially covered by three clipped rugs, one of which lay in front of a substantial sideboard on top of which a series of racks held plates and saucers.

David's eyes moved to the mantelpiece. 'What's yon?' he asked Adam quietly, nodding in the direction of a long white rod-like shape which seemed to be twisted in a spiral. It stretched almost the width of the mantelpiece.

Adam rose from his chair and lifted up the object of David's curiosity. He brought it over to the table.

'A unicorn's horn!' gasped David, recalling a picture he had once seen at school.

Adam laughed. 'That's what a lot o' folk think it is, but it's from a small whale called a narwhal.'

David reached out and felt the smooth twisted surface.

'Will we hunt them?' he asked, imagining his family's awe if he arrived home with one of these.

'Nay,' replied Adam. 'They're too small to bother with. We hunt big whales.' Seeing disappointment cloud David's face, he added, 'But you niver know, we might find one for thee.' Adam returned the souvenir to the mantelpiece where it lay between two highly polished brass candlesticks.

'Show David the bottle,' Emma prompted with a glance towards the sideboard.

When Adam brought a bottle and placed it on the table, David, with the tankard halfway to his mouth, gawked disbelievingly at the model of a full-masted ship inside.

'How did that get in there?' he asked, lowering his tankard slowly to the table, his eyes fixed on the ship.

'I'll show thee one day.' Adam grinned. 'Can you draw?'

David shrugged his shoulders. 'Niver really tried.'

'If you did you could be like Pa. He did all these pictures.' Adam indicated several which hung around the room. He indicated two in particular. 'That's Lerwick in the Shetlands – you'll see that afore long. T'other's Spitsbergen.'

'Where's that?' asked David.

'Way to the north,' said Adam.

Any more queries were halted when a thin, pale-faced girl came in shyly, followed by a youth who looked about two years younger than Adam.

'These are my other two,' said Emma with some pride. 'Lucy and Ruben. This is David Fernley.'

David smiled and said, 'Hello.'

Lucy's dress was of similar material to her mother's probably from the same bolt of cloth. It came to her ankles and had a high square neck which was trimmed with a pleated lawn collar. She wore a white muslin cap which emphasised the dark ringlets at the sides of her face.

She dropped her head shyly and nestled close to her mother's side. David estimated that she must be about the same age as Betsy but there all comparison stopped. Whereas Betsy was robust and rosy, Lucy was pale and wan, in marked contrast to the rest of the Thoresby family.

Ruben had on a loose jump-jacket and matching grey shirt open at the neck. His trousers of a brown woollen fabric came to brown leather buckled shoes. He had a kind, open face which lacked the weather-beaten appearance of his father's and brother's but his blue eyes had the same expression of restless curiosity.

'David's from Cropton,' said Adam. Excitement entered his voice as he went on, 'Saved me from the press-gang.'

'He what!' Ruben gasped. Anyone who outsmarted the press-gang must be exceptional.

'I fell, but Davey put two of 'em down and we got away,' explained Adam.

'Good for you.' Ruben grinned at David.

'Pa's going to tak' him on the *Mary Jane*,' enthused Adam.

'If you're taking Davey, tak' me, Pa. Go on. Will you?'

Seth smiled at his son's enthusiasm. 'Not yet, Ruben. But your time will come.' He turned to David as Ruben scowled at his father's refusal. He knew better than to protest. 'Lad's keen to gan to sea, but what can you expect? The Thoresbys have known nowt else. There's sea in their veins instead of blood. Adam, tak' David to see the *Mary Jane* when he's finished eating. Maybe he'll change his mind when he sees what'll be his home for five or six months.'

'David, have you anywhere to stay in Whitby?' Emma asked as if concerned for one of her own.

'No, ma'am.' He looked concerned. In all the excitement he had forgotten all about finding somewhere to stay.

'I'd have you here if we had room.' She glanced at Adam. 'Take him to the Black Bull. Tom has a spare room and I'm sure he wouldn't mind letting David have it.'

When he had finished eating, he thanked both Emma and Seth again for their hospitality and left the house with Adam.

'We'll gan to the *Mary Jane* first,' said Adam as they stepped out of the house into Church Street.

The river was swelling with the incoming tide, the vexed waters pulling at the ships, fast to the fixed dolphins in the middle of the harbour. Vessels at the quays on the east bank rose and fell with the water's gentle movement but this did not hinder the bustling activity of unloading.

Men stripped to their shirts and breeches, in spite of the nip in the wind, piled timber on the quayside. On another, six women, their bonnets keeping their hair in place, their sleeves rolled up, deftly wielded sharp knives as they gutted and cleansed a haul of fish. Guts and scales glistened on the quayside and gulls screeched overhead, ready to swoop and pinch a tasty morsel.

'Yon's just come back from Africa,' said Adam, indicating a third vessel from which a line of men were
carrying sacks and loading them on to carts lined up to
take the cargo to nearby warehouses.

Drinking in all the activity, David asked, 'What's it
brought?'

'It? Nay, Davey. She. Call a ship she,' corrected Adam.
'Don't ask me why. Maybe 'cos men love 'em as much as
their womenfolk. Or maybe,' he added with a wry smile,
''cos they can be as contrary as women.'

David grinned. 'She, then. What's she brought?'

'Mainly spices,' replied Adam. He sidestepped round a
couple of urchins wrestling for a ball.

David's gaze sped across the river. New masts were
rising from the shipyards, hulls of new vessels were taking
shape. Whitby was alive with all the activity of a major
port.

With his attention taken up, he failed to see a rut in the
pathway. He staggered and almost collided with a young
woman hurrying in the opposite direction. She cast him a
withering look, and as he looked back, murmuring his
apologies, he tripped and would have fallen if he had not
bumped into a bearded, well-dressed, middle-aged man.

'Steady, young fellow,' growled the man but his tone
was not unfriendly. He grabbed at his top-hat to stop it
tumbling in the dirt.

'Sorry, sir, sorry,' David spluttered, his face showing
concern.

'All right, young man. Just watch where you're going.
Don't get bowled over by the young ladies,' said the man
with a half-smile twitching his moustached lips.

David stepped round him to find Adam waiting for him with a broad grin on his face.

'Know who that was?' he asked as they fell into step. 'Mr Sanders. Owns four ships and one of these wharfs along here.'

Astonished at this information, David stopped and looked back. Mr Sanders strolled slowly, taking in the throbbing activity which brought wealth to Whitby. His clothes were immaculate and David was pleased that the elegant hat had not fallen into the grime. He hoped that in bumping Mr Sanders he hadn't marked his light-blue trousers nor his fawn tailcoat cut away at the waist. The tapered lapels swept into a large collar and the fitted sleeves ended at the wrists with goblet cuffs. He wore black leather boots and carried a malacca cane with an ivory knob.

David stared. He had never seen anyone so smart. A man of the shipping world. If that's what the sea could bring, he too would be like that one day.

'Hi, c'm on.' Adam's sharp call brought David back to reality. 'Stop day dreaming.'

David started and turned to find Adam with an amused frown creasing his face.

'Sorry,' he apologisd. 'But this is a new world to me.'

'Aye, I knows.' Adam laughed. 'Country lad, seen nowt like it.'

'What are they loading?' asked David as they made their way past a chain of men carrying sacks on to a two-masted ship.

'Alum. Comes from the mines just north of Whitby. Used in tanning leather.'

David nodded, enjoying all the activity around him. He saw butter, hams and bacon, and sailcloth being loaded on to coastal vessels, and flax being brought ashore.

'Down here, Davey,' instructed Adam as he turned into a short narrow street, known as Tin Ghaut, sloping down to the river.

Overhanging houses shut out the light from a street just wide enough to allow wagons to pass through to the small stone quay at which the *Mary Jane* was moored. The 350-ton ship lay serene, moving only gently on the restless water. She was a three-masted square rigger, a hundred feet long with a beam about a quarter of her length so that she looked much more tubby than the merchantmen frequenting the harbour. Though she lacked their slimmer lines, she had about her a purposeful air, a reason for being as she was. She had no need for speed as had the clippers but she needed to withstand the rigours of more vicious seas and be able to defy the Arctic ice which might threaten to crush her.

To this end she had been doubled by the addition of an extra thickness of oak planking from the main-wales to the water mark. For even greater strength to her stem and bow, she had been fortified by the addition of extra timber and stanchions, placed inside so that the whole framework would counteract any blow, no matter which side of the vessel received it.

The four sets of davits were empty, ready to take the four whaleboats, now stored amidships. Because of the war, she was fitted out with letters of marque. Accordingly, twelve guns peeped from the gunports, ready to deal with the Croppies – as sailors called the Frenchmen.

The ship was flush-decked, allowing greater space for dealing with the cutting up of the whale. Now, that deck was gleaming from regular scrubbing since the *Mary Jane* had returned from her last voyage. Seth Thoresby was particular about the appearance of his ship, saying that it gave the crew a pride in their vessel, and a crew which had its pride was happier, worked harder and was therefore less likely to be trouble-makers.

The sun brightened her new paintwork and sent glistening reflections from the polished wood.

David was thrilled by the sight of the ship on which he would sail but there was a touch of surprise in his voice when he commented to Adam, 'She's smaller than I expected. The whalers seemed huge when I was here before.'

'Aye, they would.' Adam half-turned to David. 'They did to me when I was nine.'

'Suppose so,' he replied, and turned his attention back to the ship.

The quay was quiet as Adam and David strode towards the gangplank. A man straightened up from the rail when he saw them. When he reached his full height, he looked huge, but with a body that was well proportioned. David gasped. He could not recall ever seeing anyone so big before. He glanced enquiringly at Adam. 'Who's that?'

Adam grinned at David's startled expression. 'That's Jamaica. And don't look so alarmed. He's not as fierce as he looks.'

Jamaica's broad shoulders and straight back gave an impression of power even from across the quay. But it was the man's face which held David's gaze. A black patch covered his right eye, and David knew from the ugly marks which spread beyond the patch that the eye had suffered severe mutilation. Further evidence of suffering lay in the ugly scar which ran from the ruined eye across the cheek to the chin. The right eye seemed to glow all the more because of its isolation and added to David's first impression of a fearsome face. The dark eyebrows were bushy, and short dark hair showed round the edges of a small woollen cap which covered the crown of his head.

'He's mate on the *Mary Jane*,' explained Adam. 'Keep right side of him and you'll be all right. Best harpooner in the trade after Pa. You can learn a lot from them both.'

Adam led the way up the gangplank and David realised that he had come under close scrutiny from the one-eyed sailor.

'David Fernley, Jamaica. Pa's just taken him on,' said Adam as he stepped on to the deck.

The tall man nodded. 'Welcome aboard. Been to sea afore?' His voice was harsh but not unfriendly.

'No, sir,' replied David tentatively, feeling small in the presence of such a powerfully built man.

Jamaica's grin wrinkled his scars into grotesque lines. 'Sir! I like a lad that knows 'is manners. Where you from?'

'Cropton, near Pickering, sir.'

'Another from the country.' There was a slight touch of despair in Jamaica's voice and he raised his one eye heavenwards as if asking the Lord to preserve him from having to deal with another country youth who knew nothing of the sea. Before David could say anything Jamaica's eye flashed back at him with a piercing glare. 'You've come to a rough, tough life, but you looks a likely lad to mak' it. Come to show him around?' His one eye glanced at Adam.

'Yes, sir.'

'Get on with it then, and be on board by eight in the morning,' ordered Jamaica, stretching his shoulders.

'Aye, aye, sir!' Adam turned to David. 'Leave your bags here.'

As Adam led the way forward, David asked, 'Why guns on a whaleship?'

'We're at war, Davey.' Adam scowled. 'Bloody Croppies an' damned Spaniards, who've sided with the American colonies, prey on us, but we'll give 'em a taste of our broadside guns if they try to interfere. There's talk of whaleships sailing in convoy for protection but Pa won't join 'em. He prefers t' sail alone. Besides, the *Mary Jane's* faster than most.'

When they reached the fo'c's'le companionway, Adam paused. 'I'll show you where you'll sleep first, just in case you change your mind about coming,' he said with a wry smile.

David made no comment as Adam opened the hatch that led down the companionway into the fo'c's'le.

At the bottom David stopped and looked round almost disbelievingly. Fifteen bunks were crowded into this small space where the only concession to comfort was a table, fastened at one end to a main stanchion, around which eight men could sit. The only daylight came from the companionway, and with that closed light must be provided by the two oil lamps which hung from the beams. David was speechless as his eyes pierced the gloom. Five months in this cramped, dark, almost airless hole! Five months in this tight, tiny ship, tossed and buffeted on the wild seas, and he was used to open spaces with room to move through the fields and across the moors. What the hell had he let himself in for? All the glamour, the excitement, the adventure had been swept aside. He frowned at his disturbing thoughts, aware of Adam watching him.

'Wishing you'd stayed at home?' he asked.

The question broke upon David like a clap of thunder. Doubts? He must not have any! 'No!' he answered sharply, not wanting Adam to know the thoughts he had entertained, if only for a moment.

Adam shrugged his shoulders. 'Well, there it is.' He indicated one of the bunks covered by thick blankets smelling of sweat and tar. 'You'll share that with me. Two in most bunks, three in some, 'cos it's bloody cold in the Arctic and there's nowt like another body for warmth.'

A scuttling in one corner of the fo'c's'le brought David swinging round.

'Rats,' said Adam. 'Tak' nay notice of 'em. We catch 'em when we can but there's always some about.'

David shuddered. 'Damned filthy things! I detest 'em.' He had seen plenty around the cottage and in the ditches but there there was space and dogs and cats to catch them. Here, in a confined space, between decks and with no predators to keep them down, they were a different matter. 'Let's get some air,' he added, turning to the companionway.

When they reached the deck, David stopped to savour the salty tang of the air. It was good to be in the open again.

Adam looked seriously at him. 'If you've got second thoughts about becoming a sailor, leave now. Once you sign on and sail, there's nowt you can do about it. You're stuck even if you hates it.'

'Trying to put me off?' David observed him with a serious eye.

'No, but you don't know what this life's like,' Adam pointed out as he moved to the rail. He leaned with his back against it and regarded David with an expression which was grave and steady. 'You've seen where you've got to live. It's bad enough now but it'll be worse afore we see Whitby again. Imagine thirty men sharing that place – bodies stinking with dried sweat, and smelly underwear they're hardly ever out of 'cos its warmer to keep 'em on and they're half-dressed if whales are sighted. I'll smell. You'll smell. And you'll have to put up with the stench of whales as well. There's blood, grease and slime everywhere when we're cutting up, clothes get soaked so the smell comes below decks with us. And if you can put up with that there's the damp and the cold. We sail rough seas, coldest and cruellest in the world, and some of it gets below decks. You'll be lucky if you can keep owt dry. It's a rough life, Davey, and we aren't certain to return.' Adam's slight pause emphasised his meaning. He went on again before David could speak.

'There's ice up north that can crush the *Mary Jane* to matchwood, or send us to the bottom in less than five minutes. If you're lucky enough to escape from the sinking ship and get on to the ice, there's only a remote chance of being rescued. It's luck if another ship is nearby or sights thee. Thee could have a 'orrible, freezing death. Arctic's a big, lonely place. And then there's the whales. We hunt them in those tiny whaleboats.' He indicated the boats stowed amidships. 'A whale's fairly quiet but it can be vicious. It can smash a boat to smithereens or tow it out of sight of the ship and maybe you'll niver find her again. It's a hell of a life for five months, Davey.'

He had listened intently. He knew Adam was doing him a favour by telling him all the worst sides of whaling.

David's features compressed into a penetrating gaze. His voice was low and level when he asked, 'Why do you gan, Adam?'

'It's different for me, sea's in my blood. My family have allus been sailors. I know nothing else,' replied Adam, his eyes never wavering from David's.

'Come on, Adam,' said David, half-disbelieving this simple explanation. 'There must be more to it than that.'

'Nay, there isn't. If sea's in thee, it's difficult to tear yoursen away,' explained Adam, knowing it was a difficult thing for a landlubber to understand.

'But why a whaleship?' insisted David. 'There are other ships plying less dangerous trades.'

'True,' agreed Adam with a condescending nod. 'But my father's a whaleman and this is his ship so it's natural for me to sail with him. And there's summat about whaling which grips you, in spite of the drawbacks.'

'Well, if it's good enough for thee, it's good enough for me.' There was a firm no-nonsense timbre to David's voice.

'C'm on then, I'll show thee the rest of the ship.' Adam led the way across the deck towards the companionway aft of the mainmast.

David paused to look at the whaleboats stowed upside down amidships. They looked so small and frail, hardly the type of boat to combat the Arctic waves. He turned to Adam who stood beside him. From the querying look, tinged with doubt, which came to David's eyes, Adam anticipated his question. 'They're tough. They'll stand it, Davey. One of the best craft afloat. You'll soon find out when you has to row one.'

Returning below deck, Adam showed David the blubber room where the blubber would be crammed into casks before being stored in the hold. He took him to the magazine, now locked, which received its light from the light room. The quarters for the line managers and harpooners were a little more spacious than those in the fo'c's'le and the cabins for the mates gave them some privacy.

'I'll show thee Father's quarters,' said Adam, his voice half-hushed as if in conspiracy when they neared the stern. 'I'm not allowed in, but c'm on, let's have a look.' Adam pushed open a door and they stepped into a spacious cabin in which there was a padded armchair, a desk with a wooden swivel chair, a sofa and a bed which swung on gimbals to counteract the roll of the ship. 'Nice, eh?' commented Adam, casting a glance at David.

'Aye, it is that,' he replied, taking in every facet of the cabin. 'Some day I'll have one like this,' he added half to himself as he thought of the quarters he would be sharing when they sailed.

Adam caught the words. 'Oh, getting ambitious already?' He grinned.

'This'll be thine one day,' returned David in all seriousness. 'And, as I said, what's good enough for thee is good enough for me.'

Chapter Six

The raid by the press-gang was the main topic of conversation amidst the multiplicity of voices, united in one loud din, which burst on David's ears as he followed Adam into the Black Bull. Conversations throbbed with hatred of the men who brought so much misery to Whitby families. Talk ebbed and was lost in the raucous shouts and laughter of the crowd. The oak-beamed ceiling was low, holding down the tobacco smoke which veiled the room in a blue haze.

David's nose twitched at the pungent smell of ale and spirits mingled with sweat from the close-packed bodies. He followed Adam across the uneven, flagged floor, weaving his way between tables and jostling figures to the wooden counter which ran the full width of the room. As a sailor carrying two brimming tankards of ale turned to find his table, they slipped into the place he had vacated. Orders were shouted and ale slopped as three barmaids did their best to serve the customers as quickly as possible.

'Jenny!' Adam called above the clamour, trying to

attract the attention of one of them. The girl looked up, acknowledged the shout with a smile, and, when she finished serving a ginger-haired sailor, came to them.

David stared, drawn by her captivating appearance. Fine eyebrows curved on a flawless, ivory skin above dark-brown eyes, turbulent with life, yet filled with an air of vague mystery. Her linen dress was striped with brown on a yellow background. A bright-yellow kerchief was tied around her neck and tucked into the close-fitting bodice which set off her nineteen-inch waist to perfection. She moved with the grace of a gliding bird. Her hair, swept to the top of her head, was covered by a small white cap from which wisps peeped provocatively. David imagined it, released from its encumbrances, tumbling like a sparkling, peat-coloured stream to her shoulders.

'Oh, Adam, I'm so glad to see you! I heard the press-gang nearly got you.'

David detected a special feeling for Adam in the concern and relief which showed on Jenny's face and in her voice.

'Aye, it would but for Davey here. Jenny, meet David Fernley.'

Jenny inclined her head to David and he felt embraced by the warmth of the smile she gave him. 'Nice to meet you, and thanks for saving Adam. New to Whitby?' Her voice was smooth with a gentle, flowing Yorkshire lilt and none of its roughness, very different from that which David expected of a barmaid.

'Yes,' he replied.

'Pa's given him a job on the *Mary Jane*,' Adam went

on. 'Davey has nowhere to stay until we sail. Ma wondered if Tom would let him have the spare room? Is he about?'

'He's having something to eat. Come through,' said Jenny. 'I'm sure he'll let David have the room.'

She raised the hinged section of the counter and held it up for them to pass behind the bar. She followed the two friends, stopping to have a brief word with the other barmaids.

Adam led the way to a door and into the house. A small stocky man with a frank, open face was sitting at a table enjoying a meal of cold meat, bread, cheese, apple pie and a tankard of ale.

'Hello, Adam,' he said with marked friendliness.

'Tom, this is David Fernley. He's the lad we heard about that saved Adam from the press-gang.' Jenny made the introduction.

'Glad t' meet thee, David.' Tom stood up and offered his hand. 'Anyone who can outwit the press-gang is a friend o' mine.'

'He's new in Whitby,' Jenny went on. 'Going to sail on the *Mary Jane* and needs somewhere to stay. Mrs Thoresby wondered if you could oblige with the spare room?'

'For Emma, yes.' Tom smiled. 'And of course for thee, David.'

'Thank you, Mr. . .'

'Holtby, Tom Holtby.'

David couldn't believe his luck. This room had such a warm, friendly feeling. Clip rugs were strewn across the stone-slab floor. A settle faced the fire. The large table at which Tom had been eating stood along one wall in which there was another door. The wide fireplace was spanned by a thick beam and a fire glowed on the raised hearth, above which a kettle hung on an idleback. The steam puffing from its spout, and the inglenook seats, looking temptingly warm, casting a homely feeling over the low-ceilinged room. It was as if someone, a woman, for it bore a woman's touch, had tried to create a world apart from the rowdy public room.

'I'll show you your room,' offered Jenny.

She led the way up the narrow stairs. The sneck on the bedroom door moved easily and David stepped into a room with white-washed walls. A bed covered with a white spread, a plain oak chest of drawers, a small, round, three-legged table and a kitchen chair filled the room.

'Will you be all right in here?' Jenny asked.

'Fine,' he replied, dropping his bags on the board floor. 'I'm most grateful to thee and Tom for your kindness. I won't forget it.'

Jenny glanced in a jug which stood in a bowl on the table. 'There's some water. Would you like it hot?'

David smiled. 'No, thanks. I'm used to cold.'

'You'll find a towel in the table drawer. Come down when you're ready. We'll probably be busy with customers,' she added, moving to the door.

As David washed away the stains of grime and travel, his mind turned to Jenny. Even from this short meeting, he had a feeling that there was a marked difference between her and her surroundings. She fitted the warmth and friendliness of the house but seemed out of place in a rowdy, seafaring inn. When David joined Adam in the bar, he had this feeling confirmed. There was something about Jenny which set her apart without her being aloof. She was friendly with everyone, but David noticed that she was given a certain respect which was missing from the attentions and familiarities directed at the other barmaids.

The following morning David was up early. The tempting smell of fried bacon and egg and freshly baked bread brought him hurrying downstairs. He shared the table with Jenny and Tom who wished him well when he left for the *Mary Jane*.

As he crossed the market square he was stopped by a shout. 'Hi there, young fellow. Get fixed up?'

David turned to see Silas. 'Aye. I'm gannin' to sea on the whaleship *Mary Jane*.'

The carrier's eyes widened with surprise. 'Good ship, good cap'n from what I'm told, but a rough life. Hope you survives.'

David laughed. 'I will.' He started to turn away, but stopped. 'Can thee let my folks in Cropton know?'

'Aye, lad, I will.

When he went on board the *Mary Jane*, Jamaica ordered him, along with Adam and two other men, to report to Zebediah Grimes, the skeeman who would control the storage of the blubber, but who now supervised the loading of water-filled barrels for ballast.

For most of the day they worked in the hold, and, after the open fields and far horizons of the country, David found the gloomy confines oppressive.

Once he had climbed out at the end of the day and was able to breathe the sharp evening air and see beyond the wooden interior of the ship, he even began to doubt the wisdom of agreeing to sail on the *Mary Jane*.

'Well, Davey,' said Adam, slapping him on the back, 'your first day on a whaleship is ower. How do you feel?'

'Sore and tired,' he replied, pressing his hands into the small of his back to try to ease the stiffness. He grimaced at the aches which racked his body.

Adam grinned and stretched himself with greater suppleness. 'We'll soon have thee right for whaleman's work. C'm on, thee deserves a drink.'

After a tankard of ale, Adam left the Black Bull, and, with a lull in the evening trade, Jenny prepared a meal for David, while he washed.

'That's a right good smell,' he observed when he entered the kitchen and saw her bending over a pan on the fire. She had put on a white apron with full bib to save her linen dress from splashes.

Jenny glanced round. 'Sit yourself down, it'll be ready in a moment.' She nodded at a place set on the table scrubbed as white as his mother's in Cropton. A wave of nostalgia swept over David but, in Jenny's presence, it was gone in a second. His mind settled on the trim figure who was beside him almost as soon as he was seated. She ladled some stew from the pan on to David's plate. Its appetising smell, coupled with that of home-made bread, newly cut, made him realise just how hungry he was.

He tucked into meat, potatoes and vegetables, all in tasty gravy, which he mopped up with his bread.

'By gum, this is good,' he said when Jenny sat down opposite him. 'Did thee mak' the bread?'

She nodded. 'There's no one else.'

'It's as good as Mother's and that's saying something,' he said, with an appreciative nod.

Jenny smiled at the compliment. 'I wonder what you'll think of my apple pie.' She indicated the pie set beside a wedge of cheese and a jug of ale.

'I'm looking forward to that.' David picked up the jug and poured some of its contents into a tankard.

'So how did your first day on a whaleship go?'

'Tiring, and I didn't like being below deck but I reckon I'll get used to it,' replied David before he took another mouthful of stew. He savoured it and said, 'It tastes as good as it smells.'

'Good. I'm glad you like it.' She leaned back on her chair, her eyes on David. She liked the open friendliness which she had seen in him yesterday and again this morning at breakfast. His rugged looks which still had a touch of youth about them had a marked appeal. 'What made you want to go to sea?'

'I've thought about it ever since I was nine when Pa brought me to Whitby,' he replied.

'But you're country,' said Jenny. 'What about your folks, didn't they try and stop you?'

'Aye, but I was determined to come. Besides, I wanted a job so's I could send money to help 'em.'

Jenny nodded, admiring his good intentions. David felt the intensity of her concentration on his words and knew she wanted him to go on, to tell her more about his home. He did not feel offended at her curiosity for there was nothing to shy away from in Jenny's friendly, open face. His experience of women was confined to his mother, his sisters and Ruth, yet he felt at ease with Jenny, as if she

101

too was part of his family. This surprised him for he had expected a tavern girl to be brusque and loud, sharp in her speech and intolerant of a young man trying to make his way in Whitby. Instead he found a girl who was well spoken, understanding and easy to talk to.

Once he started telling her about his home and family, the words poured out as if he was talking to an intimate friend rather than someone he had known little more than twenty-four hours.

Suddenly realising how fast he had been speaking, he stopped and an embarrassed smile crossed his face. 'I'm sorry,' he spluttered, 'I've been rambling on. I must be boring you.'

'No, David, no.' Jenny was quick to reassure him. 'You aren't boring me. I find it all interesting.'

To try to hide his embarrassment, David quaffed his ale. As he placed the tankard back on the table and wiped his mouth, he asked, 'Have you allus lived in Whitby, Jenny?'

'Yes.'

David raised a quizzical eyebrow. 'Jenny Hartley, Tom Holtby . . .' His voice trailed away as he suddenly realised what he might be implying.

Jenny recognised his discomfort, but laughed it off. 'Nothing strange, David. Tom took me in when my parents died. He served on my father's whaleship.'

David's eyes widened in surprise. 'Your father was a captain?'

'Yes,' she replied.

'Was he killed in the Arctic?' The question was out clumsily before David could stop himself.

'No.' She gave a slight shake of her head, but offered no further explanation. The laughter in her eyes had been replaced by a veiled sadness.

David was aware of the change his question had brought and felt ill at ease at the distress he seemed to be causing. He diverted his own embarrassment by taking another slice of apple pie.

Jenny looked down thoughtfully at her hands clasped together on her lap. She shuddered, her mind returning to the moment when she had found her father hanging in his study.

A sailor from the poorer part of Whitby, he had an extraordinary talent and ability which had taken him to the top of his trade and the biggest share in a whaleship of which he was captain. He and a girl from a well-to-do family on the west side of the river fell in love and married against the wishes of her family. They were deeply happy until she began to miss the way of life she had known. She persuaded her husband to move across the river. Although he tried to change his way of life, he couldn't be anything else but himself – a bluff whaling captain. Jenny was born and the baby seemed to heal the rift which was growing between them, but only for a while. He was accepted less and less by his wife's friends, so she used to visit without him, and with his being continually away at sea the rift widened. The inevitable happened. She took a lover and eventually they decided to leave Whitby. The coach in which they were travelling overturned and they both were killed.

When the news reached Jenny's father, it was the first he had heard of his wife's affair. The whole story came out and he was heart-broken. He took to drink, his money slipped away, and he sold his shares in the whale ship. He lost everything and, unable to cope any longer, committed suicide. Jenny's father had no relatives and her mother's family would have nothing to do with her. Alone at thirteen, she found a saviour in Tom Holtby, who had been saved by her father when his whaleboat had been stoved by a whale. Though he could not give her the type of life she had been used to, he gave her a father's love and a secure home.

Jenny looked up. 'David,' she said quietly, and waited for him to meet her gaze. When he did he was taken aback by her troubled look. He paused with his spoon halfway to his mouth. 'Forget the sea!' Jenny's words, though softly spoken, had a rapier-like thrust to them. They were meant to pierce, to be taken seriously.

He lowered his spoon slowly to his plate without taking his eyes from her. 'Why?' he asked, his brow creasing into a puzzled frown at the warning.

'You don't know the sea, David. It's so powerful – it can destroy lives.' The impassioned tone in Jenny's voice was coupled with an earnest look in her eyes, as if it was imperative for her to convince him.

He realised that she meant not only those of the men who went to sea, but also those of the people left behind, and wondered if that applied to her own life in some way.

'Thanks for the warning,' he said, 'but it's a risk I'll have to take.'

Jenny sensed David's resolve and she knew that he was a person who would never shirk; he was someone who wanted to find out for himself and in him there was a determination to rise above any problems and trials which he might have to face.

She sighed.

'Have you tried to persuade Adam to leave the sea?' asked David gently to emphasise further his own determination.

Jenny smiled wanly and shook her head. 'I'd love it if he never went to sea again, but I'd never try to persuade him not to. The sea's in his blood, and when it is there's no denying it. But it's not in yours.'

'But it will be,' he returned.

Jenny shrugged her shoulders. 'Maybe, maybe,' she said wistfully. She stood up and reached for the jug of ale. 'More?' she asked, shaking off her mood and putting an end to this train of conversation.

'Thanks,' said David, and leaned back in his chair.

As he watched the foaming liquid, he was aware of Jenny shooting him a quick glance. 'Got a girl back home, David?' She replaced the jug on the table and sat down and awaited his answer with the concentrated interest she had shown when he had talked about home.

'Ruth,' he replied. This slight hesitation made Jenny wonder just what the relationship was but her curiosity was allayed when David told her everything. He held back only the fact that he had promised to return to marry Ruth and bring her to Whitby.

As he lay in bed that night, he wondered why he had done so. Why hadn't he wanted Jenny to know of the possible marriage? Suddenly he felt he had betrayed Ruth. Exasperated with himself, David tossed in his bed, unable to settle. He tried to sleep but two girls kept haunting his mind and gradually one occupied his thoughts more than the other. Jenny's bright eyes beckoned and he wondered more and more about her story.

It was something which occupied his mind over the next couple of days. He found the answer after he and Adam had been helping with the victualling of the ship, aiming to have everything ready for the time laid down by Seth Thoresby.

'Now Pa can boil t' kettle tomorrow,' observed Adam as he and David relaxed against the rail.

'Boil t' kettle?' David enquired.

Adam laughed at his puzzled expression. 'Means the fire can be lit in the galley, signifying official start of work. All the crew'll be mustered, and there'll be no let up until the fire's raked out when we get back. The crew and their families look forward to the lighting, it's the time when Pa'll pay the men a month's wages in advance, and from then on they'll eat on board. After a hard winter that's a help as money is probably running out and it's a job to find food for the family. Pa allows each man to bring his family to share the first food on board.'

'Does Jenny come?' asked David, glancing at Adam.

'She isn't family,' he replied.

David pursed his lips. 'Just thought your pa might make an exception.'

'Nay, not even for me.' There was regret in Adam's half-smile. 'If he did there'd be all sorts of hangers-on. Besides, I don't think Jenny would come.'

'Why not?'

'Boiling the kettle has bad memories for her.'

'How?' pressed David, his curiosity roused.

'It was the day her mother was killed,' replied Adam.

'Killed?' David's brow furrowed. 'What happened?'

Adam hesitated, but then, knowing the story was general knowledge, saw no harm in telling David.

He listened intently, without interruption, and when Adam had finished he knew why Jenny feared what the sea could do and why she had tried to warn him away from it.

And he also knew why she had seemed different. Her breeding, inherited from her mother's family, set her apart, though she had no grandiose ideas about herself.

'Does Jenny niver desire the old life?' he queried.

'Nay. Not that I know of,' replied Adam. 'One day we'll marry but I'll never tak' her to live on the other side of the river. I know the memories of what life over there did to her father are still painful.'

Marry! David was startled by the way the word had affected him. Jealous? But he had Ruth. He had told her he loved her and would return to Cropton for her, yet now he was experiencing feelings he had never had before. Now he was aware more than ever that there was Jenny and a life outside Cropton.

Chapter Seven

Ruth stretched her limbs, enjoying the luxury of the soft feather bed. She had it to herself. Jessica and Betsy had just gone downstairs and she was determined to savour it for the few minutes she could snatch before she too should be up.

She sighed with pleasure. The week since the Fernleys had taken her in had brought an easing of her bodily pains. The cuts were healing and the bruises had lost their fearsome glow. Jessica had been pleased to let her have some of her clothes and each time she put them on Ruth moulded them to her body, revelling in the soft cleanliness, so different from the rags she had had to wear at home.

For the first time in years she had enjoyed good, wholesome food, having lived for so long off the scraps her step-father had deigned to throw to her. During the first two days she had eaten with a wolf-like swiftness until she realised that in the Fernley house meals, especially in the evening when all the family sat at the table together, were more leisurely, and with sufficient food for everyone there was no need to fight for it.

There was no luxury in the daily lives of the Fernley family but there was comfort, warmth and love. Ruth was drawn into it, liked it, and the harshness of her life at home began to recede.

She would never go back. Never! David had promised he would come for her and take her to Whitby. Ruth snuggled down and drew the bedclothes around her. Whitby! Yes, he had been right to go. Whitby offered her escape from the cruel life she had known, and from an existence in Cropton which offered David nothing. The more she thought about it, the more she agreed with his decision.

And now the good news, brought by the carrier, that David was to sail with the whalers, made that decision all the more agreeable. Whitby beckoned with a new life. She dreamed. She saw ladies in fine clothes; handsome men, courteous, attentive; fine houses; servants. Her mind flooded with imagined sights. Born where? Ruth did not know. But they had always been there, coming in those moments of escape when she had been alone, seeming to come from deep down in her very being as if she had known them in some past life. Her mother had never described such things, nor could she have known them, for she had been born to a poor labourer across the hill at Lastingham and had been no further than Cropton.

Her father? Were they the legacy of her real father? Ruth wondered. Maybe they had been part of his life; maybe he was born to them and could have inherited that right. But who was he? Ruth's lips tightened in exasperation as she recalled the times she had asked her mother, only to be met with a hostile silence or a cuff on the ear with a sharp 'Damn him to hell and his brat!' Who? Would she ever know?

Ruth stirred. Time she was up. She drew the final awareness of warmth from the bedclothes before pushing them aside. She swung out of bed on to the clip rug, tensed herself against the cold and scampered across the wood floor to the washstand beside the chair on which she had carefully laid her clothes the night before.

She glanced out of the window around the edges of which the frost had painted intricate patterns. The world was white again. The snow would be thick on the heights. David had been right to leave when he did.

She poured water from the ewer into the patterned bowl and, bracing herself against the immediate cold, washed her face and neck. As she dried, she slipped her shoulders out of the shift and let it fall to the floor. She rubbed her shoulders, ran the towel over her small, shapely breasts, across her thin but firm stomach against which the bones of her hips stood out sharply, lacking the flesh she desired. She towelled her thighs gently, aware of the bruises on her spindly legs. She revelled in the touch of the towel and in the new experience of actions which had surprised her by coming naturally in the first private moments she had ever had.

In spite of the chill she enjoyed dressing, thrilling to the contact of the clothes against her body. Her thoughts flew to the finely dressed ladies in Whitby. Maybe one day she too . . .

'Ruth, breakfast.' The shout from the bottom of the stairs broke into her thoughts.

'Coming,' she called.

She grabbed a shawl, swirled it round her shoulders and hurried from the room.

'Ah, there thee is, Ruth.' Martha Fernley straightened from the frying pan on the fire as the kitchen door opened. 'Sit thissen down, lass.' She motioned to the table where Jessica and Betsy were already seated.

Martha watched the girl with an appraising eye as Ruth crossed the flagged floor. In spite of her thinness, in spite of the harsh life which had been inflicted on her, Ruth held herself erect, head up, an automatic reaction of dignity and self-respect that had not been smashed. If the rumours which had circulated when she was born were true, there was much of her father in Ruth.

Since Jessica had brought her home, Martha had answered David's request and looked upon Ruth as one of her own. The colour had started to come back to Ruth's cheeks and now Martha swore she would not rest until she had put some flesh back on those bones.

The only thing she feared was that Ruth's step-father would come to take her back. She knew that would lead to trouble, for Kit had sworn never to let Nathan Cornforth lay a hand on his step-daughter again.

The days passed with never a sign that this would happen and Martha's uneasiness vanished in the delight she took in training Ruth in all the household duties she had never had a chance to learn.

For her part, Ruth was a willing learner. She assimilated knowledge easily, and soon recognised that she had a nimble brain which had never been allowed to blossom. She relished this new life, so different from her previous one, for with it came new experiences and feelings which brought a deeper curiosity about her real father.

Fanciful thoughts about him grew until one day she could bear them no longer. Determined to do something about it, she seized her chance when she was alone with Mrs Fernley after Jessica and Betsy had gone to the village and the men were checking the squire's sheep.

'Mrs Fernley.' Ruth spoke quietly as she stopped kneading the dough for the bread she was baking. 'Can I ask thee summat?'

Martha hesitated a moment, trying to see behind the serious expression in the eyes which were firmly on her. 'Aye, lass, but I may not answer it.'

'But thee will if thee can?' pressed Ruth.

'I can't promise,' Martha cautioned. 'Depends what it is.'

'Well . . .' Ruth glanced down at her doughy hands and then quickly back to Martha. 'Do you know who my real father is?'

Martha was startled. Ruth read in the hesitancy an acknowledgement that she knew the truth.

'Thee knows, don't thee?' Excitement quivered through Ruth's body.

Martha gathered her racing thoughts quickly. 'Nay, lass, I don't.'

'But thee has an idea?' urged Ruth.

'I don't heed rumours.' Martha's sharp retort came with an angry glance at Ruth.

'But . . .'

'Nay buts! Your ma is the only one who can tell thee,' broke in Martha firmly to put a stop to the questions she saw coming. 'It's not for me to put ideas into your head.'

Disappointment shadowed Ruth's face. 'Mrs Fernley, if thee only knew what it's like not to know your father. To be called a . . . a bastard.'

'That's enough, Ruth,' replied Martha sharply. 'If thee wants t' know, thee must ask thy mother. Now, wipe your hands and off to Liza Leckonby's for me. I forgot to tell Jess and Betsy to call. Tell her I'll gan to the hall directly and I'll see her there.'

Ruth bit her lips, hiding the frustration and anger she felt. She was sure Martha knew but realised she would never divulge the secret. Maybe Martha was right. Maybe she should ask her mother again, even though she had refused to tell, but it would mean returning to the hovel she had determined never to set foot in again. She wanted nothing to interrupt the pleasant life with the Fernleys, but she wanted an answer to the gnawing yearning inside her.

With annoyance prickling her skin and setting her mouth in a thin line, Ruth took her cloak from the peg beside the door and wrapped a shawl around her head. She fastened pattens to her shoes and left the house without a word.

Martha sighed, glanced at the door, gave a little tut and slight shake of the head before giving her baking her attention again.

She must warn Kit that Ruth was asking about her father. The lass was wily enough to question him when no one else was about.

Ruth crossed the fields to Cropton, thankful to have

pattens to keep her shoes out of the mud left by the melting snow. It was not long ago that she had run through such mud barefooted. How life had changed for her.

Four women chatting at their doors in Cropton fell silent at her approach. They watched her with hawk-like eyes, making their assessment, ready to discuss the changes which had taken place in Ruth Harwood during the last few weeks. She, knowing they were watching her, held herself more erect and tossed her head disdainfully as she hurried past.

Whispers started, some loud enough to make sure Ruth heard.

'Shameful hussy.'

'She's gettin' a side on.'

'Wonder Martha allows her under her roof.'

Not so long ago, Ruth would have pulled faces at them, put out her tongue, called them names and given them as good as she got. But not now. New clothes and a better way of life had wrought changes in Ruth and stirred feelings she had never known before. Now she felt it beneath her to take any notice of these witch-like gossips.

She hurried on, also ignoring the six ragged urchins who criss-crossed the rutted village street in loud pursuit of each other.

She knocked on the door of a stone-built cottage which was in better repair than most, for, in spite of its being the squire's property, Fred Leckonby did much of the maintenance work himself. There were those muttered against Fred, for they maintained if he did it the squire would expect them to do the same and it wasn't their job. But Fred reasoned that the squire wouldn't do a great deal and that, as he had to live in the cottage, he may as well keep it as comfortable as possible.

Ruth's knock brought a well-built woman to the door. Her rosy cheeks shone as if they had been polished and her bright eyes quickly scanned Ruth.

'I've come with a message from Mrs Fernley,' she said.

Liza Leckonby peered at Ruth as if something was puzzling her. 'Hast thee, now?' She paused and leaned forward slightly to get a better look. 'Ruth Harwood, is it?'

'Aye, that's me,' she returned, rather pleased that Mrs Leckonby hadn't recognised her immediately.

'Well, well, who'd a thought it?' said Liza, straightening to her full height. 'Thee hast changed.' She moved to one side. 'Thee'd better come in, lass.'

Ruth stepped inside and Liza closed the door. 'Tak' thy pattens off, lass, and have a glass of my cowslip wine.'

'Thanks, Mrs Leckonby.' Ruth sat on a chair beside the door and unfastened her pattens.

Liza went to a cupboard and brought a bottle and two glasses to the table almost before Ruth was ready.

'C'm and sit by table, lass.' She nodded to a chair beside the scrubbed wood table in the centre of the room.

A couch of worn, black leather stood under the uncurtained window. The limed walls brightened the room and a woman's hand, determined to make the most of what she had, small though it may be, gave the room a comfortable, homely feeling.

'Well, what's message fra Martha?' asked Liza as she poured the wine.

Ruth delivered the message and smiled to herself as she watched Liza butter some newly baked bread.

She was enjoying this newfound status; she was no longer the waif to whom Liza Leckonby wouldn't have given a second glance. Ruth felt she was somebody and it stirred those strange feelings about her birth. Who was her father and what had he passed on to his daughter?

Liza sought the latest news of David and chatted amiably while they enjoyed the wine and bread spread with jam made from bilberries, laboriously gathered from the nearby moor.

When she had finished, Ruth said she ought to be getting back and Liza did not delay her. Ruth put on her pattens, thanked Liza for her hospitality and left the cottage.

The urchins were still racing around in their game of makebelieve and the four crones, as Ruth thought of them, still had their heads together, no doubt seeing how long she spent at Liza Leckonby's.

She had only gone a few yards when she heard the clop of horse's hooves behind her. She stopped and turned to see who was riding through Cropton.

Her eyes fixed on Squire Hardy, tall in the saddle, his body moving rhythmically to the regular movement of the well-groomed chestnut mare.

His waist-length jacket had a turned-down collar which revealed a fine linen shirt with a matching neck-cloth, neatly tied and pinned at the throat. The tight fawn buckskin breeches emphasised the taut muscular thighs and were tucked into knee-length, leather riding boots. Wisps of hair, greying at the temples, showed beneath a black tricorne hat.

There was a haughtiness to his bearing and to the way he held his head. The oval shape of his face was broken by an angular, determined jaw. His cheekbones were set high; his nose, small but aquiline; his eyes, grey, sharp, ever darting, noting, but once they settled they were penetrating.

And they settled, now, upon Ruth. Almost immediately she knew he did not see her as Ruth Harwood; he did not recognise her. Once she would have diverted her gaze and turned away but now she stared back, matching look for look. She did not feel vulnerable, even though she sensed his gaze stripped her naked. She tossed her head in a gesture of contempt for the way he was looking at her, and knew if their roles had been reversed he would have done the same.

She had seen the squire only occasionally in the past, when he had curled his lip at her waif-like state, ill-clothed and barefoot, but now she was seeing him in a different way, drawn to him in a way which puzzled her.

Then he was past and Ruth stood, staring at the broad back, straight as a ramrod, power in the shoulders.

The urchins, excited in their game, were oblivious of his approach. As one twisted out of reach of his pursuer, he looked back over his shoulder, still running fast. As he outstripped the boy behind him, his teasing laughter rippled through the air. Joyous in his escape, he turned his head and was startled to see the rider in his way. He swerved, stubbed his foot, stumbled and staggered a few more paces. Unable to keep his balance, he fell in the mud. Fear in his eyes, he struggled to get up.

The horse, startled by the upheaval, shied. With the skill of the expert horseman, the squire kept his seat and controlled the animal with uncanny ease. But his face clouded with anger. As the horse settled, he glared down at the muddy urchin scrambling to his feet. He leaned forward and casually lashed out with his riding crop. It tore at the boy's cheek, bringing a cry of pain. A dirty hand automatically caught at the wound as the boy ducked to avoid the second strike. The crop caught him across the shoulders. With tears streaming down his face, he stumbled out of range and, finding his balance, ran to his horrified companions, still standing mesmerised by the attack.

The squire glared at them, jabbed his horse with his heels and set himself at the group in a canter. For one moment it looked as if he would run them down but suddenly they scattered. The squire kept the animal at a fast pace and headed out of Cropton.

The four women hurled unheard curses after the squire. 'Damn thee, Squire Hardy! Damn thee and thy own to hell!' They ran to the boy who had felt the crop. One of them crouched down and held him to her while another examined his cheek.

Throughout the whole incident, Ruth stood transfixed. She had felt no urge to interfere or go to his aid, and now as she watched the boy being comforted she realised that she felt no pity for him. Not so long ago she would have been the first to help him; then she would have felt an empathy with him, but not now. Instead she sympathised with the squire. He could have been unseated, injured, and all because some no-good urchin had been careless, too eager for his own pleasure.

Ruth watched the women lead the boy away to tend to his wound followed by his playmates, their happy chase forgotten. When they had disappeared inside one of the cottages, she resumed her walk to the Fernleys' home, her mind dwelling on the squire and the feelings he had raised in her.

When she reached the cottage, the back door was slightly open. As Ruth slowed her step, she heard voices which she recognised as those of Kit and Martha Fernley. Her step faltered.

'Kit, she's curious to know about her father, but it ain't up to us to tell her. I've told her to ask her ma,' Martha said firmly.

Ruth stood still. Her head inclined, she listened intently. Maybe she would learn something . . .

'Aye, thee's right, lass, but it means she'll have to gan home, and if Nathan's there . . .' Kit left the consequences unspoken.

'But her ma's the only one who can tell her t' truth. We know the rumours but only her ma can say if the squire's her father,' pointed out Martha.

Ruth's mind reeled. With her thoughts tumbling, she heard no more of the conversation. But she had heard enough. Her father – the squire! This must be the answer to her feelings today, this must be why she had felt sympathy for the squire instead of the boy. The squire's blood was in her!

Mrs Fernley had said so, but Ruth must be certain, she must find out from her mother. She turned and walked quickly but quietly away from the Fernleys' cottage. She headed for home, with no thought of what might happen if Nathan was there, and even if she had dwelt on that possibility she would not have hesitated. The urge was too strong. Now she knew why, as she had grown up, she had felt different from the other village girls. No wonder she had felt better than them, even better than David's sister, Jessica. The squire's blood was in her! The thought sang in her mind again and again.

The breeze drove the last remnants of the clouds away, leaving behind a sun which promised new life to a saturated countryside.

Ruth, her heart pounding with excited anticipation of what she would learn, squelched her way along the hillside. Resentment rose like gall in her. Why hadn't her father ever come near them? Why hadn't he sent money? Why had he let his child rot in squalor and poverty? Why? She bit her lip, driving back the ill-feeling. That was not important now. What was important was the truth – to know with certainty that the squire was her father. Buoyed up by elation, the possible confrontation with Nathan did not deter her. Nothing, no one, would stop her discovering the truth.

Her half-brother and half-sisters, who were playing outside, were the first to see her. One of the girls ran into the house while the other two raced towards Ruth. As they neared her they slowed and then stopped to stand and stare.

Beyond them Ruth saw her mother come to the door with her half-sister beside her. Her mother shaded her eyes as if trying to make out who was coming. Only then did Ruth realise that the children had not recognised her.

She looked back at the two nearest children and saw their eyes widening with surprise.

'It's Ruthie!' The gasp of amazement came from the boy whose tattered breeches hung low on his hips. His shirt was only half tucked in and the coat, sleeves torn, flapped open for the lack of buttons.

Her sister, her nose running, gawped timorously at the 'stranger' who approached them. As her brother started forward, she grasped at his hand as if to seek some protection from the unknown.

Seeing their miserable plight, Ruth suddenly felt sorry for them, but that sympathy soon evaporated in the mockery which flowed from the lips of her half-brother.

'Fernleys chucked ya out?' he asked with a bold contempt.

Ruth ignored the pair.

'Come for another beating? Missing 'em?' The sadistic gleam in the eyes of one so young disgusted Ruth.

The girl, drawing confidence from her brother and the knowledge that this really was Ruth, reached out and fingered her dress.

'Like it, Sis?' asked her brother. 'Isn't our Ruthie the one. Posh now, ain't yer?' He mocked and grinned up at her. 'Is everythin' posh about yer now? Might see when Pa gets that dress off yer for Ma an' gives yer a beatin'.' He chuckled at the thought, then raced ahead to his mother. His sister glanced at Ruth, sniffed and ran after him. When she reached the others, they all stood watching Ruth.

She shuddered at her half-brother's insinuations but kept a determined step and a resolve not to weaken in her quest.

'Hello, Ma.' Ruth's voice was quiet, apprehensive of the reception she might receive.

Her mother did not speak for a moment. Envy in her eyes, her gaze swept over Ruth. 'What do thee want?' Warmth and love were missing from her tone.

'To see thee,' replied Ruth firmly, drawing herself up straight.

Rebecca gave a half laugh of disbelief. 'How touching,' she mocked. 'Since when did thee care about me?'

Ruth met her mother's gaze unflinchingly. 'I once did, when there was just the two of us.'

Rebecca grunted. She was startled by the likeness to Ruth's father in her daughter; the set of her chin, the petite nose, but more than anything the startling shimmer in her eyes. Rebecca had never noticed it so marked before. Maybe it was because Ruth was cared for. It was as if the attention she had been given and the clothes she wore had given her a new life which had brought out the inheritance of her father. Memories stirred in Rebecca, of what might have been; of promises made but broken because of who she was and where she came from. Seeing resemblances stoked her hatred of the man and the brat she had borne.

'I see thee's got some fine airs about thee now.' Her eyes ran over her daughter. 'Fernleys given thee ideas?' Contempt mounted in her tone as envy tightened at her chest. 'I niver thought t' see thee back.' Her eyes flashed. 'We don't want thee here.'

Ruth gazed into Rebecca's eyes. She hesitated a moment and then in a sharp, incisive voice said, 'I want to know who my father is!'

Rebecca smirked, but before she could speak she was pushed roughly aside and Nathan lurched out of the doorway to stand swaying, his eyes roving over Ruth with a lust which made her shudder.

Her heart beat faster. Would he dare? Her eyes

narrowed as she drew on her reserves of determination to see this through. 'I want to know who my father is,' she repeated, her voice firm.

'Oh, oh, so my pretty's curious, is she?' slurred Nathan. A grin split his unshaven face, revealing yellowing broken teeth. 'What airs an' graces brought this on?'

'You gannin' t' beat her, Pa?' The gleeful anticipation in the boy's voice made Nathan aware of the children's presence.

He swung round and aimed a blow at his son's head. 'Gerraway with yer.' The boy ducked and the miss angered Nathan. 'Gan on,' he snarled. 'Gerraway.' He made a move as if to grab the children. They scurried out of his way and ran off down the path to stop about thirty yards away. They turned to stare at the three adults. Nathan picked up a stone and hurled it after them. 'Gerroff with yer.' The children scuttled away to find their own amusements, afraid of what their father would do if they did not make themselves scarce. Nathan turned back to Ruth. 'And now to deal with thee,' he leered.

Ruth, who had detected that neither her mother nor her step-father would answer her query, decided to confront them with the knowledge she had gained.

'The squire's my father, isn't he?'

The question caught Rebecca and Nathan unprepared. The glance that passed between them cleared all doubt from Ruth's mind.

'I'm right, aren't I?' she pressed.

Rebecca, ready to carry on with a denial, was too late to stop Nathan.

'How the hell did thee find out?' he snarled.

'No matter. It's true, isn't it?' urged Ruth.

'What if it is?' snapped Rebecca. 'What are thee gannin' t' do about it? He won't own thee.'

'Maybe not. But it answers a lot of questions,' replied Ruth, her eyes gleaming because the truth of her birth had been verified by her mother.

'What questions?' rapped Rebecca.

'Niver you mind,' answered Ruth.

'I'll mind!' Nathan lurched towards her, his broad, hairy hands reaching out to her shoulders. 'I'll beat it out of thee, and enjoy more besides.'

Ruth stepped back quickly. 'Don't thee dare touch me, or thee'll not only have David to answer to but my father as well.' Her eyes blazed with defiance.

She saw alarm flare in her mother's eyes. Rebecca sprang forward and grabbed Nathan by the arm. 'Stop it, Nathan, don't give her cause to do that, thee knows what'll happen.'

He tried to shake himself free of her grip but Rebecca held tight.

'Don't gan to your father, Ruth. Please. If thee does, he'll throw us out of this cottage an' off his land an' we won't get a penny more.' Rebecca's face creased with the horror of something she dared not contemplate.

The words had a sobering effect on Nathan. He stopped struggling to be free and the antagonism drained from him. He was trapped, helpless. His bullying bravado was useless. He just stood there, drooping, all the fight gone from him.

The words rang in Ruth's mind: '. . . we won't get a

penny more'. 'Thee got money for me?' she hissed, leaning forward, her eyes narrowing with disgust.

Rebecca shrugged her shoulders helplessly. 'I met your father when I had looks – there were those who said I was a beauty – he told me he loved me and I would share his fortune, but the bastard betrayed me, married into money instead.' Rebecca's voice hissed with venom. 'I was pregnant and threatened to expose him but he said he'd deny it and his word would count more than mine. I married Nathan, hoping he'd give thee a name, but t' bugger wouldn't.' She spat contemptuously at the swaying figure. 'Your father had some pity. He allowed us this place, some work for Nathan and a small sum every month, provided I niver divulged that he was the father of my child. I had no choice but to agree. Oh, I know this is nowt more than a hovel but it's a roof, such as it is, over our heads. Please don't iver gan to him?' Tears of entreaty were filling Rebecca's eyes.

Ruth's mind was racing. All these years there had been some money, no doubt meant to give her a better life, and what had she had? Nothing but rags, scraps and beatings while this swaying sot had drunk the pennies away.

Ruth's lips curled with disgust. 'Thee had money and did nowt for me!' she cried, her eyes flaming with fury. Her throat tightened. 'I ought to gan and tell him.'

'No! Please, Ruth! Don't!' Rebecca's cry pierced the sharp air like the cry of a doomed bird.

'It's what thee deserves. I ought to let him chuck thee off his estate.' Ruth's tone was like the shattering of glass. She glanced at the pathetic, defeated figure by her mother's side. 'I'm sorry for thee, Ma, to have that for a man, but thee don't deserve any better.' Ruth turned her gaze back to her mother. She felt the power she had over these two people and the brats they had borne, and she liked it. She could make their lives miserable just as they had made hers. The pretty mother she remembered was a broken figure, her looks gone in the harshness of the life she had brought on herself. Ruth could feel no pity, just as she guessed her father would feel none.

She drew herself up and gazed down at her mother with abhorrence. 'Goodbye, Ma.' She turned on her heel and started away.

'Don't gan to him, Ruth, please!' It was a last cry, a last plea from her mother.

Ruth stopped and turned. She met her mother's snivelling request with a disdain bred by her father.

Her eyes swept over the grovelling pair with disgust. With not one word of assurance, she turned and hurried away without a backward glance.

Chapter Eight

'Get singled up!'

The mooring lines were let go.

'Loosen fore tops'l!'

'Hoist it!'

Jamaica's commands demanded instant obedience from those members of the crew still sober enough to carry them out.

Below decks, men sprawled in various stages of stupor, left to recover from their previous night's carousing. Thoresby didn't blame them for taking excessive advantage of their last night in Whitby. He knew they would sober, feel as if their heads didn't belong to them, and then, fully recovered, work as well as those who had stayed sober enough to start the *Mary Jane* on her voyage to the Arctic.

'Let go fore and aft!'

The *Mary Jane* slipped away from the quay on the ebb-tide, manoeuvred through the narrow, open draw-bridge, gained speed as the wind filled the topsail and headed for the sea beyond the protective piers.

'Get aloft!'

Men swung on to the bulwark, gripped the rigging and climbed to loosen the main topsail. Adam and David, concerned with hauling in the loose ropes, finished their task and watched the people thronging the staithes and cliffs.

The buzz of excited chatter formed a constant background to the cheers and shouts which encouraged the *Mary Jane* on her way and wished her a safe voyage. Mothers held children in their arms, giving a last picture of domesticity to husbands condemned to the cramped, uncomfortable quarters of a whaleship. Others were pleased to be relieved for five months of a marriage gone wrong, with freedom to turn elsewhere for love.

David and Adam searched the crowds on the cliff top for Jenny.

A red shawl swirled above the mass of people. Jenny! David's heart leaped with delight. He raised his arms in salute. He glanced at Adam and saw his face wreathed in the joy of this last contact with Jenny, yet touched with the sadness of parting. David's mind jolted. Jenny was Adam's sweetheart, and didn't he have Ruth? He wished she was on the cliff waving to him, as Jenny was waving to Adam, and then be there to welcome him back with arms ready to enfold him, as they had in Cropton.

David swallowed hard, trying to hold back the homesickness which threatened to overwhelm him.

The *Mary Jane* passed between the two piers. Her bow cut into the quiet ocean, curling the water back in a clear, foaming sweep.

David felt the swell. The strange sensation drove a

peculiar feeling through his stomach. He braced his legs against the motion.

'Hoist y'r main tops'l!'

The command boomed across the ship, drawing David's attention away from himself. The men manning the lines hauled on them. Glancing upwards, he saw the main topsail move into position and catch the wind.

'Hoist the top gallants!'

'Topmost mast of all,' explained Adam. The sail moved upwards and billowed. 'It's a good wind coming from the south-west,' he went on. 'Pa's taking advantage of it by using those sails.'

David nodded, aware that the queasy feeling in his stomach was getting worse.

The men who had been aloft swarmed down the rigging. The *Mary Jane* moved into a graceful dipping motion as she adjusted to the demands of the sea.

'Let's get these ropes coiled,' said Adam.

David moved towards the rope he had hauled on board when they left the quay. The ship lurched. He staggered.

'Don't fight it, Davey.' Adam grinned. 'Move with the sway.'

David said nothing, but tightened his lips, envious of Adam who had had no trouble and was already coiling a rope. David seized his rope, made a coil and started his second – only to see it slip across the deck. He cursed under his breath and, fighting the nausea welling inside him, knelt down and started again. He had positioned his second coil neatly when a bulky figure swung off the rigging on to the deck. David was not aware of the man until he saw a boot close to his rope. David glanced up to see a broad-shouldered man towering above him. The hatred in the dark-brown eyes shocked David as the weather-beaten face broke into an evil grin. The man kicked the rope to one side.

'Out of my way. Farm wags aren't wanted 'ere.' There was enmity in the words he spat at David.

He started to climb to his feet but the man pushed him back. David's eyes flared angrily.

'Andrews, leave him alone!' The words were from Adam who was on his feet, glaring threateningly at Andrews.

'Keep out of this, Thoresby.' Andrews's lips curled with contempt. 'Thee can't shelter behind your pa. Thee's just one of us on board ship.'

David seized his chance and scrambled to his feet while Andrews's attention was diverted during this brief exchange. He grabbed the bully's arm. Andrews swung round, eyes flaring with hostility.

'Keep your damned hands off me!' he hissed, and pushed David hard in the chest.

The *Mary Jane* dipped her bow deeper into the water. Off balance, David flew across the deck, crashed into the bulwark and only saved himself from tumbling overboard by grabbing a lanyard.

Andrews hunched hawk-like as he glared at David. 'Thee ain't going t' like this voyage!' He moved threateningly towards David.

Adam moved quickly between them. 'Don't do it!' he rapped harshly.

'Nursemaid, are y'?' sneered Andrews. He bent forward, pushing his face close to Adam's. 'Well, keep a weather eye on him, and thissen. A friend of a farmboy's no friend of mine.' He swung round and strode away.

'You all right, Davey?' asked Adam with concern.

David's face was white with the shock of nearly falling overboard and from the seasickness which threatened to overwhelm him.

He nodded weakly. 'Who the hell's he?' he gasped.

'Will Andrews,' said Adam. 'Nasty bit of work, but a good whaleman. Watch out for him, David, he doesn't like lads from the country.'

'Why not?' he spluttered, trying hard to conquer the awful feeling which was rising from his stomach.

'Blames a country lad for the death of his brother while serving on the whaleship *Aurora*,' explained Adam. 'Disliked all people from the country ever since.'

The words hardly made an impact on David. He felt awful. Bile rose in his mouth. He swung round, leaned over the bulwark and retched until he felt as if he had no inside left. The most miserable feeling he had ever experienced gripped his whole body. He felt weak. His knees wanted to buckle. His eyes glazed. But still he saw the water sweeping past the side of the ship, hypnotising him with the very movement which was causing him so much misery.

'Fernley! Get your eyes off that water!' The sharpness of the voice bit into David's befuddled mind and he recognised it as Jamaica's.

David glanced weakly over his shoulder, not caring that this was the mate who was speaking. The ship rolled and pitched in a regular motion. Would it never stop? Would this misery go on for ever? If only he could die and end it all.

131

'Stand up!' rapped Jamaica. His one eye gleamed ferociously, yet there was a hint of amusement in it.

David pushed himself upright slowly. The ship rolled. He stumbled, his eyes on Jamaica, who seemed to be standing there as if nothing was the matter, as if he was on solid land instead of subject to this unearthly motion.

'You'll have worse than this, Fernley, but hopefully by then you'll have your sealegs. Get yourself to your bunk. Excused duty.' Jamaica's voice was sharp but there was a touch of sympathy in it.

'Aye, aye, sir,' muttered David weakly. He turned and weaved his way across the deck.

Below decks he was greeted with groans and moans of seamen trying to throw off the effects of last night's hard drinking. The air was stifling with the stench of vomit. David felt everything closing in. He retched again. His stomach muscles felt as if they were being torn apart. Crawling into his bunk, he flopped back with eyes closed. A small measure of relief swept over him, yet he still wished he was dead.

Three hours after he had rolled into his bunk, he was roused by someone shaking him. A distant voice came louder and louder.

'Come on, Davey, wake up.'

David was back to the rolling, pitching ship. Sleep had relieved the agony but now the nausea returned. Maybe not quite as bad but still there, with the longing to drift back into the soothing sleep and into the ultimate panacea. He became aware of the stifling atmosphere, the groans and smell. Why had he come? Why hadn't he realised it would be like this? Oh, to be back in Cropton on firm land. Oh, for the fresh tang of the wild moorland air instead of this awful stench.

He moaned and turned his head to see who had dragged him back to this awful life.

'Come on, Davey. I've brought thee summat to eat,' pressed Adam.

David's eyes rolled. 'Ugh!' His mouth curled at the corners with disgust.

'Come on. It'll do thee good. Better if thee can eat something. Better still if thee can keep it down.'

'I couldn't,' David spluttered, his stomach turning at the very suggestion of food.

'Thee can and must,' urged Adam.

'In here?' David wrinkled his face.

'Get up then, thee can have it on deck,' insisted Adam.

'Leave me,' groaned David.

'Come on.' A touch of annoyance had come to Adam's voice. 'Thee'll never cure it if thee don't mak' the effort.'

David rolled over and started to swing out of the bunk. It was the only way he could stop the voice which cajoled him. The sooner he did that, the sooner he could lie down again. Immediately his feet touched the floor, he was sent staggering by the roll of the ship and only prevented himself from falling by grasping the wooden support between the bunks.

He followed Adam on to the deck.

The cold air tore David's breath away, but then he enjoyed the freshness which cleared his lungs. He held on to Adam, steadying himself to sway with his friend in motion with the ship.

'Breathe deep, Davey, it'll clear your head.'

He nodded, only too eager to follow Adam's advice and get the stench of the half-deck from his nostrils. He leaned on a hatch as the *Mary Jane* plunged northwards in the heaving sea.

'Get summat inside thee.' Adam held out the plate.

David looked at the beef and bread and his stomach heaved. He felt terrible. All he wanted was to get back to his bunk.

'Thee'll be better if thee eat,' said Adam. 'Come on,' he urged when David still showed reluctance.

He reached out and took a piece of bread. He bit into it without enthusiasm.

'Get it down,' snapped Adam.

Much to David's surprise the beef and bread, instead of making his nausea worse, relieved his stomach of the empty feeling.

'Right,' said Adam when David had finished. 'Now we'll walk.'

He kept his friend moving along the deck, back and forth, again and again, repeating the exercise throughout the day until David began to get his sealegs.

That night he tolerated the smell which still pervaded between decks even though the area had been swilled with salt water. He received tolerant, teasing banter from the experienced hands and was surprised when Andrews did not join in, but he remembered Adam's warning. Maybe Andrews had something else in mind. The following morning, when the majority of the men had recovered from their headaches and seasickness, the crew was mustered and assigned to watches, with David allocated to the same group as Andrews.

'Now ain't that nice, farm wag?' said Andrews with a chuckle which boded ill for David.

His watch was first on duty and set by Jamaica to scrub the deck and clean the galley.

'Fernley, you and I'll do the galley,' said Andrews as the watch collected their buckets and brushes.

David and he worked without a word passing between them until, with two slop buckets full of greasy waste, Andrews said, 'Better throw that lot overboard, Fernley, stink'll make you turn green again.'

David picked up the two buckets and made his way towards the starboard side of the deck.

'Larboard, Fernley!' snarled Andrews.

Puzzled, David turned to the man who had followed him. 'What do you mean?' he asked.

'Bloody hell, Fernley, don't tell me you don't know larboard.' Andrews looked heavenwards in exasperation. 'Larboard! Left side to farm wags.'

David moved towards the rail.

The six men engaged in scrubbing the deck stopped and, while maintaining a working attitude so that David could not notice that they were watching him, exchanged knowing grins and winks.

David stopped by the rail, put one bucket on the deck and started to raise the other to throw its contents over the side.

'Hi, Fernley.' David stopped and looked back. 'That way.' Andrews nodded towards the bow.

Unthinking, David automatically turned and swung his bucket in the direction indicated. The slops swept out only for the wind to drive them back over David,

135

leaving him covered from head to foot in left-overs, and greasy slime.

He gasped for breath, his nostrils quivering at the obnoxious smell. His anger flared, and, with the laughter and catcalls from the working party echoing around, picked up the full bucket. In one swift movement he flung the contents over Andrews, whose amusement was cut off instantaneously. Andrews's face, dripping with greasy waste, froze in disbelief. 'You bastard! snapped David between clenched teeth. 'Cross me again and I'll . . .'

'You'll what?' cut in Andrews, brushing slime from his face. 'Let's see what you'll do.' His eyes smouldered with anger as he started forward.

'Belay there, Andrews.' The words lashed from Jamaica. 'You got what you deserved.' He turned to the men scrubbing the deck. 'Dowse 'em.'

The men scrambled to their feet and threw their water over David and Andrews. Jamaica kept them at it, with sea water, until he was satisfied that tempers had subsided in the two antagonists.

'Get changed,' he ordered, 'and don't let your differences interfere with the running of this ship.'

The two men scurried away with Andrews muttering dire threats of what he would do to David once they got below deck, but his intentions were thwarted by Adam's presence in the fo'c's'le.

Surprised by their appearance, he heard the story from David with some amusement, but when Andrews left the fo'c's'le he reiterated his warning: 'Thee did well to stand up to him, but watch out – thee's made an enemy there.'

* * *

136

Two days later the wind freshened and began to blow harder from the north-east, deeping the troughs and throwing up hills of curling water. The sky darkened, rain lashed the deck. The *Mary Jane* plunged into the head sea which crashed against her bows with the force of a sledge-hammer. Sea sprayed high, joining the rain in soaking the hands as they precariously raced about their tasks to batten down and secure everything against the pounding ravages of the vicious sea. Ropes strained in their blocks; sails filled and cracked with thunderous noise.

David thought the world had gone mad and could only follow the actions of his fellow crewmen, helping in what-ever they did, while trying to maintain a hold against the force of the sea swilling around his legs.

'Away aloft! Take in sail!' The order, rapped from Seth Thoresby, was repeated loudly by Jamaica.

The fear which the wild wind and seething sea had knotted in David's stomach gripped his heart. Aloft, in this, on masts and yards which heeled and plunged in the heaving water.

'C'm on, wag,' a voice yelled close to his ear.

He saw water streaming over a leering face which was taking delight in the fear in David's eyes.

'Aloft!' Andrews's hand tightened on David's arm and propelled him towards the bulwark. 'It's a scary climb, sheephead.' Andrews gripped the rigging and judged the moment when the sway of the ship would help him. He swung on to the bulwark, grasped the shroud lines and climbed two rungs upwards. He paused and looked down, staring straight into David's eyes.

He met the mockery and the challenge.

'Move, Fernley, move!' Jamaica's voice rasped through the howl of the wind.

David seized the lanyard swung on to the ratlines and started to climb. The ship heeled over, swinging him down towards the sea. His stomach heaved and he flung himself forward against the ropes, hooked his elbow round one and hugged it close.

Rain lashed him. The wind whistled through the rigging, wailing a noise like death. When it seemed that he would be pitched into a watery grave, the *Mary Jane* came upright again. David looked up. The lines of rope disappeared far above his head. He shuddered. He couldn't go on. His eyes focused on the grinning features of Andrews. David took a grip on his feelings. He'd show the bastard. He unhooked his arm and started to climb.

The ship shuddered under the fierce impact of every wave. Ignoring the shaking, David concentrated on following Andrews.

Without realising it, he was at the yard-arm. Rain ran into his eyes, blurring his vision. He stared at the ghostly figures who were inching their way along the foot-rope beneath the yard, holding on to every possible support as the ship rolled and pitched in a sea bent on exerting its will.

'On your way, clod!' The yell close to his ear startled David.

Andrews, wide-eyed with evil intent, threw his head back and laughed loud into the wind.

David followed the men on to the yard which sloped precariously towards the heaving waves. The narrow rope swayed beneath the pressure of their feet. David hugged the yard, thankful for the solid feel of the wood. The *Mary*

Jane plunged down a trough, threatening to fling him from his perilous position. He hung on in sheer terror. Fear churned his stomach. He retched and was sick.

A pain shot through his hand, almost causing him to release his life-preserving hold on the yard. The second stab jolted his sense of self-preservation and he was aware of Andrews thumping him again and again, trying to break his grip. David gritted his teeth, in the slashing rain, and shuffled along the rope away from Andrews. He automatically followed the movements of the men furling the sail and when the task was done was aware of Andrews beside him. A sharp jab in his side made him gasp on the howling wind but he clung to the yard for his life. As Andrews aimed another blow, David swung down on the rope and Andrews's fist missed, almost causing him to lose his balance. Eyes wide with terror, Andrews grasped at the yard and held on.

'Move,' yelled David, indicating to Andrews to head for the shrouds.

Men clambered down to the deck where David swung Andrews round by the arm.

'Try anything like that again and I'll kill thee,' he snarled. Ignoring Andrews's innocent look, he turned away.

An hour later, with the storm showing signs of abating, the watch changed and David stumbled between decks anxious to reach his bunk. He was met by a stench which almost overwhelmed him. He shot a glance at Adam who was about to go on deck.

'Gasses from the water slopping about in the bilge,' explained Adam. 'Thee'll get used to it. Been aloft?'

'Aye, and that bastard Andrews tried to pitch me off,' replied David, a vicious hate in his voice.

'He what!' gasped Adam. 'Hell, we're stuck with him. We'll have to keep alert.'

The rest of the watch clattered into the fo'c's'le and Adam left.

'Been snivelling t' yer nursemaid?' hissed Andrews close to David's ear. 'Well, it won't do thee any good, nor him.'

David did not answer but changed into some dry clothes, rolled into his blanket and was soon asleep.

Roused by a rough shaking, his drowsy mind became aware of a raucous voice. 'Fernley, Fernley.'

David twisted over to see Andrews standing beside his bunk. As his mind cleared, he was aware that the ship no longer rolled and pitched with the fury that had beset her earlier. The storm was over.

'You did well up aloft.' Andrews's voice was softer, almost friendly. His face had lost most of its hostility. 'Thought I'd bring thee some grub.' He smiled as he turned to take a plate from another member of the crew who stood beside him. His right hand clamped on the bowl which was acting as a cover and he held out the plate to David.

As David, suspicious of his motive, reached for the plate, Andrews removed the bowl with a swift gesture.

Released from its prison, a rat leaped on to David's bunk. He cringed, gaping with horror at the creature, which, matted with slime, stared at him with hypnotic power. Terror gripped him. The rat turned tail. David started. As it ran across his blanket, he whirled sideways out of his bunk. He jerked the blanket, tumbling the rat on to the floor, where it escaped through a hole.

Sinking back against his bunk, David shuddered with relief. Then he straightened, his eyes fixed coldly on his tormentor.

'You've had it in for me, Andrews, but I can't be blamed for what some other country lad might have done to your brother.' The menace in his voice brought a silence to the fo'c's'le.

David launched himself at Andrews, driving his head and shoulders into the bigger man's chest. The impact took them crashing to the floor. David lashed hard at Andrews's stubbled face, drawing blood from his cheek and nose. Andrews heaved upwards, throwing him off, and slammed his huge fist into David's nose. Blood spurted. Andrews swung again but David rolled sideways, twisted round and lunged on top of him. He pounded at the man's features with both fists. All he could see was the grinning, rain-streaked face on the yard and he had to be rid of it.

He was unaware of anything else. He did not know the rest of the men had stopped shouting until he felt himself being dragged away from the bloody face beneath him. Jamaica and Adam, realising that something untoward lay behind the shouting coming from below decks, had burst into the fo'c's'le.

'Fernley, belay there! Belay!' Jamaica's voice, sharp and penetrating, drove sense back into David's mind.

'Back off, Davey.' He heard the urgent note in Adam's voice.

Men dragged him to his feet and supported him as his chest heaved air into his lungs.

'Enough!' rapped Jamaica. 'A bucket of water,' he added over his shoulder.

A man scurried away to return a few moments later with a bucket. Jamaica took it and dashed it into the face of the half-senseless man on the floor. Andrews started and gasped for breath. Spluttering, he sat up, shaking the water from his dripping hair. His face hurt. He felt it carefully and licked his cut and bruised lips. He scrambled to his feet and fixed his gaze on David who was trying to staunch the blood flowing from his nose.

Jamaica glared from one to the other. 'I ought to clamp you both in irons. Any more of this and I will. Andrews, I know you've baited Fernley, but there'll be no more of it this voyage.'

Jamaica left the fo'c's'le. Adam gave David a reassuring pat on the shoulder and followed Jamaica. The men turned to their bunks while David and Andrews tended their wounds.

Andrews leaned close to David. 'One day I'll get thee for this,' he hissed so only David could hear.

'Shetland, Davey!' Adam pointed across the larboard quarter.

'Yonder.'

David searched. His eyes were not yet used to sea distances and he envied what he thought was Adam's superior eyesight.

'Got it,' he cried, when he saw a smudge on the horizon. A thin black line gradually took shape.

'Sumburgh Head,' said Adam. 'Sumburgh Roost just south of it. A bedevilled sea. Treacherous currents run along that coast. Always give 'em a wide berth.'

'How long will we stay here?' asked David.

'We'll tak' on fresh supplies and sail later in the day. Pa doesn't believe in giving the men too long ashore, but he couldn't hold them if he didn't give them some time off. This is the last place they'll see for five months, last human beings unless we sight another ship, certainly the last women. The Shetlanders are good sailors, good with boats. Pa would like to take some of them to the Arctic, reckons they'd make good whalemen.'

'Why doesn't he?' asked David.

'Government won't allow it. Taking them might do some homeport men out of a job. The ban will have to be removed one day; it's getting harder to raise a whaling crew in the home port. Whaling isn't everyone's fancy in spite of the wages, and the war is taking men away.'

'I'm looking forward to seeing Lerwick,' commented David when the *Mary Jane* joined five other whalers at anchor off the town which straggled along the water's edge, its grey stone blending with the hills around it.

Adam laughed. 'Wait 'til thee's seen it all. Then, you'll think it better from the deck of a ship.'

Small boats had put out from the harbour and were soon alongside the *Mary Jane*. Their occupants, old and young, shouted their wares to the sailors leaning over the bulwark. Fresh fish, chickens and eggs were offered for money or in exchange for salt beef or clothes. Amid the raucous banter bartering developed. Bargains were struck, but when permission to go ashore was granted the boats bobbing beside the *Mary Jane* were forgotten.

David found that the town did not hold the same enchantment as it did from the sea. The streets were narrow and, as they entered the poorer section, David was nauseated by the filth and rotting rubbish which lay strewn in the mud. The small houses were little more than hovels. Shopkeepers tried to tempt them with their wares and dubious-looking females invited them to visit. Reeling sailors, roaming the streets with bottles in hand, were prevented from falling by the women who held them.

'Come on, Davey, thee hasn't seen it all yet,' said Adam, amused by David's expression of disgust.

He led the way into a side street, sought out a particular shop, and, ducking low, went inside. David followed and pulled up sharp. An impenetrable darkness blinded him and smoke seared his lungs. He grabbed Adam's arm. He did not want to lose his guide in this Stygian gloom.

'Where the hell are we?' he whispered as his watering eyes became accustomed to the dim light.

A peat fire burned on the mud floor in the ingle end and, as there was no chimney, nor windows through which the smoke could escape, it hung lazily over the room. Close to the ingle sat six old women, their backs hunched, coarse shawls pulled tightly round their heads. Their eyes peered from deep sockets, their noses were hooked as if smelling out some prey. Smoke curled from the blackened bowls of their pipes as they rocked to the skirl of a piper, standing in one corner of the room which was strewn with both sexes in various stages of inebriation. A group of sailors, arms round unkempt girls, sang a lewd song in opposition to the wild, wailing notes of the bagpipes. As the tempo quickened, a girl in her teens, her eyes wide and wild with the fire of desire, jumped to her feet, picked up her skirt and started dancing in the small space in the centre of the room.

She teased and enticed with her gestures and the smouldering sex in her eyes. The singing stopped and in its place came a stamping of feet in time with the wild notes of the pipes. Drunken sailors cheered and shouted obscenities as the girl danced faster and faster into one mass of whirling clothes until, at the height of a frenzy, which coincided with the final wail on the bagpipes, she collapsed on the ground, her eyes staring upwards. She made no resistance when the nearest sailors grabbed her and pawed her heaving breasts.

David's eyes, which had been receiving an education, were fixed on the scene when his concentration was broken by a tug at his sleeve. He glanced sideways to see who demanded his attention. He started and shrank back from the hollow eye of a shrivelled old woman who was wrapped in a filthy dress and tattered shawl. The clawlike hand still grasped his coat.

'Tell ye fortune?' Her voice rattled in her throat.

Bile rose in David's mouth choking the words he tried to utter. He shook his head.

'Tell ye fortune? Tell ye o' days at sea, o' loneliness. Like a bonnie lass afore ye gan?' The old crone cackled. 'I saw ye fancied her.' She nodded in the direction of the dancing girl who was receiving much closer attention from two sailors oblivious to the leering faces around them. 'I'll tak' thee to yan who'll gi' thee a better time.'

David pulled his sleeve from her clutching fingers. At the sign of his disgust, her dry, thin lips curled back in a malevolent sneer, revealing broken, tobacco-stained teeth.

Disgust changed to revulsion and the old crone laughed with a high-pitched screech. 'Innocent, are ye? She'll like ye aa the better fer that. She'll larn ye somethin' t' remember when ye're in t' Arctic.'

David swung round, gave Adam a tap in the ribs, and made for the door with the old woman's mocking laugh ringing after him.

Once outside, he breathed deeply in spite of the stench which rose from the street, preferring that to the smoke-filled atmosphere tainted with the smell of whisky and human sweat.

'What the hell is that place?' he demanded.

'That's a whisky house,' replied Adam. 'I didn't tak' thee there to shock you but so you'd learn what to expect from the majority of the crew.'

'But that's no part of whaling,' protested David as they set off along the street.

'That's where thee's wrong,' Adam replied. 'All those men are Englishmen from the whaleships. What they do is very much the concern of the captain if he's to have a successful voyage.'

'A lot of those men won't be fit to sail,' commented David.

'They'll sail. Their captains will see to that. They need a full crew.'

'What will your . . . er, Captain Thoresby do?'

'You'll see. He'll be along here shortly. We'll go to the end of the street to meet him.'

They hadn't long to wait, and when Seth arrived with Jamaica he asked, 'Seen it all, Fernley?'

'Yes, sir.'

'He's wondering what thee does about our crew,' said Adam with a wry smile.

Seth grinned and glanced at Jamaica whose scars mellowed with the broad smile which came in response to Seth's. 'We'll show him, Jamaica, eh?'

'Aye, aye, sir. It'll be a right good education for him.' Jamaica chuckled.

'Keep your eyes open and your fists handy, Fernley,' instructed Seth.

He strode off with Jamaica by his side. As they followed, Adam instructed David, 'We protect their backs. There'll be those who'd use a knife.'

David realised the wisdom of that precaution when Seth and Jamaica stormed through the whisky shops and brothels. Sailors, deprived of their pleasures, used their fists and drew their knives but the four men from the *Mary Jane* struck first. Only once did David feel the nick of a blade before his fist sent his assailant reeling.

'Well done, Davey.' Adam grinned, slapping him on the shoulder as they hurried to the next brothel.

David laughed, exhilarated by the uncanny understanding he and Adam had struck up in these encounters.

Seth and Jamaica dragged protesting men from beds, leaving David and Adam to deal with the clawing nails of naked girls who screamed abuse when they saw their sources of money disappearing.

A girl with eyes flaming with anger flung herself at David. He grasped her wrists before her nails raked his face and flung her back on the bed where she crouched, glaring at him with hate. A second girl offered no protest but still lay invitingly on the bed.

147

'You've time afore ye gan, sailor. I'll gi' ye fine memories for ten shillings.' Her dark eyes flashed as she smiled at him.

David turned away without answering. Nearly a week's wage for one short moment. He glanced back. The girl was pretty and tempting but he had need of his money, for he had a future with a girl so different from those he had encountered in Lerwick. He hurried from the house.

Within the hour Seth had assembled all his men, knowing that, although they moaned and cursed him as the boats bobbed their way to the *Mary Jane*, they would thank him later.

Chapter Nine

Ruth paused in washing the breakfast pots and stared unseeingly out of the window.

Martha had taken Jessica and Betsy with her to the hall and the men were in the fields. Ruth's mind drifted. Washing-up? She should be living a lady's life, not standing here, her hands in water, a pile of pots to wash and dry.

Oh, she was grateful to the Fernleys for taking her in, and she appreciated their kindness. Never once had she paraded her true parentage to them. She had told them she had found out, and that was that as far as they were concerned. What went on in her mind was another matter.

She was somebody. No longer Rebecca Cornforth's bastard. She might not reveal the truth but it had given her purpose, a need to fulfil the feelings which she had experienced deep in her being.

She cursed her true father for never owning her. She cursed her mother for never giving her the benefit of the regular payments from her father and she cursed her step-father for the abuse he had heaped on her.

Her eyes narrowed. One day she would show them and they would wish they had treated Ruth Harwood differently. She would use her true background to her advantage. The bearing and confidence which the truth had brought made David's success more imperative, for in Whitby she could be somebody to look up to.

Her lips moved in silent prayer for his safe return so that he could fulfil his promise to take her to Whitby, away from the surroundings in which she was known and which held so many bad memories.

The first dip of the bow, when the *Mary Jane* left Lerwick, brought the empty feeling to David's stomach but it soon passed, unlike the moment of sailing from Whitby.

'You're coping well, Davey. Reckon we'll make a sailor of you yet.' Adam grinned.

With all the 'Lerwick headaches' gone by the next morning, the preparations for whaling began in earnest.

The crew was mustered and the selection of the men who would man the boats, from which they would hunt the whale, started. Seth allotted a harpooner to each of the six boats and they selected their men in turn, choosing a boat steerer first. Adam, newly promoted to line manager, was chosen by Jamaica to look after the whale lines in his boat. The mate also picked David as one of the three remaining rowers needed to make up the complement of six men to his boat.

Jamaica eyed his crew. 'You've all been with me afore, except Fernley, so y'know what I want.' His one eye glared at David. 'All thee has t' do is row hard and keep your wits about thee.' He cast one more glance across his crew. 'Stand by to prepare boats,' he yelled.

As Jamaica hurried away to check that all the other boatcrews were ready, Adam slapped David on the shoulder. 'Glad thee's with us, Davey.'

'So am I.' David grinned.

'Jamaica's the harpooner,' Adam explained. 'He rows bow oar and is in command. Bob Harrison's boat-steerer. Important job. Steers us towards the whale. Rowers can't see with their backs to the whale so the boat-steerer is responsible for getting us to it. He has to know its habits so that if it sounds – dives, to thee, Davey – he can anticipate where it might resurface. He'll direct our rowing and warn the harpooner when to get ready. From then on the harpooner will be in charge. A good boat-steerer will be able to anticipate the harpooner's commands and work closely with him. It's all a matter of teamwork between every member of the crew.'

'Why an oar instead of a rudder for steering?' queried David.

'Twenty feet long, that oar,' said Adam. 'It doesn't cut down the speed of the boat as much as a rudder, turning the boat is easier and it can also turn a boat when it is at rest. If we get among ice or into places where the oars can't be used, the boat can still be kept in motion by a sculling action with the steering oar.'

David nodded. 'Thee's the line manager. What do thee do?'

'I row after-oar, that's the stroke oar, so thee all take your rhythm from me. I'm immediately in front of Bob who'll indicate the speed he wants. I'm also responsible for the lines which are stowed in two square wells – thee'll see when we prepare the boats. There's also a stray-line which is put in the stern ready to connect our line to that of another boat should all ours be taken out by the whale.'

'Does that often happen?' asked David.

'Oh, aye. If a whale sounds or even runs on the surface, it can take out all the rope we have, about seven hundred and twenty fathoms – over four thousand feet in your language.' Adam grinned.

Any more explanation was halted by Jamaica's return. He allocated the three remaining rowing positions and then, on the command, all boat crews prepared the boats which had been stowed in-board for the passage to the whaling seas.

While David and the other two oarsmen cleaned out the boat, Jamaica, Bob and Adam prepared the whale lines. Six equal lengths of finest hemp were spliced to each other and were carefully coiled into the two compartments specially designed for them. Jamaica supervised this with the utmost care. Any faults in the ropes or their positioning could mean a lost whale or, if a man became entangled with the line as it was being run out, the loss of a limb or his life.

'Fernley, you're new to this. Come and learn, lad,' Jamaica called.

'Aye, aye, sir.'

'Thee's in favour,' whispered Adam. 'He wouldn't do this for any new hand unless he thought highly of him.'

The mate picked up one of the two harpoons and a piece of rope about nine yards long. 'This rope is called the fore-ganger and I'm going to splice it to the harpoon – it's called spanning the harpoon. It's vital that this is done without a flaw otherwise the throw can be affected.' Jamaica spliced the foreganger tightly to the harpoon. 'See how the end of the harpoon is splayed,' he pointed out. 'That prevents the rope from being drawn off and also forms a socket for the stock or handle.' He selected a six-foot stock and fixed it into the socket and then tied a cord from the stock to the rope.

'What's that for?' asked David.

'The stock will most likely come off after the harpoon hits the whale. The cord holds it loosely to the rope so that we seldom lose one.'

Jamaica carefully covered the point of the harpoon with an oiled piece of canvas to preserve it until it was required, and then placed it in position with its stock in a wooden rest and its point on the bow with the foreganger coiled carefully beneath so that Jamaica could take it up and use it in an instant. The other harpoon was placed close by in case a second throw was necessary.

'Thee'll have to be accurate to kill a whale with that,' commented David.

Jamaica's one eye gleamed with amusement. 'I'm good, lad, but not that good.' He chuckled. 'The harpoon's just to attach the boat to the whale. Once that's done we've got to get the boat alongside and then I use the lances to kill it.' He indicated the six stocks, each with a long, sharp, metal attachment which had been stored close to the bow of the boat.

While Jamaica had been instructing David, the rest of the boatcrew had been fitting it out with all the other items necessary for the hunt.

'Axe placed handy for the harpooner, in case we have trouble and he has to cut the rope. Bucket for throwing water over the bollard. That's the bollard,' Jamaica explained, pointing to the thick piece of wood fixed upright near the bow of the whaleboat. 'Harpooner makes a couple of turns of the line round the bollard so that it will veer the boat steadily after the whale is struck. If the whale runs or sounds, the line can go out that fast that the friction on the bollard causes it to overheat. It could even fire it. The water cools it.'

'That?' asked David, pointing to a lance-like instrument except that its blade was long and thin like a knife coming to a sharp point.

'Tail knife, used for perforating the tail of a dead whale so that we can secure it to tow it back to the ship. Then there's a jack or flag staff which we display so that other boats and the ship, if in sight, know we have harpooned a whale and can assist if required. That's a fog horn for calling should we get caught out of sight of the ship. Snow shovels, boat hooks, grapnels, all fairly obvious in their use. Piggins –' he indicated a small wooden receptacle with a short handle '– for bailing. We're sure to ship water. And there's a lantern.'

As each boat was ready, it was hoisted into position on its davits by the side of the ship from which it could be launched at a moment's notice. Seth and Jamaica made their inspections and, satisfied that all was ready, stood the crew down, except those on watch.

For the next four days, the *Mary Jane* sailed steadily north-east through favourable seas. Life became a round of keeping occupied with repeated tasks and the crew began to get fidgety, anxious to start the purpose of their voyage – whale hunting.

The ship rolled and pitched with never-ending regularity but David had found his sealegs and spent most of his time on deck, enjoying the days of longer light, going below only when it was necessary.

On the evening of the third day David was leaning on the bulwark with Adam. A natural silence crept over them, broken only by the swish of water and the creak of timbers. The sea ran smooth and the breeze was gentle. David felt cradled in the ocean's vast loneliness, his whole being at peace. To the north a pale silver-like light suffused the sky, across the thin layer of cloud, drawing David to it with an irresistible command which he could not deny.

'Thee's felt it, Davey, the call of the north.' The quiet tone intruded and yet was in keeping with the silence.

'The call of the north?'

'Yes. It isn't everyone who feels it, but thee has,' explained Adam. 'It'll hold thee, ensnare thee and bring thee back.'

David looked to the north. He was transfixed. Nothing else existed but himself, the sea and the north.

'There she blows!' The yell came clear on the crisp air.

Excitement seized the crew. Whales! All eyes turned upwards to see the man on the main-top-mast pointing to the larboard quarter. Eager to see the spout, men hurried to the rail.

There it was! A white plume of water rose and fell about a mile away.

'There she blows!' The cry came again and again as a second and third spout appeared.

'Away two and three!' Seth Thoresby's voice rapped harshly across the deck.

Twelve men obeyed instantly and within minutes the two boats were being rowed swiftly across the water.

'Bend that back, lad!' Jamaica's voice came quietly but firmly from behind David. He heaved harder, straining his bulging muscles on the oar. In spite of the chill in the air, David was soon sweating. In the stern Bob Harrison leaned against the long steering oar, pressing it to his will. His gaze was fixed ahead searching for the spouts. Each sighting brought a slight swing of the steering oar to keep the boat on the shortest course to its quarry.

Blood pounded in David's head with the exertion. Sweat poured as he heaved on the oar. Were they never going to reach the whales? He wanted to turn round to see what was happening but he knew it could be fatal if he took his concentration off the job in hand.

At a signal from the boat-steerer, rowing ceased instantly. Relief surged through aching bodies which were still tensed, for the men knew they were near the whales. They tried to quell the rasp of the air in their heaving lungs, for they wanted no sound to alarm their quarry. The boat glided in a bobbing motion. Jamaica slipped his oar, allowing it to turn fore and aft with the boat, and, as he stood up, braced himself against the sway.

David's urge to get his first sight of a whale was irresistible. He half-turned so he could glance over his shoulder. The broad-backed Jamaica towered above him and, a short distance beyond, the whole view was blocked by a huge, black mass which made their twenty-eight-feet-long whaleboat seem tiny. David gulped.

Jamaica reached for a harpoon. David turned his attention back to his oar.

Jamaica weighed the harpoon carefully in his right hand, altered his grip, glanced at the lines, and then riveted his attention on the unsuspecting animal. The boat steerer sculled the boat gently forward. Twenty yards. Fifteen. Tension filled the men. They hardly dared to breathe. David glanced over his shoulder. Jamaica was carefully poised, the barbed harpoon drawn back ready for the throw.

Ten yards! Five! Jamaica's body arched backwards and then sprang forwards with the viciousness of a tightly coiled spring released from tension. His powerful shoulders turned, bringing his right arm forward on a forceful trajectory. Through long practice he released his grip on the harpoon at a precise moment, sending it soaring over the sea in a curve towards the black shape towering in front of the flimsy boat. Its point struck, pierced and buried into the blubber where the barbs took a grip.

'Stern all!' The order rapped out and was obeyed instantly by the rowers who drove the boat away from the whale with all their power. They were not a moment too soon, for, with its peace shattered, the whale lashed at the water with its huge tail. The sea churned into a foaming mass which rocked the boat viciously. The black monster brought its tail high out of the water, turned and sounded.

As soon as the harpoon struck, Jamaica quickly made two turns of the whale-line round the bollard. The whale took the line out so fast that it was necessary to throw water over the bollard to stop it firing from the heat of the friction. Four lengths of line were run out but gradually the speed slackened until no more rope was taken. Immediately there was a frenzied haste to take up the slack by coiling the rope back into the tubs.

The tension on the rope slackened.

'She's rising!' hissed Jamaica.

The crew, wondering where the whale would break the surface, cast fearful glances at each other. Suddenly it blasted the sea into heaving waves close to the boat. Water swamped them. Men bailed as fast as they could while others hauled the rope in.

The whale lashed, turned and ran, dragging the boat with it. As the rope tightened, there was nothing the crew could do but hang on and hope. Bounced and buffeted, the boat sent water spraying over the crew as it hurled across the sea.

Suddenly the whale stopped, turned tail and sounded again. The line hurtled out once more, but this time the whale took only three lengths before it decided to surface.

As soon as it broke water, the crew hauled on the lines as quickly as possible, dragging the boat nearer and nearer their prey. Jamaica yelled instructions and cursed his crew, urging them to pull harder.

He reached for a lance and steadied himself. The black shape loomed larger and larger, filling his whole vision. As the men hauled, anxiety gripped them. This monster could send their world into a maelstrom from which there might be no escape. Then they were alongside and Jamaica struck accurately. Blood gushed as Jamaica churned the lance round and round. Hurt deep, the whale started to run again. Jamaica let the lance go. The rope hurtled out once more but it was not long before the whale settled again. Bending their backs, grasping the rope in firm hands, the men hauled Jamaica into a position to use a second lance. Each time the mate struck, he churned the death-dealing instrument in the whale's body. Blood spattered Jamaica from head to foot and his hands and arms ran red. Suddenly he yelled, 'Stern all!' The urgent note in his voice brought instant obedience. Jamaica's experience had judged it right. The whale made one last bid for life. It thrashed the sea in a final frenzy. Suddenly it spouted blood, rolled on its side and lay still.

Jamaica's yell of triumph was taken up by his crew. He secured a line to the whale and another was fastened to the second boat which had stood by throughout the attack. The long hard row back to the *Mary Jane* began. Every man's back strained and muscles ached as forty tons of bone, meat and blubber were towed slowly through the undulating sea to the larboard side of the *Mary Jane* which Seth Thoresby had been directing towards the boats. The whale was manoeuvred alongside the *Mary Jane*, positioned with its head towards the stern and secured ready for flensing.

David slumped over his oar, his chest heaving cold air into his aching lungs. His back muscles cried out for relief and his arms protested at the prospect of more exertion.

'Get on deck, lad!' Jamaica's voice boomed above him.

'Aye, aye, sir,' David mumbled wearily. He shipped his oar, struggled to his feet. Only when he had clambered on board the *Mary Jane* did he appreciate the full implications of what he had witnessed. He felt sickened as he recalled the sea running red with blood.

159

As no more whales were sighted, Seth judged that the others had deserted the immediate vicinity and ordered flensing to begin. The prompt response was a whirl of feverish activity as men, eager to be searching for whales again, set about the tasks in which they had been drilled.

The harpooners fitted iron spikes to their boots and went over the side on to the whale. Gripping the smooth, slippery surface with the iron 'spurs', they balanced and moved with the ease of experience, taking their flensing tools as required from the men attending them in the two whaleboats alongside the whale. Cuts were deftly made along the back and down the side of the dead animal. Blubber knives and blubber spades flashed, edging the blubber away from the body in long strips. These were fastened to tackle attached to the ship, peeled from the whale and hauled on board the *Mary Jane*. Here the boat steerers cut the huge strips into pieces which were transferred by the line managers, armed with pick-hacks, to a hole in the main hatchway. They were received between decks by the linesmen who packed the blubber to await a more suitable time for removing any unwanted matter in the final operation of making off. The whalebone was removed from the huge mouth and split into chunks of five to ten blades before being stowed.

As a new hand, David watched the proceedings with interest but was nauseated at the sight of the blubber being torn from the body, leaving the sea and deck running in blood and grease.

'Thee'll get over it,' said Adam, noting David's revulsion.

'But that magnificent, harmless creature . . .' he started.

'We need 'em, Davey. Blubber for oil for our lamps, whalebone for ladies' stays, umbrellas, sieves, whips and all sorts of things. Whaling's important to Whitby's economy and prosperity, many families depend on it, and thee's earning your living from it.'

'I suppose thee's right,' he admitted.

When everything of use had been taken from the whale, the carcass was freed and, as it sank, a great cheer rose from the crew of the *Mary Jane*. The proceeds of their first whale were safely on board in about three hours. Now they could start hunting again, and if Seth Thoresby lived up to his reputation they could be away from the Arctic early.

The following day whales were sighted and all boats were lowered but only the captain succeeded in making a strike. With three of the boats close by at the time, they were quick to make the kill, and the remaining two arrived to make the task of towing easier.

The weather remained fair the next day and, as there was no sign of more whales, Seth ordered the proceeds from the first two to be made off while the *Mary Jane* lay to.

Blubber was passed from the hold to the deck where it was skinned and, when all extraneous matter had been cut away, chopped into smaller pieces. These were transferred via canvas shutes into barrels and stowed for the voyage home.

David thought the activity a whirling mad-house but he quickly realised that it was a carefully planned routine with a regular rhythm. The whole crew were in good humour, working with a will, for this meant money in their pockets and the sooner they completed the making off the sooner they could hunt more whales.

About ten o'clock the following morning, with the *Mary Jane* holding a north-easterly course, Jamaica noted the changing colour of the sky and, with the appearance of a brightness along the horizon topped by a greyish hue, he predicted they would soon see ice. Ten minutes later the man at the main-top-mast yelled, 'Ice ahead!'

Seth Thoresby ordered extra hands to lookout positions. He himself went to the bow, placing one man midships to pass on his directions to the man at the helm, who had Jamaica beside him.

Arctic ice! A fear of the unknown gripped David but he drew reassurance from the calmness of the experienced hands. He stared ahead fascinated as they approached the ice. Huge, flat sheets lay almost motionless. Greys, greens, blues and whites were reflected from the rough surface. Long lanes of water criss-crossed the expanse, and David soon realised the necessity of fortifying the bow of a whaleship as they crashed and ground their way through the ice.

The monotony of the calls passed along the ship grew trying. 'Hard-a-starboard!' 'Steady-as-you-go!' 'Hard-a-larboard!' the commands droned on for seven hours, but, despite the vigilance of all concerned, all the ice could not be avoided.

Impact after impact shuddered through the ship but Seth held the *Mary Jane* to her course. He kept an eye on the weather which deteriorated in the third hour but then held, much to the relief of the crew, who did not want to be caught in the ice in a storm.

Tension, which had crept into the crew, with the prolonged contest with the ice, suddenly evaporated when the lookout at the main-top-mast yelled, 'Clear water!'

As soon as they were free of the ice, Seth set course for the east coast of Greenland. Thirty-six hours later, land came in sight and Seth altered course to a northerly heading. Keeping close inshore, he eyed the coast critically. Half an hour later, the intensity of his search eased.

'Why are we going in here?' David asked Adam as the *Mary Jane* sailed into a fjord bounded by high cliffs and towering mountains.

'Pa's smelled foul weather,' explained Adam. 'It's going to be bad, otherwise he would never have come in here.'

Suddenly the weather improved and a brilliant sun shone from a clear blue sky but Seth would not be tempted to put to sea. The crew grew restless. They could be hunting whales. Some of the hands, who had not sailed with Seth before, began to murmur and question his judgement but their criticism was silenced on the third day when the sky filled with black clouds which shut them into a tiny world. Thunder boomed between the towering cliffs like some roaring beast tearing at David's heart. Lightning ravaged the sky, illuminating their surroundings into menacing shapes which chilled David's mind. He was thankful that the captain had read the weather signs correctly for he dreaded the thought of what it must be like in the open sea in a storm of such ferocity. He determined that one day he would be as capable as Seth Thoresby.

The wind strengthened and howled at the frail ship as it whirled thickening snow over the mountains, down the cliffs and across the fjord. The ship became a dead thing covered in a white shroud.

The storm blew for three days with no let up but it took five days before it finally abated, leaving the *Mary Jane* on peaceful water.

By the last week in July, one more whale would make a full ship. The crew wanted that whale quickly, and then to be on their way home. Whales were sighted but, before the boats could reach them, something disturbed them and they sounded and were not seen again. The next day the ocean seemed to be deserted. Seth got his harpoon into a whale the following day, but the rope snagged on the bow of his boat and had to be cut before the vessel was dragged below the waves by the sixty-ton creature. Whale, harpoon and stock were lost. The same afternoon the harpooner in the third boat lost his balance at the vital moment of the throw and missed the quarry.

Men began to despair of catching the final whale. 'Lucky' Thoresby's luck had deserted him. Murmurings rose among the crew. He should be satisfied with the catch. They wanted to be away from this God-forsaken ocean which could release its viciousness at any moment. But no one dared voice these opinions to a captain whose roaring answer would demolish them in two words.

Their misgivings and despondency vanished with the cry from the mast-head: 'There she blows! There she blows!'

Jamaica's boat was the first to hit the water and David, with the rowers on his side of the boat, pushed their vessel away from the ship. Oars were in the water, backs bent, muscles strained, and men heaved with a will to get the last whale. They were two lengths ahead of their nearest rival.

'Bend to it, lads. Heave. Heave.' Bob's voice came sharp and clear, urging them to greater effort. 'Faster, faster.'

Adam increased the pace and the rest of the men kept with him. The boat flashed across the gently undulating sea. Conditions were perfect. This must be their day. They rowed with an excited will. Chests heaved, gulping air into aching lungs. Sweat soon covered their bodies in spite of the cold air.

'Come on, bend yer backs! More. More.' Bob did not let up. Already they had drawn two more lengths ahead of their nearest rival.

David's brain seemed as if it would burst with the strain. Hell! When was Bob going to call a halt? David's eyes focused through the beads of sweat which dripped into them. He saw the gleam of excitement in Bob's eyes and knew they were nearing their quarry.

'Ease it, lads.' His voice was low but clear to the rowers.

The pace slackened. Bob's orders were directed at Adam and every man matched his stroke to his until Bob signalled them to stop rowing. Oars were shipped. The boat glided silently. Jamaica stood up and turned into his position as harpooner. They were so close that Jamaica's actions were almost instantaneous. He grabbed the harpoon, balanced and threw.

The harpoon sped through the air. Men held their breath. They heard it thud home. Their oars were out. 'Stern all.' They bent their backs to propel the boat away from the rising flukes. But the whale was quick. The flukes crashed down inches from the boat. It rocked viciously, sending Jamaica over the side. The sea heaved. David released his hold on his oar, which swung into the side of the boat, and turned to grab the hands of the mate who grasped at the gunwale. David got a firmer grip on Jamaica's arms and, as the boat tossed on the churning sea, heaved him into the boat.

The whale had sounded and the rope was going out fast. The bollard was already smoking.

'Bucket, Davey!' gasped Jamaica.

David grabbed the bucket and doused the bollard and rope as fast as he could.

With the boat threatening to sink under the weight of water, which had swamped it in the maelstrom from the whale's flukes, men wielded the piggins and bailed with a desperation born out of a determination to survive.

The rope stopped moving.

'She's coming up!' yelled Jamaica, ignoring the cold from his sodden clothes.

The men were tense. Where would the monster surface? If she came directly beneath them, they were finished.

The sea heaved and the black bulk burst from the water fifty yards away. She settled and started to run. More rope ran out.

The boat bucked along over the waves. Men, fearing to be thrown out, held on with all their strength.

The whale stopped. The boat moved on, slowing with every foot until the men grabbed the lines and hauled eagerly, taking them nearer and nearer their quarry.

Jamaica tapped David on the shoulder and indicated he should move out of the way. He took up a lance and positioned himself in the bow.

Slowly now. Slowly. The men knew the signals, knew the pattern which Jamaica wanted. The boat inched nearer and nearer the black mass lying on the water. Jamaica, tense, cautious, struck. His aim was true and he had no difficulty in inflicting the final death thrust. Blood burst from the animal and sprayed the boat, but Jamaica ignored it. He had triumphed!

Eager to return to the ship with their prize, the crew quickly made holes in the tail and secured ropes through them. The long haul to the ship started, and the boatcrew were only too glad to hand over the task to two of the other boats. Men rowed willingly until sweat dripped from their foreheads in spite of the Arctic cold. They had the whale they wanted and soon they would be on their way home.

Seth directed the positioning of the whale alongside the ship. The men were happy, keen to flense and make off as soon as possible.

David was ordered into one of the boats to attend on the flensers. His companion sank a boat-hook into the carcass and held the boat steady while David got the flensing tools ready for the men coming on to the whale.

'Thoresby, Andrews, on to the whale.' The order rapped from Jamaica and as soon as they had fastened spikes to their boots they were over the side and on to the whale alongside the other flensers.

They worked quickly, making the cuts deftly to a prearranged pattern so that the blubber could be peeled from the whale to be dealt with on deck.

The work went on unceasingly with men ignoring the cold, the blood and the slime. As the flensing proceeded, pressure intensified on David to keep the flensing knives sharp and ready when wanted.

Andrews turned for a fresh knife. David fumbled. The sharp blade sliced through Andrews's jacket and only his quick reaction prevented it from cutting into his thigh. Andrews staggered and only just managed to save himself from falling off the whale. As he righted himself, his face clouded with fury.

'Bloody fool,' he snarled, his eyes wide with anger. 'Tried to kill me.'

'I didn't,' yelled David.

'Like hell! Thee did. I'll have thee for this.' Andrews threw his blood-stained flensing knife at David.

The wooden shaft caught him in the chest. He lost his balance and fell heavily in the bottom of the boat, which was only prevented from capsizing by the sailor who held it to the whale.

'Cut it out, Andrews,' snapped Adam. 'It was an accident.'

'It bloody well wasn't.' Andrews glared at Adam. 'Thee's as bad as him. I warned thee before not to . . .'

'Belay there!' The shout came from Jamaica who had just come to the rail and had seen the men not working. 'Get on with flensing. Fernley, thee having a sleep in that boat?'

David scrambled to his feet. He handed a knife to Andrews, meeting the hostility in his eyes with equal defiance. Andrews snatched the knife and turned back to his flensing.

Knives flashed in steady unison. Another hour and they would be finished.

A sudden lurch startled David. 'What the hell was that?' he gasped as he steadied himself. He glanced sharply at his companion and saw a look of apprehension.

'A swell running?' The yell ran through the ship.

Whale and boat heaved and dropped again in unison. The flensers stopped the swish of their blades, and David caught a touch of fear in their eyes. Flensing in a swell was dangerous. The movement could break the ropes to the tackle, endangering the flensers whose foothold on the whale became more precarious with the motion.

'It's not bad, get on with it,' Seth roared.

Anxious to be off the whale, the flensers swung their blades swiftly, increasing the risk of carelessness.

Ropes screeched and woodwork creaked in angry protest at the extra strain exerted by the heaving sea. David glanced anxiously at the swell beyond the ship.

It was growing, threatening to sweep high along the side of the *Mary Jane*.

'Look out!' David's warning shout was too late. The heavy swell was upon them. It lifted the fifty-ton whale with ease and dropped it contemptuously into the following trough. The sudden strain was too much. Ropes snapped. In the moment that Andrews saw them part, he snatched the opportunity for revenge. He staggered sideways against Adam, pushing him in the path of the falling tackle. Andrews jumped clear of the whale into the boat, the blade of his knife aimed at David.

Shocked into action by the evil look of triumph as Andrews hurtled towards him, he stepped sideways. Andrews fell heavily, hitting his head on the side of the boat, but David ignored him. His attention was riveted on Adam.

The heavy tackle caught him on the side of his head as the full weight pounded against his shoulder. Already fighting to keep his balance, he lost his hold, spun round and hurtled unconscious into the sea between the bow of the boat and the *Mary Jane*.

Adam! Horror swept through David.

He was into the water almost as soon as his friend. He grabbed but his numbed hands felt nothing. Gasping for breath, he broke the surface, saw a form close by and grabbed again. Instinctively he knew he had a grip. He must not lose it.

The swell swept along the *Mary Jane* again. The two men were carried with it. David grabbed for the boat but his clawing fingers only scraped it as it moved away. The man in the boat moved quickly. He knew that the two men must be out of the water within minutes if they were to survive.

He jerked the hook out of the whale and thrust it in David's direction. He and Adam were sweeping down into the trough. The boat hovered on the top of the swell and suddenly plunged towards them. It came faster and faster, swung round viciously, narrowly missed the two men and crashed hard against the whale. David, half aware that the shaft of the hook was close, grabbed. His fingers closed automatically round the wood. He must hold on. It was their only chance.

Two of the flensers, helpless to do anything from their precarious position on the whale, jumped as the boat slammed their perilous foothold. Their spikes tore at the woodwork. They steadied themselves, and in a moment were in the bow, dragging the men from the water into the bottom of the boat, ignoring Andrews whose head was only just clearing.

Seth bellowed encouragement as the three men used the next heave of the sea to get the boat alongside the *Mary Jane*. Ropes were thrown and the boat made fast. Even as this was being done, Jamaica and Bob Harrison were over the side, reaching down to give support to the men in the boat who were lifting Adam. They took his weight and hauled him up to the men on the deck.

'To my cabin,' yelled Seth, his mind tormented by the sight of his son frozen in unconsciousness.

Knowing that there was not a moment to lose, four men scurried away with Adam followed by Seth, who shouted over his shoulder, 'Bring Fernley too.'

Jamaica and Bob reached for David as boat and ship rode the swell together.

The boat lurched. Men on the deck tried to steady it with the ropes but the sea dragged it down into a trough. Jamaica and Bob held on to the side of the ship watching the boat carefully as the swell carried it upwards again, trying to judge the moment when it would be almost stationary.

'Now!' yelled Jamaica.

David was pushed upwards. Jamaica and Bob grabbed. They held on as the boat slid away. Muscles strained, lifting David towards the men on the deck who reached down to take his weight.

Half-frozen in spite of his thick clothing, he was heaved on to the deck where waiting hands carried him quickly to the captain's cabin.

Still dazed, Andrews was helped on board and the rest of the men left the boat quickly.

Once in the captain's cabin, Adam and David were stripped naked, their frozen clothes cast aside. The two friends were laid on the floor and immediately four men were on their knees beside them, rubbing vigorously. Rough hands swept forcefully over their limbs and torsos. After ten minutes Seth called, 'Enough.' He dropped to his knees beside Adam and carried out a quick examination of his son. Nothing seemed to be broken but his shoulder was severely bruised and there was an ugly gash down the side of his head. He turned to David. A quick glance was enough. 'Bloody frozen,' he muttered. 'Get them into my bed. Thompson, Wells, Brown, strip off and into bed with them. Hurry.'

The men stripped to their thick, woollen underclothes and clambered into the bed, one on either side of Adam and David and the third in the middle. Blankets were thrown over them and they pressed close to the two unconscious men, trying to drive more warmth into them.

Seth, his thoughts on getting the *Mary Jane* to Whitby as quickly as possible, hurried to the deck where he found Jamaica had already anticipated his command. The boat had been brought on board, the whale cast off and he had started to get the ship under way.

'How are they, cap'n?' Jamaica asked.

'Both unconscious,' replied Seth. 'Cram every inch of sail, Jamaica, and send three men to my cabin at ten-minute intervals.' As he spoke, Seth sought out Andrews who was removing the spikes from his boots. 'Andrews,' he barked.

'Aye, aye, sir,' he said, scrambling to his feet. There

was little enthusiasm in his voice for his head still reeled from the blow.

Seth's dark eyes filled with anger as he faced Andrews. 'You tried to kill 'em, tried to kill my son!'

The accusation bit into Andrews's mind. 'What? I niver did. Not me, cap'n.' His eyes widened with astounded innocence.

'I saw it all,' Seth rapped. 'Thee pushed Adam under that falling tackle and . . .'

'I lost my balance,' broke in Andrews in loud protest.

'Thee pushed him,' thundered Seth. 'And then on pretence of having to leap into the boat, thee tried to get Fernley with the flensing knife.'

'No, cap'n, no,' cried Andrews.

'Put him in irons!' ordered Seth, not wanting to hear any more protestations of innocence. He had more urgent matters to see to.

Seth hurried to his cabin with abuse and threats hurled at him by Andrews who was being bundled below decks.

Seth kept watch for the first sign but after three hours began to believe he would never win the battle to keep Adam and David alive.

Jenny tossed restlessly in her sleep, the nightmare threatening to engulf her like the pounding sea. The choking sensation grasped at her throat. She jerked upright, gasping for breath, her eyes wide with fear. The moon suffused the room with an eerie light. She shuddered, her body chilled in spite of the warm soft air. She grasped the blankets to her, hugging herself tight, rocking slowly as if to soothe away the hauntings in her mind.

173

Adam! David! They had been there, but they weren't real. Somewhere else. They were in trouble and it threatened their lives. Jenny moaned. 'Oh, dear God, help them.'

Within twenty-four hours of recovering consciousness, Adam was on his feet. He took over the vigil at David's side, willing his friend to show signs of recovery. David's stamina, undermined by the cold and the lack of decent food, worsened through his inability to take any nourishment, but Adam took hope when, a day later, David showed signed of restlessness.

'Davey, Davey, can you hear me?' urged Adam as he bent over the unconscious form. There was no response. He tucked the blankets closer round David. 'Come on, Davey, come on, you've got to live. Remember Ruth. You've got to get well for Ruth.'

David moaned. Deep down in his subconscious a girl appeared, waiting, watching for him. She reached out to him, needing him to rescue her from an unseen menace. Ruth. He must help her. He struggled to reach her but she was gone, and in her place was a red shawl waving to him, calling him back to the safety of Whitby. He felt compelled to answer, to relieve Jenny's anxiety. He must defeat the threat which was threatening to take him away from Jenny.

David struggled hard, fighting every backward slip towards oblivion. He forced himself to live for the sake of two girls.

Once he had regained consciousness, Adam tended his every need in his battle to shake off the ague, stemming from the intense cold which had driven into his very bones. He could not control the shivering which raked his body. He tossed in agony and cried out in torment. No one on board had the knowledge to deal with David's condition. He was kept warm and given such food as was available, but that was meagre for they were down to a few pulses and hard biscuits, both of which were showing signs of contamination. Fit men would manage but David, who had never been used to such frugal fare, needed sustenance and that would only come when they took on fresh food at Shetland.

Seth prayed and drove the *Mary Jane* southwards with the utmost speed.

Chapter Ten

'Land, ahoy!'

The shout from the man at the mast-head brought joy to the crew. Though the *Mary Jane* had been running in sight of land for some time, that special call meant Whitby had been sighted. Home.

David swung from the bed before Adam could stop him. Gaining strength daily, after reaching Shetland, had raised a false impression, for, as soon as his feet touched the floor, his knees started to buckle. He grabbed the side of the bed and steadied himself.

'Hell!' His head spun.

Adam was beside him, lending support. 'You all right, Davey?' he asked with concern.

'Didn't think I'd feel so weak,' he gasped. He breathed deeply, trying to clear his head and draw strength.

'Better get back into bed,' Adam advised. 'You're . . .'

'No!' David cut in sharply. 'I'm going on deck. I want to be there when we sail into Whitby.' He was determined to see the red shawl.

'Stubborn cuss.'

David smiled. 'Wouldn't have survived if I hadn't been.'

Adam grinned. 'Come on, then, let's get thee dressed.' He helped David into his trousers and woollen shirt and pulled a high-necked, thick jersey over his head. 'Can't have thee catching cold first time on deck.' He knelt down and pulled long, woollen socks over David's feet and fastened on strong sea-boots. Adam straightened. 'Right, let's try.'

David gripped Adam's arm and moved across the cabin slowly. Each step was an effort, but he gritted his teeth and hid his true feelings from Adam.

The day was sharp, cleared by the chill in the wind of which the *Mary Jane* was taking every advantage. David breathed deeply. It was good to be in the open again, to feel the air biting into his lungs, to see the sea and feel the spray. He glanced upwards and was thrilled by the power filling the sails, driving the ship home.

'What are the jawbones doing up there?' he asked, indicating the whale's bones fastened to the main mast-head.

'A signal. Lets the folk at home know we have a full ship,' explained Adam.

David watched Whitby rise from the sea. A choking feeling swelled in his throat. Home! What a sweet sight after months of nothing but water and ice. The sight of land meant solid security, no more danger from the unrelenting Arctic. David's thoughts stirred. He felt a contest. A beckoning fought the freedom from peril, drove it from his mind, and he realised he could never resist the call of the north.

As Seth brought the *Mary Jane* between the two piers to meet the calm waters of the river, David's eyes searched the cliff top, where crowds had gathered to welcome a whaler safely home from the vagaries of the Arctic.

The crowds waved and cheered, excited that there was bone at the mast-head. David swelled with pride at being a member of a ship's crew which was being given such a reception. The crew acknowledged the welcome enthusiastically. David searched for the tell-tale shawl, imagining that Jenny would wave it just for him.

'There, Adam, there,' he cried when a flash of red swirled above the crowd.

Then the red shawl was gone.

David relaxed and enjoyed their progress up the river, with people on the staithes cheering the *Mary Jane* every inch of the way. She passed through the bridge, drawn up to give her passage to the inner harbour.

People swarmed the quay where the *Mary Jane* would dock. Wives, eager for their husband's arms, mothers, thankful their sons were safe, fathers, once whalemen themselves, anxious to hear about the voyage, and merchants wanting news of the catch buzzed with excitement as the *Mary Jane* drew close to the quay side.

Children jumped about, while their mothers held the youngest high to get a glimpse of their fathers. Youths bustled to the edge of the quay. Girls strained on tip-toe to catch the eye of their sweethearts, while flamboyantly dressed prostitutes waited patiently to relieve, at a price, tensions built up by five months' absence.

Ropes were thrown out, gathered by sailors on the quay and wound round bollards so that the *Mary Jane* could be hauled into position and tied up. As soon as she was settled, the gangway was run out and the crew swarmed ashore to be enveloped in the hugging, kissing, back-slapping welcome of their families and friends.

'She's there,' cried Adam, spotting the red shawl around Jenny's head. 'Thee be all right, Davey?'

'Aye.' He nodded. There could be no denying the eager light in Adam's eyes. 'Away wi' thee.' Wishing he had Ruth there to welcome him, he watched Adam bustle down the gangway and thrust a path through the crowd.

Eyes bright with welcome, Jenny watched Adam leave the ship and impatiently threaded her way through the jostling folk towards him.

'Jenny!' He swept her into his arms and held her tight.

With tears of joy in her eyes, she clung to him. 'Adam, it's good to have you home.'

Their lips met in passionate welcome.

'Let me look at you.' Adam eased her from him. His eyes devoured her, pleased to see her looking so well and that her face sparkled with delight at seeing him. The red shawl slipped from her head and her hair tumbled free, to frame her face with the beauty which had filled Adam's mind on the long, lonely voyage.

Jenny searched his face. It was weather-beaten but there was a touch of pallor about it which concerned her. There was always a wan, drawn look about men returning from the hazards of the Arctic. The fresh food, taken on board in Shetland, had not had time to eradicate all the depredations of five months in the far north.

But this was different. Adam looked as if he might have

179

suffered. She was about to ask him when a disturbance focused their attention on the *Mary Jane*.

Adam strained to see above the heads of the crowd. David? He was not at the rail where he had left him. Anxiety gripped Adam. He grabbed Jenny's hand and pushed his way unceremoniously towards the ship, where several men were hurrying across the deck.

'It's Fernley.' The words swept from those near the ship.

'What's happened, Adam?' gasped Jenny.

He had caught a glimpse of David sprawled on the deck. 'Looks to have fainted,' returned Adam, though his thoughts were worse. He pushed even harder to get through the crush, with Jenny clinging tightly to his hand. Her thoughts raced, recalling the nightmare which had brought worry and concern about Adam and David. Had there been any truth to it?

They were at the gangway. Two men had reached David with a ladder to use as a stretcher. Adam dropped to his knees beside David. 'What happened, Pa?' he asked, glancing at his father who, together with Jamaica, bent over David.

'Just keeled over,' replied Seth. 'Reckon it was too much for him, first time out of bed.'

'Is he going to be all right?' Jenny asked, her brow furrowing with concern.

'Just fainted, ma'am,' replied Jamaica. 'On to the ladder with him,' he added to the two sailors with the ladder.

The men lifted David gently on to the make-shift stretcher.

'Let them take him straight to the Black Bull, Captain Thoresby.' The half-request, half-order came from Jenny who, when she saw doubt coming over Seth's face, added quickly, 'It's his home. I'll look after him.'

Seth nodded to the two men who lifted the ladder and started for the quay.

Jenny and Adam followed, she seeking an explanation of what had happened in the Arctic.

As he watched the crowd make a path for the stretcher party, Seth said to Jamaica, 'Get Andrews.'

'Aye, aye, sir.' Jamaica hurried away to return a few minutes later with the prisoner who blinked and rubbed his eyes at the sunlight, so bright after a prolonged stay below decks.

Seth eyed him with anger and disgust. 'Fernley's in a bad way thanks to thee. I should get thee transported.'

The threat startled Andrews. His face became a frightened mask. 'No, cap'n, no. Please not that.'

'As far as thee's concerned, there's no good reason why I shouldn't.' Seth was repelled by the snivelling attitude adopted by Andrews. 'But there's thy wife and kids. Why should they suffer because of thee? Thank thissen lucky thee have them. Get thissen off, and niver come for a job on the *Mary Jane* again.'

'Thank thee, cap'n, thank thee.' Andrews touched his forehead and scurried away to be reunited with his wife, who had waited anxiously after learning her husband was in irons.

Jamaica watched him go, wondering if the captain had done right, for, from Andrews's changed attitude, once he had left the ship, he figured there were curses being heaped on Fernley and the Thoresbys.

'That young man's in a poor way,' said the doctor, when he joined Jenny and Adam outside the bedroom, after carrying out his examination. 'He's lucky to be alive, but we'll get him well again.' The doctor's fragile appearance belied an unquenchable strength and determination. his nose was aquiline, his eyes bright and alert. He was not given to softness, he figured he couldn't be in a port such as Whitby, but after the severity of the first contact, people found him concerned and gentle. 'He's over the worst, but he's in a very weak state. There's nothing much I can do but keep an eye on him. What he needs is rest, quiet, no company until he's stronger, and plenty of good food.' His eyes darted at Jenny. 'Think you can see to it, lass?'

'Yes,' she replied quickly.

'Good. A small amount of broth to start with, increased as he feels he can take it. This first week will be crucial if he's not to have a relapse.' He glanced at Adam. 'It's a wonder he survived with the food he'd get on a whale-ship. And you needn't protest, Thoresby. Your father's ship's no worse than any other and probably better than most.' He shrugged his shoulders. 'I'll come tomorrow, Jenny, but if there's any change in his condition send for me immediately.'

She saw the doctor out and returned to the bedroom to find Adam trying to straighten the bedclothes which had been upset during the doctor's examination.

'Here, let me do that,' called Jenny as she crossed the

room and gently pushed him out of the way. She quickly readjusted the clothes with an expert's touch.

'How did I get here?' David croaked, his voice scarcely above a whisper. He remembered nothing from the moment he was standing on the deck of the *Mary Jane* until he found the doctor bending over him, yet here he was in his bed in the Black Bull, all cleaned up, his night-shirt on and between clean sheets.

'You passed out,' explained Adam. 'Brought here on a ladder. Two of the lads from the *Mary Jane* and myself got thee t' bed.'

'And I'm going to look after you and see you get well,' put in Jenny.

David nodded. 'Thank you.' He merely mouthed the words before exhaustion after the examination took over and he fell asleep.

As they came out of the bedroom, Adam took Jenny in his arms. 'I'm not going to be of much help, at least not after the first week, when we go to Memel for timber.'

'Oh, Adam, so soon. I'd hoped you'd be here until next whaling season.'

'That's how it is with a sailor. Thee knows what to expect when thee marry one.'

Adam insisted on spending as much time as he could at the Black Bull during the next week, relieving Jenny of her work of serving clamouring sailors and sitting with David at night. But for all the attention lavished on him by Jenny, David showed no sign of improving. He took minute sips of broth, hardly enough to keep him going. His face became drawn, his cheeks hollowed even more than they were when the *Mary Jane* docked and there was no lustre to his eyes.

Jenny's heart was heavy with fear of losing him, but she made no mention of that when sadness filled her at Adam's leaving for Memel. David smiled wanly when he made his farewell and was asleep when Jenny returned after his departure.

He awoke to find her sitting beside his bed knitting. At a sign of movement, Jenny put down her needles and straightened the pillows into a more comfortable position.

'Some broth, Davey?' she asked, her voice light and hopeful that he would be enthusiastic.

'Thee should be on the cliff top.' David's words came slowly as if it was an effort to speak.

'The *Mary Jane* sailed two hours ago,' said Jenny.

'Thee . . . thee didn't go?' he croaked.

Jenny gave a slight shake of her head. 'I couldn't leave you.'

He felt a stirring in his mind. Jenny had stayed with him even though she always waved goodbye from the cliff top.

'I'll get you some broth,' she went on. 'You must try and take more.'

When Jenny returned and spoon fed David, he made a determined effort to have more than usual. He must please the girl who had stayed with him when Adam was sailing.

Progress was slow during the next four days, but the small signs of improvement were encouraging, so much so that Jenny, determined to win the battle, lavished more and more attention on David.

During the morning of the fifth day, she was dusting David's room when she noticed him stir.

'Good morning,' she said, coming to him.

'Hello, Jenny.'

She noted the stronger sound to his voice and his eyes had an unfamiliar brightness when he smiled at her.

'How are you feeling?' she enquired with new hope.

'Better, I think,' he replied, struggling to sit up, the first time he had attempted to do so.

'Wait, let me help you.' Jenny flew to his side and supported him with one arm while she adjusted his pillows with the other. She eased him gently backwards so that he was in a sitting position, comfortably supported by the pillows. 'David, this is wonderful,' she cried enthusiastically as she straightened and smiled at him. Her heart pounded with joy. She knew they had won. David would be well again. She leaned forward and hugged him. 'Oh, it's so good to have you back. I must tell Tom.'

As she straightened again, David grasped her hand. 'Wait, Jenny. Thank thee for all thee's done.'

'It's nothing,' she replied, sensing a little more than friendship in David's grip.

'Of course it is. I'll never be out of your debt.'

'Nonsense! You saved Adam's life.' Jenny felt David's fingers relax at the mention of Adam's name. Did he feel he was trespassing? She slipped her hand from his and hurried from the room, her heart beating with a confusion which troubled her mind.

'Be careful. Don't overdo it,' warned the doctor three days later when he gave David permission to venture

185

outside. 'You've done remarkably well. Fresh air will bring your appetite back and then you'll soon get stronger. Keep your eye on him, lass,' he added glancing at Jenny.

David's eyes were on Jenny as she accompanied the doctor from the bedroom. His affection for her had grown each day. She was gentle, kind and watchful, administering to his needs, determined that he should make a full recovery as soon as possible. But David's feelings went beyond appreciation. He looked forward to her presence in the same room, to having her near. She made time pass more easily and in the hours he spent alone he found his thoughts dwelling more and more on Jenny.

Had fate thrown them together this way, directing that their futures should be shared?

'This is good news,' said Jenny brightly when she returned. 'But you must be careful.'

'I will,' replied David. 'You'll come with me?' His fingers brushed hers lightly, sending a shiver through her.

'I thought maybe Tom . . .' started Jenny, her thoughts in confusion.

She had sensed David's feelings beginning to run deeper. She found him attractive and felt beguiled and flattered by his interest. His gentleness, his quiet ways, were so different from Adam's bluff, straightforward, no-nonsense approach to life. In the narrow confines of this sick room, could two people be forgiven for coming close? David, new to Whitby, lonely, a stranger, now sick and alone, had need of her. She could not deny that need, but more than that . . . ?

'I'd rather thee came,' cut in David.

Jenny met the plea in his eyes and could not deny it. 'All right. Do you want Tom to help you get dressed?'

'No. I'll be all right. I'll shout if I need him,' said David, his heart racing at the delight of being able to walk with Jenny.

When he stepped into Church Street, he nearly turned back into the protection of the house. He felt overpowered by the noise, and the swirl of people seemed to threaten him.

'You'll be all right.' Jenny smiled her encouragement. 'Where would you like to go?'

'I'd like to see the sea,' he replied.

'We'll go to the end of Henrietta Street.'

They walked slowly along Church Street, Jenny allowing David to dictate the pace.

Tense at first, he gradually relaxed and ignored the rush of people and the sounds which filled the street. Jenny, knowing that the physical effort of walking was probably as much as he could endure, did not enforce any conversation.

Reaching the end of Church Street, where it gave way to the one hundred and ninety-nine steps, known as the Church Stairs, they moved into the quieter Henrietta Street which ran along the cliff-side towards the sea. On the left the row of houses backed on to the cliff edge overlooking the river. On the right the rock soared steeply to the cliff top. At the end of the street the rough roadway, ridged and rutted through mud and dust, gave way to a tiny track.

'I think this is far enough,' suggested Jenny.

'Aye, maybe you're right,' agreed David.

He fell silent and took in the scene.

To the left, below them, the river slipped quietly between the piers to merge as one with the sea. The quays of the outer harbour were alive with the activity which kept Whitby thriving as an east coast port. Beyond the cliff-point, ahead of them, the sea stretched endlessly in gentle, ever-moving undulations, shimmering in the sunshine. David's gaze probed the distance.

He felt drawn to the water. The sea was his passage to the north, to that enchanted feeling which could be experienced only there. But more than that he felt the sea itself calling him, offering him a freedom that he could find nowhere else. And he knew he wanted it, needed it.

When he turned to force his leaden legs back to the Black Bull, Jenny spoke. 'You'll be going back to sea?'

'Aye.'

'I thought so. After what happened I thought you might want to stay ashore, but I can see by your eyes that you'll not rest away from it.'

'Thee's right. It's got to be my life.'

'If it's what you want, then I wish you well, but be careful of what the sea can do to you. She's an exacting mistress.' A sad, faraway look had come to Jenny's eyes.

'What is it?' David wanted to share the sadness he saw and ease the trouble which seemed to worry her.

'Nothing,' she answered wistfully.

'Tell me. Let me help.'

Jenny started. 'It's nothing, really.'

Although her tone was brighter and her eyes showed none of the preoccupation which David had witnessed but a moment before, he knew something bothered her.

'Come on, we'd better get back. You've been out long enough,' Jenny urged to avoid any more questions.

They returned to the Black Bull in silence and when they reached the inn David sighed wearily as he sat down.

'Tired?' queried Jenny.

'More than I thought I would be.'

'You'll soon gain strength. Should I let your folks know? I think it will be all right to have visitors.'

'No!' David's tone startled Jenny with its sharpness. 'I don't want them to know. It will upset them. I'll go home as soon as I'm fit to travel.'

'You can't do that yet,' she pointed out quickly.

'I know, but I'd rather thee didn't tell them.'

'Very well, as you wish,' she agreed. 'Now, I think you'd better go back to bed.'

With his daily exercise and increased appetite, David grew stronger. Then, one day, he suggested a walk on the cliff top.

'It's a hard climb,' Jenny pointed out. 'Think you can manage it?'

'Yes, so long as you are with me,' he replied, looking at her in a way which set her heart racing.

Her brown eyes looked steadily at him for a few moments. Her mind raced. She had a feeling that David was seizing a chance to be alone with her. She could refuse him, and maybe that would be for the best. She was Adam's girl. But he was away so much and she had enjoyed David's company. She wanted to go, wanted to hear what he had to say.

'Very well,' she replied quietly. 'If that's what you want.'

189

As they climbed the Church Stairs, David used the excuse of admiring the view across the red roofs, glowing in the sunshine, to give himself a rest.

After the third stop, Jenny looked troubled. 'David, maybe we should go back.'

'No, I'll be all right. Not far now. Come on.' He wanted Jenny alone, with no one else about. The cliff top should give him the solitude he sought. He took her hand as they turned and started up the steps again. David took hope from the fact that she made no attempt to release his hold.

They walked in silence, a silence shared, a silence charged with emotions. These moments would never return, but they would remain with them for eternity.

They reached the top of the steps, skirted the church-yard with its grim reminders of what the sea could do, and started along the path twisting close to the cliff edge. Far below the waves beat at the rocks which broke them into spraying foam.

As the path dipped into a tiny hollow, David stopped and turned Jenny to him.

Before he could say anything, she spoke quickly, trying to stem the words she felt he was going to say. 'Maybe you've come far enough, we should go back.'

'No, not yet. I'd like to walk some more.'

'But I feel responsible.'

David took hold of her hands. 'But you're not any longer. I'm to blame if owt happens to me. You've had the responsibility long enough. Thank you for all you've done for me.' He bent forward slowly and kissed her.

Jenny's lips trembled at his touch. They held his for a moment and then broke away.

'No, David!' she cried. She would have turned away but he grasped her arm.

Their eyes met, his searching, hers pleading to be released from the torment which was welling inside her.

'Jenny, I love thee,' David whispered.

'David, you can't, you . . .' Jenny's protest was cut short.

'How could I not after the way you've looked after me?'

'That's just it. We know little of each other. That room drew us together, I the nurse and you the patient.' Her brow furrowed. Oh, there was no denying David's attraction. She could so easily care for him deeply if she did not have Adam.

'There's more to it than that, Jenny,' cried David. 'I felt it when I first met thee.'

'You were away from home for the first time. I was someone new,' said Jenny, 'and you needed friendship.'

'Give my love a chance, Jenny! Please.' David's mind pounded with the roar of the sea and the memory of the girl who waved the red shawl. She was here. Close. He saw a wild beauty which could be matched only by the wildness he had seen in the sea and in the beauty he had felt in that inexplicable call of the north, a call which beckoned him, a call which he could not deny, just as the beauty before him called him and was one he could not resist. He crushed her tight. His lips sought hers.

For a moment she resisted then she returned his kiss.

When their lips parted, Jenny gasped, 'Oh, David, I do love you but . . .'

'I knew it!' He whirled her round in sheer joy.

191

'. . . but,' Jenny was still speaking, ignoring his ecstasy, 'not in the way you want me to love you. There's Adam.'

David's face clouded at the mention of Adam. 'But there's us. We matter.'

'We've been thrown together and it's only natural that we have special feelings for each other,' urged Jenny as she slipped out of his arms.

'I think there was more to it than that.'

'No, David, there wasn't.' Jenny hoped her denial sounded convincing. She could so easily have agreed with him. 'And what about Ruth?'

David ignored her question. He grasped Jenny's shoulders. 'It's thee I love. Thee!'

'Oh, David, I cannot say the same . . . not . . . not in the way you mean.'

'But thee will one day. I'm sure of it. Give us time.'

Jenny looked at him gravely. 'David, be sure you really do know your feelings.'

'But I . . .'

She reached out with slim fingers and halted the protest which sprang to his lips. 'Please, David, no more.'

He moved to take her in his arms but she twisted away. 'It's better if we go back.' She turned and started along the path. Jenny's heart was torn in two. She had seen the pain and hurt in David's eyes. She wished she could have spared him.

David's lips tightened. No word was spoken on the way back to the Black Bull.

When they entered the house, Jenny would have gone through to the kitchen but David grasped her arm, opened the parlour door and slipped inside. As he closed the door behind them, he turned Jenny into his arms. Before she could resist, his lips closed on hers with a passion she had never experienced before. She stiffened, attempted to push herself away, but David held her tight. Overwhelmed by desire, she relaxed, her arms slid around his neck and she returned his kiss with equal ardour.

'I love thee, Jenny,' gasped David. 'I need thee.'

'David! David!' She clung to him, her lips seeking his again.

Two aching bodies were swept on to a tide of longing which threatened to swamp them. Their hungry lips sought to assuage the passion which coursed through them but only heightened the desire pounding inside them.

Their lips parted. David hugged Jenny, his lips close to her ear. 'Come upstairs with me?'

She clung to him. Her mind hammered with yearning, her body hurt with need. She knew there would be delight in giving herself to David, that she would be committing herself to him, there would be gentleness and compassion, love and friendship for the rest of her life. She started to agree, then her glazed eyes focused on the grooved twists of a narwhal's tusk lying on the mantelpiece – a present brought by Adam from the Arctic.

Adam! Jenny's thoughts jolted. She was betraying him. Adam, the man she loved. Had she not, but a few minutes ago, told David that she did not love him in the way he wanted? Yet, now, she had almost . . . she shuddered.

David felt the desire drain away from her. He straightened to look at her and in that same moment she twisted from his arms.

'What is it, Jenny? What bothers thee?'

She swung round to face him. The eagerness which had been in her eyes had been replaced with sadness, a mixture of regret that she was unable to take the step David desired and shame that she had nearly been disloyal to Adam.

'I can't, David,' she said, her voice scarcely above a whisper.

'But thee can't deny the way thee felt,' he urged.

'I told you on the cliff I didn't love you in the way you want,' replied Jenny, her eyes damp.

'But thee felt differently just now,' cried David.

'I was swept up in the desire of the moment,' she said, turning towards the window. 'David, if anything happened between us it would ruin four lives.' She turned to face him, having drawn strength from those few steps and the space which now separated them.

'No, Jenny . . .' David was not allowed to go on.

'There's Adam. He loves me and I love him.' Jenny's voice was firmer, more purposeful. She needed to convince David that she was right. 'There's Ruth. She needs you, you've made promises you'd regret breaking. Do you think you and I would be happy knowing we had betrayed and hurt Adam and Ruth who love and depend on us? We wouldn't have any peace of mind.'

'But what about our feelings for each other? Don't they count for anything?' cried David, his brow marked with furrows of anguished concern.

'Of course they do,' she replied. 'They always will, but they are special to us. Please don't mar them by wanting something that I'm sure isn't there.'

'It will always be there for me,' said David, a touch of sadness in his voice.

'You can say that now but I'm sure that, when you think about it more coolly, you'll see that I'm right and you won't regret staying loyal to Ruth and Adam.'

David's lips tightened. 'Maybe thee's right. But I can't easily forget my feelings for thee.'

Jenny came to him and placed her hand on his arm. 'You will, David, but please don't lose them altogether. We must remain friends. Nothing must come between us to spoil that or our feelings for Ruth and Adam.'

He nodded. 'It will be best if I go home tomorrow, I'm strong enough now.' He kissed her lightly on the cheek, opened the door and went upstairs.

Jenny touched the cheek where David had kissed her until she heard the door of his room close.

Chapter Eleven

The plaintive cry of a grouse, poignant with the loneliness of the moors, stirred David's memory as he strode through the vast stretches of heather towards home. It was good to be back.

He paused at the edge of the hill and gazed at the cottage beyond the wood below him. The wind had dropped during the afternoon and there was that air of calm peace which settles on the countryside at the onset of September's twilight. A wisp of smoke curled lazily from the cottage to hover in a low, dark streak, reluctant to depart. Home! Only now did he realise how much he had missed it, but it would never have the same hold that it once had.

He started down the slope, followed the path through the wood and was emerging from the trees when Betsy came out of the house carrying a small pail. She stopped in her tracks and gazed unbelievingly at the person walking through the grass towards the cottage. Suddenly she dropped her pail, yelled over her shoulder and raced towards him.

A broad grin broke across David's face as he held his

arms wide for his sister. Betsy flung herself into them and he whisked her high into the air.

'Is thee home for good?' she cried with a ripple of laughter.

David laughed with her as he swung her to the ground. He looked beyond her to the cottage. John was running towards him with Jessica close behind. Ruth still stood beside the cottage. He saw his mother look at her and say something, then Ruth hurried forward, leaving his mother and father standing in the doorway.

David waited, lost in the joy of the excitement of this reunion. Then John was close, drawing his attention. His laughter was infectious as he hugged his brother and slapped him on the back.

'I'm glad to see thee, Davey!' cried John.

'And thee.' David laughed, as he turned from his brother to receive Jessica's warm embrace.

'Jess! It's good to see thee.'

'And thee,' replied Jessica, holding back all the questions she wanted to ask him about Whitby and his future.

David turned his eyes to Ruth to watch her cover the last few yards to him. How different she looked to the last time he had seen her – pale, wan, cut and bruised. Now her skin was unblemished and her cheeks were fuller with a rosy hue. It was as if a faded rose had suddenly bloomed into full glory again.

Care and love had uncovered a hidden Ruth, a Ruth who was the same but different. There was a vibrancy about her, a new pride in herself. The tilt of her head revealed a self-confidence which he had never witnessed in the subdued girl he had known.

'Ruth.' He took her in his arms and kissed her.

She returned his affection with a joy which was unmistakable. Her eyes sparkled with pleasure and in their grey depths there was a teasing beckoning. Her body, supple in his arm, tantalised him with a tempting nearness. Ruth was lovelier than ever and he ached to be alone with her to answer the urges deep within him.

'You look so much better,' he said, as he stepped away from her.

'I am, thanks to your mother and all your family.'

'No more trouble from home?' queried David.

'None. I think Ma's been glad to get rid of me.' Concern came to Ruth's eyes. 'But you? You look thin.'

'I'm all right.' David laughed away her anxiety.

The happy group hurried to the cottage where Kit and Martha waited, pleased in the knowledge that their eldest son was home and that there was such a close bond between their children.

'Thee's pale and thin, David,' his mother commented when the first greetings were over. 'Hast thee been ill?'

David hesitated.

'Don't hold out on me, son. I can see thee's not been well,' she insisted.

'Well, yes, I have been ill,' David admitted reluctantly. 'But I've been well looked after. There's nothing to worry about. Just need some of your cooking to build me up.' He gave his mother an extra hug.

'Aye, your ma will see t' that,' commented Kit as he led the way into the cottage.

Once inside, Martha pressed for the full story. They all listened with rapt awe as David gave them the details, though he played down the heroics.

'But thee might 'ev been killed,' cried Martha, her eyes wide with horror.

'But I wasn't, Ma.' David laughed.

'Who looked after you?' asked Ruth.

'I have a room at the Black Bull and Jenny, who lives there, looked after me,' said David. 'You'll all like her. She's about our age, Ruth.'

David did not realise the impact of those words on her. Ruth's lips tightened as she saw the extra sparkle come to David's eyes and sensed the special affection he had for this girl.

'Thee should have come home,' said Martha.

'I wasn't fit to travel until today.'

'Well, thee's here now, and I'd better start getting some flesh back on thee.' Martha pushed herself from her chair.

David grinned. 'Right, Ma, have you got some of your apple pie? I'm ravenous.'

From then until bedtime it was round after round of questions until they knew exactly what David had been doing and what his life had been like in Whitby and on the whaleship.

They were aghast when he gave his mother the greatest part of his wages for they had never seen twenty guineas at one time.

'It's accumulated,' he explained. 'There's nowt t' spend it on when thee's at sea. And I have more to come – my share of the catch. We returned with a full ship.'

Though his mother did not want to take it, he insisted. 'Isn't that one of the reasons why I went, to get work so I could help you?'

'Thee's gannin' back then?' queried his father.

Ruth glanced at David. She feared that his nearness to death might have brought a change of mind, and that she did not want. Whitby beckoned with so much promise.

'Aye, Pa.' David replied without hesitation. 'I hope to sail on the *Mary Jane* again. If I do, I have every chance of promotion. Who knows? Maybe one day I'll have my own whaleship.'

Ruth's eyes closed momentarily in relief. Her heart was filled with joy. She felt something stir inside her at David's mention of owning his own ship.

'Don't get over-ambitious, lad,' cautioned his father. 'Thee aren't signed on for next season then?'

'Not yet. Captain Thoresby will be making up his crew come the new year.'

Kit nodded thoughtfully. 'Remember, if things don't work out there's always a home for thee here.'

'Thanks, Pa.'

During the following week, David relaxed in the motherly care which brought back his strength and banished the wanness from his face.

He walked the moors with Ruth and Jessica, helped his father and John with some hedging, told stories of the Arctic to a wide-eyed Betsy and alleviated their curiosity about life in Whitby.

On these later occasions, Ruth was particularly attentive, and each time her desire to leave Cropton for a new life intensified. But she also felt uneasy, for whenever Whitby was mentioned Jenny was part of it and Ruth detected a special enthusiasm in David. He seemed to have forgotten that he had promised he would return and marry her. Since his return, he had never once mentioned that promise. Did she have a rival in Jenny? What had happened between them, thrown together so intimately through David's sickness? The pangs of jealousy bit deep and strengthened her resolve to marry David. He was the means by which she could escape her past, all but her true birthright which she was certain she could use to further David's ambitions. With that she was sure she could win him.

'When is thee gannin' back to Whitby?' Ruth put the question tentatively as she and David strolled through the fields, free of the attentions of his family for the first time. The day was warm, the sky overcast.

'As soon after Christmas as possible,' replied David. 'I mustn't get trapped by the weather.'

'I? Don't thee mean we?' Ruth's voice was cold, calculating. She was determined not to let their relationship founder. She had expected David to sweep her into his arms once they were out of sight of the house. She had wanted to hear words of love in these first moments alone together. Instead there was nothing more intimate than a touch of hands. She stopped and faced him. 'Remember, thee said thee'd marry me when thee returned from Whitby?'

David's mind had been a turmoil, knowing that this moment would come. Jenny had haunted his dreams. He knew she was right and yet he held a glimmer of hope that maybe on his return to Whitby . . . but there was Adam and Ruth. He had tried to seek out his real feelings for Ruth. He had loved her; they had been close; they had shared so much and he had fought because of her. Did this all count for nothing because of Jenny? Did he still have the same feelings for Ruth as he had when he left home? And she had changed. Living with his family had wrought so much in her appearance and demeanour, but it went further than that. David was not sure how, but at times he had detected an aloofness, a haughty disposition, as if she held herself above the family which had befriended her.

David bit his lip as he nodded slowly. 'Yes, I remember.' The words were drawn out as if he was reluctant to agree.

'Well, what's gone wrong? Thee hasn't kissed me once as if thee meant it since your return.' Ruth stiffened, her eyes blazing with challenge.

'We've never had the opportunity . . .'

'Thee makes opportunities,' flared Ruth. 'What about now? You've made no attempt. There's someone else, isn't there? This Jenny! Thee allus brings her up when thee talks of Whitby. It's Jenny, Jenny! I'm fed up with hearing about her and how good she was to thee. Maybe more happened than just friendship, maybe thee thinks more of her than me – but she won't be able to do for thee what I can.'

Ruth's tirade stung David. 'There's nothing between Jenny and me,' he cried. 'She's just a good friend.' He met doubt and accusations in Ruth's eyes and saw jealousy burning in their depths. Those feelings must be extinguished.

He grabbed her and pulled her roughly to him. His lips met hers with a fierce, demanding, cleansing passion as her warm body softened and moulded to his. His hands left her shoulders and his arms closed tightly round her

202

waist, crushing her closer. She relaxed in his power then slowly enveloped him with her arms, caressing his neck with her long, supple fingers. Her lips returned passion for passion.

'Oh, Davey, Davey, I love thee,' she gasped as their lips parted.

'And I thee,' returned David gazing down into Ruth's adoring eyes, all semblance of jealousy driven from them. She clung to him as if she would never let him go.

'Thee'll marry me and take me to Whitby?' she whispered.

'We'll see,' he replied. He brushed her lips lightly with his as if to wipe away the query.

Ruth pushed herself away from him. 'What do thee mean?' she demanded.

'It's just that I've nowhere to live. I have a room in the Black Bull, as thee knows, but that's no place for thee.'

'Thee means y' don't want me there 'cos Jenny's around,' pouted Ruth, with anger in her eyes again.

David grinned, trying to laugh away her hostility. He pulled her back to him. 'She has nowt to do with it,' he replied. 'I want to be able to take thee to our own house. Thee's all right here until I find somewhere. Maybe after my next voyage.'

'But that'll be another year,' protested Ruth.

'It'll soon pass.' And he kissed away any more objections.

With those kisses Ruth decided that for the moment she would not press David further, but already she had started to lay her plans to get her way.

As their lips parted, she said, 'I have summat to tell

thee, summat which could have a bearing on our life in Whitby. Let's walk.' She turned out of his arms and took his hand in hers.

She told him how she had learned that the squire was her real father.

'So the rumours were true,' said David. 'Have you been to see him?'

'No. What would be the point? He'd deny it. It wouldn't do me any good. It would only bring trouble to Ma. And though my feelings for her are dead, I don't want her evicted because of me.'

As she was speaking, David wondered if this was the answer to some of the changes he had seen in her. Had the knowledge that she had aristocratic blood in her veins given her a different outlook on life? Was this the answer to the moments of aloofness and haughtiness, and did it have anything to do with the self-confidence and the new anticipation of life he had seen in her eye?

'But this won't make any difference to us?' Ruth said tentatively. She thought she saw misgivings in his momentary hesitation and hastened to add, 'It shouldn't. It mustn't. I still love thee. I want to marry thee and go to Whitby.'

David took her in his arms. 'It makes no difference, love.' He kissed her gently. 'What did thee mean when thee said it could have a bearing on our life in Whitby?'

'I must have inherited something from my father. I believe that is why I felt different to the other village children,' explained Ruth. 'I sense a difference now. Thanks partly to your ma and all the family, people no longer treat me as a slut. But it's also due to the newfound confidence I have, and that I believe comes from my father.'

'So how's this going to help us in Whitby?'

'Your ambitions, that whaleship you spoke about, are going to involve other people. We'll have to mix with them, make new friends, folk who'll be able to help us.' The vibrant excitement in Ruth's voice reached out to David. He had never heard such enthusiasm before and had never seen the light of ambition shine in her eyes. This was a new Ruth who must indeed have culled something from the depths of her ancestry. 'Do thee think I could do that if I'd remained the brat thee once knew? No, David, I couldn't. But now, knowing who I really am, I'll be able to. Oh, there are still some rough egdes to knock off, but I'll do it. One day thee'll be proud of me, Davey. So marry me now and take me t' Whitby.'

He smiled. 'All the more reason to wait until I find a house. I can't take the squire's daughter to any old hovel.'

The first spots of rain touched their faces. David eyed the sky, darkening from the west. 'Reckon we'd better make tracks for home.'

The rain sharpened, threatening a downpour.

'Our byre's nearer,' cried Ruth, grabbing David's hand and starting to run.

He matched her stride for stride. The rain came faster. They quickened their pace. Ruth stumbled and would have fallen but for David's support. Infectious laughter rippled from her as she enjoyed the effort to beat the rain. David laughed with her, revelling in the sparkle in her eyes, and called on her to keep up with him as he lengthened his stride.

They burst through the hide covering the byre door

and stood drawing breath into their heaving lungs. The rain beat louder, then hit the byre with a deluge.

'A good job we came here,' gasped David.

'Aye, for more reasons than one,' said Ruth, half to herself. She ran her hands through her hair. As she leaned forward it tumbled in glistening strands around her face. She shook the rain from it, then flung her head backwards to send it streaming down her back. Her body arched, her breasts stood firm, and joy and laughter still suffused her face.

She caught David watching her intently.

'Our byre, Davey. Much as we left it six months ago, remember?' Her voice was low, husky, defying him not to. She held out her hand. 'We may as well be comfortable until the rain stops.' She moved to the end of the byre and sank into the hay, drawing him with her.

He turned, leaned over her and stared deep into the laughter in her eyes, watching it slowly change to a sultry challenge filled with tempting desire.

David dampened his lips. 'You're a temptress, Ruth Harwood,' he whispered. His lips met hers gently, teasingly. He brushed them lightly again. He felt her tense, then her arms came round his neck, drawing him to her, and this time she did not let his lips stray. She matched him kiss for kiss, the rising passion coursing through their bodies.

'Oh, David, I love thee,' she gasped in a momentry parting of their lips as they rolled over in the hay.

In the instant before he drew her close to kiss her again, Ruth saw a desire in his eyes which would not be denied.

She did not hold back but returned his kisses with a

passion intensified by yearning, matching that which she felt in him. Her soft body, moulding to his, added temptation with every movement. She felt his hands start to fumble for the buttons on her dress. She helped him through his inexperience until she lay naked for him to gaze with admiration and rising desire at the milky white body which could be his. She reached up to the buttons on his shirt but he brushed her hands aside and impatiently tore the clothes from his body.

For one moment he stood above her. Their eyes met in a deep understanding. She held out her arms to him, and he came to her.

Chapter Twelve

Throughout the following days, Ruth's head was full of anything but the routine of life in the Fernley household. Soon she would escape even this for the exciting prospects of life in Whitby.

David's presence and their visits to the byre brought joy which carried her along on a magical tide. Her eyes shone or else were deep with mystery. Her merry laughter was filled with the wildness of the moors. Her charm enveloped David and drew him ever closer. Her body was supple and yielding in his hands, setting his mind and pulses pounding.

Ruth's enthusiasm to know all about life in Whitby and the prospects in the whaling trade stoked David's ambitions. Maybe she could help him attain them; maybe she was right in saying that her aristocratic background could be used to their advantage. She was attractive, pretty, and sparkled with an effervescence and confidence which at one time he would have thought impossible. His own whaleship? One of those houses on the west side of the river? Were they beyond his reach? With Ruth's help, maybe not.

One bright November morning with the sun flaming the brown and yellow leaves into an intensity of colour, Ruth and David walked hand in hand, carefree and happy in each other's presence. They felt in their touch an unspoken understanding and turned towards the byre.

Glowing with sensuality, she knew David was malleable to her very will.

'Davey,' she whispered huskily as they lay in each other's arms, blissful in the pleasures they had experienced, 'I've summat to tell thee.'

'Well?' he prompted.

Ruth hesitated. Then: 'I'm pregnant.'

'You're what?' David, galvanised by the announcement, sat up and looked at her.

Hair tumbled around her face, framing an expression that was glowing with pleasure. Her eyes held deep joy and laughter at seeing the stunned look on his face.

'I'm pregnant,' she replied, her lips twitching teasingly.

'You're sure?' His demand came automatically.

'Of course I'm sure,' said Ruth, a touch of indignation in her voice. 'I hope thee's pleased.' Her eyes probed him, defying him not to be.

'I am. Of course I am.' David's voice rose and laughter drove the disbelief from his eyes. 'It's just that thee gave me a shock.'

Ruth laughed and flung her arms round his neck, pulled him to her and kissed him.

David's mind reeled with the implications of Ruth's news.

'What are we going to tell Ma and Pa?' he asked, his mind coming back to the immediacy of the situation.

'Nothing,' said Ruth. 'There's no need to tell them I'm pregnant. We'll tell them we want to get married before thee has to gan back to Whitby so that I can come with thee.'

Whitby! The word exploded in David's mind. Whitby, the whaleships and Jenny had all receded from his thoughts in the joys and pleasures of the last few weeks. Now they were back. Jenny, whom he had pressed with his love – had he held a hope that when he returned to Whitby she might have changed her mind, or was that merely an infatuation which had been banished by the love which he and Ruth shared?

But that was the past. Now there was the future and the child which was his.

'Right, we do that.' David seized on the chance. That way there would be no disgrace on the family; no finger could point at Ruth. In Whitby, no one need know when they had married. He swept her into his arms. 'I love thee, Ruth, and now we've someone else to fire our ambitions.' He met her lips with a passion which purged every thought from his mind except his love for her.

Christmas in the Fernley household, though set to the pattern of all their Christmases, joyous and humble, was overshadowed by preparations for a New Year's Day wedding.

Though Martha and Kit had tried to dissuade David and Ruth, they gave their blessing when they saw that the young ones would not be put off.

'Thee'll stay here, lass?' Martha had offered but Ruth had refused.

'No, Mrs Fernley. It's kind of thee, but if David is making his life in Whitby I want to be there.'

Ruth's statement did much to dispel their doubts about the wisdom of the marriage. Martha went to the wedding easier in her mind and saw all her efforts to make this a memorable occasion rewarded.

From her meagre savings, she bought material for Ruth's wedding dress and, in the secrecy of the bedroom, she and Jessica, assisted by an excited Betsy, made a gown which, as Ruth walked down the aisle, on Kit's arm, sent David's pulses racing. The cream embroidered linen gave a magical quality to Ruth's slim figure. It added a lustre to the happiness on her face, thinly veiled behind the finest of lace. Her eyes sparkled and the soft, silky hair, piled on her head glistened in the light which drew out the glint of copper.

David knew he would be the envy of every man in the church and wondered why he had ever thought of anyone else. In Ruth he had all that a man could desire.

'Wrap up well, lass, especially tomorrow. It'll be cold across the tops,' advised Martha, fighting the choking feeling that threatened to smother her words.

Ruth had changed into a brown woollen dress adorned with a cream crocheted collar matching the edging of her bonnet from which wisps of her curly brown hair peeped tantalisingly. David wished he had carved her a whalebone brooch; it would have looked well on this dress.

211

She shrugged herself into the thick, warm coat held by Kit, then turned to the older Fernleys. 'Thank thee, both of thee, for all thee's done for me.' She looked from one to the other and saw love and affection in both of them.

'It's nothing.' Martha waved away the thanks. 'Thee's a good lass who's niver had a chance.'

'Thee's shown me a family life I've niver known.' Ruth gave Martha a grateful kiss on the cheek and hugged her appreciatively. She kissed Kit and felt an answering tenderness in his strong arms.

'Look after Davey, lass,' he said with quiet seriousness.

She nodded. 'I will.'

'Take care, both of you,' said Martha with tears in her eyes. She came to David. 'Come back soon, son.'

'We will, Ma.' He embraced his mother and said goodbye to the rest of the family, saddened at the departure. He picked up their two bags and followed Ruth to the door.

Their appearance raised a cheer from the wedding guests who had returned to the Fernley cottage to enjoy a feast from the table groaning under the weight of the mouthwatering food prepared by Martha and her daughters.

Good wishes and advice were shouted as they climbed into the trap, driven by one of their neighbours, for the ride to Pickering.

'The lass has changed,' commented Kit quietly to Martha as they watched the young couple drive away.

'Aye, she has. Much more sure of herself.'

'And determined,' added Kit.

'Aye. I reckon a lot of that's hereditary. I hope she's

inherited her father's good points and none of his bad ones,' sighed Martha with a shake of her head.

'The perfect end to a wonderful day,' murmured Ruth as she lay contentedly in David's arms in the Black Swan in Pickering's Birdgate. She had what she wanted. David was hers and she was on her way to Whitby! The past was the past, its ugliness only sweetened by the last ten months. The future was hers for the taking and take it she would.

'Aye, it was. Ma and Pa were so good, I felt deceitful at not telling them about the baby,' said David, running his broad fingers across Ruth's breasts.

'It was best that way, David,' she reassured him.

'Aye, thee's right. It would only have worried Ma.' He turned on his side and gazed at Ruth. 'Mrs Fernley.' David savoured the sound. 'Like it?'

A ripple of laughter sprang from her 'Love it,' she replied.

His eyes lingered over her smooth, silken body, so different from the days when he had seen her bruised and beaten. Ruth stretched provocatively, revelling in the sensuality which flowed from her, tempting the man beside her in every way.

'You're a wanton hussy, Mrs Fernley,' gasped David, his voice thick with desire. His eyes smouldered as hers lured him towards a greater ecstasy than he had already known.

'Then take me, David Fernley, as thee sees me,' she said huskily.

* * *

213

The following morning Ruth and David were up early, breakfasted quickly and were with the carrier five minutes before he was due to leave.

'Good day, young fellow,' greeted Silas. 'Heard tell thee made out well i' Whitby. Bit of a hero.'

David brushed his compliments aside. 'This is my wife, Ruth,' he said.

'So thee's got wed?' Silas grinned and winked at David. ''Morning, ma'am.' He touched his forehead as he turned to Ruth.

''Morning, Silas,' Ruth greeted him pleasantly.

'Thee's out early. Gannin' t' Whitby?' asked Silas.

'Aye,' replied David. 'Can thee tak' us?'

'Aye. Can't turn an old friend away,' said Silas. 'Thee ride on t' cart, ma'am.'

'Thank you.' Ruth accepted Silas's offer of help and climbed on to the seat.

David noticed the air of deference in the way Silas fussed around Ruth, making sure she was comfortable. He did not care for the rag-rug which Silas tucked around her but such kindness could not be denied.

'We're lucky with the weather,' remarked the carrier, eyeing the sky shot with the first streaks of dawn. 'It's cold but it'll keep fine.

'Nice lass,' he commented in an aside to David as they walked beside Sal, leading her up the track which led to the moors.

'Aye, she is that,' he agreed.

'Doing well for thissen,' said Silas.

'What do you mean?' David shot him a glance of puzzled curiosity.

214

'There's breeding there.'

'Breeding?'

'Aye. Don't deny it.' Silas's expression hardened. 'Well bred, I'll wager. Well-to-do, no doubt. It's there in t' lass. If thee don't want to tell me, that's your privilege, but Old Silas can tell.' He chuckled deep in his chest, then fixed his eyes seriously on David. 'A word of warning, lad. Mind she don't get big ideas – and thee just a whaleman.'

'Won't be for long,' he countered.

'Ah, it's *thee* with the big ideas,' snorted Silas. 'Reckon thee can get on in the whale trade, do ye? Ah, well, we'll see.'

The two men lapsed into silence and, after a few minutes, David fell back to walk beside Ruth.

'All right, love?' he asked.

'Yes, thanks.' She drew her shawl more tightly around her and huddled into her coat against the freshening wind.

After a further mile Silas came to join them. 'It's easier going. Reckon we can all ride for a few miles.'

They climbed on to the seat beside Ruth and the cart rumbled and creaked as the horse gently strained at the harness.

Silas chattered, satisfied Ruth's curiosity about his job as a carrier, and pointed out features of the countryside. They were high on the moors when he gestured to his left. 'Yon's a right hole.'

Even in the morning light, the huge, bowl-shaped hole, scooped from the moors, held a sinister atmosphere. Its depths were lost in the shadows of the hillside. A few twisted pines leaned precariously on the edge of the steep incline, driven into their perilous positions by the constant wind which swept across the wild heights. On the track, near the lip of the bowl, Ruth felt as if she was looking into a great, mysterious abyss.

'It's eerie,' she whispered with a shudder.

'Maybe, ma'am.' Silas pursed his lips and nodded as his eyes narrowed in thought. 'There are those who say it's the Devil's work, and they've called the track ahead, where it drops down to Saltersgate, the Devil's Elbow. Devil or no, there's Wade to contend with.'

'Wade?' queried David.

'Aye. Giant who wanted earth for the road he was building across the moors. Scooped it out with his bare hands.'

'Tales,' scoffed David.

'There's many a truth . . .' muttered Ruth. 'I don't like it.' She huddled closer to him.

The trackway curved with the lip of the bowl which became a narrow ridge as the ground dropped away to the right.

'Off, lad,' called Silas, jumping from his seat. 'Hold the cart back.'

David swung to the ground and turned to help Ruth down before going to the back of the cart.

The track, rutted by rain, descended steeply through a sharp bend away from the hole.

Ruth followed David and helped to hold back the swaying, groaning cart.

Once the track levelled at the bottom of the steep slope, she was pleased to be free of the strain.

'Thanks, ma'am,' said Silas. 'Thee ain't afraid to get y' hands mucky.'

Ruth chuckled. 'They've been worse than this in my time, Silas. What's this place?' she added indicating the building ahead.

'It's an inn, the Wagon and Horses,' explained David.

'Don't look very inviting,' commented Ruth, eyeing the shuttered building.

'It ain't, ma'am,' said Silas. 'We should know, Davey, eh? Avoided stopping there ever since.'

'Ever since what?' asked Ruth.

'Davey saved my life. Hasn't he told thee?' Silas's brow furrowed with surprise.

'No.' She glanced questioningly at David.

'Then up on the cart, pair of y'. I'll walk with Sal a ways. Y' can tell her then, lad,' said Silas.

David made no comment as they climbed on the seat. He was haunted by a face, glimpsed in the moonlight; a face forgotten in the upheavals of his own life but now resurrected with an impact which made his head reel.

'Well, how did thee save Silas?' asked Ruth as she pulled the rug around her.

David told Ruth how he and Silas had escaped being murdered and how they gave their pursuers the slip.

'Oh, Davey, thee might have been murdered and we'd never have known,' cried Ruth, clinging close to his arm. 'Did thee know any of these men? We could . . .'

'We couldn't do owt, Ruth. Forget I've ever told thee. The gangs have a way of finding anyone who informs, or they think might have informed, and then it's . . .' He drew his hand sharply across his throat.

Ruth shivered.

'But you recognised someone?' she pressed, studying

217

him curiously. David hesitated. 'I know you did, I can tell. Who was it?'

David glanced at his wife. His mind was in a turmoil. Should he tell her? Was it better to hold back his knowledge, keep her in ignorance, or would it be as well if she knew?

'Davey, tell me,' urged Ruth, jerking his arm.

'All, right,' he replied quietly. 'The man I recognised, the leader, was Jonathan Hardy.'

For one brief moment the name did not seem to make an impact, then its implications sent waves of excitement coursing through her. 'Thee's sure?' gasped Ruth.

David nodded. 'Certain.'

'My half-brother!' The words came as a long drawn-out whisper. Ruth tried to recall him but it was no use, she could not put a face to the name. Jonathan Hardy had spent a sheltered life as a child and, though she must have seen him drive through the village with his parents on the odd occasion, she had taken no notice of the privileged child. When he had gone away for schooling, his visits to the hall were less frequent, and in manhood they were no more regular. Rumours abounded about his life but no one was sure which of them was near the truth.

'But how did thee recognise him? I wouldn't have,' queried Ruth.

'Last year I was helping Pa with hedging in the north pasture where it overlooks Laskill Dell. Two riders came along the Dell. I recognised one as the squire. They couldn't see me for the hedge and Pa was at the far side of the field. They stopped just below me. I couldn't catch all their conversation but I did hear the squire call the other "my son". He seemed to be asking Jonathan to take the estate seriously as one day it would all be his. I got a good look at him, and the rider I saw on the moors that night was the squire's son, I'm certain of it.' David caught the thoughtful look in her eye. 'We can't do anything about it, Ruth, best forget that I ever saw him.'

She nodded slowly in agreement but she was storing the information away in the depths of her mind. One day it might be useful.

Chapter Thirteen

'See yon houses?' David indicated the fine buildings lining Bagdale. 'When I saw them for the first time I swore that one day I would have one for thee.'

Ruth viewed the houses with keen interest, taking in every detail. She had never seen the like before. They were elegant, seeming to assure a life of solid security, of money and well-being. Ruth imagined the ladies in their fine afternoon clothes, taking tea together and passing on the latest gossip of the busy town. She agreed with David – Bagdale was where they would live one day. She'd make sure of that.

She glanced at him, pleasure in her eyes. 'For us both, Davey, for us both.' The determination in her voice left him in no doubt that Ruth burned with an ambition to match his own.

They said goodbye to Silas, and Whitby life swirled around them, sweeping them into its noise and bustle as David guided Ruth towards the bridge spanning the river. Although almost overwhelmed by the new experience, she was excited by it too.

Artisans hurried to a last job; clerks rushed with a final message; housewives hastened home to prepare a meal; girls strolled along the quays eyeing sailors settling their boats for the night; weather-beaten elderly men drew on their pipes and told one last tale before departing to their homes; and urchins still ran in excited chase.

Lost in the wonder of such sights, Ruth also observed girls dressed as shabbily as she had once been, and vowed she would never be like that again. Then she turned her eyes in admiration on a group of four ladies, whose patterned skirts showed beneath their bright cloaks. Their bonnets were held by a big bow, tied neatly beneath their chins, and matched the small bags they had looped to their wrists above their gloved hands.

By the time they reached the bridge, she knew she was going to enjoy life in Whitby.

The weak sun lowered towards the west, taking any semblance of warmth with it, leaving the day ebbing to that stillness which heralds the onset of evening.

They reached the bridge.

'There she is, the *Mary Jane*!' David pointed to the whaleship resting at her moorings in midstream. He was thrilled to see the vessel which had given him his first taste of the sea, his first encounter with the Arctic and let him experience that magical call of the north. His voice rose on the pitch of excitement and from his expression, which was fired with a special admiration, Ruth knew she had a rival for his affection.

'I'm jealous of her, Davey,' said Ruth, leaning close to him.

'Why?' he asked, his brow furrowing with a puzzled frown.

'She'll take thee away from me.'

'And she'll bring me back,' he countered. 'And she's the way to our fortune.'

His eyes were bright. His mind, heady with a vision of the future, far removed from the bleak life which had faced him in Cropton. Ruth realised that their destiny was intrinsically entwined with the whaleships.

'Thee make it sound so easy,' she commented.

'It won't be. It'll be hard. We'll have to scrimp and save . . .'

'And plan and scheme and plot,' cut in Ruth, warming to his enthusiasm.

'Aye, and those,' he cried. 'But we'll do it, Ruth, we'll do it.'

He took her hand and guided her through the crowds into Church Street. A few moments later they were crossing the end of the market place.

'Here we are, the Black Bull.' David indicated the inn occupying the corner of the market place and Church Street. He stopped at a door in Church Street and knocked hard.

A few moments later it opened.

'David!' The enquiring expression that comes with answering an unexpected knock on the door evaporated from Jenny's face into a broad, excited smile of pleasure. She stepped forward and hugged him before she was fully aware that he was not alone. Her eyes met Ruth's and there she saw momentary shock, resentment and jealousy.

'It's good to see thee, Jenny.' David smiled as he stepped back. 'This is Ruth.'

'Pleased to meet you,' said Jenny, holding out her hand.

Ruth had been taken aback by the welcome Jenny had given David. She saw an attractive, pretty girl of about her own age, someone who had raised enthusiasm in David whenever he had mentioned her name, until that day when she had won him in the byre. Now she caught a glint of pleasure in his eyes. Jenny had been his nurse; they must have been close. But how close? How deep had the feeling between them been? Ruth's jealousy forced an armour around her, steeled her with a determination to drive a wedge between David and Jenny.

'And thee,' replied Ruth, her voice devoid of warmth. She took Jenny's hand. 'Thank thee for looking after David.' In a sign of gratitude, Ruth also placed her left hand on Jenny's so that she could not avoid seeing the ring on the third finger.

'It was a pleasure,' returned Jenny. 'He was a good patient.' She glanced down. Her head came up sharply, her face wreathed in astonishment tinged with delight. 'You're married!' Her eyes darted from one to the other.

'Yesterday,' replied Ruth.

'Oh, I'm so pleased.' Jenny's delight appeared genuine but Ruth wondered if disappointment lay behind the enthusiasm.

She embraced Ruth and then turned to David. Unspoken words passed between them as their eyes locked and sealed a moment in time, born of a special bond which still existed. She kissed him on the cheek and hugged him. 'Be happy,' she whispered close to his ear.

'You'll be wanting to stay here until you find a place of your own?' said Jenny as she ushered them into the kitchen.

'If that's all right with thee and Tom,' replied David.

'Of course.' Jenny smiled. 'Tom's in the bar. I'll go and tell him.'

When she returned with Tom a few moments later, Ruth was warming her hands at the cheery fire where a kettle puffed away on the reckon.

Tom greeted David with the zest of a man welcoming his own son, and then turned to greet the new bride. 'You can stay as long as you want. I'm pleased to have you.'

'Thanks, Tom,' replied David gratefully.

'We'll find a place of our own as soon as we can,' said Ruth, determined to separate David and Jenny as quickly as possible.

'Treat this as your home until you do,' said Tom. 'Now, I must be back in there.' He inclined his head towards the bar. 'Jenny'll look after you.

'Adam about?' asked David as Tom left them.

'Not yet,' replied Jenny. 'He could be in any time. David, take Ruth to your room, it's all ready. I'm sure she'd like to have a wash after your journey. You must be starving. I'll get you something warming.'

David led the way up the narrow stairs and, once Ruth had settled in the new surroundings and was preparing to change, he returned to the kitchen where Jenny was placing some rashers of bacon in a pan.

'It's good to see thee, Jenny.'

She sensed affection in his voice.

'And you,' she returned. 'I'm pleased you're looking so

much better, and I'm thrilled that you're married. I hope you are very happy.'

'I'd have come back for thee but . . .'

'David!' Jenny was shocked by his words. 'You're married, you must love Ruth.' Worry filled her eyes. Her voice was charged with alarm. 'You mustn't think of me in that way. Besides, I told you, I love Adam. Oh, maybe there were times when I had my doubts, but then I had a dream.

'I dreamed of you and Adam, but in different ways. Adam blew through my dream like a wild north-easter, lashing the sea in thunderous waves against the cliffs, just as if he was picking up life and willing it his way, living it to the full while he had it. In the calm afterwards, you appeared, moving steadily and purposefully towards fulfilling your ambition.

'Later I had the same dream again but this time it went further. You both reappeared in the calm, but suddenly there was a most violent and frightening storm which swamped you both. I cried out for your safety. I reached out to help but it was no good – you had both disappeared, leaving only the roaring sea. Then you appeared at my side. I was overjoyed, but joy turned to deep despair when Adam was not with you. I was left with a feeling of utter loneliness. I knew then that it was Adam I really loved – the despair was deeper than the joy. So, you see, I was right when I told you I loved Adam.' She paused, then added, 'But you will always have a special place in my heart. I hope we will always remain close and that nothing will ever come between us.'

'It never will,' he promised, and stepped closer to kiss her.

Jenny would have drawn away but in the tremor which swept over David's face she recognised his need to have this memory of what might have been.

The door from the bar crashed opn.

'Jenny!' Adam froze and stared in disbelief. Jenny and David stepped apart. In that moment of tense silence Adam's anger boiled to the surface. His eyes flared with suspicion. His anger swiftly erupted and in one movement he crossed the room and smashed his fist into David's face.

David reeled backwards, spinning against the table. Pots scattered and shattered on the floor. Adam sprang at him.

'No, Adam! It's not . . .' Jenny's words were lost in Adam's roar.

'You bloody bastard! While I was away, you and Jenny . . . Hell! I might have known.'

He hit David again, sending him crashing to the floor. Blood spurted from his nose and flowed from the cut at the edge of his lip.

Jenny grabbed Adam, trying to hold him back. 'Adam! No!' she screamed. 'It's not like that!'

His eyes blazed. 'You're no better than him.' He pushed her roughly off and she would have fallen if she hadn't grasped the table for support. 'Andrews was right about what he saw on the cliffs. I didn't believe him, thought he was getting back at thee, but now . . .'

She stared at him wild-eyed. 'Adam! I'd just told David it is you I love!'

'It looked like it!' he yelled, and swung menacingly at David who was struggling to get to his feet. Adam hit him again, sending him back to the floor. His body shook with rage as he towered over David. His eyes narrowed with hate. 'You'll never sail on the *Mary Jane* again, nor any other whaler – I'll see to that!' He glared at Jenny. 'It's as well I came in now. I'll deal with you later when that bastard's out of here. See that he's gone within the hour!'

Tears streamed down Jenny's face. 'He saved your life, Adam,' she sobbed. 'And it's you I love. Besides, David's married!'

Adam started. 'Married?' His voice was filled with bewilderment.

The door, which had been standing ajar, suddenly swung wide. 'That's right. I'm his wife!' The words came out imperiously and Ruth stared coldly at the man who had hit her husband. She cast only a cursory glance at David as he struggled to his feet.

Adam spun round, astonishment and confusion clouding his face. He stared at Ruth, disbelief fogging his mind, then glanced sharply at David and Jenny.

'It's true, Adam,' Jenny whispered.

'Aye, it is,' snapped David. He wiped the blood from his split lip and felt for his kerchief to staunch the blood from his nose.

'Then what was ...' Adam still held a note of suspicion.

'It was a friendly kiss of thanks for Jenny's nursing,' returned David. 'This is Ruth, and what's more I'm going to be a father! Does that convince thee?' He glared at Adam and dabbed his nose again.

'Father!' Adam gasped.

'A baby?' Jenny's words sounded surprised. Her mind

raced. Was this the reason why David had married? Did he love Ruth, or did he still nurse his love for her? She quickly pulled herself together and crossed the room to Ruth. 'I'm so pleased,' she said with a warm smile. She hugged Ruth but felt her stiffen, and knew that the other girl had overheard more than the final exchange.

'Well, Adam, are you convinced?' Ruth demanded.

'Aye . . . er . . .' spluttered Adam with embarrassment. 'I am.' He turned to David in confusion. 'I'm sorry, Davey. Come on, let's get thee cleaned up.'

'I'll do that,' snapped Ruth. 'You'd better get this room straightened. Come on, David.' She stiffened her spine and walked from the room.

David followed without a glance at Adam.

As she cleaned his face and stemmed the flow of blood, Ruth watched David closely. There was a vulnerable look about his face and she knew he was wondering how much she had overheard. Well, she'd let him wonder. Let him be tormented. There had been deep feelings between David and Jenny, she was sure of it, but she'd make certain they were not rekindled. Her mind began to burn with jealousy at the thought of the moments the two of them must have shared. But David was hers – and she'd make sure it stayed that way. She would lock away her thoughts but ever remember them and be on her guard.

When she was satisfied that the blood had been staunched, Ruth stepped back. 'There thee are. Now we'd better gan down and set matters even straighter.' Her words were aloof and cold.

David caught her arm as she started towards the door. 'There was nothing in that kiss,' he said.

'If you say so.'

David's lips tightened. 'I do,' he hissed. 'There was nothing in it.'

Ruth shrugged her shoulders. 'All right.'

She started to turn away but David jerked her back and crushed her in his arms. His lips came to hers fiercely. For a moment Ruth resisted, but, as she felt passion rising, her arms encircled his neck and she kissed him with a hunger which wanted to purge the antagonism that had come between them.

'Let's not gan down,' whispered David as their lips parted. He looked down at his wife, his eyes twinkling with a challenging hint.

Laughter turned up the corners of Ruth's mouth. Her eyes said yes but her voice said, 'Later, David. Jenny might come to see if thee's all right.' Her teasing expression flashed into thoughtfulness. 'Though what she would see might convince her thee really is all mine.' She did not give David a chance to reply but slipped from his arms and was out of the door.

When they entered the kitchen, they found that the furniture was in place and Jenny had set the table for four. Adam was on his feet immediately the door opened.

'Davey, I'm so sorry. Please forgive me.' He made his apology with abject contrition. His eyes pleaded with David not to hold it against him. He wanted nothing more than to take up the friendship where it had been before he had come to the Black Bull.

'There's nothing to forgive,' replied David. 'I'd have reacted just the same.' He held out his hand and Adam took it with an overwhelming sense of relief and gratitude.

Jenny and Ruth watched the reconciliation with different feelings. Jenny was pleased that Adam and David were still friends for they had a special affinity, while Ruth viewed the friendship as necessary if David was to get promotion in the whaling trade.

'Good.' Jenny smiled. 'Let's all sit down and have something to eat.'

Adam turned to Ruth. 'It wasn't the best of introductions so we'll begin again. I'm Adam and you must be Ruth.' He bent forward and kissed her on the cheek. 'I'm so pleased for Davey that he's got you, and I'm delighted about the baby.'

'Thank you, Adam,' she replied. 'I'm pleased to meet thee. David has talked so much about thee.'

'Hope it was all good and still will be after what I just did.'

'Forget it,' put in David.

Jenny had prepared bacon and fried bread, ale and apple pie. As the meal progressed, she sensed excitement come over Adam as if he knew something they did not. So it came as no surprise to her when he pushed his empty plate away from him, sat back in his chair and said, 'I have summat to tell thee.' He glanced at his friends, eyes twinkling at the way they were all waiting his announcement. 'I've been made harpooner for the *Mary Jane's* next voyage.'

'Congratulations!' cried David, his eyes shining with pleasure. 'That's promotion,' he explained to Ruth.

'Adam!' Jenny's gaze, fixed firmly on him to the exclusion of everyone else, showed her delight. 'That's wonderful.'

'It's more wonderful than promotion.' He grinned. 'Remember what I once said?'

Happiness filling her eyes, she nodded.

'And will you?' asked Adam.

'Yes,' whispered Jenny.

A huge smile broke across Adam's face. In one swift movement, he pushed his chair back, sprang to his feet and swept her into his arms. He whirled her round, bringing laughter pouring from her as she clung to him. He stopped to face David and Ruth. 'When I first went whaling I said I'd marry Jenny when I was made harpooner.'

'Adam! Jenny! That's marvellous,' cried David. His grasp of Adam's hand expressed his pleasure at his friend's happiness. He turned to Jenny and kissed her on the cheek. 'Hope you don't mind that one,' he joked with a glance at Adam. He turned away to allow Ruth to add her congratulations to the newly betrothed couple, but also to conceal a pang of envy.

As he gently lowered Jenny, Adam's voice boomed across the room. 'There's more, Davey.' He turned to face his friend, curiosity swamping the momentary jealousy. 'I want you to be my line manager,' Adam went on.

David stared unbelievingly at him. 'But . . . you can't mean it?'

'I do.' Adam grinned.

'I've only done one voyage,' David pointed out, feeling weak at this unexpected news.

'Doesn't matter. You learn fast.' Adam's voice rang with conviction. 'You're line manager if you want the job.'

For a moment David seemed confused, then his voice

rang out confidently: 'Want it? You don't have to ask me again! Thanks, Adam.'

'What's this mean?' asked Ruth, bewildered by it all.

'It means I'm sailing on the *Mary Jane* again, and it's promotion for me too.' David hugged her tightly and whispered only for her ear: 'The first step towards our ambitions.' Envy and jealousy had been swept from his mind. He would never have sailed on a whaleship again, let alone be promoted, if he had come back for Jenny; the whaling fraternity would have ostracised him. He already had something to thank the baby for.

Chapter Fourteen

The following day, eager to show Ruth more of Whitby, David took her hand and they climbed the Church Stairs to the cliff top.

On reaching the top of the steps, they paused to recover their breath.

They gazed across the roofs tumbling like a red cascading waterfall towards the river. Smoke curled lazily from the numerous chimneys. Across the water the older houses clustered low on the cliff. Higher, the mansions of the newly rich added a different dimension to the thriving port.

David's eyes narrowed. 'Ruth,' he said softly, 'this is our home. Here is our future. I feel it. I know it. We'll do well, and one of those big houses across there will be ours.'

'I feel it too,' she said. 'Oh, David, I do love thee so.' She turned to him and met his kiss.

'And I love you.'

Hand in hand they walked through the churchyard, past the squat tower of the ancient parish church, towards the edge of the cliffs, without a thought of the hazards foreshadowed by the greening gravestones – of bodies washed ashore from shipwrecks, of men lost in the distant icy wastes and remembered here in carved letters.

The shore stretched away, lost in the distance towards Sandsend beyond which cliffs climbed to towering heights. Ruth paused to take in the view, the like of which she had never seen before. She gazed across the sea.

'It's so vast, David, so much water,' she whispered in awe.

He smiled. 'Aye, it is that, and there's a lot more beyond the horizon. It stretched far, far away, limitless.' He gazed across the ocean with a yearning which needed to be fulfilled. 'And out there, there's a call which is irresistible.' His voice filled with passion for the lure of the north. 'Oh, Ruth, I wish I could make thee feel it, I wish I could describe it, then you'd know why our future must be with the whaleships.'

'I'm happy to be here with thee,' she said, moving closer. 'What thee wants, I want. We'll make our dreams come true.'

Far below, the waves beat against the cliffs as their lips met again, sealing the future.

They walked, a lovers' silence between them. The path took them past the old stones of the ruined abbey, a landmark of home for all Whitby sailors, a sign that the loneliness of the sea was over for a few days at least.

When they reached the Black Bull, they found Jenny overflowing with excitement.

'Oh, I've been dying for you to get back,' she cried as they entered the kitchen. 'I've had Adam and his father here. They're sorry they missed you, but told me to give you the message – there's a house you can rent.'

'What!' Ruth and David gasped together. They exchanged bewildered looks and then pressed Jenny for more detail. They could not believe their luck.

'Apparently Seth got to thinking after we told the family about Adam and me, and about you, last night,' Jenny went on enthusiastically. 'He knew of two houses coming up for sale and decided to buy them, one for us and the other for you to rent. We went to look at them this morning. We'll have the one on Church Street and you can rent the one on Henrietta Street. Isn't it wonderful?'

'It's unbelievable,' said David.

'Overwhelming.' Ruth's voice was low, choking in her throat as she recalled that less than a year ago she was a beaten waif in a hovel. Now she was somebody with the knowledge that she had aristocratic blood in her, she was married and she had a house.

'But I can't afford . . .' David started on a note of despondency.

'Seth said you're not to worry about money,' cut in Jenny quickly, 'he'll wait until you return from your next voyage. I think it's a way of showing his gratitude for saving Adam's life.'

The weeks which followed were hectic as the two couples prepared their houses and Jenny and Adam planned their wedding.

Ruth and David settled into the small house in Henrietta Street which clung tenaciously to the cliff overlooking the outer harbour. They colour-washed the sitting room and the two bedrooms and white-washed the kitchen. Ruth added colourful touches with patchwork cushions and crocheted chair-backs, gifts from Cropton. From tiny windows at the back of the house they looked beyond the piers along the coast with the ever-present sea to remind them of the life they had chosen.

Whitby rejoiced in the expected union of the likeable Adam Thoresby and pretty Jenny Maxwell. Happiness radiated from the couple as they laughed their way from the parish church on the cliff top to the Black Bull between lines of people who shouted and yelled their good wishes and advice. Tom had organised food and drink for all to celebrate the marriage of the girl he had come to regard as his daughter. Afterwards, the couple left to spend four days with Adam's aunt in Staithes, a small fishing port, a few miles to the north, before returning to Whitby ten days before sailing day.

As the day of departure for the Arctic grew closer, Ruth became quieter. David too regretted the five months' separation, but helping to prepare the *Mary Jane* for her voyage diverted his mind from the parting.

'I'll miss thee, Ruth,' he said, taking his wife into his arms on the evening before they sailed. 'Think of me.'

'Oh, David, of course I will.' Tears welled in her eyes. 'I'll miss thee terribly.' She buried her head against his chest.

'Think of the parting as a step towards achieving our ambitions.' He stroked her hair gently.

Ruth nodded and tightened her lips. When she had

taken a grip on her feelings, she looked up at him. 'Now, I'll give you something to remember all those long lonely days in the Arctic.' She took his hand and led him towards the stairs.

As the *Mary Jane* slipped slowly down the river to the sea a white shawl swirled above the heads of the crowd on the cliff top and beside it a red one, both signalling love and hopes of a safe and successful voyage.

'It is hard the first time,' said Jenny quietly, noticing Ruth's tears. 'But it gets no easier. You'll learn to be a sailor's wife.'

Ruth made no comment but waited and watched with Jenny. Her tears dried, and as they did so she resolved never to cry again when David went away. After all, it was what he wanted to do, it was his contribution towards the realisation of their dreams. She must play her role here in Whitby.

The crowds dispersed but the two girls were still watching the speck on the horizon when Jenny spoke quietly. 'There is no baby, is there, Ruth?'

She stiffened and hesitated. This was something she hadn't wanted. If only David hadn't said anything about the baby, everything would have been straightforward. Now Jenny's intuition had put another aspect on the situation. 'No, there isn't,' replied Ruth coolly. She turned slowly and fixed Jenny with an icy stare.

'You tricked David into marrying you,' returned Jenny.

Ruth gave a slight shake of her head. 'No. He would have married me one day. I only hastened it. You see, I was determined to come back to Whitby with him.'

'And he had refused to bring you?' The question was half-statement. 'So you told him you were pregnant.' A note of disgust had come into Jenny's voice.

'Does that bother thee?' returned Ruth with a quizzical raise of her eyebrows. 'Did thee hope he was coming back t' thee?'

The barb bit deep into Jenny's mind, recalling those moments with David when she might have wished just that. She stifled the outrage which sprang to her lips for she knew Ruth would see it was feigned.

In the hesitation Ruth read agreement. 'I knew it!' Jealousy tinged her eyes. 'Maybe Andrews told Adam the truth about what he saw on the cliffs. Maybe there's been more between thee and David than just a kiss. After all, thee had the opportunity when he was supposed to be ill.'

The innuendos stabbed at Jenny's heart. Her eyes blazed with anger. 'No!' she hissed, her voice low, held in check by a vice-like control. 'Nothing happened between David and me.' She matched Ruth's piercing look. 'I'll not deny we became close, and I still think a lot about him, but it's Adam I love, always has been.'

'And what about David?' snapped Ruth. 'How much of his love hast thou still got?

'You're married to him. You ask him if you can't trust his love for you.' Jenny turned away in disgust and hurried towards the church.

Ruth drew herself up and watched her go. 'Thee may be from a well-to-do family, thee may have lived on the other side of the river, but I've aristocratic blood in my veins, and David's mine,' she whispered. 'Try to take him from me and thee'll regret it.'

Chapter Fifteen

Ruth pushed open the door of the church and saw Jenny kneeling with bowed head in one of the box-pews near the back. She closed the door gently and moved quietly on her toes, trying to deaden the tap of her shoes as much as she could.

She slipped quietly into the pew beside Jenny who remained in prayer. With no reaction to her presence, Ruth slid her hand slowly on to Jenny's. She looked up, her eyes non-committal.

'I'm sorry,' whispered Ruth. 'I shouldn't have flared up like that.' She had realised she needed Jenny's friendship, at least for the immediate future. She was alone in Whitby now David had gone and needed someone's help. Jenny was her only link with other people; Ruth needed her contacts and introductions if she and David were to fulfil their ambitions.

Though still harbouring a suspicion of the relationship between Jenny and David, Ruth was prepared to view it with guarded doubt for as long as she needed the other girl.

Jenny looked at her with probing eyes, trying to fathom the genuineness of the apology.

'That's all right, Ruth. I shouldn't have been prying,' she returned, her voice low. 'The baby's your affair and no one else's.'

'Then, please, say nothing to David. He would be . . .'

'I won't say a word,' cut in Jenny quickly, to reassure her. She squeezed Ruth's hand and offered her a smile. 'Let's say a prayer for their safety. I always come here after I've watched the *Mary Jane* sail.'

They knelt quietly at the back of the church for a few moments.

When they emerged into the bright sunlight again, Jenny said, 'Will you come to church on Sunday?'

Though Ruth had not been brought up as a regular churchgoer, she had been encouraged during her stay with the Fernleys to attend a Sunday service. But now her nimble mind saw churchgoing as a means of getting to know people who might be useful to her and David in the future.

'Yes,' she replied.

'Good, then I'll call for you.' Jenny smiled.

The *Mary Jane* was a full ship by the first week in August. The harpooning skill of Seth Thoresby seemed to have been inherited by his son and his kills, together with those of Jamaica, accounted for most of the blubber and baleen which would provide oil for the lamps of Whitby and beyond, and whalebone for the clothes of the fashion-conscious upper classes, helping to stimulate the economy of the busy Yorkshire port.

'Lucky' Thoresby had the best of the weather after his

early start, but those whalers which had left England later, and were not full when Thoresby sailed from the whaling grounds, suffered damage in severe storms.

David was pleased with the praise he received for his skilful handling of the lines but it came as a surprise when Jamaica sought him out as they approached Whitby.

'Sailing again next year?' asked the mate.

'Aye,' replied David enthusiastically.

'Good. Thee learns fast. Bob Harrison's missing next season so I'll be without a boat-steerer. Want the job?' David gaped at Jamaica. 'Well, do thee?' boomed the mate, his one eye gleaming brightly as he saw David's bewilderment.

'Do I?' cried David. 'Thee needn't ask me again.'

'Good!' rapped Jamaica. He turned and strode away, leaving David staring at his broad back.

David's mind was awhirl. Boat-steerer to Jamaica! One of the best harpooners in the business! He could hardly believe his good fortune. This was something he had never dreamed of happening so soon.

He hurried to find Adam to tell him his exciting news.

'I'm sorry to lose thee but I'm glad for thee, Davey. Thee's doing well. Ruth'll be pleased.'

The news that a whaleship had been sighted had swept through Whitby and brought folk hurrying to the cliffs, eager to identify it and to see if there was bone at the masthead. The men on the *Mary Jane* were just as desirous to identify their loved ones by prearranged signals.

When the *Mary Jane* passed between the piers into the calm of the river, David and Adam saw shawls swirl and then disappear and knew their wives would be on the quay to greet them. David's eagerness to tell Ruth his news was tempered by his anxiety about the baby. Should Ruth have been on the cliffs?

The *Mary Jane* sailed proudly towards the bridge which opened to allow her to pass into the inner harbour. Commands flew and were obeyed instantly as Seth Thoresby manoeuvred the whaleship to her berth on the east bank. The quay was crowded with families, sweethearts and well-wishers, their faces reflecting their relief and happiness at the safe return of the crew. Ropes curled quaywards and eager hands soon had the *Mary Jane* tied up.

David and Adam searched the crowd.

'There they are!' cried Adam, pointing in the direction of Jenny and Ruth. He drew a sharp breath. 'Looks as though thee's a pa and I'm gannin' to be one,' he cried as he started towards the gangplank.

They jostled with other members of the crew, all eager for the touch of loved ones, and bustled their way through the folk thronging the quay.

'Ruth, is thee all right, lass?' gasped David, worry mixing with the joy of seeing her.

'Aye, Davey.' Laughter trembled on her lips and danced in her eyes.

'The bairn?' His eyes were on her and they clouded with concern as he saw the laughter fade. 'What is it? What's wrong?'

'I lost it early on,' returned Ruth quietly. 'I'm sorry, Davey.'

'Oh, my luv.' David reached out and enfolded her with loving care.

As he held her, Ruth's eyes met Jenny's. She knew Jenny had heard the exchange. Ruth's face compressed with an unfriendly warning. Tell David the truth and . . .

'I'm all right,' whispered Ruth close to David's ear. 'Don't worry. It wasn't meant to be. The important thing is you're home.' She hugged him tight, eased herself in his arms and drew him into her kiss.

'Oh, Ruth, it's good to feel thee again,' gasped David as their lips parted.

'It's good to have you back,' she whispered.

Adam's face was clouded with loving concern as he took Jenny's outstretched hands and asked, 'Why didn't thee tell me afore we sailed?'

'I didn't want to worry you while you were away,' replied Jenny. 'And don't look so worried now.' She laughed. 'I'm all right.'

He kissed her gently and their eyes held each other's in a love which set them apart from everyone else on the quay.

'When is it?' Adam asked.

'Another three months.'

'Thee shouldn't be here, shouldn't have been on the cliff top. Let's get thee home,' he blustered.

'Steady, Adam.' The laughter on Jenny's lips mingled with the happiness in her eyes. 'Everything's all right. I've been watched over by your mother and I'm certainly not just sitting around waiting for the baby to be born.'

'I'll get Pa to release me from the Memel voyage.'

'You'll do no such thing,' said Jenny indignantly.

She overrode his protests with her insistent determination. Adam shrugged his shoulders in resignation and, after

243

David had made his congratulations, turned to him and said, 'Told Ruth yet, Davey?'

'Told me what?' queried Ruth with a puzzled smile.

'I'm to be Jamaica's boat-steerer next season!' announced David proudly.

Ruth's eyes lit with excitement as she embraced him with a renewed fervour. 'Congratulations! That's wonderful.'

'Well done, David!' Jenny added her delight. 'Jamaica must think highly of you to give you that job so soon.'

'Davey's a quick learner,' said Adam. 'He'll go far.'

'What's the next step?' queried Ruth.

'Harpooner.' David laughed at Ruth's seeming impatience. 'But that won't be for a while yet.'

'You never know, David.'

He had already noticed a change in Ruth. Her voice was softer and there was less of the marked Yorkshire accent to it. The timbre seemed to match Jenny's. As they walked home, he detected a more confident bearing in her. It showed in the set of her head and the way she held her body.

'Thee's changed, Ruth,' he said, noting the reaction of pleasure to his comment.

'Thee's . . .' Ruth pursed her lips in annoyance. 'You've got me slipping back, David. I've been trying hard to speak better. You'll have to, too, now that we're moving in different circles.'

'What does thee mean?'

'Through going to church with Jenny I've become friendly with Frank and Hesther Watson.'

'Who are they?' queried David.

'He's a timber merchant and could be useful when we own our own ship. We'll need someone to buy the timber from your winter voyages, and from my enquiries Frank is the fairest man to deal with. I believe he's starting to look around for other investments so he could be interested in shares in a whaleship.'

'Oh, I see you're not wasting any time.' David smiled.

'Of course not. We're going to get what we want. Through the Watsons I'll cultivate other people who'll help us.' The ring of determination in Ruth's voice left David in no doubt of his wife's ambitions.

Excited by the possibilities, they hurried home.

The longing and desire, heightened by five months' separation, burned so deeply that it needed no spoken word nor gesture to take them straight to their bedroom.

As the door swung shut, David grabbed Ruth and pulled her close. She came to him with willing eagerness, her face tilted upwards with an invitation that couldn't be denied. His lips sought hers with a hungry passion which sent her pulses racing. She needed him, needed to feel the power of his body inside her.

'Oh, Davey, Davey,' she moaned, her voice husky with a lifetime of longing.

A sensual shudder ran through her body as she felt his hands fumbling, in their urgency, to unfasten the buttons of her dress. She released the fastenings on his trousers and, unable to wait, cried out, 'Let me, Davey.'

In one swift movement she threw her dress and petticoats over her head. As she stepped out of her underdrawers, she eyed every action with which David revealed more of his muscular body, patently yearning for her.

Her last garment scattered across the floor, she flung herself on the bed and spread her nakedness for him to take.

With the satisfaction of a long parting appeased, they lay quietly entwined in each other's arms. David felt a deep contentment. Ruth, gratified by his male strength, was puzzled by a strange, underlying desire for a gentler sexual pleasure. To ease the conflict, which sent turmoil spinning in her mind, she broke the silence.

'You like the new Ruth, Davey?'

He twisted over to look at his wife. She let her head flop back on the pillow and gazed up at her husband with a twinkle in her eye. She ran her forefinger down the length of his chest.

'Of course I do.' David grinned. 'Everything about thee.' He kissed her breast.

She moaned as desire rose in her again. She flung her arms round his neck. 'Oh, Davey, everything's right for us. I'll get the right introductions through the Watsons and we'll get our own whaleship,' she cried.

The ring of certainty in her voice thrilled him and he was determined he would match every move she made.

'Of course we will.'

His lips fell hungrily upon hers. Though she responded to his forceful urges, her desire to be taken that way had subsided into a desire to linger in the ecstasy, something which David did not seem to need.

'Ruth,' he said as they lay quietly beside each other, 'the *Mary Jane's* doing a winter voyage to Memel for timber, so . . .'

'You'll be going?'

'Yes.'

'I'd hoped to have you all winter.' Disappointment clouded her face.

'Don't look like that, luv. It's all experience for me and that's what I need as quickly as possible,' David reminded her.

'I'm sorry. Of course it is.'

'And maybe I could get a job on another vessel for the winter. The more knowledge of seamanship I get the better,' David suggested.

Ruth did not protest.

Chapter Sixteen

'Let me carry her awhile,' said Ruth as she and Jenny threaded their way through the flow of people climbing the Church Stairs to watch the whalers leave for the Arctic.

'Thanks,' said Jenny as she handed three-year-old Anne to Ruth. 'She's getting heavy.'

'Come to Aunty Ruth,' she cajoled with a smile.

The child put her arms round Ruth's neck, hugged her and settled in her arms.

'Time you had one of your own,' said Jenny with a searching glance at her.

'Not yet,' returned Ruth with a slight shake of her head.

'But wouldn't David like . . . ?'

'Maybe,' cut in Ruth sharply, 'but I've other ideas.'

'Those ambitions, I suppose,' commented Jenny. 'Don't sacrifice happiness for them, Ruth.'

'There are things we want to do,' she said, irritated by Jenny's concerned advice, 'so I'm careful. Might be different when David becomes a harpooner. I'd hoped he'd be one by now.' Her lips tightened with exasperation.

She longed to fulfil ambitions which were being held back by David's lack of progress. She knew it was no fault of his; the *Mary Jane* always sailed with a full complement of harpooners and, until one of them, through one reason or another, failed to sign on, David would remain a boat-steerer. Until promotion came, the Fernleys were not able to take advantage of the contacts which Ruth had made.

Once she had been introduced at Hesther's tea party, other invitations were forthcoming, for Whitby ladies were curious about her. They were sure, from her bearing and smart appearance, that there was more to her than a mere country girl.

'Heredity. Certain of it, the girl's from good stock.'

'But I heard she was from a very poor family who had nothing to commend them.'

'Maybe, my dear, but I tell you, there's breeding there. It will out, you know.'

'Country aristocracy, I shouldn't wonder.'

'But how . . . ?'

'Oh, really. You know these country squires. Like their fling and nothing said. Shouldn't wonder if Ruth isn't from such a liaison.'

So opinions were exchanged and the ladies became keen to include someone who might have an 'interesting' background in their monthly afternoon get-togethers.

Ruth chuckled at their obvious curiosity and played up to them. She smartened the house in Henrietta Street and returned their hospitality. She despised their tittle-tattle but tolerated it, for she realised that through them she would eventually gain invitations to the evening dinner parties where she and David would meet the menfolk whom they needed to further their ambitions.

Ruth absorbed as much as possible of the life of the whaling port, learning the way of the trade – who were the best shipbuilders, which ship's chandler gave the fairest deal, how people invested in a whaleship and who was likely to be interested in such a venture.

She felt she and David were on the brink of being able to start more positively on the road to achieving their desires. All it needed was for him to be made harpooner. Harpooners were men apart; they were the true hunters and, though teamwork was necessary when hunting the whale, it was the harpooners' skill which finally meant a kill, more money in their pockets and more wealth to Whitby. For those who wanted, the harpooner's position was only a step away from becoming captain. And she and David craved it!

'Be patient, Ruth,' said Jenny. 'David got on very quickly after his first voyage.'

'Well, he deserved to,' she returned a little sharply.

'Oh, I know he did. But it made you think promotion would continue just as quickly. David's time will come. It's sure to. He's ready for it, Adam's told me. It's just a matter of a vacancy amongst the *Mary Jane's* harpooners. As soon as that happens . . .'

'Well, I wish it would,' snapped Ruth.

The sharp, crisp air drew at their lungs and they were gasping hard for breath by the time they reached the path beside the parish church on the cliff top, where Ruth handed Anne back to her mother.

'They're on their way,' announced Ruth, glancing towards the river.

With top sails taking advantage of the breeze, the *Mary Jane* was the first whaleship heading towards the piers.

Ruth and Jenny quickened their pace and jostled their way through the crowds to the cliff edge.

High on the rigging, two men leaned outwards, their right arms held aloft in a farewell signal.

Jenny and Ruth swung their shawls high above their heads and received an answering wave. Jenny held Anne high and received an extra wave from Adam. They saw Seth Thoresby, standing beside the man at the wheel, turn and salute. Jenny drew a sharp breath. She had only every seen Seth do that once before – the day on which Adam made his first voyage.

The *Mary Jane* met the swell.

Jenny and Ruth watched in silence while the whaler grew smaller and smaller, taking their men to the dangers of the Arctic. The crowds around them dispersed slowly until they were alone except for one figure who held a grey shawl tightly around her head. Jenny sensed an aura of sadness around the woman, which was accentuated by the vast reaches of the sea and sky. It was Emma Thoresby.

Jenny touched Ruth lightly on the arm and indicated Emma. Ruth nodded. When they reached her, Emma gave no indication of being aware of them.

Jenny glanced at her mother-in-law and saw silent tears flowing. She made no comment but turned her attention to the *Mary Jane*.

'I thought you only came for a Thoresby's first voyage,' Jenny said quietly.

'I do.' Emma Thoresby was tall and thin and her face had the careworn look of most sailors' wives, but there was an air of serenity about her and Jenny knew that deep down there was a remarkable reserve of strength.

'Ruben?' Jenny asked.

'Aye. A last-minute decision.' There was a touch of sadness in Emma's voice, the sadness of a mother who cannot stop the inevitable, the growing up of the youngest son.

'He's nearly twenty,' pointed out Jenny, trying to comfort her. 'Adam was younger when he first went to sea.'

'Aye, but somehow that was different, Adam seemed older.' She smiled wistfully. 'I suppose it was because I had Ruben left then.'

'He'll be all right with Captain Thoresby and Adam,' said Ruth.

'Of course he will. Take no notice of me. I'm just a mother wishing they hadn't to grow up.' Emma wiped her eyes with her handkerchief.

They watched until the *Mary Jane* disappeared over the horizon.

'Let's go and say a prayer for them,' Emma suggested quietly.

After one more glance across the desolate sea, they walked slowly to the church.

Ruth still fumed as she thought of the *Mary Jane* sailing once more to the Arctic with David still a boat-steerer, stultifying their craving for success and with it a different life on the other side of the river. She felt sure that, once she was able to announce that he was to be a harpooner and that they were ambitious for him to become a captain, people would extend fresh invitations and that would provide opportunities to solicit investment in a whaleship. She had it all planned. How she wished just one harpooner would drop out of the *Mary Jane's* crew!

'Steady as you go.' Seth Thoresby's voice was firm. He hoped it hid his true feelings and instilled confidence in his crew. They needed something to raise their spirits, to counteract the regular crunch and grind as the *Mary Jane*, heading north, forced her way through the ice floes.

Peace had returned to the seas with the cessation of hostilities with the American Colonies and their allies three years ago. Though this meant more men available to serve on the whalers, Seth still employed some Shetlanders, as he had done since the ban on them had been lifted, for he found them willing and able sailors.

This voyage had started well and the crew hoped for as good a season as the last three when the *Mary Jane* had returned a full ship, but now it was late in the season; the year was already into the third week in August.

For once the tag of 'Lucky' had not stuck to Seth. The whaling had been poor; the ship was only a third full. Other vessels had left the whaling grounds, their captains convinced they would do no good if they stayed, for it seemed as if the whales had deserted the Arctic seas. Seth knew he ran a risk by staying. If the weather turned bad earlier than usual, he could be caught in the ice. But he slept for one more night on his decision to return home.

When he stepped out on to the deck the following morning, he found a calm sea and a fine day with the sun shining from a clear blue sky. It was a day to raise morale.

He filled his lungs with the cold Arctic air and felt new life drive into him. He turned his gaze to the north, his eyes narrowing, piercing the distance as if seeing beyond the horizon.

He sensed the tension in the ship. He knew the crew were hanging on his next order and that they were willing it to be 'Head for home.' But, damn it, whales were there for the taking. He was certain.

The crew had not known whether to be pleased or not when Seth's order taking them on a northerly course rang across the deck. They were heading for the ice floes but they had faith. The captain wasn't called 'Lucky' for nothing.

But now, in the second day of bumping, creaking ice, they were beginning to have their doubts about his luck.

The constant changes of direction, the crash of the ice against the ship, occurred with such monotonous regularity that it began to prey on men's minds. They grew restless and began to murmur among themselves.

'Hell, why doesn't Thoresby gan home?'

'He's whale mad.'

'There ain't any left.'

The ship shuddered.

'Damn the ice.'

'It'll trap us.'

'Then a bloody freezing death.'

David was no better than the rest. The constant bumping and grinding, the ever northward movement taking them further and further away from home, pounded at his brain until he felt he would be driven insane.

'Water! Clear water!'

The cry from the lookout cut through the sharp air, startling the crew out of their apathy. Morbid and disgruntled thoughts were banished. Relief surged through the ship, though the menace of the ice remained astern. Maybe the captain's luck had not deserted him.

Seth kept the *Mary Jane* on a north-easterly course for another twenty-four hours when, with the wind dropping completely, he decided to make fast to a large ice floe.

The boats were lowered and tied to the *Mary Jane*. Breath chilled on the cold, still air as men heaved the oars to bring the ship on to a southerly heading so that her starboard side was against a grotesquely shaped mass of ice to which an ice anchor was attached. Seth was content to use the southerly drift while scanning the ocean for whales.

Four hours later, the cry came from the mast-head, 'There she blows! There she blows!'

The spout was no more than half a mile away. Then more and more whales broke the surface. They were there for the taking. 'Lucky' Thoresby indeed!

'Away all boats!'

Men raced across the deck. Ropes were unfastened and boats lowered with haste but accuracy. Men swarmed down to join those already in position. They scrambled to their oars and in a matter of moments six boats were moving quickly across a calm sea.

Men bent their backs willingly. The season was late but here was a chance, in one spell of whaling, to be away from the Arctic before the ice closed in.

Muscles strained against the oars. Chests heaved and bodies, heavily clothed against the cold, sweated. The boats skimmed across the water.

David's eyes were bright, watching the whales, judging the direction and distance, steering the boat with a skill quickly learned and achieved on his last three voyages. His whispered orders eased aching backs and oarsmen, tense but thankful, rested. The boat glided on. David sculled it gently towards the whale he had chosen. A quick glance showed him that two other boats were moving for a kill simultaneously.

He signalled. Jamaica got to his feet, reached for his harpoon and steadied himself into a stance from which he could get the best possible throw. Then they were close to the dark, shiny body.

Jamaica's powerful frame swung back, then sprang in a smooth flowing curve, bringing his right arm swiftly forward to launch the harpoon in a perfect trajectory towards the whale. The barbs struck and were driven home by the force of the throw.

'Stern all!'

Instantly oars were back into the sea, broad hands drove them through the water in an endeavour to take the boat away from the turmoil as the whale, wounded from the attack, sounded. Water foamed. The line started to run out. Faster. Faster. More and more. Then suddenly it stopped and went limp.

'Damn!' Jamaica's excitement turned to annoyance. He grabbed the line and hauled it in quickly until the frayed end told him that the fore-gore had parted from the line, leaving a whale, with a harpoon sticking in its back, escaping in the depths of the ocean. Jamaica cursed and threw down the rope in disgust.

The whale which Adam sought sounded at the moment

he released his harpoon and the weapon fell harmlessly into the sea.

Excited with his perfect strike, the third harpooner lost his balance and his leg became snared by the fast-running line. His piercing screams sent a chill of terror through the rest of the men as he was dragged overboard. He hit the water, went under, then cleaved through it behind the fifty-ton monster endeavouring to escape a deadly fate. Almost at the same moment as the harpooner met the icy sea, the nearest rower released his oar and in one, swift blow of an axe, severed the line.

The harpooner, helpless in the tight grip around his leg, suddenly felt it slacken. The rope slipped. It was moving, running around his leg. Then it was gone. The buffeting ceased. The harpooner kicked for the surface. He burst into daylight, bringing shouts of relief from his crew who pulled the boat swiftly to him. Willing hands dragged him quickly from the deathly chill and lost no time in getting to the *Mary Jane*.

Seth Thoresby, seeing the reactions of the whales, led the two remaining boats beyond the position where the huge monsters had first been sighted. One moment the crews were rowing steadily, then next they were the centre of a maelstrom.

A long, broad back broke the water not five yards in front of them. Matching his balance to the bobbing boat, Seth came to his feet and in one blur of movement plucked his harpoon, swung his body and hurled the iron at the great, black body. The harpoon struck and held. Seth grabbed a second and flung it with all his strength into the towering bulk. The boat was fast. The whale began to run, taking Seth and his crew away from the violence which struck without warning.

A whale drove upwards beneath the second boat, flinging it into the air. Wood shattered. Men screamed in terror as they fell amongst splintered wreckage scattered across the icy sea. The monster's flukes waved high and paused, seeming to gather strength, before slashing down on to the bow of the remaining boat. The harpooner saw the descending tail in one wide-eyed second of horror before he was smashed into death. The flukes cleaved the boat in two, flinging men into the freezing sea. The whale sounded.

Men bobbed in the water, seeking some escape. Adam and Jamaica bellowed their orders but David and his fellow boat-steerer were already leaning hard on the steering oars, swinging the boats round in a sharp curve. They were among the victims in a matter of moments and sodden, cold, but thankful men were dragged from the sea and taken quickly to the *Mary Jane*. Many wondered why Thoresby's luck had deserted them.

'Anyone seen the captain?' asked Adam anxiously when he reached the *Mary Jane's* deck.

'Just before the whale struck us I saw him fast to a big one,' someone called.

'Ahoy, lookout. See anything of the cap'n?' yelled Adam.

'Whale running north,' came the reply.

'Tak' three boats, Adam,' instructed Jamaica. 'He'll need help towing that whale back. I'll see t' things here.'

Adam lost no time in getting the boats under way, taking up the position of boat-steerer in his own boat so that he would have a view of the way ahead. The men rowed steadily, eager to find the captain and have one whale as some compensation for the ill-luck which had hit them.

After an hour Adam's brow was furrowed with anxiety. He knew that the whale could have run far while all the time the steadily drifting floe was taking the *Mary Jane* further away from them.

Fifteen minutes later, fear surged through him when he saw the grey wall filling the horizon ahead. Fog! Pack-ice would not be far away!

Adam glanced across at David and saw that he too had seen the fog. He looked back at his own men. They were rowing steadily, unaware of what lay beyond their backs.

Eighteen men. I daren't risk their lives. We must escape the fog. But, hell, Pa's out there! Adam's mind was torn by the horrific decision which faced him.

He knew these men would row anywhere for their captain but he could not ask them to risk their lives. If they were caught in the fog so far from the *Mary Jane*, they could lose her altogether and be condemned to a ghastly, freezing death in the Arctic wastes.

'Return to the *Mary Jane*! Line astern!' Adam yelled.

'Adam!' David's plea froze on his lips when he saw Adam's tortured expression mixed with anger that David had dared to challenge a command.

David pressured his steering oar. His boat swung round and he lined it up behind Adam's. The third boat circled and closed on David's stern. They headed south.

Adam's mouth tightened into a hard line. His nails bit into the palms of his clenched hands.

Hell! What am I doing? I can't leave Pa. He tensed himself to make the command but the words which would have taken them searching through the fog were never uttered. He looked round. Eighteen men! Oh my God, I can't condemn them. I can't risk eighteen lives for six. The men rowed on, their action condoned by Adam's silence. Lines of anguish creased his face. He hated himself and his tormented mind cried out for help and forgiveness.

He glanced to the north, hoping to see some break so that he could go back. But there was none. The fog moved relentlessly after them.

'Row! Faster, faster!' he shouted.

Although backs and muscles ached, the men found some new source of energy. For an hour and ten minutes, they managed to keep ahead of the fog. Adam reckoned that they had little more than the drift of the ship to make up.

Then cold, damp, swirling fingers brushed his cheeks. He shuddered. The hand of death had touched him. He glanced back at the fog. The other two boats were still visible but the grey mass towered over them, ready to plunge and cut them off.

'Make fast!' Adam's order snapped through the cold air.

Lines were fastened rapidly between each boat and the men quickened their strokes. The fog swirled, cloaked them, then whisped away, only to come back, drifting around them. These outriders warned of what was to follow.

Adam searched the sea frantically.

The fingers of fog became more tenacious. They grasped

and swirled around the boats. The third was almost hidden from Adam's sight. It kept drifting in and out of view like some ghost. Adam shuddered. He scanned the ocean again. The ship! Fog enveloped him. Had he been mistaken? Was it his imagination? A case of wishful thinking? He cursed the fog. It moved before his eyes, parted and fell like a curtain, but, in that brief parting, Adam felt sure of his identification. He altered course slightly to starboard and passed the encouraging news to the other two boats. The fog closed in.

He swore to himself. Why didn't the damned fog hold off a little longer? 'Steady as you go. We'll soon be there, lads.' He tried to instil certainty in them. He was anxious to try to attract the attention of the *Mary Jane* but knew that no reply could sap the hearts of tired men. The crews rowed on through the thickening fog. When he began to sense an uneasiness in them, he waited no longer.

'*Mary Jane*, ahoy!' Adam's voice boomed.

The fog swirled, swallowing up the sound. There was no reply.

'Ship, ahoy!' Every ear in the boats strained. Every man willed an answer which would mean safety and release from the possibilities of a slow death in the cold Arctic seas, but there was only the swish of the water.

They rowed on.

'Ship, ahoy!' Automatically everyone stopped rowing. The cut of the oars into the sea must not hide any answering shout. '*Mary Jane*, ahoy!' Silence.

They drifted.

'Answer, damn you, answer!' The hysterical shout came from somewhere in the boat.

'Steady, there!' called Adam, admonishing yet imparting hope with his tone. 'Ahoy the *Mary Jane*!'

He stiffened. Had he heard something or was the fog mocking him? Tension in the boat heightened. Others had heard it but could hardly believe their ears. There it was again. Faint but nevertheless there. A buzz of excitement ran through the crew.

'Quiet!' Adam barked. The chattering stopped. '*Mary Jane* ahoy!'

Eighteen men waited in suspense.

'Aye, here we are!' It was faint.

'The *Mary Jane*!' David shouted.

The cheer which confirmed the men's relief was muted by Adam's command: 'Row!'

The men bent their backs willingly.

'*Mary Jane* ahoy!' Adam's call became more frequent, the reply louder. Each time he tried to estimate the direction of the welcome shout.

The fog ahead darkened. Automatically he started to give the order to turn away but it stopped when he realised that the darkening fog was the *Mary Jane*, fastened to the ice floe. They were safe!

Thankful men tied up alongside the ship and scrambled on board.

'You didn't find them?' The question, a half-statement of hopeless disappointment and horror, came from the men on board the ship, anxious for news of their captain.

'No.' Adam's shake of the head and the desolation in his eyes prevented any further discussion.

'Pa! Where's Pa?' cried Ruben, grabbing Adam's arm.

His face twisted with agony as the full impact of the tragedy bit into his young mind.

'We saw nothing,' replied Adam in a dull voice.

'Thee left him out there?' Ruben's voice was shrill with accusation and disbelief. His father couldn't be missing. He always returned. He was 'Lucky' Thoresby.

'I had to come back. Other men's lives were at stake,' Adam said, but the words seemed to hold no meaning.

'But thee left him! Thee left him to die!' Ruben's words cut and pierced Adam's mind. 'Thee's a murderer! A bloody murderer!' Ruben leaped forward, raining blows on a brother too shocked to defend himself but who felt some exorcism in their pain.

Strong hands grabbed Ruben, dragging him away from his brother. Wide-eyed, he struggled, his mind urging him to avenge his father. He fought to get at the man who had left his father to a slow, horrible death. Jamaica stepped forward and drove his fist hard against Ruben's jaw. He staggered and would have fallen as unconciousness flooded in if he hadn't been held by the mate.

'Tak' him t' his bunk,' ordered Jamaica. He turned to Adam, still staring unseeingly in front of him. 'Sorry,' he said. 'Only thing I could do, though.' Seeing little response from Adam, he grabbed him firmly by the shoulders and looked hard at him from his one eye. 'Forget it, Adam, Ruben didn't mean it.'

Adam's eyes came up slowly to meet Jamaica's. 'He called me a murderer and he's right. I left my pa out there to die.'

'He's not right!' Jamaica's voice was harsh. 'And he didn't mean it. He was hysterical. This is his first voyage and for this to happen – well, he can't be responsible for what he said or did.'

'But I left Pa.'

'And saved eighteen men from death. Your decision, authority and skill got them back here. Thee did the right thing, Adam.'

He looked wearily at Jamaica. 'I hope thee's right,' he said, his voice scarcely above a whisper.

'I am, thee'll see,' said Jamaica. 'Now, it's rest thee wants. We'll have t' stay fast t' this floe 'til this bloody fog's gone. Davey, tak' him to his bunk. I'll go t' see Ruben.'

David led his friend below decks.

'What have I done?' moaned Adam as he flopped into his bunk.

'What thee had to do,' replied David, but his mind was less convinced. Could he have done the same? He must not let his friend see his doubts. Adam needed his strength and understanding.

'How can I face Ma?' Adam's torment brought the cry from the depths of his soul.

'You can and will,' replied David firmly.

For twenty-four hours, the crew of the *Mary Jane* cursed the fog. Every moment lessened their chances of finding their captain. It answered with mocking silence, their regular shouts to indicate their presence should Seth be searching for his ship. Each moment of silence brought greater despair to the crew, growing restless and irritable with their inactivity.

When a gentle breeze swirled the fog, excitement and

hope gripped them. The wind freshened, clearing the fog but revealing a greater menace. Where there had been open water, now there was ice.

Jamaica frowned. 'Looks grim,' he said. 'That ice could close in fast. If it joins that to the south we're trapped.'

'What do we do?' asked Adam, torn between the hope of finding his father and the possibility of endangering the lives of the entire crew.

Jamaica looked thoughtful. He surveyed Adam with his one eye. He knew if he made the wrong answer Adam might never face future decisions decisively. 'Adam,' replied Jamaica, 'the captain always said thee'd tak' the *Mary Jane* one day. Thee'd better start right now.'

Adam stared at the mate. He wanted help, he needed advice. He beseeched the mate with his eyes but Jamaica's face remained impassive. Adam knew that he was right. If he was to be his father's son, he could not shirk the responsibility thrust upon him in this untimely way.

'We leave and search the edge of the ice once more!' Adam's instructions were crisp and decisive.

The ropes were cut off and, with the strong current underneath her, the *Mary Jane* was soon clear of the ice floe.

'Hoist topsails!'

The wind caught the canvas and the *Mary Jane* forged ahead through the open water.

Adam headed the vessel for the ice. He ordered a man to the main-top-mast with instructions to keep a sharp lookout for any sign of the missing boat or its crew.

Every eye on the *Mary Jane* was alert, straining to pierce distance for a sight of their captain and his crew – alive.

The sun, normally welcome at such high latitudes, was merciless, dazzling with its brightness, and when men shaded their eyes it mockingly threw itself back from the sea. Adam took the ship west along the edge of the ice and, finding nothing, went to the east, while all the time they were being pushed southwards by the relentless movement of the ice.

The longer they sailed, the deeper the gloom which enveloped the ship. The creek of the timber, the slap of the sails and the swish of the sea, emphasised the eeriness which had come with the lack of talk and the absence of laughter. The ship sailed on like a floating coffin.

During the late afternoon, the lookout broke the death-like silence. With reluctance in his voice, he reported ice to the south. Adam bit his lip. He glanced at Jamaica but the mate's face was blank.

Adam hesitated, then his command rang clear. 'Steer south!'

'South it is, sir!' answered the helmsman.

'No! Thee can't leave him!' Ruben rushed across the deck.

David, fearing another attack, stepped in front of Ruben and grabbed him by the arms, forcing him to stop.

'Thee can't leave him,' he cried, his eyes wild, as he pushed against David.

'Calm down, Ruben,' rapped David. 'Do thee think he wants to quit?'

Ruben stared past David and saw the torment which raged in Adam. He knew how hard it had been for him to reach a decision. He let his arms drop and stepped past David to his brother. 'I'm sorry. I shouldn't have said what I did.' Ruben's voice pleaded for forgiveness.

'I'm sorry too.' Adam's look pleaded with Ruben to understand. 'But I've got the crew to think of. We've searched. If anyone had still been alive, we'd have found them.' He grasped his arm in a comforting gesture.

Ruben nodded and absolved his brother from any blame. There were tears in his eyes.

'I reckon the whale took them into the fog and they met the ice before they realised it. The whale would dive under the ice taking them with it,' commented David, quietly underlining Adam's decision to leave the Arctic.

Ruben, tears streaming down his face, turned away. He looked to the north through blurred eyes, willing his father to appear. He must come. They couldn't return to Whitby without him. 'Pa!' The cry of anguish was held back to a whisper. Would his pa wish to see him weeping like a schoolboy? Ruben stifled his sobs and knuckled his eyes to quell the tears. He straightened his shoulders, tightened his lips and became a man.

The *Mary Jane* came on to her southerly heading. The crew were relieved to find the ice to the south was still cut by lanes. Adam called for more sail and pressed on with the utmost haste to clear the ice before it closed in solid for the long Arctic winter.

Chapter Seventeen

There were no cheers from the crowds gathered to watch the return of the *Mary Jane*.

Whitby folk had seen too many whalers return not to recognise the melancholy air about the *Mary Jane's* homecoming. Something was wrong. Tragedy had marred this voyage.

'Adam's bringing the ship in.' Jenny's words were scarcely above a whisper. 'Pa! Where's his pa?' Her voice trembled. The undeniable intuition that exerts itself in moments of distress brought terror gripping her heart. She feared the worst. She turned and forced her way quickly through the crowd. She must be at the quay when the *Mary Jane* docked. Adam would need her.

Ruth sense the dread which had seized Jenny and knew she should be with her.

When they reached the quay, people were already congregating in silent groups, watching the *Mary Jane* manoeuvring to her berth. There were no joyous calls of recognition, no yells of pleasure, even the necessary commands were subdued.

Jenny searched the faces anxiously. Adam! There, beside the rail. But his face! Even from this distance she could see how he had aged. His features bore the unmistakable marks of tragedy and, instead of joy, there was pain at a homecoming which held only anguish and sorrow.

As soon as the gangway was run out, Adam strode down to the quay, closely followed by David and other members of the crew, knowing what was expected of them. It was their duty to break the news which would shatter the families of the lost men.

Adam's face was grim. His eyes lacked the lustre Jenny had always seen on his return from the Arctic. They did not sparkle even when he took her and Anne in his arms.

'Oh, Jenny, my love.' The words were strangled. He held her tightly but it was in a way that Jenny had never experienced. There had always been life and passion before, now it felt as if he was seeking comfort.

'It's your father, isn't it?' she whispered.

She felt him nod. 'He and his crew didn't return.' His voice faltered. 'I . . . I had to make the decision to leave them.'

'Oh, Adam,' she gasped. She sensed the guilt he was feeling and knew she must be strong. Adam needed all the loving and understanding she could give.

He felt a touch on his arm. He turned his head and saw Ruth with tears in her eyes. 'I'm so sorry, Adam.' Her voice choked. No words were adequate. But inside her mind was already turning the tragedy to her advantage. She hadn't thought of it happening this way when the

269

Mary Jane sailed, but now there would be one harpooner less. This could be David's chance.

'Thanks,' Adam croaked.

David took Ruth's arm and they moved away.

'Thee gan home, love,' he said. 'There's things to do here. I'll be home as soon as possible.' He kissed her gently. 'Oh, it's good to see thee.'

'And you.' Ruth held his gaze for a moment then turned and hurried away, thankful that David at least was safe. He could have perished instead of Seth. This tragedy had emphasised the dangers more forcibly but it had also brought a new perspective to life. Now every moment was more precious; they must be lived to the full and every opportunity must be taken.

Though he felt comfort in Jenny's arms and wanted to stay there forever, Adam knew he must face reality. He eased himself from her. 'Jenny, I must be the one to tell Ma. Come with me.'

'Of course I will,' she said gently. 'We'll take Anne to Tom on the way.'

'I've told Ruben to let me break the news first. He'll follow in a few minutes.' Adam swallowed hard, trying to keep a firm grip of his feelings.

'Come, love.' Jenny took his hand and they walked along the quay on which little groups of people stood silent or offered their commiserations in whispered tones, while others searched the faces of the sailors who had reached home and in their absence received the news they'd dreaded.

They found Adam's mother busy with some sewing. She had never been to see her husband's whaleship return, saying that he would be home in due course and that their greetings for each other were private and not for display upon the quay. There were those who said she was insensitive but they did not really know her. She was a gentle person, but firm, as she had to be, being mother, father, confidante and adviser to a sailor's family for most of the year.

'Hello, Adam, Jenny.' Emma rose to kiss them. She kept hold of Jenny's hand, sensing the need to comfort in its grip, for she had felt tragedy the moment they had entered the room.

'Ma, I . . .'

'It's your pa, isn't it?' said Emma quietly, taking charge of the situation.

Tears swam in Adam's eyes as he nodded. Emma sat down slowly, still keeping hold of Jenny's hand. As Jenny knelt down beside her, she saw a serenity in the finely featured face and a sadness in the eyes which seemed to stare into the vast distances of the Arctic, moving with the lonely wind, searching for her husband.

Ruben came in. He glanced at Adam. 'I couldn't wait any longer.' His mother felt his tears as he hugged her.

'Tell me about it,' she said quietly but firmly.

'Pa died, that's all thee needs t' know,' protested Adam.

Emma did not miss the glance which passed between her son and his wife. 'Tell me. Spare me nothing. I will not rest until I know what happened to him.'

Adam slowly and deliberately went through the whole episode but his voice faltered more than once when he told her of the decision he had had to make. There was a pleading for forgiveness in his voice as he finished, 'Ma! I killed him! I left him to die!'

271

He dropped to his knees in front of her. Emma looked directly at him. Adam shuddered at the sight of her eyes dimmed with tears which she would not allow to flow. But through the hurt and sadness love for him still shone. 'Adam, thee didn't,' she said softly, and reached out to stroke his cheek with gentle fingers.

'But, Ma, I left him out there!'

Emma bit her lip and glanced down at her hands which she rubbed unconsciously, one against the other. She looked up slowly. 'Thee did what was right. Thee did thy duty as thee saw it. Thee gave thy father time to return. Thee searched. What more could thee do? If thee'd stayed, thee'd have risked a lot more lives and that wouldn't have been right.'

'I know, but it was Pa!'

'Don't reproach thissen, son.' Emma took his hand in hers. 'Don't live with it for the rest of thy life. In fact, not for one moment.' She glanced at her younger son. 'And don't ever blame him, Ruben. This earth is for the living, not the dead. Thee has thy lives to live. Do what thy pa had in mind for thee, Adam. Captain the *Mary Jane*. Keep faith with him. And to do that thee'll have hard decisions to make but thee'll manage. Thee'll never have another as hard as this one.' Her eyes embraced both her sons. 'I love thee both the same as I love him, but I couldn't keep thee from the sea. It's in thy blood as it was in his. I never tried to hold him back even though I knew some day this might happen.'

Adam could say nothing. He just knelt there and loved his mother all the more.

After a while Jenny went to make a drink. 'I'll lay the

272

ship up for winter,' Adam told his mother, 'and we'll stay here and spend it with thee.'

Emma drew herself up indignantly. 'Thee'll do nowt o' sort, Adam Thoresby. There's men dependent on thee for a living. From what thee tells me the catch wasn't good, so all the more reason for thee t' do a winter voyage. It's not good business t' leave the ship idle. And I'm used t' being on my own.' He started to protest but she stopped him. 'No more about it. The ship belongs t' thee and Ruben, it's up t' thee t' make it pay.'

He kissed her.

Sensing that she wanted to be alone, the three young people left the house a few minutes later.

When the door closed, Emma slumped in her chair. The tension she had held in check for the sake of her sons drained from her, leaving her feeling weak and helpless. The dread she had always held in her heart, unknown to anyone, had materialised, but now it gripped tighter with chilling fingers. Seth was lost in the Arctic. He would never come home again. Silent tears flowed and loneliness closed over her like an icy sea.

As David left the *Mary Jane*, he paused and looked back at her resting peacefully at the quayside. She bore no marks of the trials she had been through and the tragedies she had witnessed. She lay there as if she had come back from a successful and happy voyage. But David knew that an era had ended. He had no doubt that Adam would make a fine captain, that he would be as successful as his father, but he would stamp his own personality on the ship; it would be no worse for that, probably better, but life on board the *Mary Jane* would never be the same.

Ruth turned from the food she was preparing when she heard the front door close. She was wiping her hands on a towel when David came into the kitchen.

He held out his arms, seeking comfort and love.

Ruth flung herself into his arms. This was the real homecoming. Their lips met, eager and demanding. Her body was soft and yielding as she thrilled to the feel of his strength and power. She leaned backwards against his arms, arching her body, adding temptation to its softness as David moulded himself against her to prolong the kiss.

'It's been so long,' he whispered hoarsely as their lips parted.

'Too long, David. I was so worried.'

'It was a bad voyage.' He shuddered.

Ruth clasped him hard. 'I'll make you forget,' she whispered close to his ear, and as her hand smoothed the hair on his neck, her lips sought his again. 'I need you. Oh, I've missed you so much.'

'Ruth?' David broke the silence of contentment as his wife lay in his arms. 'Why were thee preparing all that food?'

'I thought you hadn't noticed.' Ruth twisted so that she could look into his eyes. She smiled and kissed him lightly. 'We've visitors this evening.'

'Who?'

'Hesther and Frank Watson.' She ran her fingers sensuously down his chest when she saw him begin to frown at the intrusion on his first night home. 'I hope you don't mind but I've had it arranged for some time. It's for both of us.'

'In what way?'

Ruth lay on her back. Her dark hair spilled across the pillow, heightening the white of the cotton. There was laughter on her lips and a teasing sparkle in her eyes.

'Kiss me first,' she said.

David leaned down and gave her a quick kiss. 'Now the answers,' he demanded.

'Oh, David, you can do better than that!' she admonished.

'When I've had the answers.'

'Before.'

David eyed his wife. He grinned in response to the invitation in her eyes. He leaned down and met her lips gently, lingering into firmness and then moving harder until the passion which surged in her swamped him. Her arms encircled him and drew him even closer.

'Do I get to know now?' he gasped when he rolled on to his back.

She turned and propped herself on her elbow. She smiled and nodded. 'I'll tell you as we get dressed.'

David hesitated a second then swung from the bed. 'Well?' he asked, eyeing his wife still snuggled in the feather bed.

Ruth turned back the sheets and stretched, revelling in the effect her nakedness had on David as his eyes devoured her. She slid from the bed and picked up her clothes from the floor where they lay, scattered in her haste to get undressed.

'I thought if I invited them this evening we might be asked back, then we'll meet people who'll invest in our future,' she explained as she dressed.

'Don't thee think we should put them off after what's happened?' suggested David.

'No,' replied Ruth firmly. 'We can't do that at the last minute. I've everything ready.' She eyed him seriously. 'Davey, I know how badly you must feel about Seth, but life has to go on. Don't you realise, you'll be made harpooner now? The sooner people know this and that you intend to be a captain, the sooner they'll be interested in taking shares in a whaleship.'

David frowned as the memory of Seth's tragic end flooded his mind. Somehow it didn't seem right to anticipate promotion on the death of a man who had given him his start in the whale trade.

Ruth grasped him by the arms and stared deep into his mind. 'Davey, you can't live in the past,' she said forcefully. 'You must look to the future, no matter what. It's our chance and we must take it. We want the same thing, don't we?'

He nodded. 'Yes.'

She kissed him. 'Then let's take the chances when we can.'

'Bad business about Seth Thoresby,' commented Frank Watson once greetings had been exchanged and they had settled down with glasses of wine which David had served.

'Terrible,' he replied, grimacing at the memory. 'It was a shock to the crew.'

'A shock to all Whitby,' said Frank with a nod of his head. 'A likeable man and a talented whaler.'

'Aye,' confirmed David. 'I've learned a lot sailing with him.'

'I suppose Adam will take command.' Frank sipped his wine and pursed his lips in approval as he studied the liquid in his glass.

'I expect so,' agreed David. 'He has a lot to live up to, but he'll make a good captain.'

'Could mean promotion to harpooner for David,' Ruth put in, her voice touched with excitement.

David smiled as Frank and Hesther offered their congratulations. 'Nothing has been said. Ruth's being a bit premature, but I suppose, with a harpooner short, it is a possibility.'

'You'll soon be a captain,' observed Hesther, accepting a savoury biscuit from the plate offered by Ruth. 'Your wife's told me that you're interested in having your own ship.'

David and Ruth exchanged glances. 'Aye, that's what we'd like,' said David enthusiastically.

'I think he'll be ready after two voyages as harpooner,' said Ruth, smoothing her dress.

'I'm pleased to see two young people with ambitions,' said Frank, with an approving inclination of his head. 'Don't forget it's timber I'm interested in when you get that far.'

'What about an investment in a new whaleship?' asked David, judging the moment right to put the query.

Frank smiled. 'You putting a proposal?'

'Not at this moment,' returned David. 'But possibly in the future.'

'Well, I might be.' Frank pursed his lips thoughtfully.

'Good,' said David, rising to his feet. 'More wine?'

'Please,' said Frank.

David took his glass and also refilled Hesther's who congratulated Ruth on her choice of wine.

The evening passed pleasantly and David seized the chance to learn more about Frank's timber business and his requirements. They discussed the whaling trade and its future and David felt he had found a man who would not be averse to an investment in shipping.

'We've had a very pleasant evening,' said Hesther as they were getting ready to leave. 'And an excellent meal.'

'Indeed.' Frank beamed. 'And a most interesting talk. Look here, David,' he went on, 'we're having a few friends to an evening meal two weeks today. You and Ruth must come.'

'Can't,' said David, 'I'll be sailing to Memel.'

'Oh, that's too bad. What about you, Ruth?' Frank turned to her. 'I'll only be too glad to come and escort you. They are a few business friends. You might make some useful connections for the future.'

She glanced at David, seeking his opinion, knowing he would give his approval, for she was sure that he would not miss the chance to build on this opportunity.

'Thee gan, dear, thee'll enjoy it,' he said.

'Now that your husband approves, you can't refuse,' said Frank with a smile.

'Very well,' she replied with a slight bow of her head. 'I'll be delighted to accept your invitation.'

After they had seen the Watsons out, David watched Ruth whirl round in ecstatic delight.

'We've done it, David! We've got the invitation we wanted!'

As he gazed at his wife hugging herself with joy, David was aware once again of how much she had changed. The girl who had been kept down by her step-father was but a memory. Now there was a self-assured young woman, one with a vision of the future and a determination to attain her dreams. Far-reaching ambitions had replaced the simple wish to marry David and be a farm labourer's wife. Her voice was more cultured; the thick Yorkshire accent had disappeared. Good clothes had replaced the tattered rags. David was surprised at the taste she had cultivated. It must have been there all the time – inherited from her father. So much change. He liked it, but was he losing the Ruth with whom he had fallen in love? He frowned at the doubt which had crept into his mind. It vanished when Ruth flung her arms round his neck. She tilted back her head and filled the room with laughter.

'Pleased, David?' she asked.

'What do you think?' He laughed with her as he held her tightly. 'Now we might get the connections we want. It's up to thee, Ruth.'

'I won't let you down,' she promised. 'Just you see that you get that job as harpooner. And, David, please try and speak with less of an accent.' She saw protests rising on his lips and, wanting no argument to mar the pleasure she felt, swamped them with a kiss. 'Let's celebrate in the best way we know,' she whispered tantalisingly and led him upstairs.

Chapter Eighteen

Ruth hummed happily to herself as she prepared to go to the Watsons' party. She slipped the chemise over her head and smoothed it across her breasts before running her hands down her sides and over the curves of her hips. She still delighted in the sensuous touch of the cloth against her body, driving away the memories of the days when she'd had nothing but filthy rags.

Those days were gone and ahead lay times of fine clothes, an elegant house, of riches built on a thriving business in the whale trade. Tonight could be an important step on that road. She wished David had been here, but, with his winter voyages on top of the whaling season, she had got used to the partings and being without him. He was gaining all the experience he could – an important factor for the future, she had reminded herself, until it became a matter of course for him to be absent. All the same, it would have been advantageous for him to be able to talk to the menfolk tonight.

But that was not to be. Ruth tilted her head determinedly.

She would do it. It was vital that these opportunities were not missed.

She slipped into her petticoat and chose the green striped poplin dress which fell away from the waist to the heel, leaving the paler-green, quilted petticoat showing at the front. She chose the cream lace fichu which David had given her for her birthday and decided to wear her red duffel cloak, for it would be chilly when she returned home.

'You look charming, my dear.' When he called for her, Frank Watson's praise came not only from his lips but also from his eyes.

'Thank you.' She returned his smile.

'There'll be more than one young beau with his eyes on you tonight.' Frank chuckled.

'Flatterer.' Ruth smiled coyly as he held out her cloak.

She slipped it round her shoulders and fastened the clasp at the neck. 'Right, shall we go?'

Frank answered her question with a slight bow and opened the front door.

Ruth stepped outside. 'My, the nights are drawing in.'

'Aye, they are,' agreed Frank as he tested the security of the door and then fell into step beside her. 'It's time we had street lights. It's been talked about long enough. You wouldn't think this was a thriving whaling port with plenty of oil. That husband of yours should do well in the whaling trade.'

'So you really are interested in whaling?' Ruth's feigned surprise led Frank on, as she had intended.

'Well, I'm interested in anything which might be a good investment,' he replied. 'Since visiting you, I've done

281

some checking. A man's character and ability soon come out in the hard school of whaling, and the whaling fraternity have a high opinion of David. That's not easily come by, I can tell you. They're pretty shrewd and cautious in their judgements.' He took Ruth's arm and guided her past some water-filled holes in the roadway. 'You know,' he went on, 'if David becomes a captain, in two years' time, we ought to have a whaleship ready for him.'

'We?'

'Aye. I'm keen to have a share, and there are others you'll meet tonight who could be interested, now David's more than likely to be a harpooner.'

Ruth smiled to herself. She felt pleased with the way things were turning out. Frank dismissed two beggars who pestered them and warded off a drunken sailor who would have lurched into Ruth as he gave her a leering look. Three urchins ran in a circle round them but made off when they reached the bridge.

'We used to live in Henrietta Street until two years ago. Then this property became available so we moved across the river,' said Frank as they turned into the garden of a house at the lower end of Bagdale.

'And you like it here?' queried Ruth.

'Oh, yes. A much nicer house. Mind you, there's some good property in Henrietta Street but this house is more spacious and we have a garden. A pleasanter situation altogether. It's away from the overcrowding. It's surprising how many people there are in those yards off Church Street. Merchants, ship owners, shipbuilders and captains are moving to this area. Maybe you'll think about it one day.'

'Maybe,' replied Ruth, keeping secret that this had always been in their minds.

Her determination to have a home in Bagdale soon strengthened when she saw the inside of the house. The spaciousness was more noticeable after the restricted confines of their house on Henrietta Street, pleasant though it was.

Hesther hurried into the hall on hearing the front door open. She greeted Ruth with a warm smile and kissed her on each cheek. 'So delighted to see you, Ruth. A pity David couldn't be here.'

She shrugged her shoulders. 'Can't be helped, but I'm pleased I could come. Thank you for asking me.' Ruth swung the cloak from her shoulders and handed it to the maid-servant who stood shyly at the foot of the stairs which soared upwards in a graceful curve.

'What a delightful dress,' Hesther commented as she eyed Ruth with approval. She was pleased that she had taken that extra care, knowing that it was important for her to create a good impression.

'Thank you,' she retuned. 'But yours makes mine pale into insignificance. I do like that colour.' She admired the blue touched with white flecks, soft as a summer sky pricked by tiny clouds. The tulle which rippled over it added an enchanting mistiness.

Hesther inclined her head in acknowledgement of the compliment. 'Come and meet my other guests. Most of the ladies you'll know from our tea parties, but you'll not know the menfolk.' She led the way to a door on the right of the hall.

As she followed, Ruth savoured the spicy freshness of

the wax polish which mingled with the tang of the pot-pourri in the decorated bowl on the highly polished table to one side of the parlour door.

Oil lamps held by metal brackets cast a warm glow around the high-ceilinged room. The flower-patterned wallpaper mellowed the white-painted woodwork. The furniture revealed that the Watsons had an eye for pieces which not only complemented each other but were also a sound investment. A gentle fragrance emanated from the bowls of pot-pourri on gilded sidetables, while the flickering firelight sparkled on the glasses held by the guests, enjoying a glass of Madeira while exchanging the latest news and comment.

Ruth revelled in the atmosphere of well-being and elegance. There was a sense of richness, of money and all that went with it. Though she could not compete on equal terms at the moment, she felt no sense of being out of place. It was as if somewhere deep inside her she knew exactly how to conduct herself in such surroundings. She had no qualms about moving in this select society. The confidence gave her an air of assurance which made people notice her with appraising eyes. This was the life she should have had from birth, and now she was determined never to let it slip from her again.

'Rhoda, dear, may I interrupt for a moment?' Hesther brought Ruth to a couple who were standing to the right of the doorway. Rhoda Shepherd, whose blue poplin evening dress fitted to perfection, smiled charmingly at her hostess and then at Ruth. 'Nice to see you again, Ruth. Peter was just asking me who the young lady was who had just entered the room.'

'Ruth, this is Peter Barrett.' Hesther made the introductions. 'Peter, Ruth Fernley.'

'Charmed, my dear,' said Peter with obvious pleasure.

Ruth saw a small, compact man. His lined face declared him to be somewhere in his seventies, but his eyes were bright and alert, and Ruth knew from the twinkle in them that he still enjoyed the company of ladies.

'Here you are, Ruth.' Frank Watson arrived with a glass of wine which she accepted with thanks. 'Keep in with this young lady, Peter,' he said knowingly, 'she might want you to build her a whaleship one day.'

'Your husband is a whaler, I take it?' said Barrett.

'Peter, the name's Fernley. Don't you remember? Saved Adam Thoresby in the Arctic about five years ago,' said Rhoda.

'Of course.' Barrett grimaced, annoyed with himself for forgetting.

'You can talk later, Peter.' Frank halted the query which he saw was about to come. 'I must introduce Ruth to our other guests.'

He took her to interrupt the discussion between three men about the position of the blubber-boiling yards in relation to the quays where the whaleships deposited their cargoes. 'Ruth Fernley, gentlemen. Daniel Pearson and his son Albert deal in whale products, my dear, so keep the right side of them.' He glanced at father and son as they greeted Ruth and saw the query in their faces at his last remark. 'Ruth's husband might soon be bringing you blubber and whalebone.' He eyed her. 'And when he does don't let them beat you down in price. They drive a hard bargain.'

'Right and proper business, as well you know, Frank,'

returned Daniel, whose rotundity showed that sixty years' love of food had begun to make its mark.

'And we'll look forward to the day when we have such a pretty trader to deal with,' remarked Albert with quiet gallantry. Ruth judged him to be a couple of years younger than herself. His thin features were in contrast to those of his father.

'You'll make a change from the likes of Bill here,' cried Daniel heartily.

'Bill Shepherd, ship owner,' explained Frank.

'I'm delighted to meet you all,' said Ruth. Her smile embraced all three but each was able to take it as if meant only for him. 'If I had your business,' she went on with a knowing look at Daniel, 'I think I'd be pleased to deal with someone like Mr Shepherd.' Her remark held a hidden compliment for the ship owner's proud bearing. Six feet two, he held himself to his full height. His hair, greying at the sides, gave him a distinguished look behind which there was a hard business brain.

'Ah, but we're dealing in a man's world,' said Bill. 'I take it that it will be your husband with whom we deal?'

'Well, that will depend,' replied Ruth, smiling to herself as she wondered what he would have thought of the ragged waif of a few years ago. 'We plan to be in business together. After all, when he's away in the Arctic or on a winter voyage, someone else will have to run the business.'

'But you . . . you're a woman,' said Bill, implying that Ruth would not have the business acumen.

'Does that stop me having a brain as astute as yours?' she countered.

Bill was taken aback by the directness of her question. 'Er . . . no, I suppose not.'

'Well, then, Mr Shepherd, maybe some day we will be rivals.' Ruth pursed her lips coyly. The teasing twinkle in her eyes softened him.

'Rivals? Don't say rivals, let's say friends,' returned Bill with a bow which acknowledged them as equals.

Ruth inclined her head with a smile. 'Of course, it's the only way.'

'I can see I'll have to keep my wits about me when the time comes to deal with you, young lady,' put in Daniel Pearson as he leaned forward with a broad smile and patted her hand. 'But it will be a pleasure. A radical change but one I'm going to look forward to. The sooner the better. When is it likely to be?'

'My husband should be in a position to captain a whaleship after two or three more seasons,' said Ruth. 'Maybe some of you will be interested in having shares in a ship?' She glanced quickly at each in turn.

'Tricky business, whaling.'

'I'll see how your husband gets on.'

'I'm interested in the products, not the ships.'

So the responses came and Ruth knew that she would have to use all her wiles when the time came.

'If it's a new ship you're interested in, then get to know young Matthew Barrett. He designs ships for his father, Peter. Top-class jobs,' said Bill.

The others nodded their agreement.

'Come, I'll introduce you,' said Frank. 'Excuse us,

287

gentlemen.' He took Ruth's arm, and as they moved across the room, added quietly, 'He's talking to Felicity Shepherd, Bill's daughter.'

The introductions cut through the young couple's pleasantries, and Felicity excused herself to question Frank about the chair beside the fireplace.

Ruth judged Matthew Barrett to be about her own age, twenty-four, and saw an elegantly dressed, slim young man whose clothes of the best materials had been tailored to a perfect fit. The colours he had chosen enhanced his dark, smooth hair and pale complexion. His features were handsome, with a set to the chin which gave him a touch of intriguing arrogance – but it was the dark, alert eyes which demanded attention for they defied her not to notice him. Those eyes swept over her, appraising, seeking to approve or disapprove. Ruth felt her body tense with a sense of apprehension. She fought it, for to give way to it would weaken her determination to make this evening a success. And she certainly wasn't going to let this man ruin her chances. She drew herself up and met his gaze. The amusement which flashed into his eyes annoyed her for she knew he had sensed her feelings. His look softened and Ruth realised he approved of what he saw.

'I take it your husband is David Fernley?' Matthew's words were half-statement, half-question.

'Yes,' she replied.

'He's a lucky man,' Matthew commented, dark eyes fixed intently on her. 'I envy him.'

'Really, Mr Barrett, you have no right to assume . . .'

Amused by Ruth's feigned embarrassment, Matthew laughed, cutting her protestations short. 'Come, Ruth – and don't say you object to my using your Christian name. You can't say you aren't flattered by my observations.'

She felt uncomfortable at the way he had read her feelings, and was annoyed with herself for being unable to hide them from this man who ruffled her yet intrigued her.

'Well, really!' She drew herself up with indignation. 'How conceited are you?'

'Maybe you'd like to find out?' Matthew smiled and kept his voice low, then went on quickly to direct the conversation along a different tack before Ruth could answer or turn away. 'Your husband did a brave thing when he saved Thoresby's life.' He paused. 'What, five years ago?'

'You have a good memory,' said Ruth coolly.

'Whitby's a sea-port, it remembers such things,' Matthew reminded her. 'He's got on quickly, very quickly in fact, particularly for someone without the sea in his blood.'

'You seem very well informed,' replied Ruth, curious that he should be interested.

'It often pays to be,' returned Matthew. 'You see, the livelihoods of all of us here depend on the sailor. If it wasn't for him, I wouldn't design ships, my father wouldn't build them, Bill Shepherd wouldn't own them, and Frank would have to be content with English timber. I want to know who's who because among those sailors there could be a potential customer. Oh, I know the majority will not rise above the common riff-raff but there are those who go to sea with ambition. If the sea doesn't break them first, if they can rise above the squalor and horrors, they can achieve their aim. I believe your husband is such a one, and, if he's going to have his own ship, he'll need me.'

'But he could go elsewhere, there are other . . .' Ruth's words were a half-protest at Matthew's presumption.

'Oh, yes, but if he does he won't get the best.' Matthew gave a knowing smile. 'Besides, I don't think you'd let him go to anyone else.'

She stared at him frostily. It was uncanny the way this man seemed to read her. He knew he intrigued her, that she had not met anyone like him before and was fascinated by his manner. She knew he sensed the rebellion in her, that her first inclination was to find some other ship designer, but that the spell he had cast was irresistible.

'Let me get you another glass of Madeira,' Matthew went on, changing the topic before Ruth could reply. He took her glass, moving easily without any sign of hurrying but returning before anyone else could come to talk to her. 'There you are, enjoy your glass of smuggled wine.'

'Smuggled!' Ruth showed surprise.

'Of course. Don't tell me you didn't know.'

'I know smuggling goes on along the coast but I didn't know Frank was involved.'

'Frank's no smuggler.' Matthew laughed. 'He's just a buyer. We all are, though no one will admit it. We wouldn't get so much wine and brandy if we weren't. I'll wager you'll be a buyer before long.' He eyed her with a close look and she was fascinated to know what was coming next. 'I'll also wager you're not upset by a bit of excitement. I'll show you the smugglers at work, if you're interested.'

'You're one of them!' gasped Ruth.

Matthew chuckled. 'Not me. I have too much at stake to get involved in smuggling. But I have my ways of knowing when a cargo's coming ashore. I'll take you to watch.' He paused, trying to read her reaction, but added quickly, 'Of course, nobody must know – and I mean, nobody.' He was careful to emphasise his last word. Again Ruth had the feeling that he knew her as well as she knew herself, for at the mention of smugglers she had experienced an inward excitement. Illicit and dangerous as the trade was, it conjured up daring deeds, adventure and a blow against authority. But more than that it brought back memories of David's escape in Saltersgate on his first journey to Whitby. Her half-brother! Maybe she could learn more about him. Ruth could not deny the temptation of Matthew's offer.

'Hardly a ladylike occupation,' she commented, feigning shock at his suggestion.

Matthew smiled. 'Come, some of you ladies are quite different to the prim and proper exteriors you present to us. Take you, for instance. There were stories circulating among the ladies about your life across the moors. But now I've formed my own opinion.'

'And what would that be?' she queried, trying to hide her eager curiosity.

Matthew paused a moment, tapping his lips thoughtfully with his forefinger as he looked her up and down. 'There may be something in the rumours but I figure that you come from pretty good stock and must have some spirit of adventure to come to an unknown life in a seaport, married to a whaler.' His dark eyes sparkled a challenge. 'And I think you would be interested to watch the smugglers one night.'

Again Ruth felt that her innermost feelings had been

divined. She saw Hesther Watson glance in their direction, make her excuses to the people to whom she was talking and come towards them.

'Well, we shall have to see,' Ruth replied quickly. 'Thank you for the invitation.'

'I hope you are looking after Ruth, Matthew?' Hesther enquired.

'I can assure you he is,' replied Ruth. 'Most entertaining.'

'Well, continue to do so,' said Hesther. 'Please escort Ruth to the dining room.'

'It will be a pleasure, ma'am.' Matthew bowed gracefully to his hostess.

He offered his arm to Ruth and they followed the other guests who had split into pairs.

The meal provided by Hesther brought praise from her friends and the conviviality around the table spread itself over the rest of the evening.

When the time came for the guests to leave, Ruth knew she had been accepted into a new circle of friends and that she had contacts who would prove valuable for any business venture she and David might take in the future.

Ruth was accepting her cloak from a maid and Frank was putting on his coat when Matthew Barrett approached them.

'There's no need for you to turn out, Frank. I'll be only too pleased to escort Ruth,' he said.

'That's kind of you,' replied Frank, 'but it's up to Ruth. After all, I brought her and . . .'

'Well, Ruth, can we save Frank a walk?' Matthew cut in.

Though her mind immediately cried out for her to refuse, she knew she wanted to accept. Besides, Matthew had been careful how he phrased his question. It would be discourteous to take her host out, even though he would willingly fulfil his obligation, when such a thoughtful offer had been made.

'Of course we can,' she replied.

They made their thanks and goodbyes and left the house.

'Take my arm,' suggested Matthew as they stepped into Bagdale. 'The way is rather rough.'

They crossed the bridge to the east side where the narrow streets emphasised the darkness and Ruth was pleased that she had a considerate escort who saw that she reached the house on Henrietta Street without mishap.

'Thank you, kind sir, for your company,' she said with mock gentility.

'My pleasure, ma'am,' he returned in the same vein. 'Doesn't kind sir get the reward of a glass of wine to fortify him on his journey back through those dark and desolate regions?'

'But, sir, I'm a married woman,' replied Ruth with shocked surprise at his unexpected suggestion.

Matthew lowered his voice. 'I will exercise the utmost discretion and the kind lady can be assured that I will be nothing but charming.'

Ruth laughed quietly, opened the door and they went inside. She found the matches which she had left handy for her return and lit the oil lamp.

'Take off your coat and sit down. I'll get you that drink.'

She swung the cloak from her shoulders and dropped it on to a chair as she went to the sideboard on which stood

293

a decanter and some wine glasses. She filled two and turned to find Matthew studying her from the comfort of a Windsor chair. He smiled and expressed his thanks when Ruth handed him the glass.

'Your good health,' he said, raising his glass, 'and good fortune so that I may soon be designing the ship you want.'

'Thank you,' she replied, wondering if he had a deeper interest than the ship. But what matter? She realised he could be most useful in furthering her ambitions and his friendship would be worth cultivating.

During the half-hour he stayed, Matthew was nothing but charm and politeness. When he rose from his chair to go, he said, 'Thank you for a most pleasant evening. No doubt we will meet again on such occasions, but, before then, would you be interested in seeing my father's ship-building yard? You'll get some idea how your future ship will be built.'

'I would love to,' replied Ruth, hiding the excitement which ran through her veins.

'The day after tomorrow? I'll call for you at eleven and maybe you will do me the honour of dining with me afterwards,' suggested Matthew with a graciousness which could not be refused.

Nervous excitement coursed through Ruth as she studied herself in the full-length mirror, making sure that her dress and hair were exactly right.

She had chosen her dark-blue dress, patterned with small white flowers and trimmed with lace. She twirled around and saw that the dress hung gracefully. She raised her head, satisfied that the black ribbon around her neck gave her that extra dignity, while emphasising the V of her dress which ended tantalisingly at the cleavage of her firm breasts. She swung a voluminous pink shawl around her shoulders, allowing it to fall below her waist.

She surveyed herself once more and, satisfied, went downstairs, pondering her reason for accepting Barrett's invitation. Was it interest in the shipbuilding yard? Was it for the contacts he could bring? Was it curiosity about his interest in her, for she felt sure it went deeper than mere business? Or was it really her insatiable inquisitiveness about the man himself? Ruth tried to rein her feelings. Why was she so excited? Why was her heart and mind racing like some lovelorn young girl's? She was a married woman.

The knock almost startled her. She turned and hurried to the door, paused, smoothed her dress and drew in a deep breath. She opened the door to receive a broad smile and courteous bow as Matthew Barrett doffed his hat.

'Good morning, my dear. A splendid day.'

'Good morning,' she returned, her voice low, catching in her throat. 'Come in.'

Matthew stepped past her. She closed the door and when she turned she found his eyes openly assessing her in a way which sent a shiver down her spine, for she sensed he was seeing more than her outward appearance.

'You look charming, my dear. It will be my delight to have you as a companion today.'

'Thank you,' returned Ruth, her cheeks colouring slightly. 'And you look more than elegant,' she added as she admired the sophisticated cut to Matthew's tight velvet coat terminating at the waist where it was carefully tailored into close-fitting tails. His fawn-coloured breeches contrasting with the deep maroon of his coat, fastened over his stocking below the knee. His cravat had been carefully arranged to give it a flounce around the high-necked collar of his shirt. The silver buckles on his sparkling black shoes matched that on his high crowned, black hat which he held in his left hand while his right toyed with a silver-topped amber cane.

David must have clothes like this, thought Ruth. Oh, he was smart enough when dressed for visiting but there was always an air of practicality about him. Here was smartness to catch the eye, to focus attention, and David needed to do that if they were to pursue their ambitions successfully. He must create the right impression. That coupled with his expertise and they were sure to succeed.

Matthew acknowledged her compliment, smiling to himself for he knew she was comparing him to David.

'Will you take a glass of Madeira before we leave?'

'Do you mind if I decline? I have ordered a meal and I want you to see the shipyard before then, so we should be going.'

'Very well. I am in your hands.'

They left the house and Matthew proved an attentive escort as they walked along Church Street and crossed the bridge to the west side of the Esk, where they followed the river, drawing closer and closer to the sound of hammering.

When two partially constructed hulls, sited firmly on their slipways, came into view, Matthew indicated the nearest. 'The Barrett yard,' he said.

'The ship?' asked Ruth.

'Merchantman for a Hull firm,' explained Matthew.

'You build for other ports?' Ruth showed her surprise.

He laughed. 'Of course. Whitby's a thriving port but we couldn't exist on building ships for only this town. Our reputation's good and we'll build for anyone. We've sent ships to London, Shields, Liverpool and Berwick, among others.'

'The other ship?' Ruth indicated the second vessel under construction.

'That's Mulgrave's yard.' Ruth noted a touch of contempt in Matthew's voice. 'Smaller firm. Not as good as Barrett's.'

'Naturally.' Ruth smiled. 'I wouldn't expect them to be.'

'When you want a ship, come to us.' There was a snap to Matthew's words which made Ruth realise that he did not relish the Mulgrave rivalry.

'What sort of a ship are they building?' asked Ruth.

'That one's a whaler.' When he saw a sharpening in Ruth's interest, Matthew went on quickly, 'We do whaleships but it happened that this merchantman was a better proposition. See that splendid keel?' He diverted Ruth's attention away from the Mulgrave yard. 'Best Yorkshire oak. Once that's laid, the stem, sternpost and stern frame are put in place. The floor frames are oak crooks laid athwart the top of the keel.'

'Athwart?' interrupted Ruth.

'Across, from side to side,' replied Matthew, then added with a touch of apology, 'Oh, but I must be boring you.'

'No, no. It's most interesting,' Ruth hastened to reassure him. 'What happens then?'

'The ribs you can see running from stem to stern are shaped and put into position on both sides of the keel. That's the stage we have just finished.'

'And then?'

'The ship is gradually built up in stages.'

'Did you design this one?'

'Yes. Barrett's are ahead of many of the yards in the country in this respect. Though plans have been drawn since late in the sixteenth century, many firms still rely on the eye of the shipwright and his own special working methods and skills in ship construction, handed down from father to son. My father was a visionary. He saw that designing a ship on paper beforehand with exact measurements and details would lead to better ships so he had me trained in the art. So, you see, we offer something special at Barrett's.'

'I'll remember that,' said Ruth with a hint of promise in her voice.

'I hope you do,' said Matthew. 'Maybe I won't let you forget.'

Ruth inclined her head in acknowledgement, wondering what exactly Matthew had in mind.

'Right, if you've seen enough, let me take you to lunch. I see my gig is here.'

Ruth turned to see a gig drawing to a halt at the entrance to the yard. The driver climbed down and held the horse steady while Matthew helped Ruth on to the seat. He swung up beside her, saw that she was comfortable, took the reins and called his thanks. As the man

298

stepped aside, he touched his forehead in respect. Matthew sent the horse forward.

'Where are we going?' Ruth asked.

'The Three Swords, a quiet inn on the outskirts. We'll have a room to ourselves there.' As he spoke, Matthew shot Ruth a glance and was amused at the momentary cast of alarm which crossed her face. 'All perfectly respectable, my dear.'

She settled back to enjoy the ride. The day was fine, the air crisp. It induced a feeling of exhilaration. A smile flickered the corners of her mouth. If only her mother and step-father could see her now. But then, by birthright, wasn't this the life she should always have been used to? Now, having tasted it, she certainly wasn't going to let it go.

As Matthew drew the gig to a halt outside the inn, a boy ran out, steadied the horse and, after Matthew had helped Ruth to the ground, led it and the gig round the back of the building.

'Good day, sir. Good day, ma'am.' The stout, rosy-cheeked woman who hurried from the inn greeted them with a broad smile. The skirt of her dress was covered with a clean, white apron with a bib which fastened over her full breasts. Her hair was tucked inside a flowered mob-cap. 'A pleasure to see you again, sir. Your room is ready.'

'Thank you, Mrs Thompson. I'm sure you have a splendid meal for us.'

Mrs Thompson led the way into the inn and along a white-washed passage. Through the closed door on the left, Ruth heard voices and guessed that they came from the public room. Mrs Thompson opened the second door on the right and stood to one side to allow her visitors to enter.

The room was simply arranged with solid oak furniture. The table in the centre was carefully set for a meal for two. A bowl of punch steamed on a small table beside the fireplace, where a warming fire blazed its welcome.

'Let me take your cloak.' Matthew eased it from Ruth's shoulders and placed it carefully over a chair in the far corner of the room, where he also left his hat and cane. 'Do sit down and warm yourself.' He indicated one of the chairs which had been drawn close to the fire. 'A cup of punch will help.'

'You've gone to a lot of trouble,' commented Ruth as she sat down.

'Not at all,' he replied. 'Mrs Thompson knows my tastes. All I do is send a message to her.'

'I see. So you come here often?' queried Ruth, wondering which other females had fallen for Matthew's sultry charm in this room.

'Only when I want to entertain special friends or customers.'

'Which am I?' said Ruth coyly as she took the cup of punch from Matthew.

'I hope to number you among my special friends. You intrigue me. You're different from other country girls who come to Whitby.' He sat down, with his punch, on the chair at the side of the fireplace.

'In what way?' she asked.

Matthew pursed his lips thoughtfully. 'I might refer to them as country lasses, but you have an air about you which indicates something else.'

'Really?' said Ruth, but offered no explanation to salve his curiosity.

A knock on the door interrupted them. After a moment's pause it opened to admit a slip of a girl, dressed in a thick black dress with white bibbed apron, carrying a tray on which rested a bowl containing soup from which rose an appetising smell.

Ruth drained her punch cup, and, with her head feeling a little lighter, all apprehensions about being here with Matthew Barrett vanished. Such was his contrast to David, the man intrigued her. And he could be useful.

The clear soup was followed by goose cooked to perfection, accompanied by potatoes and savoys. Apple pie was served in the Yorkshire tradition, with cheese, and the whole meal was enhanced by a bottle of fine claret.

As she drank her last drop of claret, Ruth felt a warm, satisfying glow suffuse her body. This had been an excellent meal; the company had been stimulating with Matthew attentive yet not overwhelming, and the conversation had drifted over many aspects of Whitby life. Ruth felt sure that Matthew had led it the way he wanted and that he was really weighing her up. But no matter, she did not mind. She too had learned a lot.

'Enjoy it?' he asked, watching her across the table through narrowed eyes.

'Marvellous,' she replied. 'Nothing could have been better.'

'Nothing?' The teasing, suggestive tone was like a caress.

'I don't know what you mean,' she replied, but her eyes betrayed her pretence at innocence.

'Maybe one day you'll find out.'

'Like the smuggling?' suggested Ruth.

'Exactly. Like the smuggling. I was right, you are interested.' An excited timbre touched his voice.

'Could be. After all, the round of tea parties and listening to the petty prattle gets awfully boring,' said Ruth, wrinkling her nose.

Matthew laughed. 'I can imagine. And I can imagine how those tongues would wag if they could see us now. All right, my dear, if it's excitement you want, the smuggling it shall be.'

When they left the Three Swords, Matthew drove the gig back to the shipyard where the man who had brought it was waiting.

'Sorry, if I'm late, Joe,' said Matthew as he handed over the reins.

'That's all right, sir.'

Matthew escorted Ruth to Henrietta Street and left with a promise not to forget the smuggling.

Four days later, Jenny and Ruth climbed the Church Stairs together.

'It will be good to have them back,' commented Jenny.

'It will,' agreed Ruth. Her words held a deeper meaning than Jenny would ever realise. Although she kept telling herself that she was cultivating a friendship with Matthew to further the ambitions she and David shared, she found pleasure in being in the company of a man who woke in her feelings she had never experienced before. She needed David home again to remind her of their love. 'I hope Adam's first voyage as captain has been successful.'

'I hope so too,' said Jenny. 'He'll have missed his father.'

They turned into the churchyard to take the path by the edge of the cliff. Stone markers or simple wooden crosses were mute reminders of men on whom the ocean had shown no mercy. Behind lettered names lay unrecorded stories of the women who waited and of children who had never seen their fathers. Poised above the rooftops of the houses reaching up the cliff for room, the graveyard bore a sombre atmosphere, so that people spoke in hushed tones when they used its paths.

'See her?' asked Ruth quietly. As yet she had not learned to identify the set of the *Mary Jane* and relied on Jenny's experienced eyes.

'No.' Jenny shook her head. 'Those ships are too far away. We may as well walk for a while.'

They passed through the wooden gate set in the low stone wall and moved on to the open expanse of the commanding coastline. Ruth tied her bonnet more tightly to her head and Jenny snuggled deeper into the warmth of the red shawl around her shoulders.

'I'm sorry I haven't seen you for a few days,' she went on. 'I've spent a lot of time with Mrs Thoresby.'

'Of course. How is she?'

'Very well. Naturally, she misses Seth, but little Lucy hasn't been very well so she's kept busy.'

'Poor Lucy, she doesn't seem very strong,' said Ruth.

'She's never had good health and the loss of her father was a shock.' Jenny paused, then brightened. 'But now, tell me about the party. Who was there? What did they wear – and what did you have to eat?'

303

Ruth, amused by Jenny's excited curiosity, went on to allay her inquisitiveness without going into details about Matthew Barrett.

Jenny's mind flew back to the days of elegance she had known across the river. Her mother had enjoyed giving parties and Jenny would creep from her bed on to the landing to watch the guests arrive. The ladies in their elaborately trimmed silk gowns, their hair elegantly styled, were accompanied by husbands or their latest beau smart in frock coats, knee-length breeches with matching stockings and shining black leather shoes. And among them all her dear father, so awkwardly out of place, trying to match his wife's effervescent charm. Only one word described her mother on these occasions – beautiful. The years tumbled away as Jenny listened to Ruth.

'Ship owner, shipbuilder, merchants . . . you're moving into a different circle,' mused Jenny.

'You're married to a ship owner,' Ruth pointed out.

'Ah, yes, but a different breed. Adam has no desire to change his lifestyle, and I wouldn't want him to,' commented Jenny.

'Has he no ambitions?' asked Ruth a little disdainfully.

'Not beyond the *Mary Jane*. She fulfils his needs. But I see you have. Don't get too carried away, Ruth,' warned Jenny.

Her mouth compressed with annoyance, stifling the words in her mind: my plans have nothing to do with you, Jenny, so don't poke your nose in.

Jenny had turned her gaze seawards. 'The *Mary Jane*,' she said as she identified the whaleship.

'Which one?' asked Ruth excitedly.

'The nearer of the two.'

From the cheerful and excited signals from Adam and David, as the ship passed into the calm of the river, they knew everything had gone well.

The cargo of timber brought Adam a good profit and he laid off the crew until refitting time early in the new year. Faced with a winter of idleness, David decided to take casual employment on coastal vessels, obtaining Ruth's approval when he pointed out that he would gain valuable experience.

Chapter Nineteen

David hurried through the cold, bleak streets of Whitby's east side. The driving rain, on this dark evening before Christmas Eve, kept most people indoors.

He pulled his coat tighter around him, eased the bag in his hand and hastened to Henrietta Street, thankful to be ashore in time for Christmas. The delay for repairs at Shields had threatened to mar his Christmas and he had wondered if the extra experience of sailing on a coastal vessel was worth it, but ambition burned deep and convinced him it was. Now, he eagerly anticipated his homecoming night.

'It's good to be home,' he said as he relaxed after their evening meal.

'It's good to have you, love,' murmured Ruth. 'We have tomorrow and Christmas Day to ourselves. Boxing Day, Jenny has asked us to spend with them. On New Year's Eve Peter Barrett's giving a party. We're invited.'

'Good,' approved David. 'It'll be nice to be with Jenny and Adam, and the party could be useful.'

They enjoyed the early festivities quietly by themselves, meeting briefly with Adam and Jenny after the Christmas Day service in the church on the cliff top. As they parted, Jenny reminded them that they were to spend the following day together.

'Thee looks as though thee's bursting to tell us something,' commented David, eyeing Adam as his friend handed him a tankard of ale.

He exchanged a glance with Jenny, and Ruth noticed an almost imperceptible nod from her.

'All right.' Adam grinned, his eyes bright with delight at what he was about to say. 'I was going to save it until later but I can't keep it from thee any longer – thee's promoted to harpooner on the next voyage.'

David gasped. For a moment he stared unbelievingly at Adam then cast a quick look at Ruth. She was elated.

'Harpooner!' The culmination of his ambitions on board the *Mary Jane*. The final step before a captaincy. The future beckoned with exciting promise.

'It's what thee wants, isn't it?' asked Adam, smiling at David's bewildered look.

He started. 'Of course. Adam, thee'll never know how grateful I am.' He grasped his friend's hand firmly.

'Just what we wanted,' whispered Ruth as she hugged David.

'I'm so pleased for you, Davey,' said Jenny quietly as she kissed him.

Ruth noted an affectionate look pass between them and pangs of resentment welled inside her, but she held them below the surface and the day passed off pleasantly.

'I'm so proud of you, David,' she said as she lay in his arms later that night. 'This is the real start. People will look up to you. You'll become the best harpooner in Whitby.'

He laughed. 'Hold on. I'll niver be better than Jamaica and Adam.'

'Of course you will,' enthused Ruth. 'Three years and you'll be a captain.'

'And we'll have that house in Bagdale,' he said.

'Do you mean it?'

'Of course. Why not?' Excitement pulsed in his voice. 'We've got to push things if we want to get on. Appearances influence people. We must look the part, and the sooner the better. Folks will be more interested now I'm harpooner, especially if they know we're serious about our own ship. We can start in earnest at Barrett's party.'

'Yes, but discreetly,' cautioned Ruth. 'After all, it's New Year's Eve.'

The New Year's Eve party at Peter Barrett's was a joyful, boisterous occasion, with Ruth and David taking advantage of the gathering to cement friendships and to create new ones with people they had never met before.

In the midst of the revelling, as midnight struck, Matthew gave Ruth a special kiss which tempted her to wish David was doing another coastal voyage before he sailed again to the Arctic.

But that moment of wishful thinking was banished as she and David walked home. The sky was clear, pricked by a myriad of flickering stars. The air was sharp, invigorating, creating a sense of well-being after the warmth of the food and drink. Ruth snuggled closer to David as his arm came round her shoulder. Revellers, still roamed the streets, happily calling their New Year's greetings.

'It's been a good evening,' commented Ruth. 'But, David, I do wish you'd try to improve your speech.'

'Folks taks me as they find me,' he rasped. 'Nobody bothered tonight.'

'No, but . . .'

'It was easier for thee with thy background,' he cut in.

'I had to work hard at it, and so could you.'

'Have thee met the Humphries before?' asked David, deliberately changing the subject.

'No,' said Ruth. 'They seem a nice family.'

'Robert Humphries is a lot older than I expected,' mused David.

'I believe he's about thirty years older than his wife. He met her in London. I'm told her family were against the marriage – a man old enough to be her father from the wilds of the north. You know how it would be.'

'But Sarah defied her family for the man she loved. Good for her. I liked her,' said David. 'And Melissa and James seemed friendly enough. Could be a family who'd be interested in investing with us. Get their backing and the others would follow.'

The *Mary Jane* sailed on the last day of February.

'As thee's the new harpooner, thee can have first choice of boat-steerer,' Adam informed David, as they sailed from the Shetlands.

David thought the matter over carefully. The skill of the boat-steerer was vital to the success of the crew. Without his deft manoeuvring and anticipation of the whale's tactics, the harpooner might never get a good throw.

'I'll have Jim Talbot.'

Adam was surprised. 'Don't thee want someone with more experience?'

'Nay. I saw Jim handle a boat on the last voyage, when one of the regular boat-steerers was ill, and from what I saw, he's good enough for me. We'll both be new together. We can strike up an understanding without one of us being more experienced than the other.'

'Could work out,' agreed Adam.

David's judgement proved to be correct. Right from the start, each man seemed to know what the other one wanted.

Jim was a big, strong man who took to the work on the long steering oar with ease. He was a quiet man who kept very much to himself, yet David knew that the rest of the crew respected him. He talked very little about himself, appearing rather withdrawn, and David understood the reason when he learned from Adam that Jim had lost his wife and two children of the fever ten years ago. He had taken to drink to try to forget but found it only made matters worse. Giving it up completely, he returned to his only other interest, the sea, and now found contentment only in his work.

Jim was grateful to David for this chance. They learned the skills quickly and, after a number of abortive attempts, finally got two whales. David was the first to acknowledge Jim's skill in bringing the boat on to the whale without scaring it away, so making his throw easier. Jim, for his part, recognised David's aptness with the harpoon and skilful handling of the lance, as well as his able command of the boatcrew.

After only a fortnight in the Arctic, the crew knew that the son had inherited the father's skill and knack for finding whales. They still sailed with a 'Lucky' Thoresby.

As he sailed the far north, Adam felt near his father. He felt the soft touch of the lonely wind and knew Seth was there, sailing the *Mary Jane*, watching over his son.

The weather remained good and the ship was full by the second week in July. With the wind filling the sails, a triumphant *Mary Jane* cleaved through the friendly sea, sending spray curving from her bow as she hastened home. Adam looked back to the mysterious light in the north, knowing that he had kept faith with his father. Silently he made his farewell to the man who had taught him so much about the way of the whale. Now he would be his own man.

With bone at the mast-head, the *Mary Jane* received a rapturous welcome from the Whitby folk who were pleased that Adam had taken over his father's role successfully. Jenny, thrilled and excited by the sight, felt happy for Adam. He had achieved the high standards set by his father. Ruth was also roused by the knowledge that the voyage had been successful and wondered how many whales David had taken.

As the *Mary Jane* moved from the sea to the shelter of the river, Ruth and Jenny hurried from the cliff top, and paused briefly at the church to offer up their prayer of thanks for the crew's safe return. Coming back to the bright sunlight they moved quickly down the Church Stairs, through the narrow streets to the quay.

Adam and David had seen the recognisable shawls waved from the cliff top and, with ropes creaking and timbers protesting as the *Mary Jane* was successfully manoeuvred to the quayside, they searched the crowds for their wives. Once the gangway was run out, Adam was soon exchanging lover's greetings with his wife, and David was sweeping Ruth into his arms with the intensity brought about by five months' parting.

'I missed thee, love,' he whispered.

'And I missed you,' she replied, her voice vibrant with desire. She leaned back in his arms and looked at him. 'Successful?' she asked.

'I got two!'

'Thee should be proud of him,' called Adam. 'He did well.'

Ruth, delighted at the praise, smiled broadly. 'I knew he could do it.'

Chapter Twenty

After the winter voyage to Memel, David once again chose to spend the time before Christmas on a coastal vessel.

The ship on which he sailed was barely a day out of Whitby when Ruth answered a knock on the door of the house in Henrietta Street.

'Good day, Ruth.' Matthew bowed politely. Seeing her surprise, amusement turned up the corners of his mouth.

'Matthew, what . . . ?' The words were stuttered with shock, but Ruth's heart raced faster. He had occupied her thoughts more than once since their last meeting, and she had wondered about the insinuations behind his remarks. 'What are you doing here?' she added in confusion.

'Invite me in and you'll find out,' he replied. 'We can hardly conduct a discussion here.'

'Oh, of course.' Ruth stepped to one side, embarrassed that she had not made the invitation first. Her thoughts were in turmoil as she closed the door. Was it coincidence that he was here so soon after David's departure?

'The last time we parted I promised you I would not forget the smuggling. I hope you're still inclined to share the experience with me,' he said as they entered the parlour.

Ruth stared at him. 'You mean . . . ?'

'We will be able to watch them tonight.'

'Tonight! But . . . I . . .' Ruth was taken aback by the way Matthew had precipitated events.

'I have word that there'll be contraband run ashore near Sandsend. With your husband away, I thought this a good opportunity. He need never know of his wife's adventures.' Matthew's eyes challenged her to share the risk with him – and something else.

The blood pounded in Ruth's head. Something urged her to be cautious, but her heart cried out for her to share this experience with a man who intrigued her even more each time they met.

'Tonight?' pressed Matthew.

Ruth hesitated.

'Don't tell me you've changed your mind,' he went on. 'I can see you're excited by the prospect, so why hesitate? No one need ever know.'

'Very well.'

'I knew I wasn't mistaken in you. Do you ride?'

'I'll manage,' she replied.

The odd occasion she had ridden, when Kit Fernley had been in charge of one of the squire's horses, she had experienced an uncanny empathy with the animal. It was as if she had been born to ride. Now she knew she must

314

have inherited her natural ability from her father. With Matthew's invitation, she would look forward to being in the saddle again, riding alongside him on an adventure which might lead . . . who knew where?

'Good. I'll call for you at nine.' He broke in on her racing thoughts. 'Wrap up well. It could be a cold vigil. I'll arrange the necessary horses.' Ruth started to thank him but he stopped her. 'Save that for afterwards.'

He left, and, overwhelmed by what she had agreed to do, Ruth flopped into a chair. It was foolish, stupid. it might have dire consequences if they were seen. What if David got to know? But the more she thought about it, the more the risks added to the thrill. She knew she would not withdraw from the night's escapade.

At nine o'clock, a quiet knock took Ruth hurrying to the door. Matthew stepped quickly inside. He wore a long cloak and his wide-brimmed hat was pulled low over his eyes.

'Your cloak?' he said. 'We leave immediately.'

Ruth swung her woollen cloak around her shoulders, tied it at the throat and pulled its hood over her head.

Matthew nodded his approval, opened the door and glanced outside. He signalled to her and stepped into the street. She followed, locked the door and, pulling on her gloves, fell into step beside him. He took her arm as they hurried along the darkened roadway to Church Street.

'I've got two horses waiting at the White Horse,' he whispered. 'A good tip ensures the landlord's silence. Pull your scarf over the lower half of your face just in case we meet anyone who might recognise us.'

They reached the entrance to the White Horse yard. 'Wait here,' he whispered and hurried across the cobble stones, leaving her standing in the shadows at the corner of the building.

Nervous doubts began to fill Ruth's mind. Why had she come on such a foolhardy mission? There was still time to back down. Should she? Did she really want to? She licked her dry lips and her scarf inched down her face. She wished Matthew would hurry. The sound of footsteps startled her. A shadowy figure came nearer. Ruth wished she could lose herself in the darkness. She drew away, her back hard against the wall. Then the stranger was close, almost brushing her, before he realised someone was standing there.

'Beg pardon.' The man sounded surprised to encounter a solitary woman at this time of night. Ruth recognised the voice and froze. Adam Thoresby! His steps faltered but then he moved on without another word.

She trembled. Had Adam recognised her? The footsteps stopped. Panic gripped her. Where could she go? What could she do? Oh, why had she come? So stupid, and to end like this before it had begun. Clogs clattered on the stones. He was coming back! Oh, my God, what would she say? Ruth tensed. Had her ears deceived her? Was the clip of Adam's footsteps getting fainter? She stared into the gloom. Nothing, only the sound of fading footsteps.

The clop of horses' hooves across the yard broke into her numbed mind. She turned quickly and, as Matthew came close to her, he sensed her unease.

'Something wrong?' he asked.

316

'Adam Thoresby almost bumped into me.' Alarm touched her voice.

'Did he recognise you?' asked Matthew anxiously.

'I don't know. He didn't greet me,' said Ruth hoarsely.

'Good. He would have done if he'd known it was you,' Matthew reassured her.

'Maybe. I expect he's been to his mother's, his sister isn't well,' said Ruth, a nervous tremor still in her voice. 'Why did he have to come along now?' she added with irritation.

'Don't worry,' whispered Matthew soothingly. 'Come on, let me help you on to your horse.'

Once she was in the saddle, all anxiety left Ruth. It was good to feel the strength of muscle and flesh beneath her. As she settled down, she sensed all momentary suspicion leave her mount and knew they would move as one tonight.

They rode towards the bridge and, as they left the confines of the buildings, the half moon flirted with the scudding clouds and sent its reflection shimmering in the water.

Gaining the top of the west cliff, Matthew drew his horse to a halt and Ruth steadied her mount alongside him.

'You amaze me, woman,' he said, eyeing her with admiration. '"I'll manage", you said when I asked you if you rode. The way you sit and handle that horse, you've done a lot of riding. That surprises me if some of the rumours about you are true.'

Ruth smiled. 'Let's leave it at that, shall we?' she said,

instinctively realising that to satisfy Matthew's curiosity would be to end his interest in her.

He held close to the cliff edge for half a mile, where the coast dipped before heightening into gaunt, forbidding cliffs. The long line of white breakers beat the shore before a full running sea.

'See that cutting down there,' he called, pointing towards the shoreline.

A cloud slid from the moon unveiling a stream of light which revealed a break, as if a huge cleaver had struck the coastline.

'Yes.' Her voice was firm and eager.

The clouds cast a shadow across the scene as Matthew turned his head to look at her. The moon once again unveiled its pale light for him to see a face, though half-hidden by a scarf, touched with an allure which he had not seen in her before. She appeared to be at peace with the surroundings and the night, but he sensed the feelings bubbling beneath the surface, a craving for excitement and danger with which he instinctively empathised. He reached towards her.

Ruth turned her head and met his gaze. 'Well?' she asked, and the spell which gripped him was broken.

'That's the place where the contraband will be run ashore,' he replied after a moment's hesitation in which their eyes locked and Ruth knew that Matthew intended more than to show her the smugglers.

'Dangerously near Whitby and the Preventive Men, isn't it?' suggested Ruth, her heart beating faster at the desire she read in his eyes.

'Yes, but it's convenient. There's a quick getaway

inland, and the smugglers can soon be in Whitby where the loot can be hidden and they in bed with someone to swear they've been there all the time.'

'Do you know what time the vessel's due?'

'About another hour.'

'Do we watch from here?'

'You'd see little,' Matthew explained. He turned his horse and, followed closely by Ruth, rode away from the cliffs. He held his mount to a walking pace, picking his way across the country with care. Reaching some thickets, he halted his animal and slipped from the saddle.

'We'll leave the horses here,' he said quietly as he helped her down.

Matthew led the two horses among the thickets where he secured them out of sight. While she waited for him to return, the roar of the sea rising over the cliffs and sweeping up the gully drove a thrill of excitement into her.

'Keep close to me,' he whispered.

She felt a gloved hand tighten on hers and Matthew led the way down a narrow path, twisting through the undergrowth along the side of the cutting which deepened as it neared the sea. The pound of the surf grew louder and, as the path followed the curve of the gully, Ruth felt the spray from the breaking waves. A cloud moved from the moon and light skipped across the sea, spilled along the sand and tried to penetrate the darkness of the gully.

The path forked, one branch slanting to the bottom of the cleft which widened as it approached the shore, leaving the undergrowth behind and replacing it with a surface of stones and rocks. The other branch, with a line of stunted gorse bushes along its edge, kept to the side of the gully about twenty feet above the bottom.

Matthew put his lips close to Ruth's ear. 'Be very careful and be very quiet,' he whispered, making his words clear and decisive. 'There'll be smugglers at the end of the cleft.'

Ruth nodded and Matthew led the way along the top path. The nearer he got to the sea, the slower he moved until he stopped by the last gorse bush. As he squatted, Ruth crouched beside him. Again he came close to her. 'The path ends ten yards further on, above the shore. You'll see everything from there but you'll have to crawl. All right?'

With no thought for her clothes, Ruth nodded. Matthew lowered himself on to his stomach and started to crawl forward. Ruth followed him closely, glad that she had put on her thickest skirt and knee-length boots. It seemed an age before the shape in front of her stopped. She glanced up. Matthew waved her forward. She moved alongside him and saw that they were above a sheer drop of twenty feet to the sand while on their left the rough gully side sloped steeply away from them.

Ruth shivered. Matthew slid closer to her. They lay for ten minutes, watching and waiting, dampened by the spray sweeping over them. Two clouds left the moon and the whole seascape was bathed in a pale, white light.

Matthew stiffened. 'There!' he whispered, and pointed seawards. Beyond the cliff a darker silhouette appeared and moved slowly, further and further across their vision, coming closer to the shore as it did so.

An owl hooted from the opposite side of the cleft. 'A

signal from their lookout that he's made a sighting,' whispered Matthew. 'The ship's a Staithes yacker.'

Ruth was tense. Out at sea a light flashed. Glancing down to the shore, she saw a lantern being swung to and fro in reply. A light on the yacker flashed again.

'The yacker will have taken the contraband from a ship which can't get close enough to the shore,' whispered Matthew. 'Now they're in as far as they dare come. They'll bring the goods ashore by boat.' Figures moved away from the shadows of the land and emerged on to the open shore, bathed in moonlight. They hurried towards the breakers.

'Some of them are women,' gasped Ruth when she saw the long skirts.

'Yes,' replied Matthew. 'Brandy and gin come in bladders which are fixed to hooks on a strong leather belt worn by the women round their waists, beneath their skirts. No self-respecting Preventive Man would ask a woman to lift up her skirts,' he added with amusement.

Ruth chuckled. Figures waited close to the sea. Her eyes strained to locate the boat from the yacker but she saw only the rolling waves. Suddenly it was there, high on a foaming wave beating in towards the shore. It seemed it would be smashed to pieces but, skilfully handled, it ground into the sand. Immediately all was activity. The figures on the shore grabbed cargo from those in the boat. Men carrying small barrels on their shoulders moved quickly up the beach. Larger barrels were rolled towards the dark cleft, while other men carried bladders to the women. Once the last item of contraband was ashore, all the men pushed the boat into the waves which tried to throw it back. Then the oars were out and the boat was away, hauling hard for the yacker. The beach was cleared of the remaining barrels and the women moved off along the sand in the direction of Whitby.

'There will be three more landings,' Matthew informed Ruth. 'The bladders have been brought on the first one so that the women can get away.'

'What happens to the rest of it?' asked Ruth.

'It'll be hidden in various places close by and moved when convenient.'

'Is that the leader, directing operations on the beach?' asked Ruth, curious to know if she was watching her half-brother.

'No,' Matthew gave a low chuckle. 'That'll be Jethro Thompson. He's in charge for tonight. You won't find the leaders of the smuggling fraternity here. They're respected landed gentry.'

'You know them?' quizzed Ruth.

'No, and I don't want to,' replied Matthew, a warning note coming to his voice. 'Could be more than my life's worth. 'And don't you forget it,' he added, trying to dampen Ruth's curiosity.

Knowing it was no use pressing the matter, Ruth hid her disappointment but firmed her secret resolve to learn more about her half-brother's activities.

They watched two more cargoes run ashore, then Matthew whispered, 'We must go. After the next one the smugglers will be moving inland up the gully. We must be away before then. You've seen enough?'

Ruth nodded and took one last look at the sea pounding the beach around the smugglers before following

Matthew. She was so close to him that when he stopped suddenly she bumped into him. He turned quickly and in the same movement grabbed her, his right hand coming across her mouth to stifle the question he knew was imminent. He held her stiffly, hardly daring to breathe. A faint noise came from the path leading into the gully and Ruth saw five shadowy forms running downwards. Matthew suddenly released his hold and struck out hard and sure. A man, hurrying along the path, was sent crashing down the slope.

'Run!' yelled Matthew, grabbing Ruth's hand. The victim of Matthew's punch might, with luck, be the last of the Preventive party, sent to the vantage point he and Ruth had so recently occupied while the others went to tackle the smugglers below. If not, he and Ruth could be in trouble.

Luck was with them and they were in full flight when pandemonium broke out behind them. They were lost in the darkness when two shots crashed above the roar of the sea.

Ruth had no time to be frightened as she followed Matthew blindly. He stormed through the undergrowth, dragging her with him. Bushes tore at their clothes but Matthew pressed relentlessly upwards. Breathing hard, Ruth drove her legs on, knowing that a wrong step or a slackening of speed would leave her at the mercy of the men who pursued them. Suddenly they burst over the edge of the gully on to open ground.

'Over there,' yelled Matthew, turning towards the thickets where they had left the horses. 'Keep coming. I'll get the horses.' He let go of her hand and lengthened his stride.

Ruth instinctively tried to keep pace with him. Her face strained in desperation, her breasts heaved with the exertion, but it was no use, she could not keep up. Matthew disappeared into the thickets. She glanced back anxiously and the moon revealed a shadowy form emerging from the gully. Fear seized her. Oh, God. Where was Matthew? Why didn't he come? Time stood still and the thickets got no nearer. Her pursuer was gaining. Her mind panicked.

Matthew burst into the open with the horses and Ruth felt his firm grip helping her into the saddle. She grasped the reins as he slapped her horse on the rump. The animal leaped forward and stretched into a gallop. The wind caught at her. She steadied herself and settled in the saddle.

A shot rang out and then another. Anxious about Matthew, she glanced over her shoulder and was relieved to see him, crouched low on the animal's back, close behind her. He drew alongside.

She leaned low, moving in unison with the horse. She thrilled to the power she controlled. Excitement permeated the exhilarating gallop, banishing the fear which had held her but a few minutes ago. Her mind was heady with the pounding of thrumming hooves and she was only half-aware of Matthew alongside her.

'Slow down!' A shout reached her. 'Slow down!' She glanced across at Matthew who signalled to her. 'We're safe now.'

Ruth straightened in the saddle as she gradually slowed her horse's pace. Matthew turned closer to the path near the cliff edge, and, by the time they reached it, they had both animals at a gentle gait.

'We gave the Preventive Men something to think about.' He grinned.

'But what if we were recognised?' she asked in concern.

'We wouldn't be,' replied Matthew. 'Nobody was near enough except the man I hit and he didn't have time to identify us.'

'I hope you're right,' said Ruth. 'What do we do now?'

'We ride calmly into Whitby, take the horses back, go home and say nothing.'

'But what about the innkeeper? He might guess when he hears that two people escaped on horseback,' Ruth pointed out.

'He might. But he doesn't know for whom I hired the second horse. He won't talk. I made it worth his while. Besides, he gets most of his spirits from the smugglers. Well, Ruth, did you enjoy your adventure?'

Her rapturous laughter splintered the night air. Enjoyed? The word wasn't strong enough. This night had been thrilling. The secretive vigil, the brush with the Preventive Men, the chase and the escape had culminated in a magnificent ride on a powerful animal whose strength had been her strength.

She tipped the hood from her head and ran her fingers through her hair, allowing the moonlight to touch the copper with silver. At that moment, she caught the admiring look in Matthew's eyes and knew she held him in her power. She revelled in the feeling.

'Wait here,' he instructed as he helped her from the saddle at the entrance to the White Horse.

Ruth merged into the shadows as Matthew led the horses away, the clop of their hooves diminishing until there was silence. Ruth shivered. Recalling the brush with Adam, she glanced about her anxiously. Nothing stirred along the street. Whitby appeared to be asleep. She hoped Matthew would not be long. Suddenly she started and almost cried out when she felt a scurrying near her feet. The moonlight, which trickled between the roofs and spilled into the street, caught a rat slinking across the roadway on its nightly prowl. Ruth shuddered and stared at the horror, hoping it wouldn't return.

Footsteps! Her heart pounded. Then she realised they were coming from the inn yard. A moment later Matthew was beside her. He took hold of her arm and hurried her towards Henrietta Street. Neither spoke and they were both breathing heavily when Ruth opened the front door. Once inside she found the matches and lit the candle she had left on the table beside the door. She led the way into the room, lit the oil lamp, and with a sigh of relief turned to face Matthew. Their eyes met and held as the tension of the chase drained out of them and was replaced by a compelling attraction.

Matthew stepped forward, his dark eyes flashing with desire. He untied Ruth's cloak, tossed it on to a chair, spanned her waist with his hands and drew her slowly to him.

All the time his look challenged her to resist, but Ruth did not. She enjoyed the sensation of feeling naked under his devouring stare which stripped her clothes from her. No one had ever looked at her in this way before. Nervous excitement coursed through her.

Matthew's grip tightened and he pulled her sharply to him, his lips seeking hers with fierce passion. Her arms came up around his neck and she arched her body, pressing it close to him, while her lips met his with an equally overpowering fervour.

'Shall we finish this exciting night in the right way?' Ruth's husky words, put with a coy smile, were charged with suggestion and promise as she slipped from his arms. She held out her hand to him as she moved towards the hallway and the stairs.

By the time they reached the bedroom, she had her dress unfastened and in a matter of moments lay naked on the bed watching him shed the last of his garments.

'You're an amazing woman, Ruth Fernley. You know what you want and you'll have it.' Matthew sighed contentedly as they lay still, their passion satisfied. 'If you weren't already married, I'd ask you to marry me.'

Ruth twisted over so she could look down at him. 'You mean that, don't you?' she said, a serious note to her voice.

Matthew nodded.

'There's no reason why we can't pretend to be when my husband's away, at least at nights,' she offered. She wanted to be loved by this man again. He was so different to David. He was gentle, considerate, subtle, with a touch which made her skin feel like silk. But David had a power which charged her with a different ecstasy, and set her whole being aflame. Ruth knew that she needed them both.

'That's an offer I won't refuse,' murmured Matthew and drew her to him again.

* * *

'Tomorrow night?' suggested Ruth as Matthew dressed.

'You want to watch the smugglers again?'

She gave a half-laugh. 'I'm not that reckless. What would David say if he returned home to find his wife under arrest and accused of being a smuggler? No, once is enough.'

'Maybe you'd be interested in other excitements.'

Ruth saw an invitation in his eyes and asked, 'Such as what?'

'I'm not at liberty to say at the moment but we shall see, all in good time. Now I must be off.'

He bade Ruth goodnight and let himself out of the house.

Two days later, Jenny called on Ruth who saw uneasiness in her visitor.

'You're looking pale, Jenny. Are you unwell?' Ruth asked.

'No, I'm all right,' Jenny answered. She paused nervously, then, gathering herself, she went on, 'Ruth, we're friends, our husbands are close. I should hate anything to happen which would upset that friendship.'

She looked at Jenny in surprise. 'What could? What are you talking about?'

Jenny hesitated as if she did not want to go on. She bit her lip, regretting what she had to say. 'Two nights ago you were outside the White Horse. You rode off with someone.'

The statement startled Ruth. She stiffened and knew from the look on Jenny's face that her own expression had confirmed the truth of Jenny's words. She cursed herself. Now it was no use denying the fact.

'What if I was?' she asked haughtily.

'So it was you!' Jenny's intonation revealed the uncertainty that had been in her mind.

Ruth fumed inwardly. Then she realised she ought to find out exactly how much Jenny knew. '. . . and Adam bumped into someone outside the White Horse. It wasn't until he had gone a few more steps that he thought it might be you. He stopped, thinking you might need help, but then he heard horses coming from the inn yard. He went on but when he glanced back he saw two people riding away.'

Ruth's lips tightened. Why did Adam have to come along at that moment, and that night of all nights? Had he recognised Matthew? Near panic seized her but then she realised that Adam had passed the White Horse; he would have seen only Matthew's back cloaked by the darkness. He could not know with whom she rode.

'So?' she asked defiantly. 'What business is it of yours?' Her eyes sparked fire as they stared at Jenny and left her in no doubt that Ruth would fight to keep a clear name if there was any attempt to reveal her secret.

'None, I suppose, but I . . .'

'Then don't be inquisitive!' cut in Ruth harshly.

Jenny met her smouldering gaze. 'I'm not,' she retorted angrily. 'I don't want to know who you were with, but at that time of night it was hardly likely to be a female! And that's what bothers me.'

Ruth bristled. 'It could have been,' she retorted, hoping to throw Jenny's suspicions.

She gave a little laugh of contempt and shook her head. 'No, Ruth, no. Don't take me for a fool, and don't be a fool yourself. You've a good man for a husband.'

'Ah! So it's David you're thinking about, not me.'

Jenny ignored Ruth's remark. 'There are rumours about a clash between the Preventive Men and smugglers the night before last, the night Adam saw you.'

Ruth crossed the room to the window and stared out, trying to hide her nervousness. But unwittingly her right hand plucked at the bangle on her left wrist.

'What rumours?' she prompted.

'The story is that two people escaped on horseback. Now, the smugglers don't normally use horses on this type of operation – that's why the Preventive Men weren't on horseback and this couple were able to make their escape so easily.' Jenny watched her closely. 'Rumour has it that one of the two was a woman!'

Ruth swung round sharply, sweeping her dress behind her with a quick, irritable movement. She glared angrily at Jenny. 'Are you accusing me?' she demanded.

'I couldn't do that without proof,' Jenny pointed out. But Ruth's attitude had given her away.

'Then why all this?' she asked, regarding Jenny balefully.

'I came to warn you of what is being said. If it was you, Ruth, stop it before it's too late! Don't have any more to do with it. It could ruin David.'

'David! David again!' Ruth sneered. 'Your concern for him touches me. Are you in love with him?'

The unexpected question, thrust rapier-like, caught Jenny unawares. 'No! No, not now!' The denial came so swiftly that the words were out before she realised what she had said.

Ruth seized on them. 'Not now! So you were?' Her

330

eyes flamed with jealousy as they demanded an explanation.

Jenny's mind, tortured by the slip she had made, sought relief and there was only one way to find it. Speak the truth. For David's sake, Ruth must understand. 'I was once. I nursed him through his illness. It was only natural that we became close. Yes, I loved him, but . . .'

'And David?' cut in Ruth fiercely.

Jenny hesitated.

'He loved you?' prompted Ruth.

'I said we became close.'

'He loved you!'

'We meant a great deal to each other. It was only natural, thrown together as we were. I still have a great admiration for him and I should hate to see him hurt over something like the smuggling. People talk. It wouldn't be the first time there's been an informer in the smuggling fraternity.' Jenny had moved towards the door as she was speaking. She wanted to finish this conversation which had gone terribly wrong. 'I'll say no more, Ruth. I only came . . .'

'Because of David!' she broke in, finishing the sentence with her own interpretation.

'I'm sorry you've misunderstood my motives,' replied Jenny quietly. She opened the door and was gone before Ruth could pass any more comments.

Her body rigid, Ruth stood staring at the door. 'Bitch!' All her feelings of anger, jealousy and hatred were expressed in that one word. So David and Jenny had been in love? She felt cheated, felt she had shared where she should have been the only one. What of the

331

future? David was hers but . . . A nagging doubt crept into Ruth's mind. A fire could be rekindled! Her jaw tightened. Her eyes narrowed. That bitch wasn't going to provide the tinder. She'd have to be kept at more than arm's length.

Chapter Twenty-one

'I think I'll do another year as harpooner,' said David as he prepared to leave for the Arctic. 'I'll tell Adam I'll sail with him again next year.'

'But why? You've done an extra one already. We said two as a harpooner. Now it will be four.'

'Well, people haven't really been interested in a new whaleship. Maybe they just aren't sure of me yet.'

'But . . .'

'No buts,' he cut in. 'Another year will give us a better chance. Don't look so disappointed, luv, our time will come.'

Ruth smiled wanly. 'Maybe you're right.' She brightened. 'But we'll do it, Davey. Nothing will stop us.'

As she watched the *Mary Jane* sail, she determined that, by the time David returned, her plans would be nearer fruition.

During the summer, while extolling David's prospects, she charmed and persuaded likely investors. She enlisted the help of Matthew with whom a deeper relationship had developed during David's absences. Ruth knew she had a lover and an ally who would serve her well.

Since her disagreement with Jenny, Ruth had seen little of her except when David was at home, and with winter voyages those times were few.

Early in August, they were pleased to see bone at the mast-head when the *Mary Jane* sailed proudly into Whitby.

Once they had greeted their menfolk, Ruth called to Adam, 'Can you spare David now? I have something important to show him.'

Adam could not deny the excitement in Ruth's eyes. 'All right, be off with thee.'

'Thanks, Adam.' She grabbed David's arm and turned him away from the ship. 'Come on, love.'

Bewildered by Ruth's haste, he protested. 'Where are we gannin'?'

'Home.' Her eyes twinkled teasingly.

'What's the surprise?' he puzzled.

'Wouldn't be a surprise if I told you.' Ruth laughed.

When they reached the road which led to the bridge, she started to turn the corner.

'I thought thee said we were gannin' home?'

'We are.'

'Then why this way? Henrietta Street's that . . .' The words faded on David's lips as the meaning behind his wife's words struck him. He pulled up sharply. 'Ruth, thee hasn't . . . ?'

'Yes!' Laughter danced in her eyes.

'But . . . when . . . ?' he spluttered.

'You said we needed a house in Bagdale. One came up

334

for sale. It was too good a chance to miss. I thought it would be a nice homecoming for you,' she cut in with bubbling enthusiasm.

'It is! Of course it is!' gasped David, swept up in Ruth's elation. He grasped her waist, swung her off her feet and whirled her round, oblivious to the people around them. Their joyful laughter mingled with the cry of gulls gliding above the bridge.

As Ruth's feet touched the ground, David grasped her hand and started towards the bridge. 'Come on,' he cried. 'I can't wait to see it.'

They hurried to the west side of the river and escaped from the hustle and bustle of Baxtergate into the quieter, wider Bagdale where they sharpened their pace.

'Here we are,' said Ruth, opening the gate of the fifth house.

David stopped. He stared in amazement at the building.

'Come on.' She took his arm and turned him along the path towards the three-storeyed house. The gently curved bow windows seemed to look askance at them as they walked beside the neat garden.

They reached the front door. Ruth opened it. As she stepped inside, she swung round excitedly. 'Welcome home, David!'

She stepped aside. He was speechless with overwhelming admiration at the fine hall, spacious yet compact, from which a staircase curved gracefully upwards. The only furniture was a small table and two chairs which backed on to the green and white walls.

'Don't say a word until you've seen it all.' Ruth's laughter rippled through the house as she led David from room to room, each one elegantly decorated and taste-fully furnished. David was still speechless when they came back downstairs. It was hard for him to believe that this was his home. He felt certain he would wake up with this magnificent illusion gone and find himself in the damp, stinking below-decks of a swaying whaleship.

'Like it?' asked Ruth, stopping at the bottom of the stairs.

'It's marvellous. But we haven't been in there.' He indicated a door across the hall.

'No, I saved it 'til last.' Her eyes sparkled in anticipation. She crossed the hall and opened the door.

A large oak desk stood across one corner of the room with the fireplace to its right. Two big easy chairs looked invitingly on opposite sides of the fire which burned brightly in an iron grate, competing with the daylight streaming through two large windows which gave a pleasant view of a walled garden.

'It's yours, your own room. From here you can run your shipping empire.'

'Mine!' He grabbed her. 'Thee's a wonder.' He hugged her tightly. Her laughter still rang in his ears as he said, 'But where did you get the money?'

'I used my influence and your promotion to borrow it,' she replied.

'How much?' asked David.

'A thousand.'

He grimaced, but his frown disappeared with the thought that they really were moving towards fulfilling their ambitions. Hadn't he sworn to have a house in Bagdale? And now, with Ruth's help, it had been achieved.

'You don't mind?' she put the question tentatively.

David grinned. 'Of course not. It's what we wanted. We've borrowed so we've got to go all out to make that money. The *Mary Jane's* sailing to Memel in two days' time, we'll be back in ten. Arrange a party for that evening, the official housewarming.' His words came quickly, fired by enthusiasm. 'We can see who'll take shares in a ship with us, and then we can get the plans under way and be ready for the season after next. I'll do one more voyage to the Arctic in the *Mary Jane* and then . . .'

David's exuberance spilled over to Ruth who finished off proudly: '. . . captain of a new whaleship? David, David, we're going to do it!' She embraced him with unbridled joy. 'One more thing. Let me see how you look behind that desk.'

As he sat down, Ruth unrolled a large sheet of paper, holding it flat with the aid of paperweights and inkwells.

She straightened with pride. 'There you are, David!'

She glanced at her husband to see sheer disbelief upon his face.

The outlines of a ship's plans were instantly recognisable. 'What . . . when . . . ?'

'I asked Matthew Barrett to draw the plans for a new whaleship to be ready for your return. You've got to approve them, then building can start and will be completed by the time you return from the next whaling voyage, just as you have said.'

David was overwhelmed. Things were happening so fast. His ship! He stared at the plans. The lines twisted and turned and merged to become a ship in full sail. The man near the helmsman braced himself against the wind and the plunge of the ship as she cleaved her way through the swell. He was taking her north. Drawn by a mysterious call . . .

'Do you like her?'

David started. 'Of course I like her. She's wonderful. She'll be the pride of Whitby's whaling fleet.' The room became charged with a vision of the future into which he swept Ruth with his words. 'Just think, in a year's time I'll be taking her to Memel and then the Arctic. After that Whitby will see the Fernleys expand. Not one, not two, but three or four whaleships.'

'And other ships as well!' Ruth bubbled with enthusiasm. 'Sailing the world. We'll go with them when we want to get away from the office and the activities of Whitby's biggest shipping company!'

'No office job for me, Ruth. Whaling will be the backbone of the firm. I'll never forsake the Arctic. I'll go with one ship, and then a fleet.' He reached out. His arm encircled her waist and as he swept her on to his knee his lips met hers with a passion which set the seal of approval on her actions and laid bare the longings of long, lonely Arctic nights.

Ruth's arms encircled his neck and she returned kiss for kiss in a need to clear her mind of the thoughts she still harboured about Matthew Barrett.

'Like to try our new bed?' she suggested in a whisper close to his ear.

'Mm, let's,' he murmured.

Later, Ruth sat combing her hair and watching David in the mirror. 'Why don't you go and fetch Adam and

Jenny to see our new home and tell them our plans?' she suggested.

'Good idea,' he enthused.

'Few people know of our move, only those concerned with it,' she went on. 'I haven't told anyone. Wanted you to be the first to know. I haven't seen much of Jenny, I've been so busy. We still have the house in Henrietta Street so I doubt if she knows about the move. Besides, I thought you'd like to be the one to give her and Adam the news.'

'Right,' said David as he fastened his shirt. 'I won't tell them anything about it. I'll just say I've something to show them.' He shrugged himself into his coat. 'They will get a surprise.' He leaned over her and kissed her on the cheek. 'You were wonderful,' he whispered. His eyes met hers in the mirror, expressing fully the meaning behind his words, and she answered him in the same way.

He straightened and turned for the door. 'Won't be long.'

Ruth watched him go. A smile began to cross her face. Surprise? Yes, the Thoresbys were certainly due one. Her eyes narrowed and the smile broadened with satisfaction.

Chapter Twenty-two

David hurried down Bagdale, past the shipbuilding yards, and across the bridge to Church Street.

In twelve months, he could be captain of a ship in which he and Ruth would have shares. He had seen changes in her but was still surprised at how quickly she had adapted to life in Whitby; the way she moved with ease in a society she had never known before coming here. It must be a case of breeding would out – she must have inherited the gift for mixing from her real father.

Now she was becoming a driving force behind their ambitions. She had taken important steps: a circle of friends and acquaintances who could be of use, a house in Bagdale, and plans for a whaleship! And behind them lay a determination to succeed which he was equally determined to match.

David's knock on the door was answered by Jenny.

'David!' She seemed delighted to see him.

'Hello, Jenny. Is Adam in?'

'Yes. Come in.'

'How's Anne?' he asked as she led the way to the kitchen.

'Very well. She's with her gran.'

'What brings thee here so soon, Davey? Didn't think thee'd be able to tear thissen away from Ruth yet.' Adam greeted him with a grin.

'I've some news,' he returned eagerly. 'We've a new house.'

Jenny and Adam stared at him in amazement.

'Thee didn't tell me,' said Adam, glancing at Jenny.

'I didn't know,' she replied, mystified. 'I'm just as surprised as you.'

'Didn't Ruth tell thee?' queried Adam.

'No,' replied Jenny, puzzled that Ruth had kept this so quiet.

'She hasn't moved everything out of the house on Henrietta Street yet,' explained David, 'and she's been living there while the new house was decorated and furnished. She told no one. She wanted me to be the first to know.'

'So that's why she hurried thee from the *Mary Jane*?'

'Exactly.'

'Where is it?' asked Jenny excitedly.

'I'm not to tell thee. It's to be a surprise. I'm to take thee back with me.'

'Won't thee tell us where we're going?' asked Adam as they left the house in Church Street.

David laughed teasingly. 'No, thee'll have to wait and see.'

'I like surprises,' commented Jenny, linking arms with her two escorts.

Evening was settling over the town as the three friends

walked across the bridge to the west bank. The buzz and bustle of the port was calming. The crowds which had streamed across the bridge throughout the day had become a trickle. A few men still worked on some fishing vessels, anxious to finish a task while there was light to see. The last sounds of hammers came from the shipbuilding yards and then were still. Smoke from the many chimneys hung low, without a helpful breeze, adding to the air of disquiet that can sometimes be felt shortly before the onset of night.

David led them into Bagdale. Reaching the house, he unlinked his arm. 'Here we are,' he said. As he hurried the last few steps to open the gate he did not see the glances exchanged between Jenny and Adam.

'Oh, my God.' Jenny's words, whispered to herself, came with the shock of disbelief and apprehension. Her stomach churned, knotted and sent a wave of nausea sweeping through her. The excitement and elation which she had been experiencing drained from her so fast that she felt weak.

Adam sensed her trauma and moved closer to her. He gripped her arm. 'Will thee be all right?' There was deep concern in his quiet voice.

Jenny shuddered, and fought to get a grip on her feelings which were threatening to swamp her. She must, for David's sake. This was something special to him. He was obviously proud of the house he was going to show them.

'Yes,' she whispered.

'Surprised?' asked David, holding the gate open.

'More than thee knows,' replied Adam, following Jenny on to the path which led to the house.

Each step was an effort for her. She had to force herself onward. The house towered over her, leering, mocking. She climbed the four steps to the door in a daze. She was hardly aware of David opening it for her.

Ruth came into the hall to meet them. 'So glad you could come.' She smiled. 'Sorry I didn't tell you about this move, Jenny, but I knew David would want to tell you himself.'

'That's all right,' replied Jenny, dismissing Ruth's apparent concern with a slight shake of her head.

'Like it?' David beamed enthusiastically as he hurried across the hall. 'Thee must see this room before anything else! I've something special to show thee.'

Ruth held back to let Jenny go first. She hesitated, mustered the courage to go on but stopped just inside. Her face paled. She clenched her fists tightly, trying to control the sensations which were churning inside her.

David went straight to the desk and looked up at Adam who stood behind his wife. 'What do thee think of that?' he said with pride as he tapped the paper on his desk.

'Adam, take me home, quick!' Jenny's voice choked on a hoarse gasp. Her face, deathly white, was creased with horror. He grasped her arm, turned her and hurried from the room. They brushed past Ruth without a glance at her.

David gaped as his two friends crossed the hall to the front door. He shot a questioning look at Ruth who shrugged her shoulders. David ran into the hall. 'Adam! Jenny! What's wrong?' he called, his face bewildered.

Adam stopped and turned. The look of utter contempt on his face stopped David in his tracks.

343

'What's wrong?' His cry held a plea for an explanation. His friends were hurt but the cause mystified him.

'Wrong?' There was anger in Adam's voice to match his dark, thunderous expression. 'Bloody hell, don't tell me thee didn't know this is where Jenny used to live? And that's the room where she found her father hanging!'

Ruth had rushed to her husband's side and stared at Adam with concern. 'Of course I didn't! No one told me!'

'Like hell!' he stormed in disbelief. He quivered with rage as he drew himself into a defiant attitude. 'Thee must have known. And Jenny suffered.'

Harsh words were threatening to obliterate a deep friendship. David knew he must try to save it. He flung his words at Adam like the cry of a wounded sea-bird. 'I didn't! And Ruth has just said she didn't.'

Jenny looked frail and beaten. Her face was drawn and ashen white. He longed to take hold of her, and dispel the torment. He needed to reassure her that he had meant her no harm, that, because of the way he felt about her, he could not deliberately wound her.

'Jenny, I'll swear we didn't know you once lived here,' cried Ruth in a tone which pleaded to be believed.

Still supported by Adam, she sighed. 'I suppose I'm to blame really,' she said, her voice scarcely above a whisper. 'I should have got over it by now, it happened so long ago, and yet at times it seems so near. Impressions on a young mind act in strange ways. It was a shock, being in that room again.' She shuddered. 'Forgive me for the way I behaved. And forgive me if I can't face this house again.' She glanced at Adam. 'Please take me home.'

He nodded. His eyes scanned David and Ruth and saw nothing to make him doubt their sincerity. 'I'm sorry,' he said. He opened the door and ushered Jenny outside.

Ruth sighed and turned towards the room but David grabbed her by the arm and swung her round to face him. 'Did thee know?' he asked, his eyes narrowing with suspicion.

'No! Of course not!' She flared at the insinuation.

'Is thee sure?' he pressed.

Ruth shook her arm free of his grip and straightened defiantly. 'You heard what I said. I did not know.' She paused to emphasise her words then added, 'But maybe what happened is for the best.'

Ruth saw the opportunity to drive the wedge of discord further. Now was the time to distance themselves from Jenny and Adam.

'For the best?' David frowned. 'How could it be? Thee saw what it did to Jenny.'

'Jenny said she couldn't face this house again, so it will mean we see less of them – and that's a good thing,' returned Ruth.

'What's thee getting at?' A coldness had entered David's voice.

Ruth eyed him squarely. 'I learned that you and Jenny were once in love.'

His mind went numb at this unexpected challenge. What had happened? Was there any use denying it? He saw from Ruth's expression that there was not. 'Who told thee?' he hissed, while his mind cursed the betrayer.

'Jenny!' she replied.

David's mind reeled under the impact. Jenny! Why had

she betrayed a secret he thought only they would share? 'What did she tell thee?' he demanded roughly.

'Oh, no, David.' Ruth shook her head, with a wry, knowing smile flicking the corners of her mouth. She was in command. She held the upper hand. 'That's between Jenny and me. And don't go asking her, she won't tell you. Remember, Adam doesn't know how deep your feelings went.'

'And thee'd tell him to get what thee wants?' Anger flared in David.

'If necessary.' The words were quiet but David saw, for the first time, the depth of the ruthlessness which lay in his wife. Was this something else inherited from her father, or had it been born in the determination to survive the beatings of her step-father?

He was astounded. 'So thee talks unless we see less of them.'

'Yes.' Ruth's eyes narrowed. 'I don't want old love rekindling.'

'Don't talk ridiculous,' rapped David. 'What was between Jenny and me was long ago.'

'You never know. I've seen the way Jenny looks at you and you at her,' said Ruth. 'She still thinks a lot about you.'

'And I about her. She befriended me when I first came to Whitby, she nursed me . . . of course I think highly of her,' he pointed out tersely.

'There you are then.' Ruth threw her arms up in despair and turned away in disgust. 'It's a dangerous situation, which could threaten our ambitions.' She swung round on him. 'And that's not going to happen,' she hissed, her chin jutting with determination. 'It's better not to see them again.'

'I can't avoid Adam,' he protested. 'I sail with him.'

'You've only one more voyage and then you'll be on your own ship. You can do that one voyage with anyone. You won't have any difficulty getting a ship with your reputation.'

'That may be,' he agreed, 'but I want to do it on the *Mary Jane*.'

'That's only a whim,' snapped Ruth. 'You don't need him. We don't need them. What happened today may be for the best.'

He grasped her by the shoulders. 'I think you knew!' he flared angrily. His eyes widened with suspicion. 'Thee knew Jenny had found her father in that room and figured she'd be so affected they'd never want to see us again. I think thee worked it all out.'

'David! You don't know what you're saying!' Ruth screamed, as the truth bit deep.

'Don't I?' This should have been a happy occasion – a homecoming to a new home on the west side of the river where he had said they would live one day – but it had been tainted by Ruth's deliberate attempt to alienate their friendship with Jenny and Adam. He was watching her closely. He had made accusations, could he be wrong? But the fleeting doubt vanished when he saw her face close with a dark, secretive expression. He could not hold back. 'Once, when I told Jenny of my desire to live on this side of the river, she warned me that it wouldn't necessarily mean happiness. Maybe she was right. Maybe I should have heeded her.'

David's words sent a cold chill to Ruth's heart. He had loved Jenny, now he was admitting that he had discussed his ambitions with her. Once again, something in which she wanted to be the only one had been shared with Jenny. How much more had been shared with her? A shadow of dread touched her and sent coldness down her spine, but fury subdued it.

'Jenny! Jenny! Is she all you ever think about?' Ruth's voice was shrill. She flicked her hair away from her face with her right hand. 'Why didn't you marry her?' Her eyes blazed. Her lips curled into a sneer. 'You couldn't, because she chose Adam. She preferred him to you! So you can forget your love for her. She's out of your reach and I'll see she stays that way.'

David stiffened. His lips tightened. He glared at his wife and for one moment she thought he was going to strike her.

But she went on quickly, sending arrows of truth to his mind and heart. 'And let me tell you this, David Fernley, if you'd married her, you certainly wouldn't be living on this side of the river now, with your own whaleship in a year's time. Don't forget I've worked for this, cultivated friendships to put your ambitions within your grasp.'

David stared at his wife. His mind raced. He owed her a lot. He must not forget it. He must wipe the suspicions from her mind. Nothing must jeopardise their future just when it looked rosy. 'I've told thee, what was between Jenny and me is in the past. I married thee. It's thee I love.' He pulled her roughly to him. 'Thee! Thee! Thee!' His lips met hers fiercely. For a moment Ruth resisted, then she was swamped in the passion which swept from him and devoured her with its intensity.

'Oh, David,' she gasped, clinging close to him. 'Don't let's quarrel. We have so much going right for us. Don't let the past haunt us and spoil our future. I'm so frightened it might.' She shuddered.

David held her close. 'There's no need to be, my luv.'

'But I am. Nothing from the past must wreck our future and it's for that reason that I think it best if we don't see so much of Jenny and Adam.' Her voice was smooth, silky, persuasive. 'Besides, we have other friends now, people to cultivate, people who will be of help to us in the future. Seeing more of them is important.'

'But old friends are important too,' David pointed out quietly.

'I agree, but sometimes there comes a time when old friends have to be gently dropped. You must realise that, if we achieve our aims, life will be very different. We'll be moving in circles which Jenny and Adam wouldn't enjoy. You must see.'

David shrugged his shoulders. 'Yes,' he agreed reluctantly. His voice firmed. 'But I won't cut them off altogether.'

Ruth bit back the retort which came to her lips. She subdued the disapproval, realising she would have to compromise. She read in David's statement a half-promise not to see so much of them. For the time being, that would do, but she would see that a final break was made in the future. She'd not be threatened by an old love. And she'd see that David's mind was kept firmly on achieving their ambitions without any outside distractions.

349

Chapter Twenty-three

The voyage to Memel was uneventful and, soon after the *Mary Jane* docked, David hurried to Bagdale.

He sensed an excitement about Ruth as she hurried into the hall on hearing the front door open. They exchanged homecoming kisses but, when David's would have lingered, Ruth eased away. Her eyes danced with pleasure as she looked up at him.

'I've arranged a party for this evening.'

'Good!' He hugged her. 'Who's coming?'

'The usual. All the people who could be useful to us. Matthew, the Watsons, Pearsons, Shepherds, Humphries.'

'Matthew's father?'

'No. Can't come, prior engagement.

'Adam and Jenny?'

Ruth hesitated and pushed herself away from him. 'No.'

'Did you invite them?' David demanded, his face clouding with annoyance.

'No,' she snapped.

'Why not?' David's lips tightened with exasperation.

'You know why. I'm not risking our future.' Ruth's eyes flared angrily. 'Besides, Jenny said she couldn't face this house again.'

'The way you planned it,' snapped David in disgust.

'That's not true and you know it,' countered Ruth, her voice rasping with agitation. 'But think what you like,' she added with a shrug of her shoulders. 'Now get yourself into a better mood. There's one other guest.'

'Who?' David's tone was surly as he turned away.

'Jessica!'

'What! Jessica, here?' David swung round, his tone showing his disbelief.

'Yes, she's upstairs unpacking.' Ruth laughed at the incredulity which had flooded David's face.

All thoughts of their disagreement banished, he raced up the stairs two at a time. 'Jess! Jess!' he yelled. He burst into the bedroom, almost knocking Jessica over as she hurried to the door on hearing his voice.

'Jess!'

'Davey!'

He swept her into his arms and hugged her tightly.

'Oh, Davey, it's good to see you.' Tears filled Jessica's eyes as her brother eased her gently away.

'Let me look at thee.' There was admiration in his eyes. 'Thee's grown up, Jess. Thee's become a very attractive young woman.'

She enjoyed the approval she saw on her brother's face.

'How's Ma, Pa, John, Betsy?'

'They're all well. They all send their love. And they're all sorry thee's not been home since the wedding.'

'I've been hoping to but I've been so busy,' explained David. 'I'll gan to see them as soon as I can. But what's brought thee here? I didn't expect . . .'

'I remembered she asked you if she could come and stay after we got settled,' Ruth interrupted from the doorway. 'Well, we have, and I thought it would be nice to have her now, especially for the party this evening. She's come for two weeks.'

'Marvellous.' David hugged his sister again. 'This visit must be a memorable one. You should . . .'

'It is already,' Jessica burst in excitedly. 'This house . . . well, I never expected anything like it. Oh, Ruth, I'm so glad thee asked me. I nearly died when the invitation came.' She broke away from David and embraced her sister-in-law again.

In the short time she had been here, she had noticed big changes in Ruth, far greater than she had expected. There was about her an aura of confidence coupled with a touch of sophistication which enabled her to wear her perfectly fitting taffeta dress with an air that attracted attention. Her self-assurance was matched by an equal determination which foretokened success in whatever she did. But Jessica was struck by the change in Ruth's voice. The harsh broad Yorkshire, roughly spoken back in Cropton, had gone. Though the Yorkshire accent occasionally peeked through, it was surrounded by a more polished tone. Jessica determined to make every effort to speak like Ruth.

'It's a pleasure, my dear. Enjoy yourself.'

'Oh, I will, I know I will,' cried Jessica, gripped by feverish excitement.

'Thee likes the room?' asked David, amused by his sister's enthusiasm.

'It's wonderful.' Jessica glanced round it again. It was beyond her wildest expectations. The bed had white sheets turned back from matching pillows. A patchwork quilt of bright colours covered it, and a small table stood conveniently to one side. But it was the size which made Jessica marvel. Back home she shared one, nowhere near as big as this, with Betsy. It was the same with the room. This was spacious. At home there was only enough space for a bed, a cupboard and a chair, but here she would have to walk to reach the dressing table with its mirror and stool from which she could primp herself.

'Hast thee seen the rest of the house?' asked David.

'No, she hasn't,' put in Ruth. 'I waited until you got home. I knew you'd like to show it to her.'

'Come on, then.' David took his sister by the hand and the three of them toured the house.

Each step strengthened Jessica's determination that one day she would forsake the farming world of Cropton.

When they returned to the hall, Ruth suggested, 'You freshen up, Jessica, and then come down for some tea.'

Overwhelmed, she merely smiled and nodded.

David watched his sister start up the staircase. She was halfway up when he called out to her, 'It's nice to have thee here, Jess.'

'Come and sit here,' said Ruth when Jessica came down for tea. She indicated a chair close to a low table on which a tray had been set with three cups and saucers, milk,

353

sugar, teapot, three plates and another containing dark, sticky gingerbread.

Ruth poured the tea and handed a cup to Jessica then one to David who had been standing in front of the fire.

'We have another surprise for you,' said Ruth, glancing at Jessica. 'Won't be long before David is a captain and we have our own vessel.'

Jessica turned in wide-eyed awe to her brother.

'It's true. Just one more voyage in the *Mary Jane*,' he explained.

'That's partly the reason for the party this evening,' said Ruth.

'I see,' said Jessica. 'Anyone interesting coming?'

'Depends what you mean by interesting,' Ruth laughed.

'Three eligible young men for thee,' said David, a teasing twinkle in his eyes.

'And who might they be?' queried Jessica.

'There's Matthew Barrett – he designed our ship,' said David. 'Albert Pearson is in his father's merchant's business. They're likely to buy our whale products. And there's James Humphries – his father's a landowner so James has a goodly inheritance coming his way.'

'Mmm.' Jessica smiled. 'They sound interesting.'

'Now, don't go monopolising Matthew Barrett,' laughed Ruth, 'David will want to talk to him about the ship.'

When he saw his sister coming down the stairs, dressed for the evening, he was once again struck forcibly by the fact that she was a beautiful young woman. Her red silk dress figured with delicate motifs had a close-fitting bodice, emphasising her slender figure, but tumbled into fullness from the waist. The vandyked collar drooped graciously around her shoulders, leaving an open neckline which was filled with muslin kerchiefs. Her hair, carefully groomed, was piled high with curls after the latest fashion.

'Thee do look pretty,' commented David as he walked to the bottom of the stairs to greet her.

Jessica gave her thanks with a good-natured smile.

'What a beautiful dress,' exclaimed Ruth as she came to join them. 'You put me in the shade.'

'I think not.' Jessica laughed. 'Ma insisted I got one 'specially to come to thee, but your blue is lovely.'

'Ah, it's you who'll turn the young men's heads,' said Ruth graciously. 'Come, a glass of Madeira before the guests arrive. You'll have one, Jess?'

Determined to move into this new life as quickly as possible, she accepted.

With glasses filled, Ruth raised hers. 'To you, Jessica, may your stay be a happy one.'

'Thank you,' she replied. 'And may I wish thee both every success, and thy ship safe voyages.'

Ruth closed the door behind the last departing guest and turned to David. 'Well?' she queried with a lift of her eyebrows.

David's fists tightened with excitement. 'We're in business. Couldn't have gone better.' He grabbed and whirled her off her feet. Ruth's laughter mingled with his to ring through the house. 'They're keen on the new ship,' he continued as he put her down, 'and all, except Matthew and Humphries, will tak shares in her. Frank Watson said he'll tak all the timber I can bring from the Baltic, so, if I do a voyage next winter, it'll be a good trial before I gan to the Arctic the following summer.'

They entered the parlour where Jessica was rearranging her hair with a touch of satisfaction. 'You two seem to have enjoyed it,' she said with a smile.

''Course we did,' affirmed David. 'Most of them will tak shares in the ship.'

With a great sigh of pleasure, Ruth flopped into a chair and kicked off her shoes. 'Rather tiring but well worth it. Jessica, be a dear and pour us all a last glass. A nightcap will do us all good.' She smiled at David as he sat down on the opposite side of the fire. Jessica went to the sideboard and started to pour the wine. 'Enjoy it, Jessica?'

'Oh, marvellous,' she replied. 'Thanks so much for asking me.' She turned from the sideboard and, as she brought the drinks, said with delight, 'James Humphries asked me to go riding with him tomorrow afternoon. He's calling for me at two-thirty.'

'Indeed?' said Ruth with surprise. 'Hope you've improved since your pa let us ride Squire Hardy's horses?'

'I have.' Jessica laughed. 'I helped the new groom at the hall to exercise the horses. He taught me.'

'Sidesaddle?' queried David.

'Yes.'

'Then you should be all right with James,' commented Ruth. She glanced at David. 'I'm sorry James's father wasn't interested in our ship.'

'Oh, he was but said he would have to think about it. Wasn't prepared to commit himself this early.'

'Then Jessica's friendly relationship with James could prove useful.' Ruth smiled. 'A pity you aren't staying longer.'

356

'I'd love to, but I promised Ma I'd be back after a fort-night. Even though I've been here a short time, I know I'll miss it all when I go back to Cropton.'

'Well, you know you'll be welcome any time, especially if you're cultivating James Humphries,' Ruth added with a teasing smile.

'I'd like to be part of all the excitement,' said Jessica. She turned to David. 'Will thee show me the *Mary Jane*? Then I can picture thee aboard her, hunting the whale, when I'm back home.'

'I'll take thee tomorrow morning when I go to show Adam and Ruben the plans for the ship,' he promised.

Ruth started to disagree but, not wanting to cause any unpleasantness in front of her sister-in-law, hid her annoy-ance until she and David were in their bedroom.

'Why are you going to show Ruben the plans?' she demanded brusquely as David closed the bedroom door.

'He's had experience of whaleships.'

'Experience? Ruben?' Ruth's voice was filled with contempt.

'He's been around whaleships all his life and Adam assures me that he has a knack for seeing the lines on the paper as a real vessel, something which he inherited from Seth,' replied David, an edge to his voice.

'I'd have thought Matthew's design was good enough,' snapped Ruth.

'It probably is, but sometimes a man with practical experience can spot something which would be better.'

'I doubt it. Matthew must know what's wanted,' she said testily.

'No doubt, but I'm going to show the plans to Ruben,' insisted David.

'Thoresbys! You're obsessed with them!' Ruth's eyes were suddenly hard.

David read the signs. His big, broad hands grasped her and there was a soul-searching look in his gaze. 'I'm not. They're friends, and if they can be of help I don't see why . . .' His words trailed away. The passion which sparked between them seemed to be heightened in moments of conflict. David pulled her roughly to him and his lips sought hers with uncurbed hunger.

Her resistance was only momentary before pleasure swamped her and she returned his desire.

'Oh, Ruth, don't let's fall out again,' gasped David as his eyes sought approval in hers. 'We've had a wonderful evening. Things are going right for us.' Her face was tilted to his and she did not attempt to conceal the invitation in her eyes while her lips offered much more.

Chapter Twenty-four

David and Jessica left the house in Bagdale after breakfast and headed for the east side of the river.

Jessica demanded information about everything as her keen eyes took in the life of the seaport.

'I'm looking forward to seeing Jenny,' she said. 'I'm sorry she and Adam weren't at the party. I don't want to pry, David, but has summat come between them and Ruth?'

David hesitated, wondering how much he should tell his sister, but Jessica was someone special and there had always been a close rapport between them. Confidences had been shared in the past, so why not now? Once he had started on an explanation, he found it was good to have her to talk to.

'That's the situation,' he concluded. 'I don't see why we should have to give up our friendship with Jenny and Adam.'

'Nor do I,' she agreed.

'Ruth wants to see it broken up altogether even though

I've assured her that what was between Jenny and me is in the past.'

'But thee must gan on seeing them even if she won't. They've done so much for thee, thee just can't cut them off. Besides, with the Thoresby experience in the whale trade, they could still be valuable to you.'

'Exactly.' A thoughtful frown creased his brow. 'You know, I still have a feeling that Ruth knew about that room and Jenny's father, and maybe even planned to use it to try to drive a wedge between Adam, Jenny and myself.'

'Oh, David, she couldn't,' cried Jessica in surprise.

'I'm not so sure,' he mused. 'Ruth's changed. You must have noticed.'

'Yes, for the better,' replied Jessica.

'In many ways, yes, but I think she might do anything to get what she wants.'

'Oh, Davey, do be careful. Don't let anything ruin the chances thee has,' warned Jessica. 'Seeing Ruth with her guests last night made me realise how important she is in helping thee realise thy ambitions.'

'I know. Yet I don't want to lose the friends I have,' said David, his voice cramped with irritation.

'Then don't, but be discreet,' advised Jessica.

She was thrilled to see the *Mary Jane* and plied David with question after question. When he was able to get her away, he guided her to Emma Thoresby's, only to be told that Ruben was with Adam.

When they reached the house in Church Street, Jenny opened the door to their knock.

'David!' Jessica noted the pleasure which sparkled in Jenny's eyes.

'Jenny, I'd like thee to meet my sister, Jessica. Jessica, this is Jenny Thoresby, Adam's wife.'

Jessica stepped forward with a warm smile. 'I'm pleased to meet thee. I've heard a lot about thee.'

'And I about you,' replied Jenny with a welcoming smile. 'Davey thinks a lot about his sister. Do come in.'

Adam, too, showed his delight in meeting Jessica.

Jessica took an instant liking to them both and knew the feeling was reciprocated. There was an instant understanding between her and Jenny, as if they had known each other all their lives.

'I've brought the plans of my ship to show Ruben. Your ma said he was here,' said David when he could get a word in.

'Aye. He's upstairs. I'll give him a shout,' replied Adam. He crossed the room to the stairs and called up.

A few moments later, Ruben hurried into the kitchen. He pulled up short when he saw Jessica.

With his eyes fixed on her, Ruben stumbled over his greeting, held as he was by the radiant vitality in the face which he studied.

Jessica saw a young man whose weather-beaten face had the rugged attractiveness of a Thoresby, but in Ruben the friendly, deep-blue eyes held a gentleness inherited from his mother.

Jessica held out her hand. 'I'm pleased to meet thee, Ruben.' A little embarrassed colour flushing his cheeks, Ruben took her hand in his. He felt a tingle of excitement run through his body at her touch, and swallowed. He was used to girls but he had never felt like this. Why was she having this effect on him? Ruben realised he was still holding her hand and, flustered, quickly released it. Jessica's eyes twinkled with understanding and pleasure at his attention.

'Thee wanted me?' Ruben tore his gaze from Jessica and turned to his brother.

'Davey's brought the plans of his whaleship for thee to see,' explained Adam.

'Oh, right,' spluttered Ruben.

David started towards the table.

'Not there, David.' Jenny stopped him. 'You three men take them into the other room. Jessica and I want to chat and I'll make us all some hot chocolate.

The men left the kitchen for the parlour where Adam removed a bowl from the table so that David could spread his plans. Adam carefully placed a brass candlestick at each corner to hold the paper flat.

'I'd like you to look this over, Ruben. Adam tells me you have an eye for a ship's design.'

'Pa seemed to think so,' he said. 'He taught me a lot.' Ruben studied the plans carefully, while David and Adam waited impatiently for his verdict. When he finally straightened, he said, 'Thee's damned lucky to be getting a ship like that. Barrett knows his business but he isn't cheap. Only two things to watch. The stowage of the whaleboats, for one – he's scrimped the room in which to handle them when preparing to swing them into position. The other thing I feel is more important. I'd have the bow strengthened even higher and further back than he shows. Here and here.' Ruben stabbed his finger at the appropriate points on the drawing. 'Who's going to build her?'

'Barrett, I expect,' replied David.

'That doesn't sound as though it's been finalised.' Ruben turned a quizzical eye on David.

'It hasn't.'

'Good. Barrett is a good firm and Matthew will try to get the trade for his father, but hold out. Insist that Mulgrave's build the ship. They're a small firm but they're thorough craftsmen. Also, they're looking to specialise in whaleships, so they'll be even more particular to do a good job to build up their reputation.' Ruben glanced quickly at the plans again, then said, 'I think that's all I can tell you.'

'Thanks for your advice, I appreciate it,' said David, rolling up the plans while Adam replaced the candlesticks on the mantelpiece.

'I'll be sorry to lose thee when the time comes,' said Adam sadly.

'I'll be sorry to go,' replied David. 'I'll always be grateful to your pa and to thee for the chances thee's given me. I'd like to do one more voyage on the *Mary Jane*. The ship should be ready by the time we get back, then I'll tak her to Memel as a trial.'

'Good idea,' approved Adam. 'We'll do the Memel voyage together. I can give thee a few tips for trading there.'

'Thanks,' returned David. 'I'll never be out of your debt.'

Adam waved away his thanks. 'Let's go and see if the girls have finished gossiping.'

'Did you approve David's ship, Ruben?' Jenny asked when the men returned.

'She'll be a beauty,' he enthused. 'One or two minor

363

alterations.' He felt Jessica's eyes on him and when he glanced at her his mind raced with feelings he had never experienced before.

'Jess, will thee make your own way back to Bagdale? I'd like to go and see Matthew Barrett about these alterations right away,' said David as he placed his empty cup on the table.

'I'll see Jessica gets home safely,' Ruben put in quickly.

'That's kind of thee,' she said, dispelling the fear in him that she might refuse.

David made his goodbyes and ten minutes later Jessica and Ruben left the house.

'How long is thee here for?' he asked as they started along Church Street.

'Two weeks.'

'Good!' Elation lit his face. 'Then when can I see thee again?'

Jessica smiled wryly. 'Thee doesn't waste any time, Ruben.'

'Don't believe in doing so where a pretty girl's concerned.'

'Then there must be others.' Jessica laughed with a teasing twinkle in her eyes.

'I'll not deny it, but there's none as pretty as thee.'

'Get on with thee. I bet thee says that to all the girls.'

Ruben took hold of her arm, stopped her and faced her with a serious expression. 'No, I don't, Jess, but I mean it where thee's concerned.'

Looking into his deep-blue eyes, she saw that it was love at first sight for Ruben. She was flattered to know that she had made a conquest. And she liked the intimate way he had abbreviated her name, something no other stranger had ever done.

'Let me show thee Whitby. Let's start this afternoon,' Ruben went on with the earnestness of someone determined to seize a chance and not waste one moment thereafter.

'Oh, I'm sorry, Ruben. I can't. I've another engagement.' His face registered his disappointment. 'Don't look so glum,' she added with a smile. 'There's another day. I'd like nothing better than to see Whitby with thee.'

Ruben brightened. 'Thee mean it?'

She nodded. 'Of course.'

'Good.' A broad smile crossed his face. 'I'll call for thee at ten tomorrow morning.'

Chapter Twenty-five

After lunch, with her heart soaring with joy, Jessica hurried to her room. Ruth, who had taken up riding after the smuggling incident, had laid out a riding habit for her to borrow.

Jessica did not have the natural flair and affinity with horses her sister-in-law enjoyed. Nevertheless, she had the confidence of a competent horsewoman and was looking forward to the afternoon with James Humphries.

She slid the green velvet skirt over her head, fastened it tightly at the waist and slipped her arms into the smart jacket. She gathered her hair on the crown of her head, pinning it securely before adding the final touch of an exquisite little velvet cap.

She opened her door and waited until she heard the maid announce James Humphries before making a sweeping entrance down the curved stairway.

He was paying his respects to Ruth and David and all three looked up when they heard footsteps tripping lightly down the stairs.

Their admiring expressions sent a thrill of delight through her. She held out her hand to James as she crossed from the foot of the stairs.

'You're looking very pretty,' he said as he took her hand and bowed.

'Thank thee,' returned Jessica, wishing she could talk like Ruth and making a vow to work on her accent as quickly as possible. She smiled at Ruth and at David, who was still overawed by the way his sister had grown into an attractive young woman.

Jessica and James bade their goodbyes and he escorted her to the horse and trap waiting at the gate.

He helped her into the trap, and as she settled herself she studied him while he unfastened the tethering rein. He was of medium height and build and, although his complexion tended to be sallow, there was a handsome look about the square jaw, the finely shaped mouth and arched eyebrows. His hazel brown eyes were alert and attentive to the point of penetrating which sometimes caused an uneasy sensation in the person being observed. His brown hair with a natural wave across the front tended to lighten at the temples.

James climbed up beside her, took a rug from behind him and spread it over her knees. 'You'll be more comfortable with that around you,' he said. Picking up the reins, he flicked the horse forward and Jessica saw hands used to having horses obey them. They were gentle but firm.

Three miles out of Whitby, James turned the horse and trap through a gateway in a high wall and followed a curving path to a large house fronted by a well-kept lawn which gave way to the trees through which they were passing. James drove straight to the stables. 'We may as well go now. Mother and Father are in Whitby and Melissa's visiting friends for an hour or two.'

As the horse and trap clattered into the stable-yard, a man emerged from one of the buildings to hold the horse's head while James climbed from the trap and helped Jessica to the ground. A second man appeared leading two horses and in a few minutes Jessica and James were riding out of the yard.

James kept to the low land behind the seashore. He made pleasant conversation until he sensed that Jessica had got the feel of the horse and had settled into the ride. Then he quickened the pace and soon knew that Jessica shared his enthusiasm for a harder ride.

'Race you to the cottages,' he challenged, indicating the buildings ahead.

She laughed and sent her horse into a gallop. She stretched herself on the animal's back and thrilled to the powerful muscles beneath her. Glancing over her shoulder, she saw James urging his horse to cover the two yards which separated them. Earth flew as pounding hooves cut into the turf, with each horse responding to the challenge of the other. Then James was alongside her, but gained no more before they were hauling on the reins to pull their mounts to halt close to the cottages.

Breathing hard from the exertion, they laughed loudly as their eyes swept each other.

'Want to go further?' called James. 'There's a grand view from the top of yon cliff.'

'Love to,' answered Jessica.

They sent their horses forward, crossed a shallow

stream and put them at the slope which climbed gently to a high promontory above the sea. They halted their horses near the edge of the cliff.

'What a marvellous view,' she cried.

'Thought you'd like it.'

They sat a few moments taking in the panorama of bay and cliffs stretching away before them. The gentle sea broke quietly, touching the bay with a curving line of white foam. Beyond the next headland peeped another and another, marking the rugged Yorkshire coast which had claimed many an unwary ship. In the opposite direction the long stretch of shore ended at the river squeezing to the sea between the two cliffs at Whitby.

James slipped from the saddle and moved to Jessica's horse. 'A short walk. Give the horses a rest,' he suggested. He reached up to help her to the ground. She slipped her foot from the stirrup and eased herself into James's waiting hands. They took her round the waist and she felt a power in him she had not expected as he lifted her down. Her feet touched the grass but James did not release his hold. She met the gaze which she had felt on her all afternoon and was drawn to him. His lips met hers gently, then, as they lingered, moved into a passion which swept through him. Jessica resisted his fierceness but, becoming swamped by it, relaxed and returned kiss for kiss.

The ride back along the edge of the sea, with water splashing from the horses' hooves, was enjoyed by riders and animals and all were sorry when James turned from the beach to a cutting which climbed inland towards his home.

The sound of the returning horses brought the two men hurrying to take charge of them. James dismounted and helped Jessica from the saddle. The two men led the sweating horses away as James and Jessica, deep in conversation, walked towards the house. Lost in each other's company, they did not notice James's mother, who had come out of the front door to stand in the portico, until they reached the four steps rising from the path.

'Mother! You're back soon,' he exclaimed.

Startled, Jessica looked up to see a tall, middle-aged woman whose formidable appearance was emphasised by the severity of her grey dress. Her long, pale face wore a serious expression and the colour of her garment did nothing to enhance the sallow complexion. With her hands clasped in front of her, the long fingers entwined, she looked down from the extra height loaned to her by the steps.

'James, there is a matter of some urgency which I must discuss with you. Please take this young lady home immediately and return as quickly as possible.'

Jessica was attracted by the soft, well-spoken voice which bore no trace of the Yorkshire accent to which she was accustomed. But it was the eyes which she would remember. Even though clouded by the anxiety which was troubling her, there was a velvet warmth in them when James's mother turned her gaze on Jessica.

'I'm sorry for spoiling your afternoon. I wouldn't have done so if it could have been avoided.' She turned, without waiting for a word from Jessica or her son, and hurried into the house.

'I'm sorry,' said James simply.

'That's all right. I've had a wonderful afternoon.' She

touched his arm in an expression of thanks. 'Come along, we mustn't delay. Thee must get back quickly.'

When James returned, after seeing Jessica to the house in Bagdale, he left the horse and trap in front of the portico and hurried inside. As he closed the front door, his mother appeared from the main parlour and beckoned to him.

Although, as was usual, the log fire burned brightly in the grate and the silver sparkled on the sideboard, James felt the chill of trouble in the room. His mother went to a chair beside the fire and sat down, holding herself erect with her hands crossed on her lap.

Melissa turned from the window from which she had watched her brother arrive. Her green taffeta dress rustled as she crossed the room to sit on the couch opposite her mother. She smoothed it and waited for someone to speak.

'Father?' asked James.

'He's in the library resting. The news we have had today was a great shock to him.' Mrs Humphries's voice was quiet and even.

As his mother paused, James glanced at his sister and realised, from the almost imperceptible shake of the head, that she knew no more than he.

'Your father and I have visited our lawyer today. He wanted to make certain provisions for me in case he dies before me. As you know, he's thirty years older than me and has been far from well lately. Well, as it happened, Mr Jackson was about to come to see us within the next few days. He was verifying one or two points before doing so.' She paused, seeming to draw on some reserve of

371

strength to break bad news. 'The fact of the matter is that one of the shipping firms in which your father had invested heavily has run into trouble and is finished. Your father has lost the greater part of his money.'

James and Melissa, still not fully understanding the significance of the news, exchanged brief glances.

'Just what does this mean, Mama?' Melissa asked.

'We have very little left.'

'But hasn't Father more money elsewhere?' asked a bewildered James.

'A little, but only sufficient to live on.'

'Will we have to leave here?' asked Melissa.

'No, not necessarily. If we stay, we won't be able to keep Jane, and the grooms will have to go, the gardeners too. We'll have to do everything ourselves. We could leave and find a smaller place but I wouldn't want to do that, for your father's sake. I know he would like to spend the rest of his days here. After all, it is his family home.'

As the news sank in, James was not relishing the thought of having to alter the lifestyle to which he was used, but he knew how much living at Esk Hall meant to his father.

'Then he shall,' he said firmly. 'I'll find a way to make things easier.'

'Thank you, James,' said his mother graciously, then added firmly, 'You'll have to mend your ways – no more gambling. It will only make matters worse if we have to face any more debts.'

'You have my word, Mother,' he returned.

'And I'll do all I can,' said Melissa.

'Good.' Mrs Humphries smiled at them both. 'Thank

you for being so understanding. It may not be for too long. I shall come into some money when my father dies. Though my family have had little to do with me since I came north, I heard about two months ago that Father was unwell and not expected to live long. You remember I went to London to see him?'

'Yes,' said James, 'but I thought he'd made a recovery.'

'It was only partial and I've been expecting any day to hear that he has died,' said his mother sadly.

'So our present situation may only be for a short time?' asked Melissa.

'Yes.'

'Oh, well, I'm sure James will think of something to see us through,' Melissa added with a glance at her brother, little knowing that he was already making plans.

It was dusk when he left the house that same evening, and, by the time he reached the Angel Inn in Whitby, darkness was blanketing the town. The room was dimly lit and he paused inside the door to get his bearings. Two steps took him down to the floor of the room and, as he moved between the occupied tables, a girl with unkempt hair and a scarred face thrust herself at him with hopes of a night's payment. He pushed her roughly out of the way and ignored her curses.

A big, broad-shouldered man, whose excess weight hung over the top of his belted trousers, came to him as he reached the stretch of wood which served as a bar.

'Whisky,' James ordered.

The man eyed him, nodded and poured the drink. He was not used to well-dressed young men frequenting his inn. He knew James Humphries by sight, and knew his reputation, and was curious about his visit to the Angel.

'You the landlord?' asked James, a firm note to his voice.

'Aye.'

'Then you'll oblige me by telling me where I can find Jethro Thompson.'

The landlord leaned his hands on the counter and eyed the newcomer suspiciously.

'Jethro Thompson? Now what would the likes of you be wanting with the likes of him?' he asked hoarsely, his voice low.

'That's none of your business,' retorted James, but quickly took the edge from his voice. He did not want to antagonise the landlord and jeopardise the chances of meeting the man he hoped would enable him to keep life at Esk Hall unchanged. 'I'm told he frequents this inn.' He fumbled in his pocket and found a guinea. He placed it discreetly on the counter. The man put his broad, hairy hand over the coin quickly so that no prying eyes could see it. His hand rested there while he stared hard at James, trying to figure out why Humphries should want to meet Jethro Thompson and whether he should arrange a meeting. Maybe it would be all right. If he took suitable precautions, no harm would be done.

He slid the guinea from the counter. 'He comes in but he's not here now.'

'Can you get him?' queried James.

'Aye.'

'Soon?' The way James pressed the question left the landlord in no doubt that there were urgent matters abroad.

'Aye. Come this way.'

The landlord walked towards one end of the counter, pausing on the way to say something to the small, thin man who stood rubbing a tankard with a dirty cloth. He nodded, eyed James and then got on with his work. The fat man came from behind the bar and started up four steps which led to a door. From his glance and the inclination of his head, James knew he had to follow. They entered a short passage at the end of which the man opened a door and motioned James inside.

'Wait here,' said the landlord gruffly, and closed the door after James had entered the room.

He glanced round. Weird shadows danced to the bidding of an oil lamp's flame. The room was sparsely furnished with a table, four wooden chairs, a sideboard and an extra chair to one side of the big open fireplace which lacked a fire. James shivered and waited impatiently.

The moments dragged. Once he started for the door, determined to hurry things up, but then he stopped. If he tried to do that he would probably jeopardise the chances of seeing Jethro. He waited.

The movement of the sneck startled him. He swung round to face the door. A man stepped into the room, closed the door behind him, and stood eyeing James from deep-socketed eyes. Their usual indication of gaunt, lean features was confounded. Instead, James saw a well-formed face with a determined jaw and high forehead. Though of only medium height, the man was broad and hefty, his manner lively and alert. James figured he would be a man with whom it would be difficult to get the upper hand.

'What does James Humphries want with Jethro Thompson?' The voice was deep, demanding straight answers.

James was startled that the man knew him, but kept his voice calm as he answered. 'You Jethro Thompson?'

'Might be.' The man was suspicious.

'I speak only with Jethro Thompson.' James forced his voice to be firm. He wanted the man to know he would stand no nonsense. 'It will be to his benefit to see me.'

'And yours, no doubt?' the man rasped sharply.

'Naturally. I wouldn't be here if I didn't want something in return. Now, are you Jethro or are you going to bring him here?' James, tired of their fencing, allowed annoyance to enter his voice.

The stranger eyed James for a moment longer and then stepped towards the table, pulled out a chair, sat down and indicated for him to do likewise. James relaxed. The tightness in his stomach was dispelled. He sat down.

'I'm Jethro Thompson,' the man said. 'What possible proposition can you have for me?'

James met Jethro's narrowed gaze. He must not show weakness. If he did, it would undermine his competence in Jethro's eyes.

'You're a smuggler, Jethro.'

Thompson leaned back in his chair and laughed, revealing a row of discoloured teeth. 'Aye, I am, lad. But most of Whitby knows that – even the Preventive Men.'

He laughed again at James's look of disbelief. 'They do, lad, but the knowledge is no good to them unless they can catch me red-handed.' He stopped laughing suddenly and leaned forward on the table, his eyes piercing.

''Ere, you ain't been sent by them to trick me, 'ast thee?'

'No.' James was quick with his reassurance. 'I have a proposition for you. You need places to store your contraband as soon as you run it ashore – good secure hiding places.'

'Aye.'

'Well, I can offer you Esk Hall.'

Jethro pressed hard against the table with the palms of his hands, hiding his surprise. 'We have our places, why should we need another?' he queried. He knew the advantages Esk Hall could offer. His nimble brain was already playing with the possibilities but he knew there was going to be a price to pay.

'Its position is ideal,' James went on to press his point. 'A cutting runs from the shore almost to the house. On either side of that cutting the land is open and flat. With lookouts posted advantageously, the Preventive Men would not be likely to surprise you. Apart from that, the house offers plenty of hiding places.'

The young man had certainly studied the possibilities. Jethro knew he would not get off cheaply, but to have the use of Esk Hall could be worth it.

'Why should thee mak this offer?' he asked.

'No need for you to know the details, but I need money,' replied James.

Jethro grunted. 'I'll pay thee fifty pounds every time we use Esk Hall.'

James laughed derisively. 'What? For the risks we'll run? Besides, you've not considered payment for the time the contraband will be under our roof. Three times your offer will take care of everything.'

'One hundred and fifty?' Jethro could not fail to hide his surprise. 'No, lad, seventy-five and no more.'

James stared at him. The oil lamp flickered, sending their shadows dancing wildly on the walls. He leaned forward on the table. 'One hundred.' He paused, letting the determination in his voice register the finality of his offer, then added, 'And twenty pounds a week for every week there's contraband on the premises.'

'Thee drives a 'ard bargain,' muttered Jethro. 'I'd like to use Esk Hall but I can't give the final word.' He saw the look of surprise on James's face, and grinned. 'So thee thought I was the leader? Oh, no, and I'll 'ave to 'ave his approval.'

James's face compressed with an anger he fought hard to keep under control. 'I wanted to deal only with the top man,' he snapped indignantly. 'I thought you were that person. Who is he?'

Jethro gave a sharp laugh. 'Be more than my life's worth to tell thee. Thee can only deal with me. Come back tomorrow night, same time, and I'll have an answer.'

James nodded. As much as he wanted approval now, he knew it would be useless to argue.

'Just a few details before we part,' Jethro went on. 'Who else of your family knows about this?'

'No one at the moment. My sister Melissa will have to know as I will want her help. Father mustn't know – he's too old – and I don't want Mother to know.'

'Good. What about servants?' asked Jethro.

'If we still have any, they're utterly trustworthy. They are loyal to the family.'

'They'd better be.' There was a note of warning in Jethro's voice.

James made no comment on the veiled threat, but it emphasised the care he would have to take should this venture be approved.

Jethro pushed himself to his feet. 'Tomorrow night.' He went to the door. 'Give me five minutes before thee leaves. Better we aren't seen together.'

The following night their meeting was brief. The offer was accepted and Jethro told James that he would be contacted when a consignment was going to be run to Esk Hall.

When he reached home, he sought Melissa.

'I've solved one of our problems, Melissa. We'll be able to keep Jane.'

'How clever of you, James!' Melissa's big eyes brightened at the prospect of part of their life remaining unchanged. She had hated the thought of housework and this fresh development brought a ray of hope to the gloom. 'What have you done?'

'Will you help me?' he countered.

'Of course,' replied Melissa quickly, only too eager to do anything to help ease their present situation.

'Good. I must ask you to swear to secrecy. You must not breathe a word to anyone.' His tone hardened, leaving his sister in no doubt of the seriousness of the arrangement he had made.

Melissa's large eyes grew even wider at the prospect of a mystery. She leaned forward in her chair, anxious not to miss one word.

'I've seen Jethro Thompson.'

'You've what!' gasped Melissa. 'Jethro Thompson, the smuggler?'

379

'Yes. I'm going to let him use Esk Hall as a hiding place for contraband.'

'James, you can't!' The prospect shocked Melissa.

'I'm getting good money for it,' he pointed out.

'What will Mother and Father say?'

'They mustn't know.'

'But what do you want me to do?'

'You must be ready to divert unwanted attention,' explained James. 'See that Mama is out of the way when we're bringing contraband in. If a Preventive Man comes nosing, a pretty girl should be able to hold his attention. In other words, anything for which I might need your help.'

In spite of her fears about the whole business, Melissa was secretly elated by James's confidence in her ability.

'What will you tell Mama about the money? She'll want to know where it's coming from?' warned Melissa.

'I'll think of something,' he said, and then emphasised, 'but she mustn't know about the smuggling.'

Chapter Twenty-six

A week later, during breakfast, Ruth eyed Jessica with casual curiosity. 'Who is it today, James or Ruben?' she asked.

'Ruben,' replied Jessica.

'You've certainly been getting a lot of attention from these two,' observed David.

'Hadn't you better settle on one?' Ruth's query had the flavour of a suggestion.

'Oh, I'm not that serious . . . not yet,' replied Jessica.

'It could lead to trouble, flirting with two young men,' Ruth pointed out.

'I'm not flirting,' said Jessica. 'They like my company and I like theirs.'

'Young men can be jealous,' put in David. 'Be careful.'

'I will. Now, if you'll excuse me, I must go.' Jessica laid her napkin on the table, pushed back her chair and started from the room.

'Settle on one,' called Ruth, when she reached the door.

'Aye, and mak it Ruben,' added David. 'He's a good, honest Thoresby.'

Jessica left the ripple of her laughter in the dining room as she opened the door and passed into the hall.

Her lips tight, Ruth glared at David. 'Can't you think of anyone but the Thoresbys?' she snapped. 'Let Jessica make her own choice.'

'That's just what I intend to do, and thee'd better do the same.' David's eyes narrowed as he leaned forward, meeting his wife's smouldering dislike of the Thoresbys. 'I notice thee's pushed James at her at every opportunity. Oh, I know thee thinks he'd be a better catch . . .'

'Of course he would,' returned Ruth sharply. 'Money, land, position . . . just the type of backer we need. What's wrong with trying to cultivate a friendship?'

'Thee's thinking of more than that.' David's gaze bored into her. 'But I warn thee, don't try to use Jessica for our ends.' He stood up and looked down at his wife. 'And I mean that, Ruth!' He turned from the table and walked from the room, leaving her staring after him with an angry determination to do all she could to achieve their ambitions, no matter what it entailed.

'Thee's coming home with me, aren't thee?' Jessica asked David as Ruth filled three cups with hot chocolate in front of the parlour fire.

David held his hands towards the fire and then rubbed them vigorously. 'I'm sorry,' he replied as he turned round. 'I intended to, but there's so much to do here before I sail on the *Mary Jane* in March.'

'Oh, Davey, I thought thee would.' Jessica's face

puckered with disappointment. 'Everyone at home will be expecting thee.'

'I'm sure they'll understand when thee explains,' he said as he took the cup of steaming chocolate from his wife. He drank from his cup, enjoying the warmth as it drove out the chill of the breeze which had swirled around them on their way from church.

Jessica looked downcast. 'I was hoping thee'd help me persuade Ma and Pa to let me come to live in Whitby,' she said glumly, then added hastily, 'that is, if thee'll have me.'

David was taken aback. Though he knew this request would come one day, he had not expected it during this first visit.

'Of course we'll have you,' put in Ruth quickly before David could recover from his surprise. She did not want to miss the opportunity of encouraging her sister-in-law. Her mind was already savouring the possibilities Jessica's presence in Whitby could create. 'When you come to Whitby, you must make your home with us. The house is big enough.'

The offer had been made before he could say anything. He could not disappoint his sister now. 'There thee is then,' said David. 'But please be patient. It might even be better to wait until I've done my first Arctic voyage as a captain. When Pa sees how things are turning out, he might be more inclined to let thee come.'

'But that'll mean nearly two years!' protested Jessica.

'We'll see if anything can be done before then,' put in Ruth quickly. Two years was too long for Jessica and James to be apart. 'But let us get this winter over first.'

In spite of her disappointment, Jessica enjoyed the rest of her stay and left for home with a promise to the two men who sought her affection to return as soon as possible. Maybe she could act on her own and not wait until David came to Cropton.

'These are the final plans. I've made the alterations you suggested.' Matthew Barrett handed a roll of papers to David. 'And these are the necessary agreements and contracts to be signed.' He took a glass of Madeira from the silver tray on which Ruth had filled three glasses. 'Here's to your new venture.'

David unrolled the plans on his desk and studied them while he drank his wine. Finally, he praised the alterations and the two men got down to discussing details.

As they leaned over the plans, Ruth studied Matthew. His clothes were of the best cloth and fitted him perfectly. His lithe, supple body gave him a masculinity so different to the power of the whale man beside him. Her eyes moved to the four hands resting on the table and she was comparing the caresses of the long smooth fingers of the ship designer and the broad, hard hands of the whale man, when David's voice broke into her thoughts.

'Well, that's all settled,' he said as the two men straightened from the table.

'Good,' said Ruth, pushing herself from her chair. 'Let's have another glass of Madeira and drink to the future.' She filled the glasses and raised hers. 'To a long and pleasant association.' Her eyes met Matthew's momentarily but it was sufficient for her to receive a message that he interpreted those words in a way which was different from their apparent meaning. A shiver of excitement coursed through her body.

'I'll see Father has this ship ready for the winter voyage,' he assured them.

'No,' said David firmly. 'I don't want your father to build her.'

Matthew's expression changed abruptly. 'But why?' he asked, an edge to his voice.

'David, don't be ridiculous!' protested Ruth. Her jaw line tightened and her eyes flared with annoyance.

David ignored her and directed a question at Matthew. 'You aren't tied to your father's firm, are you?'

'No.'

'You're completely independent in your job as a ship designer?' pressed David.

'Yes.'

'Well, I hired you in that capacity. It doesn't mean that your father builds the ship.' David eyed Matthew over the rim of his glass as he took another sip of his wine.

'But . . . naturally I thought you would give him the chance,' said Matthew, seeking Ruth's support with his glance of astonishment.

'Of course we will, Matthew,' put in Ruth. As she turned her eyes on David, they hardened, daring him to defy her. 'We won't think of going elsewhere.'

'Oh, yes, we will,' replied David in that quiet tone which Ruth knew hid a deep determination. 'I want Mulgrave's to build her.'

'A newish firm,' pointed out Matthew sharply, still bristling from this turn in events which he had not anticipated. 'My father has the experience.'

'Then there's no question of who'll do it,' snapped Ruth with a half-laugh which poured scorn on David's idea.

'Yes,' he said stubbornly, 'Mulgrave's.'

'Oh, don't be so stupid, David,' snapped Ruth, irritated at his calm insistence.

'Mulgrave's are specialising in whaleships,' he informed her. He glanced at Matthew. 'Thee's worked with them before so thee can vouch that they do a good job.'

'Oh, been checking up?' Matthew's eyes were cold.

'Naturally. When we're spending so much money,' retorted David.

'I don't think that was a very honourable thing to do,' commented Ruth, her voice bearing an icy disapproval of David's action towards a friend.

He paid her no attention. 'You agree they're a good firm?' he put the query to Matthew once again.

'Yes,' he replied.

'Then it's Mulgrave's,' said David, with a nod of the head which set the final seal on the matter.

'I suppose this is a Thoresby suggestion!' cried Ruth, her lips curling with contempt.

'Yes,' snapped David, annoyed by the scorn in Ruth's voice. 'They know whaleships and their builders.'

'Thoresbys! Thoresbys! You'd think they were the only damned people who know. You're besotted with them.'

Anger swelled in David but, with a witness in Matthew Barrett, he held it in check. His lips tightened. 'Mulgrave's will build the ship,' he said firmly.

Barrett had felt no embarrassment at witnessing the disagreement between husband and wife. On the contrary, he rather welcomed the knowledge that the marriage was not what it appeared on the surface. But he judged it time to try to smooth over the situation. 'Look, I don't mind working with Mulgrave's and you'll get a damned good ship. Naturally, I'm sorry my father won't get the order but let's say no more about it. If you are satisfied with the design, let's sign the contracts and I can get everything under way.'

'Very well,' said Ruth grudgingly. 'It's generous of you to be so understanding, Matthew.' She shrugged her shoulders in resignation. 'What can I do but agree?'

'Thee won't regret it, Ruth,' said David.

'I hope not,' she replied coolly.

'Right, then let's sign the papers.' David went to the desk and in a matter of moments the agreements had been signed.

Matthew left immediately and, when David returned to his study, Ruth stopped her agitated pacing and swung round on him.

'I think you treated Matthew abominably, and it's going to be embarrassing when we meet his father.' Her voice was taut with emotion.

'Why should it be?' countered David with an equal snap to his voice. 'He knows he's in competition with other shipbuilders.'

'But he's a friend. He'd expect to get the job,' she countered.

'Well, he shouldn't.'

'And why should the Thoresbys advise us? It's no concern of theirs.'

'They have practical experience. Ruben's advice was sound,' returned David calmly.

'You go to someone like that . . . he hasn't even done as many voyages as you. Yet you talk of practical experience!' Ruth gave a tiny grunt of contempt. 'More likely it was just an excuse to see Jenny!' Unconsciously, her long fingers twisted and turned at her plain wedding ring, emphasising the irritation she was feeling.

David's eyes hardened. 'What's the use of talking to thee?' He turned away in disgust but then swung round sharply, his body inclined towards her, his head thrust forward. 'I've told thee what was between Jenny and me is in the past, but thee'll believe only what thee wants to believe.'

'Are you still going to hang around their necks when you have your own ship?' Ruth shot the question at him.

'I've told thee, they're friends. I'll not cut them off,' he rasped.

She tossed her head with disdain and her bitter laugh revealed the direction of her thoughts. 'Oh, you'll see to that – so you'll still see your precious Jenny.'

For a moment that thin line between love and hate was broken. David's face darkened with a look that frightened her. In that instant, Ruth saw her step-father towering over her. She flinched, fearing the blow which must be coming. David trembled with fury. There was a fierce, corrosive well of feeling between them, which threatened to overflow into a destructive force. David stiffened his will, swung round and hurried from the room, slamming the door behind him.

'Go to your precious Thoresbys! I don't need you!' Ruth flung at the closed door. She grabbed the bottle of wine. Liquid slopped over the edge of the glass as she poured with a shaking hand. She drained the glass in one gulp and poured herself another, breathing hard with pent-up fury as she leaned against the desk.

Damn David! But she still had Matthew. Her secret meetings with him had become more frequent as she sought a different brand of sensual excitement to that she found with her husband. She could do without David if she had to. And yet he aroused such passion in her . . . her mind wavered between the two men and she filled the glass again and again, trying to see the way ahead.

When she woke in the coldness of the morning, her head throbbing, only half-remembering how she got to bed, she was aware of the strength of the sleeping man beside her, and knew that she could not dismiss David from her life as easily as she had supposed the day before.

She awoke him and in the passion of their union they obliterated their differences of yesterday. But words had been said, accusations had been thrown, and could not be retracted as if they had never been.

'Thee's sure thee's got everything clear?' David's anxiety was evident when he put the question to Ruth as they sat in the firelight the evening before the *Mary Jane* was due to sail for the Arctic.

'Of course I am,' she replied. 'Stop worrying. I'm capable of looking after things.' She reached out and slowly entwined her fingers with his. 'David, it's been such an exciting time, laying the plans for our future.'

He smiled. 'I'm glad thee's enjoyed it. So have I.' He paused. Concern masked his face again. 'Thee's sure thee wouldn't like me to resign from the *Mary Jane*? I know Adam would understand even at this late hour.'

Ruth laughed. 'There you go, fussing again. There's nothing to go wrong. Mulgrave's are capable of building the ship and Matthew will deal with any shipbuilding problems. The rest I will look after. Get all the experience you can – it could be important. Next year you'll be taking our ship.'

'Our ship,' whispered David wistfully, squeezing Ruth's hand. 'We should have had a name for her all this time. Let's decide now, afore I gan.'

Ruth nestled closer to him, stretching her feet towards the fire, and nodded. 'Good idea.'

'I'd like the name to be connected with the north,' he prompted.

'How about *Ice Cape*?' suggested Ruth.

'Mm.'

'*Aurora*?'

'Better.'

'*Whale*, then?'

'I prefer *Aurora*.' But doubt lingered in David's voice.

They stared thoughtfully at the flames. Suddenly Ruth started. 'I think I've got it,' she said excitedly. 'You remember that day we walked at Cropton when you felt the wind, felt its pull and tried to make me understand what it was that called you to the Arctic? You spoke of the lonely wind.'

'The *Lonely Wind*.' David savoured the name. The sparkle in his eyes matched Ruth's enthusiasm as they faced each other. 'The *Lonely Wind*. Ruth, thee's brilliant!' He leaned to her and kissed her. She held his kiss and he stayed willingly. 'I'll miss thee,' she whispered when she let him go.

He stretched. 'We should have a bairn, someone to share all this with, someone who'll take it over from us.'

'Not yet, Davey. We've been careful so let's leave it that way until we get this ship, and maybe another.' She leaned closer and kissed him again.

Chapter Twenty-seven

Grey clouds hung low when the *Mary Jane* put her bow into the swell beyond the shelter of the piers. Adam looked back to the cliffs. A red shawl was still held high. David saw it too and was saddened that this was the last time he would look for it. It was a signal to Adam, and David would not be sailing with him again.

Ruben did not look back. He was disappointed that Jessica had not returned to Whitby.

While the *Mary Jane* beat her way northwards, Matthew Barrett walked up the path to the house in Bagdale.

'Hello, Matthew, a query so soon?' said Ruth, a touch of amusement on her face as she came to greet him after the maid had shown him into the parlour.

As always, he was impeccably dressed, the cut of his clothes accentuating his lithe body.

'Of a sort.' He brushed her proffered hand with his lips.

Her skin tingled at his touch. She turned to sit and indicated a seat for him. 'Well, what is your question?'

'Would you like to accompany me to a weekend party

just north of Scarborough, weekend after next? Peter Jenkins, a friend of mine, invited me, and told me to bring a friend – female. I've to let him know and a room will be reserved for Friday and Saturday nights.'

'I've heard rumours about these parties. They started about three months ago, didn't they? They sound interesting.'

Matthew chuckled. 'There's plenty of good food and wine, there's dancing, gambling ...' He paused and leaned forward conspiratorially. 'And of course other pleasures. With everyone bringing a partner and more girls brought in there's plenty to amuse everyone, no matter what their taste. You'll enjoy yourself.'

Two weeks later, with the first faint stars beginning to replace the fading twilight, Matthew drew his gig to a halt outside an imposing mansion on the edge of the lonely moors, three miles inland from Staithes.

As a groom stepped forward to hold the horse steady, Matthew jumped to the ground and hurried round the vehicle to help Ruth.

No word passed between them as the groom climbed on to the gig and drove it to the back of the house. He wondered who Matthew Barrett had with him tonight, but dismissed the query from his mind quickly. It was no concern of his. The pay was too good to be imperilled by curiosity and an unbridled tongue.

As Ruth and Matthew stepped on to the colonnaded portico, the oak door swung open and a liveried manservant bowed. They entered the house where a second manservant, identically dressed, took their cloaks.

Ruth's gaze swept quickly round the imposing hallway from which a wide marble stairway with a wrought-iron balustrade, ornamented with cupids, swept upwards. The ceiling soared high into graceful curves. Classical statuettes occupied niches in each of the walls. The whole scene was given an ethereal look by the numerous candles which flickered in brackets on the walls and from the two huge chandeliers which hung across the room.

A door on the right burst open and a young man emerged, hand in hand with a girl. Their heads together in conniving laughter, they ran to the stairs. Intent on their own pleasure, they saw no one as they climbed them quickly.

Ruth's amused attention was diverted when a second door opened and a voice called out, 'Ah, Matthew, old boy, good to see you.'

She turned to see a tall, thin man of about her own age coming towards them. He held himself erect, as if stretching to make himself even taller. He was immaculately dressed in well-fitting trousers and an impeccably tailored coat under which he wore an elaborately embroidered waistcoat. A lace cravat was tied neatly at his throat and matching ruffs protruded beyond the end of his sleeves.

'Peter Jenkins, Ruth. Peter, Ruth Fernley.' Matthew made the introductions.

'Pleased to meet you, my dear.' Peter bowed low to take Ruth's hand and brush it with his lips.

'I am delighted to meet you,' she returned with an appreciative smile. 'Thank you for inviting me.'

'Don't thank me, my dear.' Peter chuckled as he straightened. 'Thank Matthew. I invited him and told him to bring a friend. And a charming friend, I must say.' He stepped back, the better to admire her. Ruth had chosen her green silk dress which, cut low to the breasts and tight at the waist, showed her figure to advantage.

'Well, thank you both,' she said with a grace and charm which impressed both men.

'I hope you enjoy yourself and that Matthew will bring you often to charm our company when we have these get-togethers,' said Peter. He snapped his fingers and one of the footmen, who had been standing close to a table near the foot of the stairs, stepped forward and handed a key to him. Peter nodded his thanks and the man retired discreetly, to stand beside the door and await the next arrival. 'The key to your room, old boy,' Peter said as he held it out to Matthew. 'There's no need for me to intro-duce Ruth to the various activities. You know them all, Matthew. Enjoy yourselves.' He bowed to her and glided away through a doorway on the left.

'Well, what is it to be?' said Matthew with a wry smile at Ruth as he tossed the key in his hand.

'I think there are other things to show me before we make use of that,' she replied, a faint smile playing at the corners of her mouth.

'Right. That door there leads to the gambling rooms. The one Peter took leads to the dining room where there will be every imaginable sort of food and as much wine as you want. The doors on the right offer access to various pleasures.'

Curious, Ruth inclined her head to the right. 'We'll

start there, then have something to eat and then go gambling before we use that key.'

Not surprised by her choice, Matthew escorted her across the hall.

When they went to the dining room, Ruth's mind was aflutter with the things she had seen: girls in their late teens and early twenties parading themselves for men to choose; couples disappearing through a door which Matthew explained led to rooms off a long corridor running along one side of the house. She had been surprised when he pointed out one guest taking his companion for the night along with a girl of his choice. She had seen strip-tease and other actions which had been too lewd even for her taste.

Now she cast all that behind her as she chose from the sumptuous dishes which adorned a long table down the centre of the oak-panelled dining room.

Matthew escorted her to one of the several small tables which lined the walls. He was enlightening her about Peter Jenkins, the house and these parties, when Ruth's attention was diverted to a couple who had entered the dining room. It was the man who drew her gaze and sent her mind tumbling back through the years, especially to the day when she had taken a message for Mrs Fernley to Mrs Leckonby, the day when she had seen the squire confront the village boys. This man could have been the the squire in his younger days. The likeness was uncanny and sent Ruth's pulses racing.

She leaned forward to Matthew, interrupting his flow of words. 'That man, who is he?' She indicated the couple with a glance in their direction.

Matthew half-looked over his shoulder and then back at Ruth. 'Jonathan Hardy,' he said, his voice low.

Startled, she repeated the name under her breath.

'You know him?' queried Matthew.

'No,' she replied hastily, but Matthew was not impressed by her denial. It had come just that bit too quickly to be altogether convincing. But he did not press the matter.

'He's a fairly regular visitor to these weekends. More interested in gambling than what we've just been seeing, but he's not averse to a pretty girl. He has a big estate near Pickering and a house on the cliffs beyond the abbey.'

Her half-brother! Ruth's flesh tingled. Her mind raced and floundered in a morass of confusion. Her half-brother here, and he would not know that from a few yards he was being observed by his half-sister. She brought her whirling thoughts under control and was left with a burning hatred of the man because he was his father's son. Ruth locked away the information imparted by Matthew, and linked the fact that her half-brother had a house near Whitby with that almost forgotten sighting of him by David on the moors all those years ago.

It was early August when the *Mary Jane* returned, a full ship. David had taken three whales and it was with mixed feelings of regret and excitement that he faced the arrival in Whitby. He would not sail on the *Mary Jane* again but now there was the *Lonely Wind*.

'Well, Davey, the last time together,' said Adam as he

joined David at the rail, having left Jamaica to take the ship in.

David nodded. 'Thanks for all thee's done.' The words choked on the lump in his throat.

A red shawl waved on the cliff top. David bit his lip. That shawl linked so much of the past, right back to his first voyage, and now it would not wave again when he sailed.

'Thee'll need a good mate for the *Lonely Wind*. Take someone from my crew. Anyone but Jamaica,' Adam broke in on David's nostalgic thoughts.

'Thanks,' he said, knowing better than to protest at Adam's generosity. 'I'll ask Jim Talbot.'

'A good choice,' agreed Adam. 'Thee's made a good partnership in the whaleboat. It should continue.'

David had Jim's enthusiastic yes by the time the *Mary Jane* passed into the inner harbour, when he rejoined Adam. His gaze turned to Mulgrave's shipbuilding yard.

'There she is, Adam,' cried David excitedly, pointing in the direction of the *Lonely Wind* moored to the yard's quay.

'A beauty,' he commented quietly. 'She'll be faster than the *Mary Jane*.'

'If she's half as good, I'll be satisfied,' said David.

'Well, Davey, I hope she fulfils your dreams. May God go with her and with thee.' He smiled at his friend. 'Don't forget I'm here if thee wants any help.'

'Thanks,' said David. Their hands clasped in a grip of lasting friendship.

'Off with thee as soon as we tie up. The *Mary Jane* has no more hold over thee.'

* * *

David threaded his way hastily through the crowds on the quay and quickened his steps towards the wharf near Mulgrave's shipyard.

When he turned on to the quay, his step slowed and finally stopped. He stood stock-still, staring in disbelieving admiration at the ship. She looked heavy and almost tub-like, yet there was a purposefulness to her appearance. The rich-coloured English oak gave an extra feeling of solidity, a comfort to the man who would captain her to the Arctic. She looked tough, ready to withstand the crushing ice and the buffeting of piercing winds which could drive the unrelenting sea into pounding barriers of water. Her masts soared skywards ready to take the mass of sail which would drive the *Lonely Wind* ever onwards to her fortune. Though she did not have the fine lines of some merchantmen, she held a beauty which outshone any ship David had seen. This was his ship and none other could match her, not even his first love – the *Mary Jane*.

Everywhere men were busy. Hammers thumped, saws screeched, ropes creaked. David knew this was a determined effort to have the ship ready for the winter voyage.

He strolled slowly alongside the vessel, thrilled by every piece of timber and rope, excited by the fact that she was his and the next time he sailed out of Whitby he would be captain of . . . David had reached the bow. He stared at the bold letters. The *Lonely Wind*. He savoured the name silently, feeling a deep sense of pride.

He returned along the quay, pausing now and again to look back in admiration, before eventually hurrying home. As he went along the path towards the house, the front door opened and Ruth ran out to meet him.

'David! David! I'm so glad you're back.' She flung her arms round his neck and her lips met his eagerly. 'Oh, it's good to feel you so close,' she gasped. 'I've wanted you so much.'

'And I've wanted thee,' he whispered.

They kissed again and then, with arms around each other, walked to the house.

'You've seen it, David?' she asked eagerly.

'Yes, she's beautiful.'

'I'm glad you like it – oh, she. I'll never get used to calling a ship she. I've had such an interesting time. Matthew's been a great help. I've engaged Francis Chambers to look after all the paperwork. He's had experience in the shipping trade. And I've made preparations for the disposal of the timber when you get back from Memel. I've kept in touch with our friends and tried to make new contacts. All you need to do is to make sure your voyages are successful.'

'Steady on.' He laughed at his wife's exuberance. 'The important thing is, will the *Lonely Wind* be ready?'

'Yes, in a week,' Ruth informed him as they went into the house.

'Wonderful!' David shrugged himself out of his coat at the bottom of the stairs. 'You've worked miracles.'

'I can be persuasive.'

David held her at arm's length and looked at her with loving admiration. 'Who'd have thought that browbeaten Ruth Harwood would turn into a sophisticated woman with a head for business?'

Ruth looked at him coyly. 'And who'd have thought that David Fernley would captain his own whaleship sailing to the Arctic?' She looked at him in admiration, then added in a voice full of feeling, 'Oh, David, I'm so glad you made the decision to leave Cropton and come to Whitby.'

'So am I.'

'And I've another surprise for you.' Ruth linked arms with him and turned to the parlour. 'Jessica's here.'

David stopped and stared incredulously at his wife. 'Jessica, here?'

Ruth's laughter rang through the room. 'Yes.'

'But I thought she was going to wait until I'd been to the Arctic as a captain?'

'Yes,' agreed Ruth, 'but we expected it to be sooner than this, and I remembered how disappointed she was at the possibility of waiting even the two years we first thought, so I went to see your father and mother and persuaded them to let her come to live with us.'

'Thee must have been very persuasive,' commented David.

'I told you I can be,' replied Ruth. 'When they heard that you were to captain our own ship, and that Jessica could help us, they agreed.'

'And how is she? Where is she now?'

'She's well,' Ruth reassured him. 'Thoroughly enjoying herself. She's helping me, there's been so much to do, and she's been seeing a lot of James Humphries.'

'Ah, I see. Getting serious?'

'Oh, I don't know about that,' replied Ruth lightly.

'But you approve?'

'Oh, David, I'm not your sister's keeper. She has a will of her own, and a strong one as you probably know,' Ruth pointed out. 'But I see nothing wrong in the association. He's an eligible bachelor. He'll be very wealthy one day.' She gave a half-smile. 'It could be useful to us to have your sister married to him.'

'That may be so, Ruth, but I want no pressure put on her. Jessica must make up her own mind.' David's gaze left Ruth in no doubt that he meant what he said and that the repercussions could be harsh if his words were not heeded.

'I wouldn't dream of it.' She looked shocked by the suggestion.

'So long as you understand. I don't want Jessica hurt,' he said. 'Now, I'll get changed and we'll have some tea.'

Half an hour later, a flushed Jessica burst into the room. 'Oh, Davey, I'm so glad to see you.' She hugged her brother who had jumped from his chair to greet her.

In those few words, David noticed a difference in the tone of Jessica's voice and realised that his sister had lost that broad Yorkshire accent to which he had been accustomed. He made no comment but said, 'It's good to see thee too, Jess. Let me look at thee.' Still holding her hand he stepped back. He saw a Jessica radiant with pleasure. Her smile was broad. Her eyes brimming with vitality which sprang from sheer happiness. David had never seen his sister in such a bubbling mood. He realised that something more than the pleasure of seeing him was exciting her. 'What's pleasing thee so?'

'I'm going to London!' she announced. 'This evening!'

'What!' David was flabbergasted.

'Don't look so shocked, both of you.' Jessica laughed. 'It's just for a few days. Ruth, you must help me pack and see I have everything I'll need.' Jessica whirled round, laughing with joy.

'Hold on, Jess. What's this all about?' demanded David.

'I'm going with James Humphries.'

'Humphries? But . . .'

'Jessica, you can't!' Ruth sounded startled, though she was pleased that the relationship with James was developing favourably. Her efforts to encourage it over the last month could be important for their future. Already plans to further their ambitions had been forming in her mind, but they needed money and James Humphries could be the way to it. He would not be asking Jessica to go to London if he did not think a lot about her, and that was important to Ruth's plans.

'Oh, Ruth, don't take on so.' Jessica chuckled. 'It's not like that. Mrs Humphries's father died and there's some urgent business to see to in London, so James is going. When I said how much I'd like to see it, he said he'd take me. I refused at first, of course, as much as I wanted to say yes. But he insisted. I don't know what I would have done if he hadn't! He went straight away and booked another passage on the London Packet.'

'Thee mean, he's paid for thee?' David frowned.

'Yes.' Jessica looked sheepish. 'I wanted to pay, though I'd have had to borrow from you, but James wouldn't hear of it. He insisted on paying.'

David and Ruth exchanged brief glances. Each, knowing

403

of James's reputation, knew the other was wondering what his real motives were.

'Just thee and James?' asked David, his brow furrowing with concern. 'Without a chaperone?'

Jessica's eyes sparkled with amusement. She had never seen her brother take on the role of a father figure before. 'Of course not. Melissa's going.'

'Oh, well, you'll be all right with Melissa there,' Ruth approved quickly, heading off any further objections from David.

'Of course I will,' said Jessica, pleased with her sister-in-law's support.

David shrugged his shoulders. He knew it was no good arguing with them both. If he opposed Jessica, it would only lead to trouble and she would still go. 'Very well,' he said.

Jessica rushed over and hugged him. 'Thank you,' she whispered.

He pushed her away gently. 'Don't thank me, just take care of thissen. Thee's very dear to me.'

'I will. I'll be all right.'

'I don't know what Mother and Father would say,' he said with a half-smile.

'That reminds me, David,' said Jessica. 'I promised I would go back sometime before the winter sets in and take you with me.'

'Right, we'll do that after my voyage to Memel,' he agreed.

'There may be too much to do to get ready for your first whaling voyage,' Ruth pointed out.

'We'll make time. I should have gone before, and if Jessica has promised . . .'

'Well, we'll see. You can go while I keep an eye on things here,' said Ruth. She turned to Jessica. 'Come along, I'll help you pack.'

Calm did not return to the house in Bagdale until Jessica left with David for the ship.

'Hello, Jessica.' With outstretched hands, James came to meet them as they went on board.

'Isn't this exciting? It's so good of you to take me,' she said as he took her hand and bowed to her. She turned to Melissa and embraced her.

'Hello, David. Or should I say Captain Fernley?' James held out his hand.

'James.' David returned the friendly greeting. 'Melissa.' He bowed with less finesse than James.

'The *Lonely Wind*'s a fine-looking ship,' James went on. 'I hear you're taking her to the Baltic. I'll be interested to know all about that voyage.'

'They can't leave business alone,' said Melissa with a teasing twinkle in her eyes. 'Come along, Jessica, I'll show you to your cabin.'

'Jessica tells me the *Lonely Wind* is just a beginning,' commented James. 'Make a good trip, prove the *Lonely Wind* is as fine a ship as she looks, and I might be interested in investing some money in you.'

'The Arctic will be her real proving ground,' David pointed out. 'Thee should wait until after our first whaling voyage.'

A few minutes later, Jessica and Melissa returned.

'Like your cabin?' queried James.

'Oh, yes, thank you,' replied Jessica. She glanced at

David and added, 'It's next to Melissa's.' She saw that the inference was not lost on her brother.

'All ashore!' a voice boomed across the deck.

David kissed Jessica and said, 'Enjoy thissen.' He turned to James. 'Look after her, she's very precious.'

'She is to me too,' he replied. 'She'll be all right, won't she, Melissa?'

'Of course,' agreed his sister. 'Now don't worry, Captain Fernley. She'll have a wonderful time.'

As he walked down the gangway, doubt niggled at David. He could not really make up his mind about James Humphries.

Orders were shouted, ropes were cast off and the ship slid slowly away from the quay. She moved towards midstream and headed for the open sea. David watched, acknowledging Jessica's gestures of farewell. Then he heard the sound of running footsteps across the quay, getting louder and louder. He turned to see who was in such a hurry and was startled. Ruben.

The younger Thoresby, chest heaving with exertion, face a mask of anguished disappointment, stopped beside David. He stared at the London Packet moving further and further away, widening the impossible gap. He swung round on David.

'Why did thee let her go?' His desolate cry was like that of a wounded sea-bird. His eyes, darkening with anger, showed hurt and accusation. 'Thee could have stopped her! She shouldn't be gannin' with that devil. He's no good!'

The words hammered at David. Were his own suspicions being confirmed? Did Ruben know something about Humphries which he didn't? Or was this simply jealousy?

Startled, David eyed Ruben with a rebuking glance. 'She has a mind of her own,' he said.

'Humphries knows how to blind lasses with his charm.' Ruben's lips tightened in disgust. He glanced with desperation at the ship and would have hauled her back if he could. 'Oh, if only I'd gone to Adam's sooner, this wouldn't have happened. She wouldn't have gone. I'd have stopped her. She's had a month here with that bastard and now she's gannin' to London with him!' His eyes were still on the ship, measuring the distance between them. 'If he harms her, I'll kill him!' Ruben swung on his heel and strode away.

Ten minutes out of Whitby, with her face fast losing its colour, Melissa made her excuses and hurried to her cabin.

James smiled after she had gone. 'My sister never was a good sailor. You've been to sea before, Jessica?'

'No.'

'You must have. You're showing no ill-effects from the ship's motion,' he observed.

Jessica laughed. 'No, really, I haven't. As a matter of fact, I'm enjoying it.'

'I'm glad.'

She hugged herself with excitement and was sorry when the time came to retire to their cabins.

'Just one more turn around the deck,' James suggested.

'All right.'

A thin layer of high cloud diffused the moon's light

which cast pale, moving shadows across the deck. The sails filled with the gentle breeze and ropes and canvas creaked as the ship cleaved through the waves sending the sea hissing away from its bow.

They paused by the rail. The moonlight danced across the sea.

'Isn't it beautiful?' Jessica glanced at James. She felt herself drawn by his gaze and her eyes did not leave his as he bent slowly towards her upturned face. His lips met hers gently and the softness of their touch sent thrilling sensations along her spine, until the moment of tenderness was gone and his arms drew her fiercely against him. Jessica's heart beat faster and an unquenchable passion flowed between them.

When their lips finally parted, James took her hand and no word passed between them as they walked to the cabins.

Jessica's mind was a whirl of desire and disappointment. She wanted James to kiss her again, wanted to feel the power of his body so close to hers, and yet it was to be good night. Had her kiss not satisfied him, had he been disappointed in it? He had never seemed so before.

They reached her cabin and she half-turned to him but he reached past her and opened the door. 'Not good night yet, Jessica,' he whispered and with a persuasive hand pushed her gently into the cabin.

The door shut with a click behind her and she swung round to find James, his back pressed against the door, smiling at her.

Protests sprang to her lips but they were never uttered.

James stepped forward, pulled her close and stifled them with the urgency of his kiss.

Jessica tried to resist but was swamped by the passion of a James she had never known. Desire swept through her body and she could not leave it unfulfilled.

Chapter Twenty-eight

'Loosen for tops'l!'

'Hoist it!'

'Set the jib!'

'Let go fore and aft!'

David's orders, his first as captain, flew firm and confident. The *Lonely Wind* edged from the quay. The sail billowed, caught the extra wind, and she moved beyond the bridge towards the sea. Excitement ran through the ship in anticipation of her first communion with her rightful home. Groups of people along the quays and sailors on boats at their moorings cheered and shouted, wishing the *Lonely Wind* God speed as she sailed majestically towards the sea.

David glanced towards the cliff. There would be no Jenny. He started to turn away but was stopped by a movement which whisked a red shawl from someone's shoulders among a small group of people at the cliff top. The figure moved nearer the edge and the shawl waved in the air. Jenny! She was there! She had kept her promise to be there whenever he sailed. She had not forgotten – she must still think a lot of him. Pleasure coursed through him. He grinned broadly and waved back, then turned to his task of negotiating the harbour entrance.

The *Lonely Wind* took to the sea as if she were doing her hundredth voyage instead of her first. Old men, veterans of the sea, watching critically from the cliff top, nodded their approval of the way she caressed the waves instead of fighting them. She was a good ship, they agreed, and David would not have gainsaid. Throughout the voyage, he had nothing but praise for Matthew Barrett's design and Mulgrave's construction. If she stood up to whaling in the Arctic as well as she handled now, he knew he would have a success.

David found Adam eagerly awaiting his arrival at Memel. 'I've got you a cargo,' he told him.

With few details to bother David, the deal was soon completed. Once the ships were loaded, they left together on the next tide.

The sea to Whitby ran fair. Always in sight of each other, the two ships made a good passage to their home port.

An elite group stood apart from the familiar crowd who shouted raucous greetings to the crew of the *Lonely Wind*.

Ruth, her ankle-length dress covered by a flowing robe fastened at the throat, was chatting to Matthew Barrett, James Humphries and Jessica. She waved to David who, with thumbs up, indicated a successful voyage. Francis Chambers was making final arrangements about the cargo with Frank Watson who was eager to inspect it.

David waved to the well-wishers and, anxious to impart news of the voyage, was quickly down the gangway once the ship had docked.

Ruth greeted him with a kiss as the others crowded round.

'Everything went well. She's a fine sailer, Matthew. Francis, take Frank on board, Jim'll show thee the cargo. It's good timber, Frank. Thee gan too, James. Might mak thee think about that suggestion thee made afore thee left for London.' James nodded but said nothing. David thought he looked strained but had no time to consider the matter for he was swept up in eager questions.

'Let's see what Frank thinks to the cargo,' suggested Ruth, seeking an escape from those who held David's attention.

They hurried to the ship where they found that they only had to agree to the price arranged between Frank and Francis Chambers. They exchanged glances of congratulation. They were in business and this was the way to success.

'Did thee have a nice time in London, Jess?' asked David as they walked home.

'Oh, yes,' she answered with obvious enthusiasm for her trip. 'The voyage both ways was wonderful, and I wasn't seasick once. I couldn't have had kinder escorts. It was unfortunate that we couldn't see more of London, but we had to return three days sooner than expected.'

'Oh, why?'

Jessica frowned. 'I don't know. James and Melissa went to see about their grandfather's will. When they returned, they looked extremely worried. They had little to say except that we had to return to Whitby by the next available ship.'

'A pity,' David commiserated.

'James has not been his usual self ever since,' she said regretfully, then added with concern, 'I do hope there's nothing wrong.'

'Some minor upset, maybe,' consoled Ruth. 'Oh, by the way, Jessica, James might be interested in investing with us, so you can keep putting in a good word.'

'Oh, I hope he does. I'll do what I can,' she promised. 'You are coming home with me for a few days, aren't you, David?'

He frowned and pursed his lips thoughtfully. 'I've a lot to do here,' he pointed out.

'But you promised,' protested Jessica. 'I wrote and told Mother and Father that you'd be home when you got back from Memel. They'll be very disappointed if you don't go.'

'You did promise.' Ruth lent support to Jessica. 'I'll stay to see to things here, and then you can have a fortnight instead of a week. It will do you good. You've had no time off. There'll be a carrier's cart tomorrow.'

'But that means leaving thee again so soon.'

'What's a couple of weeks out of a long winter?' replied Ruth, her eyes holding out a promise that she would more than make up for the parting.

David made his protests but they were brushed aside by Ruth and Jessica, and arrangements were made for them to go the next day.

An urgent knocking on the front door startled them

and a few moments later Mary came in and announced, 'Mr Ruben Thoresby, asking to see Miss Jessica.'

'All right, I'll come,' she said, hurrying from the room before Ruth or David could comment.

Jessica held out her hands as she crossed the hall. 'Ruben, how nice to see you.'

He took her hands in his. 'It's grand to see thee. Jessica, I've got to talk to you.'

She hesitated, wanting to avoid what she thought might lie behind the gravity of his expression, but she did not want to hurt him by refusing his request.

They left the house and Ruth frowned as she watched them from the window. No one must get in the way of her plans, and certainly not a Thoresby.

Ruben and Jessica climbed to the cliff top behind Bagdale, exchanging only pleasantries during the walk. Near the cliff edge, Jessica stopped and admired the view across the river. Whitby's red roofs glowed in the autumn sunlight. The river flowed gently to the calm sea which barely made a mark of white foam on the sands which stretched in a golden line towards Sandsend.

'It's beautiful,' observed Jessica quietly.

'Almost as lovely as you,' whispered Ruben, coming close to her. His hand took her arm and turned her.

Jessica found herself looking into eyes which left her in no doubt about Ruben's feelings for her.

'Marry me, Jess,' he added before she had time to speak. 'I love thee. I have from the first moment I saw thee.'

'Oh, Ruben!' The words caught in her throat.

He bent to kiss her but she turned her head away. 'Jess, what's wrong?' His cry held the pain of rejection.

There were tears in Jessica's eyes as she turned them back to Ruben. 'I'd hoped you wouldn't ask me. I don't want to hurt you.'

'What do thee mean? Marry me and I'll be the happiest man in the world,' he entreated, fearing the worst.

'Ruben, please. I like you a lot but it doesn't go any deeper than that.'

His face clouded with hurt. His world lay shattered. 'Jessica, give me a chance. Liking can turn into love, I know it. Marry me. Thee'll never regret it.'

There was sadness in her tear-filled eyes as Jessica touched his cheek with the tips of her fingers. 'Dear Ruben, I can't say yes because you deserve someone who loves you in the way you are saying you love me.'

'Jessica, please . . .'

'Ruben, the answer is no.' She tried to be gentle but firm. 'You deserve someone better than me.'

'There's no one better than thee.'

Jessica smiled sadly. 'I'm flattered, but I can't say yes.'

Ruben stiffened. 'Oh, if only I'd reached the London Packet in time!'

'What do you mean?' Jessica frowned.

'I learned thee were gannin' to London with James Humphries. I tried to reach the ship before thee sailed.' His eyes burned with the memory. 'I wouldn't have let thee gan if I had.'

'You couldn't have stopped me,' she replied indignantly.

'Oh, yes, I could. Why did thee have to gan with that no-good scum?' There was a venomous hatred in Ruben's voice.

'You can't mean James! He's very considerate,' snapped Jessica.

'Oh, he'd blind thee with his charm to get his way with thee,' said Ruben with contempt for the man.

'I've had nothing but courtesy from him,' she protested.

'For his own ends!' snarled Ruben.

'Nonsense!' Jessica's face flushed and her eyes blazed furiously.

Ruben grabbed her by the shoulders. 'Dost tha love him?' he demanded.

The unexpected question surprised Jessica. She suddenly felt baffled, for she had never really faced the possibility squarely. Now the question forced her towards an answer.

'I . . . I don't know,' she whispered, unsure of herself.

'If thee don't know, then give me a chance,' he cried. 'I love thee.'

'Ruben, I've already told you, I . . .'

'If thee don't love him, please don't cut me off. Let me see thee again.'

Jessica hesitated. Was the situation too dangerous to say yes? Would Ruben interpret their meeting in the wrong way if she agreed?

'Please?'

Jessica could not cast aside the man who pleaded with her. 'All right.' She placed a cautionary hand on his arm as she saw the joy which overcame him. 'Please don't view this the wrong way. I want to be friends, good friends, but don't get serious.'

'I promise,' he said, taking heart from the fact that she didn't know if she loved James. 'Can I see thee tomorrow?'

'I'm going to Cropton for two weeks. When I come back. That's a promise.'

'I can't wait for that day,' said Ruben, and kissed her gently on the cheek.

Jessica was thoughtful as she entered the house in Bagdale. Ruth, who was just going up the stairs, was drawn by the look of deliberation.

'Something troubling you?' she asked.

'Ruben Thoresby's just asked me to marry him.'

'What!' Concern and alarm sending her heart racing, Ruth came down the stairs quickly. 'You didn't accept?' Already her mind was reeling with the consequences to her plans if Jessica had agreed.

'No, but I wonder if I should have done?'

Even as relief started to flood over Ruth, it was halted by Jessica's pondering expression.

'Of course you shouldn't,' Ruth replied quickly. She must distract Jessica from thoughts of Ruben. 'Not when you have such good prospects.'

'James, you mean?'

'Of course. You must think a lot about him to be going out with him so often.'

'I suppose I do. He's charming, attentive . . .'

'Well then, why consider Ruben?' cut in Ruth. 'Marry him and you'll be without a husband half your life, because the sea's in the Thoresbys. Marry James and you'll be rich, be able to live a life of leisure, with a fine house and servants. You'll never have that sort of life with Ruben.'

'I don't suppose I would, but I'd have sincerity, love

417

and devotion,' she said, recalling the veneration she had always received from Ruben.

'Wouldn't you have them with James?' queried Ruth with feigned surprise.

'Sometimes I wonder about him,' replied Jessica with a slight shake of her head.

'If he didn't think so much about you, he wouldn't want to take you out so often,' said Ruth, her voice low but full of conviction.

'I suppose not,' agreed Jessica.

'I know I'm right.' Ruth felt she should press home the advantage she seemed to be gaining. 'I don't think there's any reason to consider refusing if James asks you. Naturally, your happiness comes first, but a marriage to James could help your brother a great deal.'

'How do you mean?'

'If James was one of the family he'd be more likely to invest . . .' Ruth hesitated and then went on smoothly, 'But that's a mercenary way to look at things. Your happiness is the most important thing. Think of the prospects with James carefully. There are many girls who'd jump at your chance. You don't need to decide right away, do you?' Jessica shook her head. 'Well then, you'll have time to think things over while you are at home. But don't worry David – he has a lot on his mind. I'd like him to relax as much as possible at Cropton. In fact, I wouldn't mention it to him at all. At least, not until your mind's made up.' Ruth eyed Jessica, hoping she had made her point. If David knew Ruben had proposed, he'd be pressing his sister to accept and Ruth did not want that.

Jessica looked thoughtful for a moment then said,

'Maybe you're right, Ruth. Thank you for talking to me.'
She stepped past her sister-in-law and walked up the stairs.

The following morning, after seeing David and Jessica
leave for Cropton, Ruth called at Matthew Barrett's
office.

'This is a pleasant surprise,' he said as he came from
behind his desk to greet her. 'David not with you?'

'I've just seen him off to Cropton. He and Jessica have
gone for a fortnight.' She paused in a way which charged
the moment with innuendo. 'I thought you might like to
know.'

'It's a fortnight we must not waste,' he replied. His smile
anticipated further meetings as he bowed in acknowledgement of Ruth's hint.

'We won't,' she said.

He sat down on the opposite side of the large, mahog-
any desk. 'Ruth, I know all is not as it used to be between
you and David. Am I the cause of that?'

She hesitated. She did not want to spoil her relationship with Matthew. She needed him, needed his love, so
different from David's. She knew she could spend the rest
of her life with Matthew but realised that if she chose that
course she would lose the fulfilment of achieving an ambition. But most of all she would forfeit the feeling of power.
As the Fernleys' prospects advanced, that feeling grew
and Ruth liked it. It was as if an innate desire was being
satisfied, an inborn force was driving her on to wield
power over lives. And for that she needed David and his
ambitions in the whaling trade.

She wanted things left just as they were, but was

Matthew looking beyond them? If so, it would be better to make the situation clear to him.

'You're right about David and me, but you are not the cause. He doesn't know about us.' She paused. 'We had a difference of opinion over Jenny Thoresby.'

'David and Jenny Thoresby?' Matthew was surprised and curious.

'They were in love, maybe still are, but David's too loyal to Adam. It has soured our relationship.' Ruth paused and eyed Matthew gravely and firmly. 'But let's get things straight between us, Matthew. There's no chance of David and I splitting, if that's what you're thinking. I loved David very much, was determined to marry him. And when that meant coming to Whitby, I was equally determined that he should achieve his dreams for I was just as ambitious. I still love David but now it is the business and our ambitions which hold us together. We are necessary to each other.'

'I see,' said Matthew. He nodded thoughtfully, then fixed his gaze on Ruth as he went on, 'You and I understand each other so I hope you won't mind if I ask you a frank question. Your differences with David are nothing physical, as I once thought?'

Ruth laughed. 'Far from it.' She met his eyes with equal frankness. 'David's love is a powerful thing, I need it. So you wonder why I come to you? I was curious. I wondered what it would be like to be loved by you. I found out. You love differently, and now I need to be loved both ways. You need to be fulfilled the way I do, and I believe, to gain that fulfilment, you are prepared to accept the situation and our relationship as it is.'

Matthew's eyes narrowed and an amused, knowing smile twitched at the corners of his mouth. 'Not only have I found the woman I need, I've found a very perceptive one.'

'Good. Then we understand each other better for your question.'

'Yes,' he replied. 'And I'll tell you this, Ruth Fernley – whatever happens, however we lead our lives, if ever you split with David, I'll have you.'

James Humphries, his coat collar turned up, his hat pulled well down on his forehead, bent his head against the driving rain as he hurried through Whitby's darkened streets to keep an appointment with Jethro Thompson. There were few people in the Angel Inn and James, with a nod to the landlord, went straight to the room which he and Jethro used for their meetings.

''Evening,' Jethro greeted him amicably.

''Evening, Jethro.' James took his hat from his head and beat the rain from it, sending spray across the floor. He slipped out of his coat and shook it before hanging it on a hook behind the door where it continued to drip, forming a small pool.

'It's a foul night. I've got a hot whisky for thee.' Jethro indicated the glass on the table. 'Drink it down, it'll drive out the cold.'

'Thanks,' said James, reaching eagerly for the glass. He gulped down the contents, shuddered, and, feeling the glow start to work outwards from his stomach, said, 'That's better.'

'Have another while we talk,' said Jethro, lifting a jug from the table.

He held out his glass. As Jethro poured, James studied him by the light of the flickering oil lamp which sent huge black shadows swaying on the wall. He had grown to like and respect Jethro, uncouth and rough though he might be at times. He was a man who knew his own mind, a good organiser, firm with his decisions but adaptable. He was shrewd and loyal but not a man to be crossed.

'Well, what dost thee want to see me about?' asked Jethro as James sat down on the opposite side of the table.

'You remember I said that the use of Esk Hall might be for a short period only?' James reminded him.

'Aye. I hope that time hasn't come. It's a handy place,' replied Jethro, leaning forward on the table.

'No, it hasn't and it's not likely to.' James's tone was sharp with regret.

Jethro studied James through narrowed eyes. Something had upset this young man and it concerned the use of Esk Hall. Whatever it was must not jeopardise the smuggling fraternity. 'I'm glad to 'ear it, but thee didn't come 'ere to tell me that.'

James licked his lips. He had a tricky point to put to Jethro and was apprehensive of the man's reaction. 'The use of the hall is likely to be more permanent, so I'd like to be more deeply involved in the smuggling. What can you arrange?'

'Nothing,' replied Jethro sharply.

'But I need . . .'

'Boss wouldn't allow it,' cut in Jethro, leaning back in his chair and giving himself the determined appearance of authority.

'Let me speak to him.'

'Couldn't. I'm the only one who has contact with him. It's best that way. If I'm caught he knows I won't talk, so his identity remains a secret to all but me.'

James scowled at the rebuff. 'Look, Jethro, I need to raise my income.'

Jethro was quick to note the touch of desperation in the plea. He grinned. 'Ah, I thought that must be it. Whatever thee expected to release thee from the smuggling must have fallen through.' His grin broadened. 'Now thee's hooked to us for good.'

He leaned forward again, staring hard at James. The movement threw a new light on his face. Some shadows deepened, others receded, revealing a touch of cruelty in the deep-set eyes beneath bushy eyebrows. This was a side of Jethro unknown to James until now and he didn't like it. He realised the smuggler was revelling in the power that he held.

'Don't get big ideas. The boss wouldn't like it.' Jethro's voice was charged with warning and James recognised it. Step out of line, upset things, and he would be dispensed with. He was cornered and realised that Jethro knew that he knew.

'You cunning old bastard,' hissed James. 'You've got me.'

Jethro shrugged his shoulders. 'It's all in the game. My advice is to leave things as they are.'

James stared at him for a moment then drained his glass, slammed it on the table and stood up. He swung round and grabbed his coat from the door.

As James's hand closed around the knob, Jethro spoke. 'There'll be a consignment brought ashore on Wednesday night.' His voice was low level but with a timbre that spelled out a warning if James should fail to fulfil their arrangements.

David was glad he had been home, seen the family and strengthened ties with them.

Jessica returned to Whitby physically refreshed but no clearer in her mind about James and Ruben.

The news they brought, that Squire Hardy had died, did not touch Ruth's heart with pity. She felt an intense regret that she had not been able to wreak revenge on the man who had never owned her. But in the days which followed she nurtured the possibility of fulfilling that revenge upon his son.

By the first day in March, David was satisfied that all was ready. The crew was mustered, David having decided to make up half of it with Shetlanders, and once the necessary clearances had been made the *Lonely Wind* sailed with the *Mary Jane* the following day on the morning tide.

Ruth felt a flush of pride as the *Lonely Wind* eased her way to the centre of the river. There had been the maiden voyage to Memel but this was the real start towards their dreams. She and David needed each other to fulfil them. Last night she had loved him, felt the power of his body satisfy her. Until the *Lonely Wind* returned, she would temper her craving to the needs of Matthew Barrett, and in answering those needs would find a different satisfaction herself.

But last night David had sensed a subtle change. Ruth had loved him in a way to make a man yearn to be back from the long Arctic days when he had only the lonely wind to caress him, but there had not been the same tenderness. It confirmed a suspicion that had grown in him ever since his return from Cropton. It was as if Ruth sought to satisfy an appetite and, in slaking that need, had lost the tenderness of real love.

The *Mary Jane* was in sight all that day but at dawn on the second she was nowhere to be seen and was not sighted again until they reached Lerwick.

Once he had taken fresh supplies on board and had struck a bargain with the Shetlanders for his crew, David lost no time in getting the Whitby men from the whisky-houses and sailing into the vastness of the Arctic Ocean.

Boatcrews were selected, boats prepared, lookouts posted and a routine organised with a throroughness his crew respected. And when David personally struck the first whale, the men recognised they were on a winning ship.

On a fine day five months later, the *Lonely Wind* was sighted by the crowd on the cliff top, after the cry of 'Whaleship!' had swept through Whitby.

Jenny felt a pang of disappointment when she did not see the *Mary Jane* but was pleased that David was home safely with the sign that he had a full ship. Cheers broke out from the crowds when the *Lonely Wind* left the sea for the calm waters beyond the piers. Whitby was glad to have a successful new captain among its whaling skippers.

Jenny's eyes were riveted on the ship, and she sensed the pride David must be feeling. She swirled the red shawl from her shoulders and waved. David raised his arm and answered with a signal that told her that Adam was safe and not far behind.

Ruth and those who had shares in the *Lonely Wind* waited eagerly on the quay for details of the successful voyage. David met their enthusiasm with his own excitement, and Ruth eagerly returned to the subject later, after they had made up for five months' separation. 'With oil and whalebone bringing good prices, we'll make a nice profit. You had a good winter's voyage and there's no reason why this year's shouldn't be equally profitable. Frank will buy all the timber you can bring. We should be well placed. David, we could think of another ship!'

She slipped out of his arms and rolled over in the feather bed so that she could see his reaction.

'You approve?' she prompted.

David smiled. 'I approve of everything about thee,' he replied huskily, his eyes straying over her exposed breasts.

'Then you agree we could get another ship?' she queried, gripped by a feverish desire for immediate expansion.

'Yes. There's always a risk in the Arctic, but if we don't take risks we'll never get anywhere.'

'Oh, David, you're wonderful!' cried Ruth in pure pleasure at his ready agreement. She crushed her lips against his and felt his arms encircle her waist to pull her closer.

'We'll put out feelers for shares this winter,' suggested David as they dressed. 'We'll make all the arrangements and build while I'm away in the Arctic next year.'

'Will you keep the same design as the *Lonely Wind*?'

'Couldn't better it,' he replied. 'I'll see if James Humphries is interested in investing. He said he'd think about it after our first whaling voyage.'

'He must be. The results are so good.'

David found the opportunity to approach James during a pleasant evening at the Watsons'.

'Thee said thee'd be interested in the results of my first whaling voyage and then might consider an investment,' David reminded him. 'The profits were good, as you've probably heard, and I'll have the money from my coming voyage to Memel to add to them, so I'm considering building another ship next year. Interested?'

'Of course I am,' lied James, not wanting to reveal the change in his fortunes. 'But whaling's a tricky business. Next year's voyage might be just as bad as this was good. I'd rather wait another year.'

'But I want this new ship ready before then and to do that I've got to get investors soon, preferably before I sail to Memel,' David pointed out, making no attempt to disguise his disappointment at James's refusal.

'I'm sorry, David, but that's the way I see it,' said James. 'My advice to you is, don't expand too quickly. Do another Arctic voyage, maybe even two, before you think of another ship.'

'But the time is right now,' urged David.

'I know things are booming in the whaling trade, but it'll not go on,' said James, his glance darting beyond David as he sought some means of escape. 'Wait.'

'Chances must be taken whilst they're there.' David's voice was filled with agitation. 'I wouldn't want thee to miss the opportunity.'

'Another year,' replied James, patting his arm condescendingly.' 'Now, you must excuse me, I'd like a word with Melissa and Albert.' He walked away, leaving David staring after him with disappointment and anger welling inside him.

Ruth saw her husband standing alone, excused herself from Captain Shepherd, and crossed the room.

'I saw you talking to James,' she said, inclining her head in query.

'He wants to wait until after our next whaling voyage,' replied David tersely, 'and even then he isn't sure. We certainly can't bank on any support there.'

'Damn the man!' Annoyance and frustration flared in Ruth. 'Well, we'll just have to see what can be done about him,' she added, tapping her fingers in agitation against the stem of her glass.

'Not this evening,' warned David. 'He won't budge now.'

Ruth looked thoughtful. 'Maybe Jessica will be able to help,' she said quietly.

David's face hardened. 'Ruth, don't push Jessica at James. That's her own private affair. I won't have her used for our ends.'

Ruth shrugged her shoulders and kept her ideas to herself.

Chapter Twenty-nine

The *Lonely Wind* was only an hour out of Whitby, on her way to Memel, when Ruth called on Matthew Barrett.

'You don't wait long once David has sailed,' he remarked as she closed the office door. He came from behind his desk only to be greeted by a friendly cheek turned for his kiss, instead of her usual, more passionate greeting.

He opened his mouth to protest but her gracious inclination of the head and sweet smile halted his words.

'Matthew, I've something to ask you,' Ruth said lightly as she stepped past him. 'You won't like it but it will benefit you in the end.'

He raised his eyebrow quizzically. 'Ask.'

'I want you to take me to Peter Jenkins's and introduce me to Jonathan Hardy.'

'Hardy!' gasped Matthew. 'Not with his reputation for womanising.'

'I want to meet him,' returned Ruth firmly.

'Not likely,' replied Matthew, a snap to his voice as he turned away from her.

'Matthew, please do this for me.' Ruth lowered her voice to a soft lilt.

He swung round to see her smiling entrancingly. His immediate anger was gone but irritation remained. 'Why? What do you want to meet him for?'

'Trust me, Matthew,' replied Ruth, moving towards him. 'It will be for our good.'

'How?' He was suspicious.

'I can't tell you now, but it will be.' Her hands slid up the lapels of his coat and round his neck. The seduction in her eyes melted the last remnants of his protest. 'It's you I love, it's you I want to spend my time with, but please do this for me.'

She looked into his eyes with a longing that stirred his whole being.

'You're a vixen, Ruth Fernley, a beguiling witch.' He crushed her to him and his lips met hers with a passion which told her he was hers.

Two nights later Matthew escorted Ruth into the house on the edge of the moors and within the hour she was accompanying her half-brother to the gambling tables.

When he was serious about his play she watched; when he was light-hearted she entered into the fun. She cajoled and teased, she encouraged and demurred, until they left the gambling to enjoy the sumptuous delights of the dining room.

Through all the pleasantries and enjoyment, Ruth nursed her contempt for this man who had enjoyed a lifestyle which by rights should have been hers.

'I see you wear a ring, yet you come with Matthew Barrett?' Jonathan leaned closer to her.

She read this as her chance to establish a bond of frankness between them and smiled wryly. 'My husband is a whaling captain. I thought you would have recognised the name.'

'Whaling doesn't interest me,' he replied.

'I thought you must have investments in ships.'

'No,' replied Jonathan. 'Too risky for me.'

'You've never been interested?' pressed Ruth, hoping for an opening by which she might persuade him to invest in a new ship.

'No, nor ever will be,' he replied firmly. 'I'm too much of the land. That's where my money lies.'

Disappointment filled Ruth. She knew from his attitude that it would be no use pursuing the matter. To do so might only bring suspicion upon herself. There must be some other way and she was determined to find it. She hid her disappointment and said, 'Yet you live in Whitby.'

'It's not my real home. That's near Pickering,' explained Jonathan, little knowing that he was telling her something she already knew. 'But Fernley . . .' He paused thoughtfully. 'The name does mean something – one of my workers has the same name. Don't know much about the family. I was hardly ever at home when I was younger. It's only since my father died . . . They wouldn't be related to you?'

Ruth shook her head. 'No,' she lied. 'We're from along the coast.'

'So you're not averse to pursuing your own pleasures when your husband's away?' he said with clear insinuation as he studied her closely.

'No. I'm not going to sit at home bemoaning his

absence,' replied Ruth, finding herself studying her half-brother as a man. She was aware of his lithe body with its hidden strength. His gaze probed, assessed, and at the same time admired and approved, promising a deeper relationship if she wanted it. A flutter of desire shivered through her body and she wondered what it would be like to be loved by a close relation. Her mind whirled with the thought and with it came the first glimmer of a plan which could wreak even greater revenge. As it quickly matured, she relished the thought of playing Jonathan as a fisherman might a fish. She met his gaze over the rim of her glass as she sipped her wine.

He interpreted a look from which he need not shy. Its frankness broke down any barrier which might have been left between them. His features contained an unspoken promise as he leaned closer to her. 'And you find all your pleasure with Matthew Barrett?'

'Are you suggesting something else?' she asked coquettishly.

'You know I am.' Jonathan smiled, raising his glass. 'And I believe you're interested. A pity you're with Matthew this evening.'

'Then we must make it another time,' she said. 'My husband is away for another eight days.'

'Let's not waste it. Tomorrow night?'

'So soon?'

'Why not?' Jonathan chuckled. 'You aren't really shocked.'

Ruth laughed, and, as he laughed with her, the bond between them was finalised.

'I'd better return to my escort for this evening,' she

said, replacing her empty glass on a table. 'Until tomorrow night then.'

'Wait.' He stayed her departure. 'We'll not come here. My house. A carriage will call for you.' The command in his eyes and voice brooked no refusal.

Ruth smiled to herself. Not that she would have refused such a tempting offer. This was better than she had hoped for. Her half-brother hooked. Revenge would be all the sweeter if her ambitions could be furthered at his expense.

'Any time,' she returned quietly. 'My husband's sister, who lives with us, leaves in the morning to visit her parents for a week.'

'Then pack a bag.' Jonathan's voice was low.

Ruth smiled but said nothing. She turned away. As she walked from the room, his eyes were on her. She sensed his desire, and delight shivered down her spine at the thought of the power she held over him.

A fierce craving gleamed in Jonathan's eyes when he met Ruth at the door of Rigg House on the lonely cliffs between Whitby and Robin Hood's Bay.

When he made introductions to Mrs Judson, Ruth sensed animosity in the tall housekeeper with a severe face. She knew she would have to win the esteem of this woman, and emanated charm and friendliness. Mrs Judson's searching gaze eventually turned to one of approval.

Once her cloak and bag had been disposed of, Jonathan led Ruth across the hall. 'We'll not waste time,' he whispered seductively close to her ear.

As they climbed the curving stairs, his long fingers

started to unfasten her dress and, when the bedroom door closed, he slipped it from her shoulders.

Jonathan turned her to him. For one fleeting second a flash of resistance coursed through her body, a momentary repugnance at being touched by the man she hated. Then it was gone, lost in her curiosity to know what it would be like to be taken by him.

In David she felt strength and power, in Matthew she found tender and lingering love, and with Jonathan she was already anticipating the excitement of illicit pleasure.

His lips brushed hers, sought her neck and moved passionately to her shoulders.

Ruth stood, relaxed and limp, enjoying each new sensation as Jonathan undressed her, his supple hands flicking across her soft skin, sending shivers through her.

When his lips sought her breasts, she reached out for him. Her desires surged into a wild demand which would not be denied. She tore at his clothes, ripping them from his body. Jonathan, borne along on her craving, helped her.

The last garment shed, they paused. Their eyes devoured each other for a moment. Ruth shuddered. He took her and, locked together, they sank on to the bed.

Six days later, Jonathan helped Ruth into the carriage which he had summoned to take her back to Whitby.

'Goodbye, Ruth. I'll look forward to the day the *Lonely Wind* sails to the Arctic,' he said quietly. His eyes devoured her one final time as he closed the carriage door.

Ruth smiled encouragingly and blew him a kiss. Jonathan called to the coachman and the carriage rumbled forward. Ruth gave Jonathan one final wave from the window and, with a contented sigh, sank back on the seat.

She allowed herself a smile of satisfaction. Jonathan had been attentive to her every need. Nothing was spared to make her comfortable and happy. It was almost as if he was courting her.

But in the bedroom he became a different man – a man who demanded perverted sexual pleasures. And Ruth matched him as if she had inherited the same intense desires.

As she lay back in the carriage, she could still feel the giving and receiving and knew that if everything went according to plan no one would know who was the real father of the baby she had planned.

Chapter Thirty

'Tak care of thissen, Ruth. We don't want anything to happen to that boy thee's carrying.' David showed his concern before boarding the *Lonely Wind*.

She smiled. 'Might be a girl.'

'Nay, lass, bound to be a boy.' He grinned. 'But whatever, tak care.'

'I will, Davey. Don't fuss so.'

All about them activity bustled on the quayside. Families come to bid their loved ones goodbye mingled with spectators come to wish the ship well on her voyage to the Arctic.

'Sorry we didn't get the backing for another ship,' commented David regretfully. 'Maybe it's for the best with the condition thee's in. There'd have been too much worry for thee.'

'I'd have managed,' replied Ruth.

'No doubt thee would,' commented David, knowing his wife's determination. 'After this voyage they'll all be clamouring to invest in us.' His eyes narrowed. 'Then we'll be choosy who we pick. Well, I'd better get aboard.' He turned to Jessica. 'Look after her and my son,' he called.

'I will, don't you worry.' She kissed her brother. 'May God go with you.'

''Bye, Ruth.' David took her in his arms and hugged her. He held her close, kissed her upturned face, then strode away up the gangway.

'I'm going to the cliff top,' said Jessica.

'Very well,' replied Ruth, half turning to her sister-in-law. As Jessica hurried away, Ruth's attention was caught by a face in the crowd. Jonathan! He was back in Whitby. She had had no news of him since those six days spent together. Now he was here. Their eyes locked and an understanding flashed between them. Jonathan's lips formed one word and Ruth had no doubt that a carriage would call for her tomorrow.

The sun spilled weakly across Whitby's roofs, and a cold breeze whisked the smoke from the forest of chimneys as the *Lonely Wind* and the *Mary Jane* cast off, caught the breeze with their topsails and headed for the open sea. Cheers from the crowds on the quays, staithes and cliff tops encouraged them on their way.

On the east cliff, Jessica watched the two ships with pride. On one her brother was the captain, on the other sailed a man for whom she had deep feelings. It was these which troubled her as she watched the ships meet the first waves. Did Ruben command more of her love than James Humphries nowadays? It was a question which was to trouble her throughout the summer.

Beside her Jenny swirled her red shawl in a farewell

gesture which was interpreted by two whaling captains in different ways.

When Ruth left the quay, she made her way through the dispersing crowd to Matthew Barrett's office.

'So soon?' he remarked, a teasing twinkle in his eye as he rose from his chair behind his desk.

'Do you mind?' said Ruth primly.

'Of course not.' He smiled, took her hands in his and kissed her. 'I've told you I'm pleased to see you any time. I love you, Ruth. I want to spend the rest of my life with you. David's baby makes no difference.'

Ruth looked up at him with a smile. 'You're sweet, Matthew. One day we'll be together.' She slipped out of his arms. 'Now, this is a business visit.'

Surprised, he cocked a quizzical eyebrow at her. 'Business?'

She smiled. 'Yes. I want you to see to the building of another whaleship.'

'You've raised the money?'

'Not yet. Only Frank Watson was interested. As you know, everyone else says they are fully committed, and James said maybe in another year.'

'So I thought you were waiting. What's brought the change of mind?'

'I can get the necessary capital from another source,' she replied secretively.

'Where?' asked Matthew.

'That's my business. One day you'll know, but not just yet. You just put the ship under way immediately. I want it ready before David returns.'

Matthew eyed her warily. 'He doesn't know about this?'

'No,' she admitted.

'Ruth, be careful about committing yourself,' cautioned Matthew. 'You're taking a big risk. Tell me where you're getting the money, then I can better advise you.'

'No.' An edge had come to her voice. 'Now, are you going to see to this ship or not?' Her eyes hardened.

Matthew, recognising the signs, hastened to reassure her. 'Of course I will, I was only trying to be helpful.'

'You'll help by doing as I ask.'

Matthew inclined his head in apology. 'Very well. The same arrangement as before?'

'No,' replied Ruth, her voice softening to a more friendly tone. 'I was spiked by David over the building of the *Lonely Wind* and it's needled me ever since.' Her lips tightened as she recalled what she had always regarded as her humiliation in front of Matthew. 'Well, he's not here now. Your father can build this one.'

'Won't that cause trouble when David returns?'

'I can handle him,' snapped Ruth.

'Very well,' conceded Matthew. 'Barrett's yard will build you a fine ship.'

'Good. And see it's ready on time.'

'It will be,' said Matthew. 'We'll seal the bargain with a drink,' he added as he crossed the room to a corner cupboard from which he produced two glasses and a decanter.

As Ruth had surmised, a coach called for her the following afternoon. On the journey to Rigg House, she formulated her plan to get the necessary backing for the

439

new ship, and with it the revenge which had lain deep in her heart for so long.

'No bag?' observed Jonathan as he helped her from the carriage. 'With your husband away, I thought . . .' The words trailed away as she straightened. His eyes widened in a mixture of surprise and annoyance. 'You're with child!' he gasped.

'Shall we go inside?' she asked with a demure smile.

Quickly controlling his feelings, Jonathan ushered her into the house. He took her cloak, laid it on a chair and guided her to the parlour.

'Did you not know when you saw me on the quay?' she asked before he could say anything.

'There was a crowd. I couldn't see all of you.' There was still an edge of annoyance to his voice. His eyes were hard and dark and Ruth sensed the restless urge within him heightened by frustration.

'If you had been in Whitby, you would have known,' she said.

'Wasn't it better that I was away when your husband was at home?' he snapped. 'I checked when the *Lonely Wind* was sailing, and here I am – only to find this –' He cast a contemptuous glance at her stomach and turned away in disgust.

'Oh, come, Jonathan, don't act so . . .' Ruth's voice was smooth, deliberately caressing.

He swung round. His eyes were fired with a desperate longing, while his face was clouded with anger. 'I've dreamed of having you again just as I did those days you spent here. And now, what do I find?' His lips curled with repugnance.

Ruth was enjoying his torment. His words notwithstanding, she knew he was overwhelmed by abject desire, a desire which she could heighten at her wish, until it became unbearable.

She stepped closer to him and reached out to stroke his face gently. He quivered and she chuckled temptingly. 'Oh, Jonathan, I didn't know I could have such an effect on you.' She looked deep into his troubled eyes. 'There are other women.'

He stepped into her arms and shuddered like a child seeking comfort. 'No. It's not the same with them. There's something about you, Ruth . . . maybe it's because you're married. But, no, it's something else. It's as if we were bound closely in something dangerous, forbidden. I want you. I need you!'

She stroked the nape of his neck. 'Don't take on so, Jonathan. There are ways. Did we not do other things when I was last here?'

He straightened with an excited tremor. 'You mean it, Ruth?' The thought of satisfying his desire lightened his eyes.

'Anything, Jonathan,' she said quietly, stepping back from him so that she could better see his reaction to her next words. 'Anything. But you shall not enter me. I'll not risk the life of your baby.'

For one fleeting second, the implication behind that one word made no impact. Then it struck, drawing his eyes wide with incredulity. 'Mine! It can't be!' he gasped.

'It can and it is!' Ruth's words, cloaked in cold certainty, pierced Jonathan's amazement.

'But . . .' his voice quivered with bewilderment. 'I don't want . . .'

'What you want and what you'll get are two different things.' The rapier-like thrust to Ruth's tone startled Jonathan though he could not begin to guess the true meaning behind her words. Her voice softened and her smile tempered his confusion. 'Don't fret, love. David believes the child is his.'

Relief drove the bewilderment from his face.

Ruth stepped close to him, exuding the sexuality through which she knew she held him in her power. 'So forget the baby.' Her hands caressed him, and with the shiver which she felt course through his body she knew his mind. She took his hand and led him to the stairs.

With little feeling Ruth gazed down at her son, snuffling contentedly in his cot. She smoothed her dress across her stomach, pleased that she was firm and slim again. She had hated her misshapen figure and loathed its cause, but had survived in the knowledge of the revenge her baby would bring.

The birth had been almost trouble free, though nauseating and upsetting and not without pain. Jenny's good wishes, sent through Jessica, were received coolly, with a hidden delight that Jenny would not enter the house in Bagdale. Matthew outwardly paid his respects, as did other friends, but alone with her declared his continuing love, in spite of the baby.

Now Ruth prepared to meet the one person she had not heard from until yesterday. A note, delivered to the door, had borne one word – 'Tomorrow'.

Jonathan was back.

The time had come to be certain of paying for the new ship and furthering the Fernley shipping empire.

She drew resolve from her son but gave him no smile, nor offered him a kiss. Coldly, she turned to the door and went downstairs to await the carriage.

'Thank goodness that's all over,' commented Jonathan, eyeing Ruth's slim figure with pleasure. 'I can have you properly again.' His eyes sparkled with anticipation of the satisfaction he knew only she could impart.

'If I let you!' There was an ominous crispness to her voice which told Jonathan that she was not being frivolous.

'What do you mean?' he asked, puzzled and indignant.

'What I say,' replied Ruth. She turned casually away from him.

He grabbed her by the arm, jerking her back to face him. 'Don't taunt me, Ruth.' His eyes blazed.

She looked at him defiantly. 'I'm not! You take heed. You'll not have me unless you meet certain conditions.'

Jonathan gave a mocking laugh. 'Conditions? There's only one condition you have – your need. And that's as strong as mine. You can't do without me, Ruth. You know what I can do for you, and you've said no one else can fulfil you as I can.' He released her arm with a shove, a gesture which signalled his contempt of her suggestion that she could withhold her favours.

Ruth straightened and matched his look. 'Oh, I can do without you, Jonathan. But can you really do without me?' She reached out and let the tips of her fingers run sensuously over his cheek. He shuddered and did not pull away. Ruth sensed it and smiled beguilingly at him as her fingers caressed his neck. He stiffened at her touch. 'See,

443

you can't,' she added in a sultry, silken voice which promised so much.

Jonathan moaned. He had anticipated this day for so long that now it was here he could not let it slip away. He grabbed her round the waist and pulled her tightly to him. Her soft, warm body moulded to his, tempting and encouraging, while her hands stroked him knowingly. Jonathan groaned with desire.

'See, you need me too,' he whispered close to her ear.

'Oh, no,' she rapped, startling him with the sudden change in her voice as she stepped away. 'I can do without you. I've a stronger will than you. You think of the things I've done for you and you want them again and again.' Jonathan, bewildered by this unexpected side of Ruth, started to shake his head. 'Oh, yes, you do, otherwise you wouldn't have sent the carriage for me whenever the opportunity arose.'

'All right, Ruth. Please don't torture me so,' he pleaded. 'What is it you want?'

'You acknowledge your son!'

The audacity of the statement cleared Jonathan's brain. 'What?' he gasped. 'How? What about David? You said he thinks the baby is his.'

'He does and will go on doing so.'

'But if I acknowledge it . . .'

'You don't have to acknowledge him openly,' cut in Ruth.

'Then how? Why?' His features tightened in confusion.

'You acknowledge him in a will!' Ruth drilled her words home with precision. 'You leave everything to him, with me as his guardian should you die before he comes of age.'

'What!' He was astounded by Ruth's demands. 'Never! I've no proof that he *is* my son.'

'My word,' she replied coldly.

'The word of a trickster!' he snarled. 'I'll not . . .'

'And miss what I can give you?' cut in Ruth.

Jonathan drew in a sharp breath. Even now he could feel Ruth's warm soft body pliable in his hands, could feel his senses reeling under her touch until . . . He tore his mind away from her siren sensuality.

'No!' he rapped with an arrogant shake of his head.

'Then I shall have to go to the authorities and tell them who is the leader of the smugglers!'

'Smuggler? Me?' He laughed with disdain.

'Do you remember a few years ago when you and some of your associates searched for two men who had been at the inn in Saltersgate? You didn't find them.' Ruth's voice was low and precise. She knew from the way Jonathan's face blanched that he recalled the time and the place. 'Well, one of those men was David. He recognised you in the moonlight.'

'Recognised me? But how? I've never met him.' Bewilderment fogged his mind.

'No, but he remembered seeing you one day when he was working in the fields . . .'

'Wait!' cut in Jonathan roughly. 'Fernley . . . You lied when you said you were from further along the coast.'

Ruth smiled coldly. 'Yes. We are from Cropton. Kit Fernley, your tenant, is David's father.'

Jonathan's lips tightened. His eyes deepened with

contained anger. 'And you? I suppose you're from Cropton as well.'

'Yes,' she replied calmly, though an inward excitement had set her heart racing as the moment of revelation came upon her. 'I am your sister!'

Jonathan laughed derisively and turned away at the announcement. 'What nonsense are you going to trump up next?'

'It's true,' she replied firmly. 'I am your half-sister. I didn't know until shortly before I left Cropton to come to Whitby. Your father never acknowledged me, and because of that I lived in filth and poverty and survived on scraps which my step-father threw to me!' Anger and hatred had crept into her voice. She spat the words out with a venom which struck at him, convincing him that she was telling the truth.

'Half-sister!' The word hissed from between Jonathan's clenched teeth. 'You knew and yet you lay with me, you let me . . .' He shuddered with disgust.

'And I bore our son!'

He met her defiant gaze with loathing.

'So isn't he more than entitled to your estate?' Ruth went on. 'I got nothing from our father, but by God I'll see his grandson gets everything from you.'

Hatred coursed through Jonathan. He sought words to defy her but could find none.

'So you see, brother, apart from losing my favours, you would not want me to denounce you as a smuggler, and worse still someone who forced his sister into incest! Yes, Jonathan, that's the way I'll put it. My silence for a will made out in favour of *our* son.' She paused and then added, as he still floundered for words, 'And after you've handed it over, you can still have me if you want me.' She strode past him towards the door, and paused with her hand on the knob. 'I'll be back in three days! See that you have it ready.' She swept from the room to call the coachman, leaving him staring at a closed door, his mind numb at the price of silence.

Three days later, Ruth stepped from the carriage and hurried into Rigg House. 'Oh, Jonathan, you didn't come to meet me,' she said touching his arm lightly.

'Did you expect me to?' he asked, his glance cold.

'We are brother and sister,' she reminded him gently. 'And lovers.' As she spoke, she ran her fingers up and down his arm.

His first instinct was to turn away but somehow he couldn't. He was bewitched by Ruth's sheer presence. He tried to concentrate on the scene outside but it turned into a misty nothingness. His blood pounded harder and harder under Ruth's touch, calling him to satisfy his desires and attain the heights to which only this woman could bring him.

'We can still be friends,' said Ruth. Her voice lowered. 'We can still be lovers.'

He glanced at her again, but this time his eyes had lost their coldness and in its place was the fire of anticipation. There was no denying the look she gave him. It acknowledged no barriers. He crushed her roughly to him.

Ruth returned his kiss with equal passion. With the tremors she felt run through his body, she knew she could turn him to her will.

'The will?' she said with a slight movement of resistance, just sufficient for Jonathan to brush it aside without delay.

'There on the table,' he said, and led her towards the door.

Ruth matched his step in the knowledge that she had got what she wanted.

An hour later, their lust satisfied, she stirred. 'Jonathan,' she murmured, 'let's take the ride we used to when I stayed with you.'

He rolled over, grinning broadly. 'Let's,' he cried, for he knew the excitement of the hard gallop brought a new exhilaration upon Ruth.

Twenty minutes later, two horses galloped at full stretch along the cliff tops north of Robin Hood's Bay. The riders leaned forward in the saddle, urging the animals onward. The joy of speed, the thunder of hooves on the soft earth, the thrill of being close to the cliff edge where, far below, the restless sea pounded into foam on the jagged rocks, brought laughter to Ruth and Jonathan.

He glanced over his shoulder, challenging her to catch up. She responded, crying out to her mount. The animal stretched itself. The gap closed. Ruth was alongside Jonathan. He grinned broadly at her. She pursed her lips in a kiss and he lifted his head in resounding laughter. The wind tore it away and tossed it into eternity.

Ruth's eyes narrowed, exploring the track ahead. It swung dangerously close to the cliff edge. Jonathan had seen it too and made to move away from it but she held her line of gallop.

'Move over!' he yelled.

Pretending not to hear, she took no action.

'Ruth!'

Instead of turning away, she brought her horse closer. There was a clash of flesh upon flesh and the screech of stirrup against stirrup. Ruth's mount shied away. Alarm and fear flaring in his eyes, Jonathan hauled hard on the reins. Too late! His horse lost its grip on the soft earth. The edge of the cliff gave way. Rider and horse plunged downwards. A piercing scream rent the air and assailed Ruth's ears as she dragged her horse to a stop. She turned and rode back.

Anxiety clouded her face as she slipped from the saddle and inched her way to the edge of the cliff. She stared downwards. Her gaze settled on a figure sprawled on the rocks far below. There was no movement. Only the sea broke the stillness at the depths of the cliffs, but Ruth was unaware of it, intent as she was upon Jonathan. Her anxiety lifted. No one could have survived such a fall.

She smiled to herself, straightened and gazed out across the ocean, letting the wind stream through her hair, revelling in the sense of freedom which gripped her. She had gained her revenge after all these years and now the whole of the estate at Cropton was under her control. She laughed aloud. Now she had money; now she could pay for the new ship, and build others; now she could become the most powerful ship owner in Whitby. Nothing could hold her back.

She turned to her horse, idly champing at the grass, climbed into the saddle and headed back to the house, making a pretence of alarm and urgency. Shocked at the tragic news, Mrs Judson gave comfort to her. Once the search party had been despatched, Ruth gathered the envelope from the table and returned to Whitby.

Two days later, at an inquiry, Ruth gave her version of the ride with her friend and how it had ended in tragedy through Jonathan's misreading of the track.

Her story accepted, she made her way to the offices of Bickerstaff and Whalley, where she presented the will left by Jonathan for verification.

Mr Bickerstaff indicated a seat to her and extended his commiserations. Ruth was suitably demure and downcast, resting her black-gloved hands in her lap as the elderly lawyer opened the envelope with great ceremony. He unfolded the paper slowly, while Ruth fought to keep her impatience under control.

Mr Bickerstaff read the contents of the document and then, without raising his head, glanced up at Ruth. His eyes fixed firmly on her, he said, 'Mrs Fernley, I was aware what this contained because I helped Mr Hardy to draw it up but I had to make sure it was the same. Mr Hardy gave me no reason for drawing up a will in favour of your son.' The statement was made as if to elicit information.

'It surprised me,' she replied quietly. 'I suppose it was because we were such friends.'

Mr Bickerstaff nodded. 'I expect so.' He paused and gazed harder at Ruth. 'But I'm sorry, this will is invalid.'

Startled, she stiffened. 'Invalid? It can't be. Jonathan gave it to me just before we rode out together on the day of his . . .' Ruth let her voice falter and brought out the last word on a whisper '. . . death.'

'I don't doubt that, Mrs Fernley. You will see this will is dated two days before the tragedy.' She nodded. 'Well, the day after that he came in here with another envelope marked "To be opened if I die a violent death".' Bickerstaff shook his head thoughtfully. 'Strange. He must have had some premonition.'

Alarm had set her heart racing. 'You've opened it?' she pressed.

'Oh, yes,' replied the elderly man. 'I think a fatal fall merited the description "violent". Wouldn't you agree, Mrs Fernley?'

Ruth felt that he was suspicious but lacked conclusive evidence and was therefore fishing for information. She put up her guard.

'And what does it say, Mr Bickerstaff?'

'It rescinds all previous wills and leaves everything to a distant relative on his mother's side. I'm afraid there is nothing for your son, Mrs Fernley.'

She wanted to scream. Silently she heaped curses on Jonathan who, foreseeing her intentions, had taken steps to outwit her. Her world was on the verge of collapse. With no money to pay for the new ship, her dreams of creating a shipping dynasty were shattered.

She took a grip on her feelings, straightened in her chair and picked up the will in favour of her son. This evidence, a pointer to what had gone on, must be destroyed before David came home.

'Thank you, Mr Bickerstaff,' she said quietly, and rose from her chair.

He rose with her and ushered her to the door, bidding her a polite good day.

451

By the time she reached home, Ruth's anger had calmed and she had thought rationally about her situation. She had suffered greater setbacks and survived. She would not be beaten now. A plan had formed in her mind to which Jessica was the key.

Chapter Thirty-one

'You told me we'd benefit from your association with Jonathan Hardy,' Matthew accused as he poured himself a glass of Madeira. 'What happens now?'

'A damned nuisance, that horse going over the cliff,' replied Ruth. 'I'd learned he was a rich man and hoped I'd persuade him to invest in the new ship.' She shrugged her shoulders as she picked up her own glass.

'In one way I'm not sorry. I didn't like your seeing him, knowing his reputation as I did.'

She smiled. 'Your concern is flattering but you had no need to worry.'

'Good,' he commented. 'So how are you going to finance the ship? My father is becoming concerned.'

'He needn't be,' she replied easily. 'I'll get James Humphries to change his mind.' When she saw Matthew look doubtful, she added, 'He's been seeing a lot of Jessica lately.'

He pursed his lips in amusement. 'And you hope . . .' He left the rest unsaid.

'Exactly.'

'Well, there's something you should know. It might be of use to you.' Matthew sipped his wine, without enlightening her further.

'What's that?' she asked, irritated by his secretive attitude.

'You'll have to watch the smugglers again,' he announced.

'Oh, no!'

'You enjoyed it the first time.' There was a cynical note to his voice. 'You can't deny it.'

'You can tell me everything I need to know. I shouldn't risk going,' she protested.

'You wouldn't believe me. I want you to see for yourself. I promise you, it will be worthwhile.'

'Matthew!' Her voice took on a commanding tone.

He shook his head slowly. 'Sorry, I'm not telling you.'

'But, Matthew . . .' She switched to cajolery, though secretly burning with annoyance that he should trifle with her like this.

He smiled, still shaking his head. 'Come with me.'

Ruth hesitated, caught between annoyance and curiosity, before she pouted and said, 'I suppose I'll have to if I want to know. But you are sure they'll be operating? I've heard rumours since Jonathan's death that he was the leader.'

Matthew raised his eyebrows in surprise. 'Is that so? But if he was, it'll make no difference. There's always someone to take over.'

Two nights later, by the light of a waning moon, Matthew tethered their horses in the thickets above the cutting

454

which ran to the seashore. He took Ruth's hand and they moved quickly but cautiously along the ridge. Crawling the last few yards, they reached cover without mishap.

The beach was empty and only the gentle sea made any movement as it lapped and ran in slowly decreasing motion across the sand.

'A perfect night for it,' whispered Matthew close to Ruth's ear. She shivered. 'Cold?' he asked. He put his arm around her and pulled her closer to him.

She snuggled up to him, finding comfort and warmth. She had always realised the thrill of the perverted affair with Jonathan would be brief and she was thankful that she had had Matthew's sensuality during David's long absences. But a deeper feeling had grown between them now and she knew she could never give herself entirely to David again. But could she ever part from him? She needed him to satisfy her insatiable ambition.

After twenty minutes, she was getting impatient. 'How much longer?' she whispered irritably.

'Not long,' reassured Matthew. 'It's nearly high tide and they'll want to use it.'

The sea played with the light spilled by the pale moon and splintered it in a sparkling stream running to the shore.

Ruth glanced across the cutting, straining her eyes for movement, but saw nothing.

No sooner had she turned her attention away from the sea than she felt Matthew's arm tighten around her.

'There!' he whispered.

She moved her gaze quickly but sensed the light rather than saw it.

People appeared from nowhere and within a few minutes the first boatload of contraband was being run ashore. Women with bladders of brandy beneath their skirts were first away in the direction of Whitby. Men made for the cutting with barrels and boxes.

'Come on.' Matthew started to move away.

Ruth stopped him. 'What have I come to see?'

'I'm going to show you now.'

They moved along the ridge, Matthew careful to keep below the skyline, matching their pace to that of the shadowy figures below.

Approaching the end of the cutting, Matthew quickened pace and found cover behind some bushes. A few moments later, the weak moonlight revealed a steady line of figures coming out of the cleft only a few feet from them.

The smugglers turned smartly across the field away from the sea. Once the last man had passed them, Matthew and Ruth followed at a safe distance. The field dipped into a hollow and then rose steadily towards the black mass of a large house. Matthew stopped at the edge of the hollow and pulled Ruth down beside him.

'Well?' she whispered, her eyes following the line of figures moving towards the house. Even as she put the question, the realisation of what Matthew wanted her to see struck her. 'Esk Hall!' She gasped the name in a tone of disbelief. 'The Humphries!'

'Yes,' replied Matthew, keeping his voice low. 'I thought you ought to know because of Jessica's relationship with James. Come on, let's clear out before the rest come.'

He started to move away but Ruth's attention was still riveted on the house. The Humphries involved in smuggling? It was too incredible, and yet she was actually watching contraband being run ashore and taken to Esk Hall.

Matthew tugged at her. She lurched to her feet, her mind still on the scene she had just witnessed. They were soon leading their horses from the thickets and turning them for Whitby.

'Are they the leaders of the smugglers?' asked Ruth.

'No, but they allow Esk Hall to be used for safe storage. How do you fancy a smuggler as a possible future partner? And how do you think David would take to having a smuggler as a brother-in-law?'

Ruth reined her horse to a stop. As Matthew turned his alongside, she told him firmly, 'Look, I want James to invest in our business. How he gets his money is no concern of mine. Marriage with Jessica could make his investment more certain, but David wouldn't like his sister marrying a smuggler, so David isn't going to know about what I've seen tonight. I'm not going to tell him, and you'd better not.'

'Why should I?' said Matthew, with a shrug of his shoulders. 'You need the money, Father wants the business, so my mouth is closed.'

'Good,' returned Ruth. 'We understand each other.'

'Haven't we always?'

Their eyes locked and Ruth knew why he had never pressed her to leave David. He was satisfied with their relationship, for he saw the Fernley ambitions meant greater wealth all round. Only a breakdown of those ambitions would make him view their life together differently, but Ruth was certain the love between them was strong enough to meet any adversity. Hadn't it survived the affair with Jonathan?

She nodded. 'Yes.'

They sent their horses forward and Ruth knew she would be invited to Matthew's house before he escorted her to Bagdale, and it would be an invitation she would not refuse.

'James!'

He looked round to see Melissa, her face creased with worry, hurrying into the stables.

'What is it?' he asked anxiously.

'Father has Jethro Thompson with him!'

'What!' A chill gripped James and nausea knotted his stomach. 'What the hell is he doing here?' he demanded harshly.

'I don't know,' she replied testily. 'I didn't get a chance to find out. Jethro came here to see you and me on a matter of the utmost importance, but, before I could learn what it was, Mother appeared. Apparently Father had seen Jethro talking to me. He recognised him and wanted to know what he was doing here. You'd better hurry, Father knows you're back, he's had me watching for you.'

James's lips tightened into a grim line. He unsaddled his horse quickly and threw a blanket over it. 'I'll have to see to you later,' he muttered, and hurried to the house.

He threw off his coat as he crossed the hall and followed Melissa into his father's study.

Although a fire burned brightly in the grate, James felt

a distinct chill in the atmosphere. His father glowered at him from a high-backed armchair set to one side of the fireplace. Her troubled expression seemed to have pressed the marks of years into his mother's face. Melissa hurried to her mother's side to give comfort but also to seek reassurance that things weren't as bad as her father's angry glare indicated. James glanced at Jethro who stood calmly and impassively at the other side of the fireplace.

'James, what's this all about?' Robert Humphries's voice was strong as he drew himself straighter in his chair in an attempt to throw off the years and exert his authority. 'Melissa consorting with a known smuggler, a man condemned by the law . . .'

'I've not been condemned,' cut in Jethro harshly.

'Quiet, man,' stormed Robert, glaring with contempt at the smuggler who dared to interrupt him. 'You're only free because of lack of proof.' He turned his attention sharply back to his son. 'Well? No one would speak until you were here. What have you to say?'

James's hesitation, as if searching for the right explanation, irritated his father.

'Speak, boy, speak!' Robert's authoritative tone lashed James. He knew there was no way in which he could keep the truth from his father.

'Melissa was receiving a message from Jethro for me,' he explained. 'I've let him use Esk Hall to store contraband.'

Robert's old eyes flamed. 'On whose authority?'

'My own,' replied James.

'Yours! Damn you, boy. You had no right,' stormed his father, flushed with anger.

'I think I had. So will you when you hear the full story,' James blazed.

'Nothing could justify your usurping an authority which isn't yours.'

''Appen I'll be gannin',' cut in Jethro. 'This is no concern of mine.'

'Hold your tongue!' Robert snarled. 'You'll speak when I tell you.'

Jethro's eyes narrowed. 'Like hell I will. I'll say what I have t' say, and gan.'

'You'll wait until I hear from James.' Robert tried to regain the initiative but the hot-headed Jethro was having none of it. Unlike James, he had nothing to lose by defying an ailing man who clung so grimly to his authority.

'I won't!' Jethro's voice had the cold thrust of a rapier. 'What thee's discussing is private, a family affair. It don't concern me. What does is the use of Esk Hall.' He glanced at James and Melissa. 'Unless you make your father see sense, it's the end of the little sweeteners we pay thee.'

'No one will make me do anything against my better judgement,' rapped Robert, angered by the smuggler's effrontery in suggesting it.

'Then that's it, James. I'm sorry. This is a good place.' He ignored Robert.

'I'm sorry too,' said James. 'It places the family in an awkward position, as Father will learn.'

Jethro held up his hand. 'No concern of mine. I'll be off. Good day t' thee all.' His gaze embraced all the family as he hurried to the door, followed by James.

Fearing her father's wrath might turn upon her, Melissa

gripped her mother's hand tightly. Sensing her daughter's troubled mind, Sarah's comforting touch betrayed none of her own anxieties. She went to her husband and laid a hand on his shoulder, trying to calm his rage.

'Now let's hear why you dared to assume authority in this house,' Robert demanded of his son as he closed the door on his return.

'I did it with good reason.'

'He did, Father.' Drawing courage from James's attitude, Melissa moved in support of her brother.

'I'll hear it from him.' Robert threw his daughter a cursory glance and turned his eyes on his son. 'What could be reason enough?'

'You! I did it for you!' James hurled the words at his father.

'Rubbish! Don't lie to me.' The muscles in Robert's neck tightened. 'You put all of us and the good name of the family in jeopardy.'

'I'm not lying,' replied James tersely. 'I did it to save you from having to leave Esk Hall!'

'What nonsense are you talking? You know I lost money but we're all right now that your mother has received her legacy.'

James glanced at Sarah. Her face was creased with strain at having to tell her husband something which she had hoped to keep from him.

'Robert, I received no legacy.'

'What?' He stared disbelievingly. One shock was coming on top of another. 'But you said . . .'

'Yes, I know. I'm guilty of telling you a lie. I knew what the Hall meant to you and I wanted you to spend your last years here.' Tears came to her eyes but she fought them back.

Robert gaped.

'Father, I'm sorry for what I did . . .' started James, only to be hushed by a wave of his father's hand, dismissing his apologies.

Trying to assimilate the shattering news, the old man shook his head slowly.

Her eyes filled with sorrow, Melissa knelt at his feet. He was the one who needed comfort now. She laid a hand on his arm. 'What would life have been like if we had had to leave?' she said quietly. 'It would have broken your heart to lose the Hall.'

'James and Melissa did it for the best,' said Sarah.

The old man glanced up. 'They shouldn't have presumed, especially James.' The glint had come back to his eyes. He was the head of the household and no one, for whatever reason, was going to step into his shoes. 'You should have come to me, should have told me the truth. We'd have thought of something.' He shrugged his shoulders. 'All right, you did what you thought was right. It was a foolhardy scheme – what if you'd been caught?'

'It doesn't bear thinking about.' Sarah shuddered.

'But what are we going to do now?' cried Melissa, picturing herself as a spinster governess, looked down on by her employers.

'We'll think of something,' James offered. 'I'll find work.'

Robert grunted. 'What can you do? You've never needed to work. Maybe it was my fault. I never put you to anything useful. We always had plenty. I don't know . . .' His voice trailed away wearily.

'Maybe I could borrow from one of my brothers?' suggested Sarah.

'That's unlikely and you know it,' he said. 'Your family cut you off because you married me. You aren't going to humble yourself to them now.'

'I could ask.'

Robert appreciated what his wife was prepared to do and showed it as he looked at her. 'I'll not have you beg, Sarah. I'll sell Esk Hall first.'

She took his wrinkled hand and the love which had always been between them was expressed in their touch.

'We won't let that happen,' said James. 'I'll find employment, even if it's on a whaleship.'

'James, you mustn't. Not the whaleships!' cried his mother.

'I don't relish the prospect, but I will if necessary. I'm sure Captain Fernley would sign me on.'

'No need.' A smile spread across Robert's face. Sensing a solution, his family stared at him with expectant curiosity. 'Families like ours have a way round money problems.' He paused, letting his glance embrace everyone, then added with a note of triumph, 'Marriage.'

'Marriage?' Sarah frowned with surprise.

James and Melissa exchanged puzzled glances.

'It's time you were married, James.'

'What?' His eyes widened.

'Marry, James, marry. That will solve our problems,' said Robert, gripped by a feverish elation.

463

'I don't see how marrying Jessica Fernley will help,' returned James, 'she'll bring no fortune.'

'Fernley? No, no,' said Robert irritably, with a quick shake of his head. 'Not a Fernley. Caroline Howard.'

'But it's Jessica I have in mind,' protested James.

'Poppycock,' returned Robert with a wave of his hand as if to dismiss her from his son's mind. 'You love where there's money.'

'Your father's right.' Sarah seized the chance to back her husband. 'From our point of view, Caroline would be a good catch. Extensive estates next to ours and considerable wealth, all going to an only child whose mother is a widow. Well . . . you see the possibilities?'

'You used to see a lot of her,' put in Melissa enthusiastically as the vision of herself as a governess faded rapidly. 'She was disappointed when the friendship died away. I'm sure it would take little renewing.'

'Easy,' enthused Sarah. 'I'll invite her and Mrs Howard to dine with us.'

'Don't rush, Mother, I haven't agreed,' said James.

'But you must,' cried Melissa. 'It will solve everything.'

'She's attractive,' pressed Robert. 'Don't tell me you didn't find her so?'

'Of course she is,' agreed James. 'But . . .'

'Well then, why hesitate? Don't tell me you don't fancy bedding her – if you haven't already done so.'

'Robert!' Sarah looked shocked at the implication.

'Now don't try to look so prim and proper, my dear.' Robert looked back at his son. 'You can't be serious about this country wench?'

'Well . . .' James hesitated thoughtfully then added, 'No, I suppose not.'

'Then say yes,' urged Melissa.

James smiled. 'Caroline's money and land are very tempting. All right, Father, I'll marry her.'

'Good, good.' Robert slapped his knee with delight. He glanced slyly at his daughter. 'And you might start looking around. Time you got a man with money.'

Chapter Thirty-two

At the beginning of August, David and Adam met at a prearranged rendezvous on the edge of the northern ice. It was a meeting both had hoped need not take place for they had planned to meet only if the whaling had not been good.

In spite of the urgency of the situation, the two captains allowed their crews to relax for the best part of the day.

On board the *Lonely Wind*, David and Adam talked strategy and decided that, in spite of the fact that it was the end of the season, they would try for a few more days to fill their ships.

Every day added risks from ice and bad weather so the two friends decided to stay in sight of each other, and if conditions started to deteriorate they would break off the hunt immediately and set course for home.

They cruised along the edge of the ice for four days, without success. It seemed as if the whales had deserted the sea. On the fifth day, David took the *Lonely Wind* further south, into the open sea, while still keeping the

Mary Jane in sight as she continued to search along the edge of the ice. About mid-afternoon he felt a change in the direction of the wind and made the necessary adjustments to hold their course as the wind blew from the north-east with ever-increasing strength.

'Ice! Ice!' The chill in the cry from the lookout at the mast-head spelled danger.

'Jim, take over!' David yelled.

'Aye, aye, sir.'

David's heart pumped faster as he crossed the deck, leaped on to the bulwark, grasped the rigging and climbed quickly for a better view of the situation.

The lookout shouted again and David followed the direction of his arm.

A curving tongue of solid ice was being driven in their direction. The *Lonely Wind* could reach safety, but the *Mary Jane* still sailed westward. Unless Adam was aware of the menace curling towards him, he would be trapped between the opposing masses and ground into extinction.

Adam! Adam! Get out of there! The words drummed in David's mind as he willed his friend to safety. But the *Mary Jane* sailed on. The ice was moving faster in an ever-widening curve. The *Mary Jane* was under a terrible threat. Fear clutched David's heart like an icy hand.

'Jim! Head for the *Mary Jane*!' he yelled, with an urgency which alerted every man on the *Lonely Wind*.

'Aye, aye, sir.' Jim's response was immediate. His orders were quick and precise and the *Lonely Wind* swung round to head for the *Mary Jane* in a race against the ice.

'Collins, get below. Six men in the bows, ready to plug any holes.'

David, his jaw clenched, his eye calculating distances, willed his friend to safety. A momentary relief rippled through him. The *Mary Jane* was turning! The danger had been seen! Even in that instance of elation, he realised it was too late. The ice would close across the *Mary Jane*'s track before she could get clear and she wouldn't have sufficient speed to break through. David raced down the rigging to take charge while Jim Talbot took over from the helmsman.

As Adam brought the *Mary Jane* on to a southerly course, he saw the danger was more immediate than he had first thought. The realisation plunged a chill to his heart, more intense than the Arctic cold. He paralleled the curling menace, hoping he might outrun it. It was a race he must win. His features were rigid with strain. He could do nothing but will the ship to safety. He watched the ice with anxious eyes, only half-aware of the *Lonely Wind* heading in his direction. An anguished cry rose in his throat when he saw the ice beginning to move across the *Mary Jane*'s bow. She would be trapped! Adam cursed. There must be a way out. There had to be. Desperately he looked for a manoeuvre which would foil the closing ice.

'The bloody fool! What the hell's he doing?' Jamaica's harsh cry shattered Adam's concentration.

Startled, he looked round to see the *Lonely Wind* bearing down on them fast. Only the ice stood between them and a crippling collision.

'Bloody hell!' Adam's exclamation of disbelief was barely out before he read David's intention. 'If I'm right, there's just a chance of escape . . .'

The *Lonely Wind* cleaved its way through the sea

closing the distance between herself and the ice with frightening rapidity. All David's concentration was on the distance between the two ships. He must judge it exactly right; the slightest error could prove fatal. He was unaware of the tension which gripped his body, of the sweat which had broken out beneath his heavy clothes, and of the stinging sensation in his eyes from the sheer physical effort of staring at the floating ice.

'Hard a larboard!' David's voice rang clear.

Jim Talbot was keyed to obey instantly. The wheel spun. The bow came round. The helmsman sprang to held Jim. Then suddenly the bow crashed into the ice. The *Lonely Wind* shuddered and jerked under the impact which sent timbers crashing and splintering in spite of the strengthening timbers, but the speed carried the ship on, cutting into the ice.

'Hold her hard, Jim!' yelled David.

'Aye, aye, sir,' came the confident answer.

Jim and the helmsman tightened their grip as they strained to hold the wheel which fought to be free.

The *Lonely Wind* crashed on. Now the starboard bow received the full impact. Below deck, Collins and his crew of six men crowded into the bows. They had gathered timber, matting, hammers and nails with great haste and then braced themselves for the deadly impact with the ice. Every man had a look of fear in his eyes. Each knew that, if the crash was bad, a hole could be torn into the side of the *Lonely Wind* which they would have no hope of plugging, and if that happened they were doomed to a watery death. Suddenly there was an ear-splitting crash and the men were flung into a tumbled heap. Timber split with an

469

unnerving noise. They scrambled to their feet to fight the water which was pouring through a jagged hole on the starboard side.

'Get the matting over that hole!' yelled Collins. 'Move! Move!'

The two men assigned to the job were already battling against the force of the water which fought to tear the matting from their grasp. Muscles strained and gradually the hole was closed.

'Get that timber on!' yelled Collins.

Three men clamped a large rectangular block of wood over the matting.

'Shore it!'

The two men released their hold on the matting and came to help the sixth man with the shoring timbers. Water oozed in at the sides of the blockage but they were containing the force which would have doomed them. They must shore that wood before a sudden extra pressure undid all their work. Swiftly timbers were forced into position. Only after he was satisfied that the main threat was contained did Collins direct his men's attention to the minor holes cut by the ice.

The *Mary Jane* loomed large. David was tense, willing Adam to read his intention. If he didn't, the crews of the two whaleships were doomed. He heard Adam's yell cut through the freezing air. 'Hard a starboard!'

The two ships were closing rapidly. Each member of each crew was transfixed as the *Lonely Wind* bore down on the *Mary Jane*. They could do no more.

The *Lonely Wind* jerked and faltered. An ear-splitting crack turned all eyes in horror to the fore-mast. The top teetered for a moment then toppled slowly, gathered momentum and crashing downwards, tearing into the topsail before being held by the rigging, but still the ship moved on.

Both vessels were turning, forced by the pressure of the men at their wheels. Ice crashed and cracked, piled and tumbled. The *Lonely Wind*'s bow was round and past the *Mary Jane*. Their sides almost touched as they both came on to the same heading. Stern and bow scraped. The crews, tense with anxiety, watched the *Lonely Wind* pass in front of the *Mary Jane*.

'Dead ahead!'

'Dead ahead!'

Both captains shouted the order almost simultaneously and both vessels came on to the same course with the *Mary Jane* astern of the *Lonely Wind* which, still cleaving a way through the ice, created clear water for her.

The atmosphere of fear and apprehension on both ships was suddenly relieved and the crews gave vent to their feelings as the last few yards of ice were swept aside and both ships sailed into clear water.

The summer days moved into the first week of September, and, as each day passed without news of Whitby's two missing whaleships, Ruth feared for her business and for her husband, and a knot of dread tightened just a little more round Jenny's heart.

She studied Emma Thoresby and marvelled at her resilience and the way she hid the fear she must be feeling. There was an air of serenity about her but Jenny knew the anguish she must be experiencing. Having lost a husband,

471

she now had two sons overdue from the Arctic. Jenny drew strength from her mother-in-law.

'Whaleships!' The cry rang down the street.

Jenny looked up. Had she heard correctly? Her eyes met Emma's and Jenny knew that she too had heard the shout. Her lips moved in a silent prayer of hope.

'Whaleships!' There it was again, nearer and louder, and there was no mistaking the plural.

'Away with you, lass. Anne will stay with me.'

Grabbing her red shawl, Jenny ran from the house.

People were already thronging the street. They poured from the yards and alleys, eager to see the ships, to identify them and have their hopes confirmed. Jenny reached the Church Stairs and started the climb. She was halfway up, impatiently tolerating the people who slowed her, when word swept downwards through the crowd: 'The *Mary Jane*! The *Lonely Wind*!' Jenny grasped at the relief which the news brought.

Suddenly it seemed as if a heavy weight which had been oppressing Whitby had been lifted. Her ships were back. The anxiety and the fear which had faced thirty-six families, and which the whole town shared, had passed.

When she reached the edge of the cliff, Jenny's first sight of the two vessels spiked her joy.

The *Lonely Wind*, leading the way, took her attention first. The fore-mast was broken and all the fore-mast sails gone. The bow was battered, her timber splintered, and on the larboard side there was a large hole just above the waterline. Fearing what she might see, Jenny turned her eyes to the *Mary Jane*. Anxiously she searched the ship, but, apart from a few splintered timbers near the bow, there was no visible harm. Her heart went out to David. His ship damaged and no bone at the mast-head.

When the cry of 'Whaleships!' swept up Bagdale, Ruth seized on it, with hope banishing the fear that the whaling mission had gone wrong and that the new ship would be jeopardised.

She whisked a cloak round her shoulders and hurried from the house. Turning off Bagdale, she made for the top of the west cliff. Crowds were gathering and word swept back to her that the *Lonely Wind* and the *Mary Jane* were close.

The *Lonely Wind* was safe. From reports brought by earlier ships, she knew that the whaling had been bad. No doubt David had stayed longer to get a full ship. A good catch was essential now that the new ship was rising high in Barrett's shipyard. There must be bone at the mast-head. There had to be. Ruth pushed her way forward and her eyes searched for the signal of success.

Nothing! She stared in disbelief. The *Lonely Wind* was not full. Nausea gripped her. She had banked on a capacity catch to supplement the hoped-for investment from James. Ruth shivered. She had never felt so cold.

The ships were nearer. Ruth's eyes glazed with shock. The fore-mast was broken! The sails were gone! The *Lonely Wind* was bringing her own chill warning about the future. Ruth's face creased with agony. Why? Why did he have to do this to her? Why couldn't he come back prosperous, breathing new life into her plans? Instead, all her husband had brought was costly repairs and doom.

She couldn't take her eyes off the ship, staring her own

ruin in the face. Then it passed the piers and revealed the wounds of the battle with the ice.

'Oh, my God!' Ruth's white lips formed the words but no sound came.

As the *Lonely Wind* sailed slowly towards the bridge, a dazed Ruth turned and made her way through the crowd, oblivious to the whispers among those who recognised her. She walked unseeingly, drawn along by instinct. Her dreams of success lay shattered in the broken timbers of the *Lonely Wind*. Arms limp by her sides, her steps heavy, she felt herself dragged down to utter despair which held no promise of escape.

She knew nothing of the walk which took her to Bagdale and the house which mocked her with its appearance of success.

David skilfully brought the *Lonely Wind* past the bridge into the inner harbour. As he manoeuvred her towards the quay, he saw a ship nearing launching day in Barrett's shipbuilding yard. He stared across the water. The ship was an exact replica of the *Lonely Wind*! A sister ship! Ruth must have got more people to take shares, but he'd have something to say about letting Barrett's build her.

David searched the crowds on the quay but could not see Ruth. Worried, he called to Jim to tend to things once the ship was tied up. When he went on to the quay, he noticed Matthew Barrett surveying the damage.

'Well?' asked David when he reached him. No other words were necessary.

'The repair will be costly.'

474

'Thought so. Do thee think Mulgrave's will handle it?' queried David anxiously.

'What, with that over there?' From the inclination of his head, David knew Matthew meant the new ship. 'It will be one debt on top of another.'

'What do thee mean?' David's brow puckered.

'Only Frank took shares in the new ship,' explained Matthew. 'Ruth is still hoping that James Humphries will invest but, in the meantime, as Father was wanting some cash, she's borrowed from the bank.'

'What!' David's face darkened angrily. 'Damn the woman. What's she got us into?

'I doubt if you'll get more credit,' said Barrett. 'The *Lonely Wind* will have to be laid up until you can afford the repair.'

'Blast! Then we'll be dependent on a profitable first voyage in the new ship,' stormed David.

'If it takes place,' Matthew pointed out quietly.

'If?' David frowned.

'As I understand it, the bank made the loan provided both ships sailed to the Arctic, the *Lonely Wind* as a sort of insurance for the new one. Two good catches would put the whole situation beyond doubt. The bank might insist on something less risky if the new vessel has to go alone.'

David's lips tightened. 'I warned Ruth to be careful. She knew James was not keen to invest yet. Why build until she was certain?'

'I think she had some idea of persuading him to change his mind,' said Matthew.

David grunted with annoyance. He started to turn away but Barrett stopped him. 'Oh, congratulations, you've a son. Thought Ruth would have had him here to meet you.'

'A boy!' For one moment the excitement of those words drove his troubles from his mind but they were back by the time he was through the crowds covering the quay.

Thunder rumbled in the distance as David walked to Bagdale. His mind seethed. They faced ruin. Hopes, so high when he left for the Arctic, lay shattered. Why had Ruth taken such a risk? Maybe Barrett was exaggerating. Barrett! David's mind gave a jolt. How the hell did Barrett know so much about their private affairs? The bank wouldn't tell him so that meant Ruth must have done. Why should she confide in him?

By the time he reached Bagdale, black clouds hung over Whitby hastening the night. The first huge raindrops started to hit the town as David turned in the gateway. He ran up the path but the sudden downpour had soaked his coat by the time he reached the house.

Mary opened the door in answer to his urgent knocking. David shrugged himself out of his wet coat.

'I'm sorry about the *Lonely Wind*,' said the maid as she took it. 'I saw her from the cliff. But I'm glad thee's safe.'

'Thanks, Mary,' said David. 'Where's Mrs Fernley?'

'In there, sir.' She indicated the parlour door.

Thunder crashed overhead as he shoved the door open and slammed it shut behind him. He strode across the room and stared down at Ruth who had not moved in her chair.

'What the hell have thee been doing? A new vessel and only Frank interested. Thee knew that wasn't sufficient to start a new ship.' The words lashed whip-like from him, without any form of greeting. The lightning, white through the rain-spattered window, lit the anger in his face.

Ruth started. Her eyes flared as she turned them to meet his fury. 'You listen to me, David Fernley. I put that ship under construction because I was certain I could get the money.'

'Who from?' snapped David.

'Jonathan Hardy!' She stood up, defiance in her attitude.

'What!' David gasped, staring wide-eyed at her. 'Where did . . . ?'

'I met him, it doesn't matter how or where.' Ruth brushed David's questions aside. 'He'd have invested – nothing more certain when I threatened to expose him as leader of the smugglers.'

'Thee what?' David frowned incredulously.

'I had your evidence from your first coming to Whitby.'

'You blackmailed him?' The thought of the consequences of such an action began to prey on David's mind.

'I only faced him with the truth,' she replied smoothly.

'Did he know who thee really are?'

Ruth shook her head. 'No,' she lied. She saw no point in revealing the truth to David unless it was necessary.

'So what happened?'

'He was killed in a riding accident before I was able to persuade him.'

'And thee turned to James, in spite of the fact that thee knew he had said he wasn't interested.' He paused, then added when he saw Ruth's questioning look at the mention of James, 'Barrett told me. He was on the quay, looking at the damage. I asked him about the cost of the repair and he told me a few facts. He also said thee had some ideas to persuade James.' David's features tightened with suspicion. 'What are you up to, Ruth?'

'Nothing,' she answered, turning away, only to swing round and carry the attack to him. 'You're ready to blame me for our dilemma. What about you? Look at the *Lonely Wind*. If you'd brought back a full ship . . .'

'I can't catch whales if they aren't there,' he snapped.

'Look at the damage. If you hadn't done that, we'd still be all right.' Ruth glared.

'That couldn't be helped,' cut in David.

'Oh no,' she sneered. 'Something *you've* done couldn't be helped.'

'Men's lives were at stake,' hissed David between his teeth, seething at her unreasonable attitude.

'Good excuse.'

'The *Mary Jane* was in danger. We only just managed to rescue her in time.' David's voice was sharp and precise, trying to drive the words into a mind which did not want to accept them.

'And got damaged in the process. More fool you. And Thoresby escapes while we face ruin,' Ruth snapped contemptuously. 'Thorsebys again! I'm sick of them.' Her hands went white as she gripped the back of a chair.

'I suppose I should have left those men to die?'

Rain lashed at the windows with an added fury as if determined to be heard above the angry voices.

'You shouldn't have endangered the *Lonely Wind*.'

'If I hadn't, the *Mary Jane* would have been trapped.'

'Then you could have taken the men off.'

'And left the *Mary Jane* a total loss, and Adam without a ship?' David glared at his wife.

'So his livelihood is more important than ours?' she yelled.

'No, but thee saves a ship if thee can,' growled David. 'I didn't endanger our livelihood. Thee did that.'

'I took a gamble.' Ruth's anger boiled over. 'It seemed a pretty safe one. How was I to know that Jonathan would die, that the *Lonely Wind* was going to be damaged and no bone at the mast-head? You'd have been thanking me if the voyage had been successful and Jonathan had lived to invest.'

David turned away in anguish. He hadn't anticipated a homecoming like this. Through the lonely months in the Arctic, he had dreamed of coming home to Ruth's warm embraces. Now his hopes had vanished. With his back to her, he stared at the flickering flames of the fire which seemed to burn less brightly, fading like his hopes. His mind worried at the problems which overwhelmed him.

'Thee should have let the whole thing drop when thee couldn't persuade anyone else but Frank to take shares,' he snapped over his shoulder.

'There's still a chance that James will invest.'

'With the *Lonely Wind* evidence of the risks? He's not likely even to think about it now,' he said, his voice hollow with despair.

'Jessica will persuade him.' Ruth's announcement was low but it brought David swinging round to face her.

'What the hell has she to do with it?' he rapped, suspicions tumbling over in his mind.

'Married to Jessica, he'll . . .'

'Have thee been pushing her?' David's frown darkened as he glared at Ruth.

'No!' Ruth drew herself to her full height, meeting David's challenge. 'She needed no pushing.'

She swept contemptuously past but he grabbed her by the arm and turned her roughly to face him.

'Thee wants her t' marry James just for thy own ends.' His eyes bored into her. 'By God, if thee's . . .'

The threat was never made. His words were cut off by a crash which reverberated through the house as the front door burst open. David was across the room and into the hall in a moment.

He pulled up sharply. The wind howled driving rain across the hall, buffeting the girl who leaned against the doorpost and would have fallen but for its support. Water streamed from her, forming a widening pool at her feet. Saturated hair hung long and dank, dripping on to her shoulders and sending rivulets down her forehead to mingle with her tears. Sobs shook her body and anguish racked her face, contorted with shocked emotion.

'Jessica!' David's surprise was only momentary but it seemed as if an age had passed before he reached his sister's side. He supported her and forced the door closed against the thrust of the wind.

His cry brought Ruth hurrying into the hall. Shocked by her sister-in-law's appearance, she hastened to take hold of Jessica's free arm and help David take her to the parlour.

The noise brought Mary hurrying from the kitchen, only to stop and stare wide-eyed at Jessica.

'Blankets, towels, some dry clothes and a hot drink,

Mary.' David's command, above the crash of the thunder, startled her into activity.

As soon as they had Jessica close to the fire, Ruth started to remove the soaked clothing, while Jessica, oblivious to her concern, stared unseeingly.

'Jessica, where hast thee been? What's happened?' asked David. There was no response.

'She's had some sort of shock,' observed Ruth.

'But what? How?'

Mary appeared with the towels and David began to rub his sister's arms vigorously. Ruth wiped Jessica's face and rubbed the soaking hair. Once they had dried her, they wrapped her in blankers and laid her on the sofa close to the fire.

David knelt beside her and said in a gentle voice, 'It's me, David. What happened, Jessica?'

She stared at him. Then there was a flicker of recognition. Suddenly she sat up and flung her arms round his neck. He held her and let her cry.

A few minutes later, there was a knock on the door and Mary appeared with a hot drink. Ruth took it. 'Drink this, Jessica, it'll make you feel better.'

Jessica did not move. The crying had ceased but still she clung to her brother as if she would never let go.

'Have this,' Ruth said gently.

'Come on, Jess,' David encouraged as he tried to ease her away.

Jessica gave way with some reluctance. As she sat up, she brushed her hair away from her face and wiped the dampness from her eyes with the handkerchief which David offered her. She thanked Ruth quietly as she took the drink but kept her eyes averted from her brother and sister-in-law.

'Better?' David asked when Jessica had finished her drink.

'James is going to marry Caroline Howard!' The words caught in her throat.

'What!' Ruth was shattered. She glanced at David who showed equal surprise. 'But I thought you and he . . .'

'So did I!' cried Jessica. 'He's just told me.'

Outside the wind howled, lashing rain at the panes.

'But why? What's happened?' pressed Ruth. The consequences of Jessica's information could be devastating. Now James Humphries would have no incentive to invest with them. The last hope she had of retrieving the situation had gone. This was the finish.

'You know he's been seeing Caroline a lot during these last few weeks,' explained Jessica, with a sob.

'Yes, yes,' said Ruth, impatient for her to carry on. 'We thought there was nothing in it.'

'Well, we were wrong! He used to see Caroline a lot at one time. People thought they'd marry. She was very keen but he wasn't. But it seems the attraction was still there and only needed spurring by necessity.'

'Necessity? What dost thee mean?' prompted David.

'James's father lost most of his money when two firms went bankrupt. Then his mother, who had expected to receive a sizeable inheritance when her father died, inherited nothing.' Jessica dabbed at her eyes with a handkerchief.

'You mean they've lost everything?' urged David.

'Practically. So James is going to marry where there's money,' she cried.

'Caroline!' hissed Ruth, starting to tremble with rage. 'An only child, whose wealthy, widowed mother will not see her daughter go wanting! And she won't want her in-laws to be poverty stricken.' Her voice rose shrilly. 'Damn the man, damn him!'

James might come into money by marriage but she was perfectly sure that Caroline's mother would see that he hadn't free access to it. There would be no money for the Fernley shipping business. It was wrecked, and with it her dreams. Her eyes widened, fired by the irony of the situation. 'And I'd hoped that by getting you he'd invest with us and all the time there was no money.' Her short laugh was harsh.

David's mind fastened on to the meaning behind her words. So Ruth had used Jessica! She had encouraged the relationship, even though he had warned her not to push his sister. His eyes burned with the wrath he was about to turn on Ruth when Jessica's cry came like that of a stricken bird.

'I thought he loved me! I thought he'd marry me when I told him I was going to have his baby!'

'Thee's what?' gasped David.

'Jessica!' Ruth was stunned. 'He'll *have* to marry you!'

'He certainly will,' rapped David grimly. The anger he had directed at his wife was suddenly switched to James. 'I'll gan to see him now.'

'No! David, no!' screamed Jessica. 'Don't go. He thought this might happen so he said he would deny the baby is his.'

'He wouldn't dare . . .' started David.

'He would and he will,' snapped Ruth with a snort of

contempt for David's belief that under these circumstances James would marry Jessica. 'But we can force him to marry you. Esk Hall has been used by smugglers as a hiding place for contraband.'

'What? Blackmail again! Never!' Furious that she should have thought of it, David swung round on Ruth.

'For Jessica's sake or would you rather she had a bastard?' Ruth's taunt pierced him like a rapier.

'Thee'd need proof,' he pointed out, as he tried to foresee the consequences of such blackmail.

'Matthew and I saw it with our own eyes. We followed the smugglers to Esk Hall.' The information was out before Ruth realised what she was revealing.

'You what?' David was astounded. His mind raced with the inferences which Ruth's words carried. Another association with Barrett, and this one in a strange, bizarre adventure. How much more had she shared with him?

'I don't want James by blackmail!' yelled Jessica, bringing David's thoughts back to the problem of his pregnant sister. 'Besides, he would deny the smuggling charges. He told me the whole story, and you'll find no proof of smuggling at Esk Hall now. It would be your word against his, and I damned well know whose word would be believed.'

Jessica felt the whole situation bear down on her. James had refused to marry her. Ruben wouldn't want anything to do with her. She would bear a fatherless child and have the finger of condemnation pointed at her for ever. At another thunderclap, her head throbbed. She had hurt the people she loved and there was only one thing to do to put things right. She leaped to her feet and, before

David or Ruth realised what was happening, she was across the room and into the hall.

David raced after her. His cry of 'Jessica, come back!' was swept away by the shriek of the wind when she jerked the front door open. The fierce strength of it and the sting of the lashing rain stopped her for a moment. She fought the invisible wall and then suddenly she was outside, running through the driving rain. Her frenzy gave her new strength and speed. Lightning tore through the clouds to reveal her halfway down the path as David burst from the house.

Jessica reached the open gate and tore into Bagdale almost colliding with a figure whose shoulders were hunched against the wind. As she rounded him, lightning lit her face. She had gone before he registered it. As he turned to go after her, David raced out of the garden, collided with him and grasped him to save himself from falling.

'Ruben!' yelled David. 'It's Jessica. We must catch her!'

Ruben needed no further explanation. The urgency and alarm in David's voice told him that something terrible might happen. He spun round to follow David who was already rushing after the figure, dimly visible through the driving rain and gathering darkness.

His chest heaving, David was aware of Ruben alongside him. Each helped the other by his presence to run harder and gradually they narrowed the distance separating them from Jessica. If only someone would come on to the street, they might stop her, but the storm had sent everyone indoors and was keeping them there.

Thirty yards.

Thunder rumbled and crashed above the cliffs.

Twenty yards.

Lightning split the sky, silhouetting the gaunt abbey.

Ten yards.

The wind renewed its effort to keep them apart.

They were racing towards the bridge. Realising Jessica's intentions, David drove new power into his legs. He drew nearer to his sister.

Her tortured face streaming with the rain, Jessica turned on to the bridge. She reached the centre, grasped the rail and hauled herself upwards. The water, lashed into a frenzy, sent white-flecked fingers reaching for a victim, urging her to destruction.

David hurled himself forward as his sister clambered over the rail. His clawing fingers grasped her dress. He felt it tear. Jessica was falling. His brain was numb with horror as he stumbled. Then she crashed against him, brought backwards by Ruben's grip on her ankle. David was sent sprawling on the bridge and, as he twisted round, driven by the urge to save Jessica, was aware of two figures on the ground beside him.

Jessica fought to escape from Ruben's tight hold. David flung himself on his sister whose screams pierced the howling wind. The extra help released Ruben's tight grip. He brought his fist back and struck it hard against Jessica's jaw. The girl lay still and the two men knelt there, lungs labouring for relief.

David glanced at Ruben through the water streaming from his hair. 'Thanks,' he panted. He pushed himself slowly from the ground and bent to help Ruben to his feet. He stood looking down at his sister, his heart torn with pity for her, his mind filling with guilt, for had it not been for him she would not be lying in a dirt-spattered pool on Whitby's bridge.

The rain beat on her white face now peaceful in unconsciousness. Her dark bedraggled hair spilled on to the roadway. For one fleeting moment David saw her as the happy, carefree girl who had once been caught in a storm with him on the hills above their home.

He sighed and glanced at Ruben who sought no explanation. 'Help me to take her back?' he asked. Ruben nodded and assisted David to take the girl into his arms. Thunder rumbled beyond the east cliff as the two men set off for the house in Bagdale.

Anxiety passed from Ruth's face when she saw them. She followed David as he carried Jessica upstairs while Ruben watched from the hall. A pool of water widened as it drained off his saturated clothes. A bell tinkled in the depths of the house and a moment later Mary hurried through the hall, giving him only a cursory glance, and went up the stairs quickly.

Time passed slowly until David reappeared. He came wearily down the stairs, his face grim, his shoulders drooping. 'Ruben,' he sighed. 'I'm sorry, I'm neglecting thee.'

'No thee's not. Thee had to see to Jessica first. Is she all right?' There was concern and bewilderment in the question.

David nodded. 'Yes, she'll be all right, I'm sure. She's just coming round. Ruth and Mary are with her. Now let's see to thee. Thee must get out of those wet clothes. Come on, I'll fix thee up.'

'Thanks, but I'll go now, get out of the way,' he said.

'Thee won't. Thee don't want another soaking tonight.'

David took hold of Ruben's arm and led him to the stairs. As they started up, David glanced at his friend. 'I owe thee a great debt. If it hadn't been for thee, Jessica would be in the river.' His voice faltered at the thought. Then he glanced curiously at Ruben as he asked, 'What brought thee to Bagdale on a night like this?'

'I was coming to see her,' Ruben explained. 'I wanted to know how things were between her and James Humphries. When I was on my way home from the ship, I heard talk of Humphries marrying Caroline Howard. Then I find myself helping to save Jess from suicide. What's wrong, Davey?'

Chapter Thirty-three

The expression on Ruben's face demanded an honest answer. David knew he must be frank. Ruben deserved the truth now rather than later.

'It's a long story, we'd better change first.' He found dry clothes for them both and brandy to drive out the chill. Once they were more comfortable, he told Ruben Jessica's story. 'Well, there it is,' he concluded. 'I've been honest with thee because of what thee did and because I know thee and Jessica were friendly. I hope thee'll keep this to thissen.'

'Of course,' replied Ruben. 'I suppose thee intend to force Humphries into marriage?'

David's half-laugh was hollow. 'If we try that, Humphries has said he'll deny the baby is his and his word will come before ours.'

Ruben's face darkened. 'The bastard!' he blazed angrily. His lips tightened. 'I'll kill him!' He flung himself out of his chair and started for the door.

David moved equally quickly and grabbed his arm.

'No, Ruben, no! Don't be a fool. Don't make things worse.'

'It's what he deserves!'

'Think of your family. Think of Jessica. Thee'll hurt them all far more if thee kill Humphries.' David knew he must keep talking, keep persuading Ruben until some of the fire of vengeance had died down. 'Your mother, your sister, Adam, Jenny, little Anne – everyone would suffer. Don't thee think I felt like thee when Jessica told me? I could willingly have killed Humphries, but it wouldn't have done any good. As it is, Jessica can go home to have the baby – no one in Whitby need know.' David saw the fire dying in Ruben as reason began to assert itself. 'That way no one will be hurt but Jessica. She will have a father-less child. That will be her punishment, for she must have been willing. But that'll be better than knowing that she also caused thee to commit murder.'

Ruben held stiff for a moment then sighed and relaxed. 'A possible suicide, a possible murder. Thee's had your fair share of stopping people doing foolish things tonight. Thanks, Davey.'

He released his hold. 'Come, have another brandy.'

'Do thee think I could see Jessica?'

'I'll see how she is,' replied David. He poured Ruben some more brandy and then went to her bedroom.

'I'm sorry, David,' she whispered when he came to the bedside.

'That's all right,' he replied as he knelt beside his sister and kissed her on the cheek. He glanced over his shoulder. 'I'd like to speak to Jessica alone. Would thee both leave us?' His emphasis of the word both left Ruth in no

490

doubt that David really meant her as well as the maid. She sensed the coldness in his voice and knew that he blamed her for many of the things which had gone wrong.

David looked with compassion at his sister. 'That was a very foolish thing thee did; I want thee to promise me thee'll never do it again.'

'I'm bringing disgrace to you and everyone back home,' she cried. 'Why didn't you let me jump? It would have solved everything.'

'It would have solved nothing and a lot of people would have been hurt,' he said, 'especially the young man who saved your life.'

Startled, Jessica stared at her brother. 'But I thought it was you.'

'Yes, but I would have failed without his help. He grabbed thee at the vital moment. He's waiting in my room. He'd like to see thee.'

'Oh, David, I can't face anyone, not now,' protested Jessica, alarm in her eyes.

'That's foolish talk,' he retorted. 'Thee can't hide this-sen away completely. Thee's got to see people and it's better if thee start right away.' He got to his feet and, ignoring her protests, left the room.

A few moments later, the door opened slowly.

'Ruben!' Jessica gasped.

'Hello, Jessica,' he said quietly, and moved to the bedside.

'You . . . you were there?' She was bewildered.

'Yes.' Ruben nodded.

'But how? Why?' asked Jessica.

'I was on my way here when thee ran out of the house.'

'I remember nearly bumping into someone.'

'Me. I was coming to see thee.'

'Me? On a night like this.'

'Yes. I heard that James Humphries is going to marry Caroline Howard and I wondered . . . Jessica, I still love thee. I always will.'

She turned her face against the pillow. 'You mustn't, you'll only be hurt. It's useless now.' Tears filled her eyes and the words choked in her throat.

'It isn't.' He turned her face gently to him so that she could see his sincerity. 'David has told me everything but I still want to marry thee.'

'But the baby . . .'

'It will make no difference if thee wants to marry me.'

'Oh, Ruben.' Emotion stifled her. She took Ruben's hand. She smiled wanly. 'I've always liked you a lot, maybe I loved you. Maybe other things have blinded me into thinking I loved James. Oh, Ruben, I don't know. I don't deserve you.'

'If thee hast been as near loving me as that, then I have no fear for our future together. There'll be no need for anyone to know that the baby isn't mine.'

The tears which brimmed in her eyes overflowed. She held out her arms and when Ruben came to them he felt her thanks and joy. 'What can I do to deserve you?' she sobbed.

'Just be thissen,' he whispered.

As David and Ruben came down the stairs, Ruben said, 'I've proposed to Jessica and been accepted. The baby makes no difference. It will be brought up as mine.'

'Ruben, I don't know what to say.' David's emotion showed as he gripped the young man's hand.

'Then say nothing.' He smiled. 'I'm more than happy, and I hope Jessica will be too. We'll gan to Cropton and get married as soon as possible.'

After David had seen Ruben out of the house, he went in search of Ruth. There were some things which needed clearing up immediately. He found her pouring herself a glass of wine in the study.

'So there thee are,' he said, his voice heavy with contempt. 'No concern for my sister. Now another of your schemes has gone sour.'

'Schemes?' She straightened, her body stiffening as she turned to face him.

'Don't play the innocent,' he said coldly. 'It makes me sick.'

Her expression altered abruptly. Her lips tightened and her eyes matched his contempt.

'Thee knows what I mean,' he went on. 'Thee allus wanted Jessica to marry James, hoping his money would help our expansion. Thee pushed her when thy scheme with Jonathan Hardy collapsed. No doubt thee talked for James and against Ruben, blinding her to the good steady lad and making her think she should make certain of James. Thee pushed her into doing what she did – there'd have been blood on your hands if we hadn't saved her!'

'I didn't!' broke in Ruth furiously.

'Oh, thee wouldn't suggest that she became pregnant, but thee'd be very near the mark with subtle suggestions about making sure of him.'

'She was more than willing it seems,' sneered Ruth.

David's eyes burned with anger. 'You bitch!' he hissed.

'A word of warning, Ruth, and take notice of this one – don't say anything to anyone about Jessica and James. Nobody must know. Ruben is going to marry her, so don't spoil their chances.'

'And I suppose the noble Thoresby will say the baby is his?' she said sarcastically. 'More fool him!'

After the scene on the bridge, her dismissal of Ruben was too much. Fury blinded David. He struck hard with his open hand. She reeled against the mantelpiece and, unable to escape, felt the fierce lash of David's hand twice more. Her knees buckled and she staggered sideways into an armchair.

'You bastard!' Tears of pain ran down her cheeks. The desire to hurt was too much for Ruth. 'You can go to hell. It's all over. That precious dream of yours is finished. There's nothing to hold us now. Once we needed each other. You needed me for the ships and I needed you to catch whales. Now we have no ships so it's the end.' She pushed herself unsteadily to her feet. Against the pallor of her cheeks, the livid marks of his blows were clearly visible. 'I don't need you any more – not for anything!' Her voice rose hysterically. She was beyond discretion, beyond anything but hitting back at him for all the pain he had caused her. His physical mistreatment was nothing. The really bitter blow was the foundering of all her business hopes. 'Once I needed the power of your body, but I needed other things as well – excitement, subtlety, satisfying love. I found them in someone else. Power I can get from any man!' Ruth's eyes burned with contempt. 'I don't need you, David Fernley.'

She started to turn away but he grabbed her by the arm

and jerked her round, pressing his face close to hers. 'Matthew Barrett,' he hissed. 'If thee'd spend the night watching smugglers with him, thee'd no doubt do other things.'

In spite of the pain from his harsh grip, she laughed in his face. 'He's a hundred times better than you!' she screamed.

He pushed her away with disgust and loathing. She staggered and would have fallen but for the desk which she grabbed and held on to, snarling like a vixen.

'Are you such a paragon of virtue?' Her lips curled with the primitive urge to wound. 'Haven't you always loved Jenny? Maybe Anne is yours!' David stepped towards her, menacing in his manner. 'That's right, hit me again,' Ruth screamed at him. 'It's all a peasant like you is good for. You'd have got nowhere without me. You'd have been a sailor all your life.'

'I got to be a captain. You needed that.'

'But that's all you'd have remained. You haven't the business brain I have. That's what made us.' She gave a half-laugh of contempt. 'You'd never have mixed with the right people if it hadn't been for me. That ability was born in me, not you.'

David's lips tightened. He glowered at her. 'Don't thee forget that, when I married thee, thee were no more than a bastard starveling, a brat with mud on your feet.'

'That was finished long ago. Bastard maybe, but a bastard with aristocratic blood in my veins and that's something you'll never have.' She gave him a withering look. 'It's over, David, all over! Striking me sealed it forever. You're no better than my step-father. I'm leaving, right now. Do what you will with the ships, with the business . . .'

'Go! But thee leaves my son!'

'So you've heard?' A hard, hateful glow of triumph gleamed in her eyes at the prospect of dealing David this body blow. '*Your* son?' She mocked him with a sneering laugh. 'But Richard's not yours, David. Never was and never will be. Oh, you can have him. I don't want him. I don't want to be reminded of failure all my life. You can have that pleasure – only it will be a mixed one, knowing he isn't yours!'

David grabbed her by the arms and shoulder. His fury was surpassed by the need to know the truth. 'What do thee mean, not mine?'

'Exactly that!' She laughed in his face.

'Barrett's?' hissed David.

'No. Jonathan's.' Ruth's voice rose in triumph as she saw the shock contort David's features. 'My brother's,' she said with an unmistakable note of satisfaction.

He was speechless. Disbelief turned to horror. Unable to stand, he sank wearily into a chair and covered his face with his hands.

'That hurts, David, doesn't it?' she mocked. 'To be left with a bastard, born from my half-brother.'

His mind throbbed. Did he really know her, this brazen, hard-eyed slut he had been married to for twelve years?

'You may as well know the whole story,' she went on, revelling in the hurt she was inflicting. 'He was to be our way to a fortune. The heir to all those estates, in Cropton where we were born.' Ruth was fired with a fanatical compulsion to reveal everything. The words poured out without her realising the extent of her revelation. 'My way to revenge for what that bastard squire never gave me! But Jonathan outwitted me . . . he made another will. I only learned about it after I'd driven him over the cliff to his death. Well, you can have his bastard!'

She left him, appalled, in the empty room, watching the door slam behind her.

Despondency drained into him, fogging his mind. He tried to think, to get a grasp on the situation, but all he gained were impressions of his years with Ruth. Hope, love, plans – all lay broken. He felt drained. What was there left for them? Nothing but a world of bleak emptiness.

He stirred, something attracting his attention, and opened the door. There were footsteps on the stairs. Ruth appeared, a cloak around her shoulders carrying a small valise. She did not look towards the study as she crossed the hall to the front door.

David half-reached out towards her, wanting to purge himself of any wrong he had done her. He realised now that differences, subtle though they were, had been there for some time but the holding power of ambition had made him ignore them. Now it was too late. There would be no going back.

The front door crashed. Ruth had gone.

And with the shock and grief and regret came a moment of realisation. She had been right: he had always loved Jenny. He had failed to face up to the fact that she still held first place in his heart. Had that driven Ruth away from him? Had he forced her into Barrett's arms or had she gone willingly, to assuage a need which burned inside her? Had his ambitions swept her along even as far as her half-brother's bed? Had she done the things she had so that his dreams would become realities?

He clenched his fists and thumped them on the side of his chair. Those dreams could never be and maybe he was as much to blame as Ruth. He pushed himself from his chair, took a glass and a bottle of brandy from a drawer in his desk, sat down and poured himself a drink. The liquid bit into his throat, burned its way into his stomach. He poured himself another and took this in one gulp. He reached for the bottle again.

'Sir! Sir!' The voice came dimly to David through a haze which seemed a long time in clearing. The voice went on and David became aware of the anxiety in it. He stirred. He ached. His head throbbed. 'Sir, is thee all right?'

The light streaming in through the windows hurt his eyes. He blinked and finally kept them open. He looked up and saw Mary standing over him. He saw concern on her face. David tried to force the stiffness out of his body. He rubbed his hand slowly across his forehead, trying to alleviate the thumping.

'Is thee all right, sir?'

He mustered a smile. 'Yes, thanks, Mary. I must have dropped off.' He saw her eye the half-empty bottle and the glass. 'I'll feel better after a wash and some strong coffee and something to eat. Can thee manage that for me?'

'Yes, sir.'

David pushed himself to his feet, swayed unsteadily for a moment then stretched. 'What time is it, Mary?'

'Seven o'clock, sir.'

'Has thee seen Miss Jessica?'

'Yes, sir. She's awake. But Mrs Fernley's not in.'

'I know, Mary. She had to go out last night.'

The maid said nothing, it was not her place. But, after the scene she had witnessed last night, she knew there was more to it.

As David crossed the hall, he heard a knock on the front door. He opened it to find a small, bare-footed boy in a tattered shirt and trousers standing on the step.

'Thee Mr Fernley?' he demanded with bright, intelligent eyes shining from a dirty face.

'Yes.' David nodded.

'I've t' give thee this.' A grimy hand thrust out an envelope.

'Thank thee,' said David as he took it. 'Who gave it thee?'

'A lady,' replied the boy, and rubbed his sleeve across his nose.

David glanced at the envelope and recognised Ruth's handwriting. He put his hand in his pocket and brought out a coin which he gave to the boy. 'Is thee hungry?' he asked.

'Yes,' came the reply as the boy clasped the coin tightly in his clenched hand.

'Come with me.'

Staring about him, amazed at the size of the house, the boy followed David across the hall. Once he had instructed Mary to give the boy some breakfast, David returned to his study. He found a letter-opener and slit the envelope. He pulled out a sheet of paper and read:

David, I am leaving Whitby. Vacate the house immediately.

I have sold it.

Ruth

Curt to the point. No regrets. No indication where she was going. It wrote a finish to their marriage.

Feeling numb, he walked slowly up the stairs to Jessica's room.

'How is thee?' he asked.

'A lot better. I'll be all right now.' Her smile changed to a look of concern. 'You look tired, David. I'm sorry for all the trouble I've caused.'

He smiled wanly. 'It's not thee, Jessica. Ruth's left me.'

'What!' She was stunned. 'Oh, David, why?'

He sat on the edge of the bed and told her the whole story, leaving nothing out. Feeling the need, he used his sister as confidante and confessor, and when he had finished felt better for having shared his troubles with someone.

'I'm sorry,' said Jessica sympathetically. 'I had no idea about Ruth and Matthew, nor about her and Jonathan. She was always very careful about her comings and goings. What will you do about Richard?'

David shrugged his shoulders wearily. 'I don't know.' He sighed. 'I haven't even seen him yet. I don't know if I want to.'

Jessica laid a comforting hand on his arm. 'You will, David, given time. He'd be a fine little chap, in the right hands. Sally, the woman Ruth engaged, is very capable.'

David nodded.

'Can you be sure he isn't yours?' questioned Jessica, who had been doing some calculations in her mind.

'But Ruth said . . .'

'I know what Ruth said, but did she say it just to spite you?' pressed Jessica. 'As I see it, Richard could just as easily be yours as Jonathan's. You don't know with certainty that she had that sort of relationship with him.' She went on to explain her reasoning to her brother. 'And by the way,' she added, the touch of excitement giving a tremor to her voice, 'Ruth added Christopher to his name.'

'What?' David looked up sharply. Kit, the Fernley family name. 'She never said.'

'Don't you see, she wanted to punish you further?'

'But she tried to blackmail Jonathan with the fact that *he* was the father.'

'And what a triumph for her if that had worked?' said Jessica. 'The son of David and Ruth Fernley as the squire of the Cropton estates.

'My God,' he gasped. 'Thee could be right.'

'Then let me take you to him,' she urged.

A few minutes later, David was staring down at the tiny form in his cot in a room at the top of the house which Ruth had turned into a nursery. The little head turned and eyes as bright as his mother's stared at David. His heart softened despite the shocks of the last twenty-four hours. He reached down and brushed his finger against the child's cheek, causing the tiny lips to curl into a smile.

'He likes you.' Jessica smiled.

David did not answer. He took in the fine drapes around the cot, the soft pillow trimmed with lace, and the patterned eiderdown. Whatever her faults, even though she had indicated she had no love for the child, Ruth had provided well for it.

'I hope everything is to your liking, Captain Fernley,' said Sally tentatively.

'It is, thank thee,' he replied. 'In future,' he added quietly, 'we will call him Kit.'

'What will you do now?' asked his sister, when they went downstairs.

'I'll try to sort something out. I'll have to see if I can sell the new ship as it is, but maybe I'll have to sell both.'

'Oh, David, and you loved the *Lonely Wind* so.'

'Can't be helped.' He shrugged his shoulders. 'I can always get a job on the *Mary Jane*. But first things first. We've got to leave here. We'll see if Mrs Thoresby can give thee a bed for tonight and I suggest that thee and Ruben leave for Cropton tomorrow. Thee can arrange for the wedding as soon as possible.'

'Where will you live?'

'I can always go back to Tom Holtby at the Black Bull.'

'You can't take Rich— Kit there,' Jessica pointed out. 'Let me take him to Cropton. Ma will look after him until you can make other arrangements.'

David nodded. 'Maybe that's the best idea.'

'You'll come for the wedding?' asked Jessica.

'I wouldn't miss it for the world.' David smiled and gave his sister a reassuring hug.

Three hours later, brother and sister left the house in Bagdale without a backward glance. It held too many bad memories. David had explained the situation to

Mary and Sally and asked the maid to stay until the new owners made themselves known. His belongings, together with Jessica's, had been put in the hall and David had told Mary he would send for them later in the morning.

Though the sky had cleared a little, there was still a strong wind blowing and, from experience, he knew there would be a heavy sea running. He felt an urge to be on it. The sight of the *Lonely Wind* and the *Mary Jane* confirmed his feeling. He knew that whaling and the Arctic would always be in his blood and that he would never be happy if he did not return to the sea.

As they tensed themselves against the driving wind and hurried towards the bridge, David glanced at a nearby quay. He pulled up short and stared at two people who stood deep in conversation by the London Packet which he knew was due to sail for the capital in ten minutes. Matthew Barrett stepped on to the gangway and held out his hand to help Ruth. She took it and followed. When she stepped on to the deck, she turned and in doing so saw David. Their eyes held for a moment, then Ruth tossed her head haughtily, took Matthew's proffered arm and crossed the deck towards the cabins.

David felt a touch on his sleeve.

'I'm sorry.' Jessica's voice was quiet, expressing a desire to help but knowing that she could only comfort.

'Don't be,' he said. 'What's happened has happened. There's no retrieving the past. Come on, I've a lot to see to.' They started towards the bridge, David's back to the life he had shared with Ruth.

As they moved out over the river, they felt the full blast

of the wind. Jessica hugged little Kit closer and pulled his shawl more tightly around his head.

'Ruth's first voyage is going to be a rough one,' commented David.

Mrs Thoresby, although sorry about David's trouble, was pleased to have Jessica for the night.

'I'll be going to Cropton tomorrow, and if Ruben can come with me we'll fix the wedding for two weeks today,' said Jessica.

'What about this grand little bairn?' asked Emma, smiling as Kit grasped her finger with his chubby hand.

'I'll take him with me,' explained Jessica. 'Ma will look after him until Davey gets things sorted out.'

'Your ma will have plenty to do with thee and Ruben and the wedding and all,' said Emma. She glanced at David. 'I'll tak him if thee likes, Davey. With Ruben gone, there'll only be Lucy and me.'

'Well, if thee don't mind, at least until the wedding. Then you and Lucy will come to Cropton with me,' he said.

'It'll be no trouble,' Emma reassured him. 'Thee'd better let Ruben know about tomorrow,' she said to David as he was about to leave. 'He and Adam went to the *Mary Jane* after Adam had brought Anne to me. Jenny's gone to clean up for Tom.'

When David reached the whaleship and passed the news to Ruben, Adam gave his brother permission to leave the ship.

'I'm pleased about Ruben and Jessica,' he said as he watched Ruben hurry from the quay.

'So am I,' replied David.

'That makes thee almost one of the family.' Adam smiled. 'What are thee gannin' to do about the *Lonely Wind*?'

'Don't know yet,' replied David. 'I'll have to try to raise a loan somewhere but it'll be hard to do with that around my neck.' He nodded in the direction of the half-built ship in Barrett's yard. 'The conditions of Ruth's borrowing have me tied up, and who'd want to invest in a crippled business now? I might be looking for a job, Adam.'

'What about Ruth? Can't she . . . ?'

'She's left me,' cut in David.

'What!'

'She's on board the London Packet with Matthew Barrett.' He indicated the ship which was moving steadily through the open bridge.

Shocked by the totally unexpected news, Adam struggled to find words which would help his friend, but all he could say was, 'I'm sorry, Davey. If there's anything I can do . . .'

'Thanks,' interrupted David, and, to save Adam any more embarrassment, straightened from the bulwark and added, 'I must be off, see if I can get my old room back with Tom. Ruth sold the house over my head. Tell thee all about it sometime.' He crossed the deck to the gangway.

As David approached the house door of the Black Bull, he noticed Jenny hurrying along Church Street.

She greeted him warmly, and with sincere gratitude added, 'It's inadequate, I know, but I'll always be grateful to you for saving Adam and the *Mary Jane*. We'll always be in your debt. I would have come yesterday but . . .'

505

'That's all right,' he cut in. 'I only did what any sailor would have done.'

'But you risked losing the *Lonely Wind*. As it is, she's damaged. Is it bad, Davey?' she asked with concern.

He nodded, his face grave.

Jenny sensed that there was something else wrong. 'Worse?' she queried tentatively.

'Walk on the cliffs with me?'

Jenny could not disregard the plea in his voice.

Once David started, he poured out his soul. His talk with Jessica had helped him to get things into perspective. Now he purged himself.

They walked along the cliff edge oblivious to the buffeting wind; she lost in his story, listening without question or comment, he lost in its telling. Far below them the heavy sea pounded the cliffs.

There was sorrow and compassion in Jenny's eyes as she turned to David when he had finished. 'I'm so terribly sorry. What can I say? What can I do?' The cry came from her heart, as a feeling of helplessness overwhelmed her. He needed her and she could do nothing.

'Just having thee to talk to has made me see some things differently. I'm grateful for that.' He half-smiled. 'We're almost back where we started, thee and I on the cliffs, but so much has happened and thee did warn me what the west side of the river could do.'

'I think a lot of your trouble stems from the time Adam and I came to Bagdale, so I must share some of the blame for what happened. I shouldn't have acted so foolishly that day.'

'Thee can't be blamed,' cried David. 'It was the way Ruth and I handled our lives. We should have . . .'

506

'David,' she cut in sharply, 'you mustn't keep looking back. I know it's easy to say, but you must look to the future, you have a life to live. You have a son. You still have the sea, ships, the Arctic, and you still have friends in Whitby. The past is out there on the London Packet. It's leaving you. You've got to make a new life.'

But he was no longer hearing her words. With his attention directed at the London Packet, he saw she was making heavy weather at the start of her voyage. 'Good God!' he gasped. 'What's the fool doing? He has too much sail!' Alarm swelled in his voice.

Almost as if in reply, an explosive crack blasted towards them on the tearing wind. A mast tottered slowly, then fell, dragging sails and ropes with it. It crashed across the deck and trailed into the heaving sea. The ship shuddered and wallowed, spinning helplessly in the sea's gyrations as mast and canvas dragged at her. Jenny and David stood transfixed, helpless on the high cliffs, watching a tragic nightmare in which nature was the chief actor. The ship was helpless, tossed by the sea, driven by wind and waves towards the shore. Tiny figures ran in confusion on its deck, seeking some means of saving themselves.

The horror of the sight was reflected in David's face. 'She's driving in towards Saltwick Bay,' he yelled. 'If she misses the Scar, they might be saved. Get help, Jenny!' He started towards the cliff edge where it fell less steeply towards the small bay.

Hemmed in by cliffs, with a huge projection of rock lying across its opening like some massive whale, the bay offered some chance if the ship was lucky enough to miss the cliffs.

'Be careful, David!' shouted Jenny, only to have her words torn away by the wind.

Stones and clay fell away beneath his feet as he plunged down the cliff-side, sliding here, holding on there, twisting and turning, ever conscious of the ship being driven helplessly towards the shore. If she hit the beach, he might be able to drag someone ashore.

He slipped and crashed the last few feet on to the firm sand. His lungs gasped for air as he scrambled to his feet. Staring wildly around him, in a moment's hesitation, he was overwhelmed by the scale of nature. Cliffs towered huge and black. The massive humped-back rock seemed to fill the bay, blocking any chance the ship might have. Huge waves pounded the beach, sending spray high across the whole scene.

David could not see the ship. He ran towards the water, shielding his eyes against the spray.

Then he saw her. She had missed the headland and was being driven towards the bay. He stood transfixed as the ship was heaved towards destruction.

For a moment his hopes were raised. She seemed to make some effort to find the gap between the whale-rock and the cliffs. Then, as if it had been only teasing the victims with hope, the rising wind churned the sea into a boiling cauldron of destructive waves. They tossed the ship away from possible safety and threw her like some useless object on to the great island of rock.

David's eyes widened with horror. He started towards the sea but it was only an instinctive move. There was nothing he could do. The helplessness of the ship and the sheer force of nature in its power of destruction hypnotised him. The wind screeched its triumph. The sea pounded and crashed its pleasure.

David started. He fancied he heard a woman's scream. Wiping spray from his eyes, he ran into the sea but it burst around him, staggering him with its force, driving him back to stumble on the beach. He knew he could do nothing. The ship was too far away, the sea too powerful.

He narrowed his eyes against the wind and the spray. Boats! He was mistaken. No. They were there. Climbing the waves. Lost in the troughs. Appearing again. Jenny had succeeded in raising the alarm. There was hope.

Four boats battled towards the stricken ship. The large one, kept for such purposes, was oared by the port's best men, one of whom was Adam. The other three were smaller, manned by one or two seamen, eager to do what they could for those in distress.

David stepped nearer the sea as if his movement would take the boats close to the ship. He willed them on, then froze. The sea seemed to gather all its momentum into one massive wave, sending it rolling with unbridled power. It heaved the boats like pieces of driftwood and cast them down to its depths. The wave broke around the ship sending spray high into the air. When it cleared, there was not one boat to be seen. David felt numb and beaten senseless. The wind screamed at him in joyful triumph.

Battered and beaten, the ship broke up. The churning water threw timbers towards the beach. A wave held a body uplifted as in sacrifice. Then, its offering made, spewed it on to the beach. David ran forward. The receding water dragged the body away, tumbling it over and over. Another wave pounded in, throwing a second body on to the beach.

David reached out for the first but the wave knocked him off his feet and rolled the body past him.

He scrambled up. Salt water streamed from him. He ran up the beach. The body lay still as the sea swirled its way backwards, eddying around it. Gasping and panting, David reached out – then froze. He stared wide-eyed at the silent form. Barrett! He shuddered at the sight of the staring, unseeing eyes.

Ruth? Where was Ruth? He cast his gaze across the waves. His mind cried out in anguish. She was somewhere out there. She didn't deserve this fate. If only he could do something. His features creased in frustration and he yelled obscenities at the overwhelming elements.

Waves pounded and sent their long rivulets of water around the body. He bent down automatically and dragged Barrett up the beach, away from the clutching fingers of the sea. Then he turned and in helpless resignation made his way slowly back to the sea.

The rescue party found David still mechanically searching for bodies to join the six he had already recovered. He grabbed the first man to reach him. 'Adam? Was Adam out there?' he cried.

His face creased with painful regret, the man nodded. For a moment David stared wide-eyed then was past him, ignoring the rest of the rescuers as he scrambled up the cliff. He must go to Jenny.

He knew nothing of his rush to Whitby, living as he did through a fiendish nightmare in which his whole world was destroyed in shattering upheaval.

He reached the house in Church Street. The gathering of sympathisers, outside the house, parted for him. He opened the door and stepped quietly inside. He went to the room at the back of the house. Jenny was leaning with her head against the mantelpiece. She straightened when she heard his footsteps. With silent tears streaming down her cheeks, she turned to him.

'Oh, my luv.' His tone expressed all his heartfelt sorrow and distress. He held out his arms. She came to them and he cried with her.

Beyond Saltwick Bay, a tiny boat bobbed on the calming waves. The oarsman, marvelling how he had survived the tremendous wave which had battered the rescue boats, still battled the power of the sea, but knew the worst was over.

A bedraggled figure stirred in the bottom of his boat.

Chapter Thirty-four

Later that same day, David walked slowly through the narrow streets. His whole world had collapsed and he saw no future. His dazed mind seemed unable to cope with the problems which faced him. He did not know where his footsteps took him but he was jolted out of his bewilderment when he found himself outside the hall to which the victims of the shipwreck had been brought.

Puzzled as to why his steps had brought him here, he started to turn away. Then he stopped, glanced at the door and pushed it tentatively. It yielded. The noise of hammers driving nails into wood reached him. He shoved the door wider and stepped inside. The sight of a row of coffins made him falter. At the far end of the hall, four men were busy shaping two more. David walked slowly towards them. The men stopped hammering.

'G'day, Cap'n Fernley.' One of the carpenters broke the silence as all four stared at him with marked curiosity.

David nodded his acknowledgement. 'My wife . . . have you . . . is she . . . ?' He glanced at the row of coffins.

'Sorry, she's not been found,' answered one of the men. 'Adam Thoresby?'

'Behind there.' The man nodded towards a curtain which blocked a section of the room from sight.

David stepped past them only to hesitate at the curtain. The quietness, after the noise of the hammers, was charged with an almost overwhelming sense of oppression. David's mind faltered. Why had he come here? Why open his wounds? But he must say goodbye to a valued friend.

He drew the curtain back slowly.

Two bodies, covered with white sheets, lay on the floor side by side. He dropped on one knee and pulled a sheet back slowly. He stared at the pale face, peaceful and serene. The silent form bore no sign of the roughness of the pounding sea which had dragged Adam to his death.

'Oh, Adam, why did it have to be thee?' The cry came from David's heart as his eyes filled with tears. 'Far better for it to have been me. My life's in a mess. Yours wasn't.'

His mind dragged him back over the years. What went wrong? How much was I to blame? Ruth was ambitious, yes, but I had those ambitions first. I desired my own ship and a house in Bagdale. I sowed the seeds in her mind. I brought her to Whitby where the seeds blossomed in her desire to realise those ambitions. So what went wrong? Maybe I never gave the love I had for her a proper chance. If only we could start again. Did I drive her to Matthew Barrett? Did I really become so uninteresting? We shared so much, it shouldn't have gone wrong. We shouldn't have let our ambitions rule us.

Misery and remorse flooded over him. He put a brake on his thoughts. It was no good. The past couldn't be retrieved and he had a future to face. He stared at the waxen features and his lips moved silently. 'I'm sorry, Adam, I'm burdening you with my troubles even now.' He paused for one last loving look. 'Goodbye, old friend.' Straightening, he let the sheet drop.

David hurried away without even a glance at the workmen. In respectful silence, they watched him walk to the door and then resumed their sombre task.

The following morning, he watched Adam's coffin, along with so many others, lowered gently into the earth.

His eyes turned seawards. Somewhere out there lay Ruth, gone from the cares, worries and angers of their turbulent world. Silently he bade her goodbye. I'm sorry, Ruth, for my faults, for what I did to drive thee away. Forgive me.

As the mourners drifted away from Jenny's house, she asked David to stay and he found himself with Jenny, Ruben, Emma and Jessica.

Emma, hiding the hurt at the loss of her eldest son, outwardly remained calm. 'David,' she said, 'Jessica has told me of your predicament, and I have discussed it with Ruben and Jenny. They agree that we should make thee a loan to have the *Lonely Wind* repaired and set something towards payment for the new ship. The two ships can then sail to the Arctic as the bank stipulated.'

David stared at her. 'I don't believe it,' he muttered. 'It can't be true.'

'It is, Davey,' said Jenny. 'We want you to have the money.'

'But I couldn't. It's too risky. Thee could lose it all.'

'We know the risks,' Ruben pointed out. 'But I know thee and I think thee'll succeed. I know what thee's thinking – can they afford to run a risk? Well, Pa did very well with his whaling. The *Mary Jane* was his own so he took all the profits. He lived well but had no desire for fine houses, preferring the life he knew. He did not spend a great deal. We won't go hungry if thee fails, but we don't think thee will.'

'You must accept,' urged Jenny. 'Adam would have wanted you to.'

David looked at his friends with deep affection. 'What can I say? Thee's all too good to me.' He paused thoughtfully. 'There's only one way I'll accept. Thee has a share in the business which Ruth and I hoped to create.' When he saw Ruben start to protest, he went on quickly, 'I'd be happier that way, and with success thee'd get a return on your money.'

Ruben eyed him for a moment. He knew that once David got his mind set there was no altering him.

He glanced at his mother. 'If thee agrees, Ma, we'll bring the *Mary Jane* as well as the money and create a new shipping firm – Fernley and Thoresby.'

Emma looked thoughtful, smoothing her black dress across her lap and she weighed up the situation. Then she nodded. 'A good idea, Ruben. Dost thee agree, Davey?'

He held out his arms to them all. 'What can I say?' Overwhelmed by their generosity, his voice choked.

A bargain was sealed.

Though Ruben and Jessica wanted to postpone the wedding, Emma and Jenny insisted that Adam would not have wanted them to do so. Those touched by his death hid their sorrow for the sake of the bride and groom.

Two days later, David returned to Whitby, leaving his mother and father proud to be looking after little Kit. He approached the town with apprehension for the shadows of the tragedies still hazed his mind, but, once he felt the thrill of seeing the masts soaring high from the wooden decks, he knew the worst of the past was over.

He hurried to the *Lonely Wind*.

Jim Talbot gave him a warm welcome. 'Glad to see thee looking better, Cap'n.'

'Thanks. I feel a lot better,' replied David. 'How are the repairs going?'

'Mulgrave's are doing well. The *Lonely Wind* will be ready for a March sailing but I'm afraid the new ship is about four weeks behind schedule,' Jim informed him.

David frowned. 'I'll have to see if Barrett's can speed things up. I'd like both ships to sail together. I'm calling the new ship *Ruth*. I'll be taking her, and I'd like thee to take command of the *Lonely Wind*.'

Jim's eyes widened with surprise. He gaped at David. 'Me?'

'Why not?' David chuckled. 'She's yours if you'll have her.'

There was no second asking. Jim was more than grateful for the chance David was giving him.

The winter months slid by with David satisfied at the progress of the two ships, particularly as Barrett's made up time and he would now sail only three weeks after the *Lonely Wind* and the *Mary Jane*.

Jessica and Ruben returned to Whitby to live with Mrs

Thoresby until after his first voyage as captain, an arrangement which pleased Ruben for he knew that Jessica would receive his mother's careful attention throughout her pregnancy.

As sailing day drew near, and with the baby due in less than a month, Ruben's concern for his wife increased but Jessica reassured him and insisted on seeing him sail.

On the first Tuesday in March, beneath a grey overcast sky, David gave some final instructions to Ruben on board the *Mary Jane* and arranged a meeting point for two months later.

'Good luck,' he said, taking Ruben's hand in a firm grip. 'Don't worry about Jessica. I hope I'll be able to bring thee news of the baby.'

He left Jessica and Ruben to make their goodbyes and hurried to the *Lonely Wind* where he told Jim of the arrangements he had made to meet Ruben.

'Thee hurry. The Arctic won't be the same without thee,' said Jim affectionately as he shook David's hand.

'I'll soon be there. I'll see thee where the whales spout.'

As the ships slipped from the quayside, David left for the cliff top. Hurrying through the flow of people, his attention was caught by a slight figure just starting to climb the Church Stairs.

'Hello, Jenny,' he greeted, his lungs heaving with the extra effort of catching her. 'I didn't think thee'd be coming any more.'

She glanced at him with a wan smile. 'People dear to me still sail. Besides, she's Adam's ship.'

'Will thee watch when I sail in the *Ruth*!'

'Of course I will. The red shawl will wave for you.'

'And when I return?'

'Yes.'

'Maybe then thee and I . . .'

She laid a hand on his arm, stopping him before he could utter the words she sensed were coming. 'Don't say it, Davey.' Her voice caught in her throat. Tears dimmed her eyes. 'We'll see,' she added with quiet finality.

He respected her wish.

Three weeks later, a red shawl waved, sending love and good wishes for a safe and prosperous voyage to the captain of the *Ruth*.

Further down the coast, on the lonely cliffs between Whitby and Robin Hood's Bay, a solitary figure watching the ship become a tiny speck on the vastness of the ocean rent the air with a bloodcurdling cry of revenge.